I0819975

Family Unity

Family Unity

Arthur J. Skogsberg

Family Unity

Cover design by Jeanine Henning
www.jeaninehenning.com

Book design by Maureen Cutajar
www.gopublished.com

ISBN: 978-0-692-62502-6

This book is dedicated to my awesome three:
my wife Patti, my son Colin, and my daughter Alicia.

ACKNOWLEDGEMENTS

I have always wanted to write a fiction book about the Old West and after nearly two decades training in the martial art of tae kwon do, it occurred to me I should incorporate some eastern philosophy into the story line.

A special thanks to my wife, whose assistance was instrumental in reviewing my grammar.

Family Unity

CHAPTER 1

사랑

Playing in the rice paddies during the rice harvest in Korea was one of those simple pleasures only a three-year-old could enjoy. Alicia recalled how much fun it was to squish the mud between her toes as she stood in the shallow water of the paddy while all the workers including her mother and father were toiling under the hot midday sun. It was a cloudless day with a crystal-blue sky and a slight breeze from the west, which cooled the workers while they labored in the paddies. "Alicia!" She could faintly hear her mother calling her in for lunch from the rice paddy she was playing in.

"*Alicia!*" Startled by the loud voice, she realized she was daydreaming while looking out the school window on the Pennsylvania farmland fields surrounding the building where she taught Asian history in a private school. She turned and saw the headmistress standing in the doorway with a concerned look and immediately knew there was something terribly wrong. The headmistress was carrying a piece of paper in her hand, and her face was ashen gray.

"Mrs. Kilpatrick, I am sorry I did not hear you call me."

The headmistress, who was always in control, looked helpless and unable to express herself as she handed the paper to Alicia. "I am terribly sorry to give you this news, Ali. We will do anything we can to help you in your time of need. I will give you some time alone to read the telegram and then please come down to the office so we can arrange for a leave of absence."

Alicia was concerned and took the paper, which was a telegram addressed to her in the care of the school. The telegram was from her mother in Wyoming and simply read, "Alicia, please come immediately STOP Father has been shot STOP Need you at ranch STOP Love Mother."

Sarah sat in the living room of her house looking out the window at the mountains and wondering what she would do if her husband didn't survive the gunshot wound to his chest. Her mind drifted back to the memories of when she and Gus had traveled west in a prairie schooner to stake out some land and start a cattle ranch. Back in 1840, they had to endure the hardship of breaking new trails while forging into an untamed wilderness country with unknown dangers. There was always the threat of Indian attacks, but Gus told her the danger was outweighed by the reward of starting their own cattle ranch. There were few settlers out this far west, and the army posts could not offer much protection since they were responsible for patrolling a thousand square miles. That left the settler to protect himself the best he could from the elements and Indian attacks.

When they started out for Wyoming, Gus was a strong twenty-year-old-man with all the hopes and dreams of making his mark. Sarah was nineteen and completely in love and dedicated to her husband of a few months. She remembered she was thrilled and scared at the same time about their long trip to the Wyoming territory from back east. They had left the confines of a civilized Independence Missouri just three short weeks ago heading to the Wyoming territory with their prairie schooner and enough supplies to last them for the three-month trip they were to embark on.

Sarah leaned back in her chair and remembered how Gus had started working in a livery stable, telling her what a good opportunity this would be for him. She recalled how excited he was to have this job and after a while, he learned how to pick out a good horse among the ones that were being stabled. He also learned about the equipment needed for covered wagons from those that came into the livery in need of repairs from time to time.

Gus worked in the livery for two years and earned the reputation of a hardworking young man, who eagerly learned the trade from the owner, Angus McCraken. Sarah smiled to herself as she remembered cranky old Angus, who was a bachelor with no family and very few friends. He was fifty-five years old and abrupt toward most people he came in contact with on a daily basis. Gus had told Sarah, Angus did not think a scrawny lad of eighteen could do the heavy work required in this trade. However, Gus explained, no one else wanted to work for the crotchety old man so Angus reluctantly agreed to try him out. Gus didn't waste any time to prove himself and pitched in to do the worst jobs in the stable, showing Angus he could do anything asked of him.

Every day, Sarah brought lunch to Gus and tried to be nice to Angus even though he acted as if she were in the way of their work. So one day, Sarah brought down a freshly baked apple pie for Angus and thanked him for giving her beau a chance to work for him. Angus was surprised by her kind gesture and couldn't think of anything to say. He grumbled thanks to Sarah out of the corner of his mouth as he turned and walked back to his small office. A tear came to his eyes as he couldn't remember the last time someone had given him something out of pure kindness.

Even though he did not let on to Sarah, Angus was impressed by her young man's attitude and his desire to learn everything he could about the livery. He began to think he might have someone to leave the business to when he passed away or became too old to handle the heavy manual labor required of a smithy. Sarah remembered Gus telling her how as he continued to learn the business, his involvement with customers also increased, and Angus was letting him do more of the wagon repair work. Many of the wagon repair customers Gus spoke to were preparing to move west and stake land claims to start farms or cattle ranches. He was intrigued with these customers and began to ask these folks about the opportunities out west for a young man like himself. Many of the tales he knew were outlandish exaggerations. An old prospector, who stopped to have his mule shoed, told Gus the territories had fruit trees laden with apples, oranges, and other varieties year round and anyone who wanted to eat could pick the fruit. From the conversations she had with Gus, Sarah knew most folks going out west were genuinely interested in giving accurate information to the young man, and she recalled the hours and hours they spent talking about moving out west to start a cattle ranch and raise a family of their own after they were married.

Dr. O'Malley stood up and stretched his legs and arms. He had been operating on Gus for the gunshot wound to his chest for the past two hours. It had taken a long time to locate the bullet, using a probe and then extracting it from his chest. Dr. O'Malley had been practicing medicine for about ten years and had seen his share of gunshot wounds. However, Gus was extremely lucky in one respect. The bullet had struck the sternum and glanced off, missing the heart by an inch. As the doctor worked on him, he thought whoever shot him had meant to kill him. He couldn't understand why anyone would want to hurt Gus, who was a hardworking and honest individual. He was a good neighbor and always the first to offer help to his friends when they were in need. However, he did not allow anyone to cheat or insult him under any circumstance.

As Dr. O'Malley continued to work, he remembered when he first arrived in town to start his medical practice. He had heard there was a shortage of doctors in the west and thought he would have a ready-made practice in the absence of competition. He arrived in Cheyenne dressed in eastern-style clothes and felt immediately out of place. He stepped from the train onto the depot platform noticing everyone dressed in western-style clothes, with the men wearing six guns on their hips. As he walked down the street dressed in an eastern-style suit complete with a derby hat and carrying two suitcases and his medical bag, he could see the townsfolk staring at the eastern dude and trying not to snicker. Most of the children were not able to contain themselves and laughed at him as he passed them by, their parents shushing them and telling them not to be rude to strangers.

He finally located the hotel and entered in through a small lobby. Walking up to the registration counter, the clerk looked up to greet him with a smirk on his face. The clerk gave him the once-over and then said, "Can I help you?"

"Yes, I need a room and bath."

"I've got two rooms left. Both are on the second floor. One has a window lookin' out on Main Street and the other room is in the back on the same floor lookin' out on the alley. What's your pleasure, sir?"

The doctor thought a minute and said, "I think I'll take the room overlooking Main Street. Now, how do I go about getting that bath?"

"We got a room on this floor that the owner put a bathtub and washstand in for our guests. He put it on the first floor to make it easier to carry the hot water in from the stove in the kitchen. The bath will cost you an extra fifty cents," said the clerk.

"Good! Start the hot water, and I'll be down in half an hour after I unpack and get settled in my room."

"Well, Gus, that's about as good as I can do for you," muttered Dr. O'Malley under his breath. It then dawned on him that the hardest part of his profession was about to come up. *I've got to tell Sarah I don't know if her husband of forty years is going to live or die.*

As he opened the bedroom door into the living room, he saw Sarah sitting in the rocking chair Gus had made for her years ago.

She looked like she was in deep thought staring out the window toward the mountains.

"Sarah, I need to talk to you about Gus."

Sarah slowly turned her head toward him with a look mixed with fear and anticipation not knowing whether he was going to tell her Gus was dead or alive. She got up and walked across the room to where he was standing. "Okay, Doc. Is Gus going to live through this or not?"

The doctor was momentarily stunned. Sarah was blunt and to the point as usual. Most wives would be either crying or hysterical, or both. Not Sarah though, after years in the west, she had learned when to be tough and when to be sensitive and caring. He looked Sarah in the eye and simply said, "I honestly don't know. He's tough and strong but lost a lot of blood. I got the bullet out and sewed him up. If the bullet hadn't glanced off his breastbone, it would have hit his heart. I give him a fifty-fifty chance if he makes it through the night. If he wakes up, he needs to keep quiet and not try to get out of bed. Although I don't think he'd have the strength to do that. I'll come back tomorrow mornin' to check on him and change the bandage. I want to make sure the wound does not become infected. Can I get one of your friends from town to stay with you and help with Gus?"

"Doc, I appreciate the offer, but I've been takin' care of my man for the past forty years. I took care of him when he was sick, fixed his broken bones, and even dug some arrowheads out of his hide long before you came to town and started your practice. Na, I'll take care of my man tonight and 'spect to see ya in the mornin'. You've done all ya can so I'll take over from here," said Sarah.

"All right, I'll bring some medicine and clean and change the bandage tomorrow morning," O'Malley said as he headed for the front door to leave. He walked out the door and down the steps toward his one-horse covered buggy, which had been tied to the horse rail all evening. It was close to midnight, and he still had a two-hour ride back to town. He untied his horse and climbed up into the buggy, putting his medical bag on the seat beside him. He then snapped the reins in his hands and said, "C'mon Dollar, let's go home."

As Dollar started out for the town, the doctor folded his arms with the reins in them and leaned back into the corner of the buggy to try and get some sleep. He was aware Dollar knew the way back to town as well as he did so he was quite confident he could get some rest on the way back. As he started to doze off, he was still troubled by the thought that someone had tried to kill his good friend Gus. He quickly fell asleep and dreamed of the first day he arrived in Cheyenne.

O'Malley came down from his room and found the clerk pouring the last bucket of hot water in the bathtub for him. "Well, it's all filled up for you, Mr. O'Malley. You'll need this key to lock the door while you take your bath so no one will disturb you. I put some towels on this table here. Let me know if you need anything else," said the clerk.

"Thanks, I don't think I'll need anything more."

He could still remember to this day how good it felt to slip into that hot bathtub of water. It instantly relaxed his muscles, and he began to clean up after simply enjoying the warm water for about five minutes. He bathed, got out of the tub, and shaved. He then put on the clean suit he had brought down from his room. As he finished getting dressed, he took his watch out of his vest pocket to check the time. It was ten o'clock, and he needed to start making arrangements to get settled in town. He walked out of the room and started toward the front desk to let the clerk know he was done and the room was free to be cleaned up.

"I'm sorry, I forgot to ask you what your name is when I checked in," said O'Malley to the clerk as he got to the registration desk.

"My name is Jim Harbor. What can I do for you, Mr. O'Malley?" replied the clerk.

"I wanted to let you know I am finished with my bath so you could arrange for the room to be cleaned up for your next customer."

"That's fine, Mr. O'Malley. I'll have the cleaning lady take care of it. Can I help you with anything else?" asked Jim.

"Yes, can you direct me to the local bank?"

"Sure, go out the front door and cross the street, then turn right, and the bank should be about a hundred feet down the boardwalk," replied Jim.

"Thanks," said O'Malley as he turned and walked out the front door of the hotel. As he stepped out of the hotel and into the street, he immediately felt the searing heat of the sun on his face. There was not a cloud in the sky to hide the sun. The doctor was wearing his suit and derby hat, which provided no shade from the sun as it glared directly on his face. He took a moment to let his eyes adjust to the bright light and then started across the street.

"Hey Whitey, look at the dude with the funny hat," said someone close by. O'Malley stopped crossing the street and looked over to see who made the remark. "Yeah, that's right, I'm talkin' to you, dude. That's the ugliest funniest hat I've ever seen," said the stranger.

"Yeah, Stu," said the man called Whitey. "That is the ugliest hat I've ever seen, too. Let's show the dude a real western welcome."

As Whitey and Stu started walking toward him, O'Malley turned to face them. He noticed the two men were dressed in long-sleeved shirts and dirty dungarees. "Hi fellas, you probably guessed I'm new in town. I'm just taking care of some personal business. I plan on settling down here."

"Well dude, let us welcome you to the West," Stu said as he grabbed Doc's derby and stepped back. Stu had gotten close enough for O'Malley to smell the strong odor of alcohol. "Whitey, how good a shot are ya at something this small?" Stu asked as he threw the derby up in the air as high as he could while Whitey drew his colt and fired off three quick shots at the hat, hitting it once.

O'Malley looked closely at the two men. They both wore six guns with the holsters tied down to their legs and were dressed like the pictures of cowboys he had seen in books he had read. They were both dressed in jeans with chaps and typical cowboy hats with button-down long-sleeved shirts. O'Malley was no coward, but he was unarmed, and with the alcohol odor, he had to assume these two cowboys had been drinking a long time. It also meant they were unpredictable and dangerous. O'Malley hoped he could try to talk his way out of what could develop into a bad situation.

"Boys, boys, boys! I got to admit this is kind of a funny hat to be wearing out here in this part of the country. Like I told you, I'm new in town and one of the things I need to get is some new clothes. Can either one of you tell me where I can get some new clothes?"

"Well, Whitey," Stu said. "Let's help the dude get outta his clothes since he wants to get rid of 'em."

"Yeah!" Whitey said.

"Let's undress the dude right here on the street."

Gus had just picked up his repaired saddle from the tack shop when he heard three shots from down the street. He walked outside and saw a stranger talking to Stu and Whitey in the middle of the street. Then it dawned on him that yesterday was Friday and also payday for the ranch hands. Stu and Whitey had probably collected their pay from the Double X ranch where they worked. Gus knew these two had a habit of coming into town to drink and raise Cain at the Grizzly Saloon all night long on Friday, then sleeping it off the next day. He also knew Stu and Whitey loved picking on strangers who looked different and were perceived to be weak. This man Stu and Whitey were talking to certainly fit the bill. He was dressed in eastern-style clothes and probably wore the derby hat that lay by them in the street. He knew the stranger would be a perfect target for Stu and Whitey's pleasure. Gus had run-ins with these two in the past but nothing that caused one of them to draw their gun on him or a stranger even if it was for fun. He also knew the sheriff was out of town tracking some rustlers that had been plaguing the local ranchers recently. Stu and Whitey had nasty reputations for being plain mean and so no one was going to intercede on behalf of the stranger. So Gus decided he would take on the job of helping the stranger. He walked toward the three men, coming up behind Stu and Whitey. He hoped the two would not hear his approach, which would give him the advantage of surprise.

O'Malley couldn't believe his ears. He had been in town a short two hours not bothering anyone and minding his own business when the first townsfolk he talks to—other than the hotel clerk—turn out to be bullies looking to cause trouble. As he was talking to these two bullies, he saw a third cowboy walking toward them. He didn't know if this cowboy was with Stu and Whitey or a curious bystander coming in for a closer look.

"Boys, I don't think I can let you do that," O'Malley said.

Stu and Whitey glanced at each other and started to laugh loudly. After their laughter had died down, Stu looked at O'Malley and said, "Dude, I don't think you gotta choice. Whitey and me don't think you belong here with your fancy clothes and funny lookin' hat. We're just gonna take you down to our level. So start takin' off them clothes right now dude or Whitey and me are gonna help ya."

By then, O'Malley noticed the new stranger who had been walking toward them stopping about five feet behind Stu and Whitey, listening to their conversation. After hearing Stu and Whitey's comments, this third cowboy's face turned from a normal look to a look of anger over the course of a few short seconds.

Gus couldn't believe what he was hearing Stu and Whitey saying. These two were troublemakers but usually involved in barroom brawls or arrested for drunk and disorderly and then released the next morning after paying a small fine and reimbursing the saloon for any damages they had caused. But assaulting a stranger in broad daylight was highly unusual even for these two saddle tramps. Gus usually did not meddle in other people's business, but he greatly disliked bullies or anyone who purposely picked on someone weaker than themselves. He quickly walked the last two paces and stood not more than a foot behind Stu and Whitey.

"Hi, ya boys, whatta ya up to this morning?"

Both jumped, startled by the voice behind them and turned to face him. "Well, hi Gus. I didn't hear you come up behind us. We're just havin' a little fun with the dude. Do ya wanna join us? Oh, I remember. You're too good for our kind," Stu said.

"I don't consider myself better than any man. But I also don't like to see two armed men startin' a fight with somebody who is unarmed and if I'm right, was probably bothering no one. So, boys, I suggest you hightail it out of here or go somewhere to sleep it off."

"Well Gus, I don't think we're goin' anywhere till we're finished with the dude and if you don't like it, just hang around and you can be next," Stu replied.

Just as he finished his sentence, he went for his gun. Gus had seen the change in Stu's eyes and knew what he was going to do before he did it. Before Stu was even able to touch his gun, Gus hit him and knocked him out with what appeared to be an incredibly powerful right-hand punch. Then with what looked like the same motion, Gus took a half right turn toward Whitey, who had his gun partially out of his holster, and struck him with a lightning-fast back fist sending Whitey unconscious and flat on his back. Gus walked over and unbuckled Stu's gun belt, removing it, and then walked over to Whitey and repeated the same thing. He draped the gun belts over his shoulder, walked over to the general store, picked up an empty bucket that was out front, and filled it with water from the horse trough. He then walked over to where Stu and Whitey lay and poured water over both their heads.

"Gaud dang it!" Stu said. "Why'd you do that, Gus? Whitey and me were just gonna have some fun. We weren't gonna hurt the dude."

"Aw man, Gus!" Whitey said as he came to. "We were just gonna roust the dude and then let 'em go."

"Well boys, you can go back to the ranch and sleep it off. Your fun's over for the day, and I'm gonna leave your guns at the marshal's office where you can pick 'em up when he gets back to town."

"That's just plain not fair, Gus. Marshal Jackson might not be back for a long time, and we can't go back to the ranch without our guns," said Whitey.

"Well boys, you should've thought about that before startin' this ruckus. As far as I know, the marshal's supposed to be back any time now. Tell you what. You boys don't cause any more trouble, and I won't tell the marshal about how you were gonna welcome this stranger to our town. Now move on outta here, and I'll drop these off at the Marshal's Office so you can pick them up after you get sober."

"Gus! This just ain't right and me and Whitey are gonna remember this. We're gonna get even for this! Come on, Whitey, let's get outta here," said Stu.

"Yeah, let's go, but Gus, you better watch out for us from now on," Whitey said.

Gus returned an angry glare and said, "We can settle this right here and now, boys. If that ain't good, you two know where you can find me. Anytime you wanna do something about this, you just come and see me," replied Gus.

At first glance, O'Malley thought the third cowboy approaching them was just curious until he saw the look in the cowboy's eyes. As the stranger walked the last few feet, standing directly behind the two roughnecks, he thought this cowboy was going to join the two bullies. The stranger's conversation with the two bullies was short and to the point. It was immediately apparent to him this third man disliked the two bullies and had decided to take his side.

The conversation took less than thirty seconds when suddenly Stu and Whitey started to turn as if to attack the stranger and that's when the cowboy exploded into action ferociously. He first knocked Stu unconscious and then Whitey before either of these bullies could get their guns out of their holsters. O'Malley was stunned by the lightning speed in which this old cowboy dispatched the two bullies. He continued to watch in shocked silence as the stranger disarmed the two unconscious cowboys and then fetched a bucket of water and poured it over their heads.

He then heard the conversation between the three men noticing the shakiness in the voices of the two bullies, revealing they feared this third cowboy. After the two cowboys left, the stranger walked up to O'Malley and said, "Howdy son, and welcome to Cheyenne. This ain't how we usually treat newcomers. My name's Gus, and I hope you don't judge everybody in town by these two bums." Gus extended his hand to shake O'Malley's.

"My name's Dr. O'Malley, and I appreciate your help. I was beginning to think I came to the wrong town to open my office. Have you been out here long, Gus?"

"My wife and I came out here by schooner about forty years ago before there was a stage line or train. We got a little ranch about two or three hours ride north of here in a valley surrounded by the mountains. How about you, Doc? Where do you hail from?"

"I grew up back east where my family owned a bank in Boston, and I attended Harvard College and then Harvard Medical School. When I graduated, my family expected me to either join a medical practice in Boston or open up my own practice and go into business by myself. But during medical school, I read many stories about the west and that there was a need for doctors out here. So, when I received my medical license, I told my family I was moving out west to start my own practice. Of course, my parents were both shocked and disappointed at my decision. But my father told me if it was what I wanted, he would give me his blessing and some money to get my practice started. I sent inquiries to Dodge City, Wichita, and Cheyenne to see if any of these cities had a need for a doctor. Your mayor replied and said Cheyenne's only doctor had retired and they would welcome me to start my practice here. So I packed up my things, said my good-byes, got on a train, and here I am. I was on my way to the bank when I got stopped by these two. I want to thank you again for what you did, but I think I could have handled this trouble without your help," replied O'Malley.

Gus was astonished. How could this doctor, fresh out of the east, ever consider he would have had a chance handling Stu and Whitey?

"Doc, I hope it's okay if I call you Doc," Gus asked.

"Doc is just fine with me," answered the doctor.

"Well, Doc, I just don't know what to say. I mean, those were two mean cowboys, especially after one of their all-night drinking binges. Out here, when someone comes head on at ya without giving you a chance to talk, you gotta take action with either fists or guns. Stu and Whitey weren't gonna stop until they were through with what they had in mind for you. I don't usually give advice to people because they usually don't follow what other people tell 'em, anyway. But in your case, I'm gonna make an exception. To most people in town, you're not only a stranger but a stranger who is also a dude from out east. These two boys ain't gonna forget what happened here, and they're gonna come lookin' for you to finish what they started. I know you're a doctor and all but if you're gonna stay here, you best get yourself a gun and learn how to use it. Otherwise, you're gonna be headin' for some real serious trouble with those two."

O'Malley was silent for a moment and then said, "Gus, I'm a doctor who lives by something called the Hippocratic Oath. It means I cannot do harm onto others. So I won't have a gun even if someone gave me one. I don't believe in guns or violence, and I won't participate in something that would hurt others. Gus, I believe we are going to become good friends, but I refuse to settle disputes with violence. You're just going to have to trust me that I could have taken care of this situation with Stu and Whitey."

"Well Doc, don't say I didn't warn ya. I've gotta get back to the ranch. The bank is just down the street here, and I hope you find a place for your office. This town surely does need a doctor since Doc Williams retired about a year ago and went back east to be with his family. We have been trying to get another doctor since then but have not had any luck. I think you'll find the folks here are friendly once you get to know them. I'm in town every now and then, and I'll look you up next time I'm around to see how you're getting along. If you need anything, come out to the ranch, and I'll be more than happy to help ya anyway I can," replied Gus.

"That's an offer I might take you up on. Thanks for all your help today."

Gus put his hand out and O'Malley grasped it with a much stronger grip than Gus would have ever suspected of a dude from back east.

Alicia hurried downstairs to Mrs. Kilpatrick's office, which was at the end of the first-floor hallway. Mrs. Kilpatrick had left her door open and as soon as she saw Alicia walking into the reception area located in front of her office, she got up from behind her desk and met Alicia at her door. "Please, come in and sit down, dear. We want to do everything we can to help you get to your family as soon as possible. I have already approved an indefinite leave of absence considering the circumstances. I have also asked Mr. Dixon to drive you back to your boarding house so you can pack and then take you down to the train station. Mr. Dixon should be here in a few minutes. I have someone instructing his physical education class while he helps you this afternoon," said Mrs. Kilpatrick.

"I'm grateful for all your help, ma'am. You have always been very kind to me since I applied for a position here to teach in your Asian Studies department five years ago. I appreciate your assistance and the kindness you are extending me at this time. I will return to school as soon as I take care of things out west."

Just then, Mr. Dixon knocked on the door, and both Mrs. Kilpatrick and Alicia jumped, startled by the unexpected knock. "Sorry ladies, I didn't mean to give you a fright. I got here as soon as I could. Mrs. Kilpatrick, I was told you needed me to take Alicia to her boarding house and then the train station as soon as possible. Alicia, I am ready to go just as soon as you are. I will wait in the hallway until you finish up here," Dixon said.

"No need to wait, Luke. Mrs. Kilpatrick and I have just finished." She turned back to the headmistress. "Thank you for everything, Mrs. Kilpatrick," Alicia said as she extended her hand.

Instead of taking her hand, Mrs. Kilpatrick got up and walked around her desk to take Alicia's hand and then hugged her, saying, "Please let us know if there is anything we can do to help. Give our best to your family," said Mrs. Kilpatrick.

"I will, Mrs. Kilpatrick. Good-bye and thanks for everything." She then walked out to the hallway and over to Luke. "Well, Luke, let's get started so I can pack my things and start for home. I still have a lot to do, and it's a long trip to Cheyenne Wyoming, even by train."

Luke walked down the hall with Alicia making small talk about school activities, trying to keep her mind off her troubles. They got into Mrs. Kilpatrick's buggy and started the short ride to the boarding house. Alicia was considering what to pack so she could travel light on the train. As they rode down the brick street toward her flat, the sound of the buggy reminded her of the sound of the clip-clop hoof noises she remembered in Cheyenne.

"Well, here we are, Alicia," Luke said as they pulled up in front of the boarding house.

"I'll only be a few minutes, Luke. Why don't you wait out here and enjoy the nice May weather?"

"Okay. If you need any help with anything, let me know."

She jumped from the buggy and half-walked, half-ran toward the house and bounded up the stairs through the front door stopping to unlock her flat. Once inside, she went through the living room to her bedroom and started packing the clothes she felt would be right for her trip out west. She was able to put everything in one bag, which amazed her. She closed up her bag, latched it, and started for the front door. Suddenly, she remembered something and went back to her bedroom to retrieve a small wooden case with Asian calligraphy on the cover. She turned, opened the bag, and put the case inside, then latched the bag once again and headed for the door. She walked into the hall and turned to lock the door to her room. As she started for the front door to get her ride to the train station, she realized her landlady didn't know she would be out of town for an unknown period of time. Alicia walked briskly down the hall to Mrs. O'Rourke's flat and knocked on the door. The door opened and there stood Mrs. O'Rourke. She was a plump woman in her sixties with gray hair and always had a big smile and something nice to say. It dawned on Alicia that she could not remember a time Mrs. O'Rourke did not have a full apron on over her house dress. She seemed to always be baking or cooking food, and this day, the smell of freshly baked bread permeated Mrs. O'Rourke's kitchen.

"Alicia, I'm so glad to see you," Mrs. O'Rourke said as she held out her arms to give her a hug. "Child, you're looking just as pretty as ever. Come in here and visit with me for a spell," said Mrs. O'Rourke.

"I only have a minute, Mrs. O'Rourke. My mother in Wyoming wired me. My father has been shot, and I need to leave immediately on the train. I could be out there for two or three months, and I was wondering if I mailed my rent in, could you hold my room for me?"

"Oh dear, I am so sorry to hear about your father. Please give your family my best and don't worry about your flat. I will take care of everything. Now don't let me hold you up. You need to get back to your family as soon as you can," said Mrs. O'Rourke.

They both said their good-byes quickly after exchanging hugs, and Alicia hurriedly made her way to the front door and down the front steps to Luke, who was waiting patiently in the buggy. "Okay, Luke, let's get going," Alicia said as she tossed her bag behind the buggy seat.

"Well, that was quick! I thought I would have to wait at least a half hour. Fifteen minutes to pack is really quick. Do you think you left anything behind?"

"I just packed a few things that I would need. Knowing my mother, she has kept all my clothes that I left at the ranch when I came out here. There's the train depot, Luke. Let me off here, and I'll get the first train I can. Thanks for the ride and help. I hope I won't be gone more than two or three months."

"Glad to help, Alicia. You take care and give my best to your family. I hope everything works out for you."

As Alicia climbed down, she removed her bag and walked to the depot to get her train ticket. Just before entering the station, she realized in her hurry to pack she had forgotten to go to the bank and withdraw money for her trip. She continued to the depot and made arrangements with the ticket agent to keep her bag behind the counter and then walked the two blocks to the bank to withdraw two hundred dollars. Upon her return to the depot, she got in line and in a few minutes she made her way to the front.

"Hello Miss, I've got your bag back here. Where would you like a ticket to?" said the ticket master.

"I need a ticket to Cheyenne Wyoming, and I need to get there as fast as possible," she replied.

"Well, let me see there, young lady. The fastest way is to go from here to Chicago and then make a connection in Chicago, which will go straight through to Cheyenne. This is gonna be a long trip. It's about eighteen hundred miles to Cheyenne. It'll take you about three days to get there. I can put you in a sleeper compartment for thirty dollars or if you decide on riding all that way in a seat, the cost would be ten dollars. Which ticket would you like, Miss?" asked the ticket master.

Alicia thought for a moment and then replied, "For a three-day trip, I will definitely take the sleeper compartment. It sounds like it would be much more comfortable and restful considering the length of time I will be on the train. When will the train arrive in Cheyenne?"

"I am not sure when you will get to Cheyenne as the trains out west are sometimes delayed for mechanical problems, accidents or holdups. The schedule I have here says you should arrive late afternoon in three days. It's 11:30 a.m. now, and the schedule says the next train to Chicago will arrive here at 11:53 a.m. So you only have a little more than twenty minutes to wait. The Chicago station might be able to tell you a little bit better what your arrival time will be in Cheyenne. I will announce the Chicago train's arrival when it comes in. Go ahead and take a seat. Relax and I'll let everyone know when it's time to board," replied the ticket master.

Alicia turned and located a seat in the waiting area and sat down with her bag at her feet. As she settled back into the bench and started to relax, she realized just how tense she had been in the last two hours. As she sat there, her thoughts turned to the next three days on the train. She would not be in touch with her mother and so would not know the condition of her father until she arrived in Cheyenne. Just then she realized she had not sent a reply to her mother's telegram in all her hurry. She got up, went back to the ticket master, and asked, "Would it be possible for me to send a telegram before the train leaves?"

"If you can write the message out, Miss, I will have the boy here run it down to the telegraph office and make sure it gets sent out," said the ticket master.

"Thank you. I will get the telegram written and get right back to you." She sat back down and wrote a quick telegram advising her mother she was on her way. She gave the message back to the ticket master with some money to send the message plus a tip for the boy who was going to deliver it to the telegraph office.

Sarah watched as the doctor climbed into his buggy and rode off toward town. She then turned and walked back into their bedroom where she looked at Gus, who was asleep and seemed to be resting comfortably. She walked over to him and pulled the bedcovers back. The doctor had bandaged his chest expertly and there appeared to be no sign of bleeding. She bent down and kissed him lightly on his forehead murmuring softly, "I love you."

She then stood up and went out to the parlor. She picked up the rocking chair she had been sitting in and carried it into the bedroom where she could sit with her husband. She put the chair down and sat with her knitting in her lap. Knitting always helped pass the time, and she hoped it would help occupy her mind while she waited for Gus to give her a sign of life.

She knitted for about two hours until fatigue finally took over. Putting the knitting aside, she pulled a quilt over her to keep warm and remained seated in the rocking chair next to Gus. As she started to relax, a light, restless sleep came over her, and she dozed off. She dreamed of the past when she and Gus were about to start their lives together.

CHAPTER 2

사랑

She dreamed of Gus walking up the steps of her parents' house in his good Sunday clothes with a warm overcoat unbuttoned down the front even on this cold January night. As her dream continued, Sarah pictured herself in her bedroom on the second floor with her door open. She remembered Gus knocking on the front door, and her mother walking down the hall to answer the door. She heard her mother say, "Why Gus, you look very handsome tonight. I wasn't aware you and Sarah were going out tonight."

"No, Mrs. Winthrop, Sarah didn't know I was coming over tonight. I would like to see Mr. Winthrop if he is home and not busy this evening."

"Yes, I believe Mr. Winthrop is in the parlor relaxing after the evening meal. Can I get you something to drink? How about some lemonade? I just made some a few minutes ago."

"Lemonade would be just fine, Mrs. Winthrop. Is it all right for me to go in and see Mr. Winthrop?"

"Please do and I'll be right along as soon as I can fix a tray of lemonade."

Gus walked the few steps to an archway on the right and entered the parlor. Mr. Winthrop was sitting in an overstuffed chair smoking a pipe and reading his evening paper. As Gus entered the parlor, Jonathan Winthrop looked up from his paper, recognized Gus and smiled. Mr. Winthrop liked this young man, who had an excellent work ethic coupled with strong ambition. “Hello, Gus. You’re sure dressed up this evening. Is Mrs. Winthrop letting Sarah know you’re here?”

“No sir. Well, I don’t know, sir. I mean, I guess she could be letting her know. I mean, I came to talk to you, sir.”

“Oh...well, come in and sit down and make yourself comfortable,” Mr. Winthrop replied. He folded his newspaper and placed it on the end table next to his chair and then looked up at him. “What did you come to see me about, Gus?”

Gus hesitated a moment and then said; “I-I-I wanted to ask you about Sarah,” Gus stammered out. “I am a bit confused. I am not sure what I can tell you about Sarah that you don’t already know.” Gus fidgeted for a few seconds and then said straight out. “Mr. Winthrop, I am not sure how to put this but...I want to marry Sarah, and I would like you to give me your permission, sir.”

This did not come as a surprise to Mr. Winthrop as he knew Gus had been courting Sarah for the last year and a half. He had expected him to eventually ask for her hand in marriage. Mr. Winthrop was just not sure when that request would be made. He looked at Gus, thought for a moment, and then said. “Why do you want to marry Sarah?”

Gus was caught off guard by that question and then said, “Because I love her, sir.”

“Well, I assume you love her, Gus, but do you appreciate her?”

“Well, sure I appreciate her, sir, but I’m not sure what you mean or how to answer your question.”

“Let me ask you another way. Why do you appreciate Sarah?”

“Well, I appreciate her for her kindness and the way she treats people. She never looks down on anyone. She is always pleasant with a smile that never leaves her face. I also like how she is independent and can think for herself. Does that answer your question, sir?”

“Yes, Gus. I have known all those qualities about Sarah for a long time. I just wanted to make sure you also knew them, too. You know, when I first married Mrs. Winthrop, I came to realize I didn't really love her, but I appreciated her a lot. But after I was married for a few months, I fell in love with her and that love has grown every year since. I realized love really comes when the person you marry is also your friend. I hope you understand what I am trying to explain to you about how Sarah's mother and I have developed our relationship over the years. I know you love Sarah, but I come back to my question, do you appreciate her?"

Gus was silent for a moment as he thought about what Mr. Winthrop had just said. "Mr. Winthrop, I think I understand what you are saying. I know I love Sarah, and at the same time, I can talk to her about anything, and she will listen and speak her mind to me. When I think about it, only true close friends talk to each other that way. So in answer to your question, yes, Sarah is my friend, and I would hope our close friendship and love will grow stronger each day of our married life as we become closer and closer to each other," replied Gus.

"Then, my son, welcome to our family. I am very happy for both you and Sarah," said Mr. Winthrop as he stood and extended his hand to congratulate Gus. "I had better get Mrs. Winthrop in here and tell her the good news. She had also told me she had a feeling you two would get married sometime in the future. She thought I should expect you to speak to me sometime soon about asking for Sarah's hand in marriage. I know Mrs. Winthrop will be as happy for you as I am," Mr. Winthrop said as he stood up and shook Gus's hand. He then excused himself and walked out into the hallway to find his wife.

While Mr. Winthrop was out of the parlor, Gus had a few moments to himself to collect his thoughts. He was happy with how well the marriage conversation had gone with Mr. Winthrop. Now he had to think how he was going to approach Mr. and Mrs. Winthrop on what he thought would be ten times more difficult for Sarah's parents to understand.

Sarah's dream continued, and she now remembered being in her room while Gus was downstairs. There was a soft knock on her bedroom door, which she recognized as her mother's knock and immediately told her to come in. As Sarah's mother entered the room, she looked down at her daughter and said, "Sarah, Gus is here! When I told him I would let you know, he said he wanted to talk to your father. Do you know what he wanted to talk to him about?"

"Mom, I wasn't supposed to say anything, but Gus asked me to marry him, and I said yes. He said he wanted to get Dad's blessing. He is downstairs asking for my hand in marriage!"

"Oh my God, Oh my God!" said Sarah's mother as she walked over to her daughter with arms outstretched to give her a hug. Sarah stood and they hugged each other tightly with joy.

"Your father and I have talked about you and Gus getting married. We were unsure when or if you two would eventually tie the knot," Sarah's mom said as they were hugging each other. Just then there was a knock on Sarah's door.

"Sarah, I can't find your mother anywhere. Do you know where she is?" Mr. Winthrop yelled through the door.

"She's in here, Dad. You can come in. We were just talking."

Mr. Winthrop opened the door and walked in. He saw the look on both his wife's and daughter's face. It told him what they were discussing. "Well, I assume you both know why Gus was downstairs and what we were talking about. So, what do you think, Mother?" asked Mr. Winthrop.

Sarah's mom looked back beaming at her husband and blurted out, "It's wonderful! I can't wait to start planning the wedding with Sarah. It will be such fun, and we can start planning immediately."

"Well, Mom, you're going to have to do some quick planning," said Sarah.

Mr. and Mrs. Winthrop looked at each other and then back at Sarah. "Do we have anything to worry about?" asked Sarah's mom.

"No, Mother, nothing so drastic. It's just that Gus wants to settle out west, and to do that, we need to start out in the early spring so we can arrive in time to build a shelter."

Sarah's mom and dad looked at each other in total shock and then back at Sarah. "I am sure you can see from the look on our faces we are both stunned at the news you and Gus are moving out west. I'm sure you probably know we would have many questions regarding this news. Are you going far out west? When will you come back to visit? What will you do out there for a living? These are just a few of the questions I have. I thought Gus might start his own livery business here in town, which I was prepared to help with financially. We were hopeful you both would be living in town instead of moving to God knows where. How will we know you are all right?' asked Sarah's father.

"I know you are both concerned and obviously this has come as a shock to both of you. However, Gus and I have had some very long conversations about this. We have decided we want to set off on our own and start our lives together out west in the new territories. I am sure we will come to visit you as time permits, and we would always welcome you to come out to our home after we get settled. All we want today is for you both to be happy for us and to give us your blessing. Gus and I know how hard this is for you, but we also need to be able to make our own decisions and hope you will continue to support us."

"Your father and I have always put your happiness and well-being first and foremost. It will take a little time to get over the shock of you and Gus moving away right after you get married. It will certainly be a void in our lives that you will not be around for us to get better acquainted with him. We both like Gus, and it is our fondest wish you are both happy in your future lives. Of course, we will give you both our blessing. We will help you in any way we can for you to start your new lives on a positive note."

Sarah and her parents gave each other hugs and then went downstairs to join Gus in the parlor.

❁ ❁ ❁

"Doc, Doc, Doc," whispered Marshal Tom Jackson as he gently shook Doc's shoulder. "It's two in the morning, Doc. I was just wonderin' if you were goin' to get out of your buggy and go into your house. I saw you pull up from two blocks down the street as I was doin' my rounds. Figured you fell asleep on your way back from treatin' Gus. How's he doin' anyway?" asked the marshal.

"The bullet just missed his heart. If he lives through the night, he has a good chance of making it. I did everything I could think of, but he's lost a lot of blood. The good thing is we both know he's stubborn as a mule and tough as a grizzly bear. So if anyone can make it, Gus will."

"Did Gus say anything about what happened or who shot him?"

"No, he was unconscious when they brought him in, and he never came to while I was there working on him."

"Well, I need to talk to him if he makes it. Let me know when he's conscious and can talk. I gotta lot of questions for him. I went out to where he was found on the trail but couldn't find out a thing that will help me find out who shot him."

"I'm goin' out to their ranch tomorrow to check on him and see how he's doin'. I'll let you know when he can talk to you, Tom."

CHAPTER 3

사랑

"All aboard for the train to Chicago," the ticket master shouted from his counter, letting the waiting passengers know the train to Chicago had arrived for boarding. Alicia picked up her bag. She walked through the depot out onto the railroad platform and noticed a conductor standing by one of the passenger cars helping people on and off the train. She approached the conductor and asked him to direct her to the car that had the private sleeping compartments. He checked her ticket and then directed her to the last car of the train. "Do you need any help with your bags, Miss?"

"No thanks, I can manage," she replied as she picked up her bag. Alicia walked along the platform to the last car and handed the porter her ticket. He showed her to her compartment, and she tipped the porter as he held the door to the compartment open for her. There was a single-size bed on the right with a small washroom on the left by the compartment door. The compartment expanded to an area just past the washroom where a comfortable overstuffed chair was located by the car window with a small end table next to the chair that could be used to place books, writing materials, or beverages on. The wall separating Alicia's compartment from her neighbor had some shelves where she could put her bag after unpacking. Under the shelves, was a small chest of three drawers where she could put the clothing she had in her bag. Just then the train started to move with a jerk, almost making her lose her balance. *Well*, she thought, *this is just as good a time as any to unpack*. After quickly unpacking, she sat down in the chair and leaned back to relax for a few minutes. As she settled back into the soft, easy chair, her muscles relaxed for the first time that day. She realized just how tense and stressed she had been since receiving the telegram from home. She leaned her head back, closed her eyes, and immediately dropped off to sleep.

O'Malley had spent a restless night tossing and turning, and thinking about what had happened to his good friend Gus. By seven o'clock in the morning, he decided it was no use remaining in bed since sleep was out of the question. He got up, dressed and grabbed his medical bag. He was in a hurry to get out to Gus and Sarah's place. His office was in the back of the house he owned in Cheyenne. His living quarters were in the front left side of the home, making it convenient if someone came to his house seeking medical treatment. He went out the front door and headed down the street to Mary's Café. O'Malley wanted some breakfast before taking his long ride out to the ranch. In all the excitement yesterday, he had not eaten dinner and went to bed as soon as he arrived home from the ranch early this morning.

As he walked into the café, Mary looked up from behind her counter. She waved and said, "Good mornin', Doc. How ya'll doin'? Are ya goin' back out to the ranch?"

"Whoa Mary! How about one question at a time? I'm fine, and I won't know about Gus until I get out there this morning. I patched him up the best I could but won't know if he made it through the night until, like I said, I get out there this morning."

"Oh Doc, I'm sorry, I didn't know he was hurt that bad. I heard he had been shot, but no one knew how bad it was. You tell Sarah I'll be out directly to see her. Now, what can I get for you, Doc?"

He ordered eggs, bacon, potatoes, and toast along with coffee. Mary knew he was in a hurry and went back to the kitchen where she quickly prepared his breakfast. It seemed to O'Malley that he had only been waiting a minute when Mary brought out his food.

"Here you go, Doc! I know you're in a hurry to go see Gus. I baked bread this mornin', and I want you to take this loaf with you out to Sarah. I'll wait for you to get back to town so you can tell me how things are out there before I go see her."

"Uh-huh," O'Malley grunted as he continued to eat. He didn't realize how hungry he was until he started eating. He remembered again that he hadn't eaten anything since lunch yesterday. "I'm sorry, Mary. I didn't mean to be rude. I'll be glad to take the bread out to Sarah," O'Malley said as he finished his last bite of breakfast. He got up, thanked and paid Mary. Then he headed back to his house.

As he left the café, he stopped and looked down the street toward the railroad depot where Joe Hicks, the telegraph operator, was waving and calling his name. He stopped to let Joe run to him. "Hey Doc, I got a telegram for Gus and Sarah! Are you goin' out there today?"

"Actually, Joe, I'm on my way back to my office to hitch up Dollar and head out there this morning."

"Well Doc, I'm alone at the telegraph office today and can't leave. This telegram is from Alicia, and I think Gus and Sarah would like to get it as soon as possible. I'm supposed to deliver all these personally, but that means they won't get it until tomorrow. You're one of only a handful of folks in town I would trust to deliver a telegram for me. Can you take it out with you?"

"Sure, Joe. Let me have it, and I'll take it out today."

"How's Gus doin', Doc? Is he gonna be okay?"

"He was alive when I left him last night. I'll find out this morning when I get to the ranch."

"Tell 'em I wish 'em the best."

"I sure will, Joe. I'll see you when I get back."

The gentle side to side swaying of the train combined with the soft rhythmic metallic click-clack of the railroad car wheels allowed Alicia to relax and think back to her early childhood days. Sarah and Gus were not Alicia's biological parents. Alicia recalled how she came to join this loving family along with her brother Colin. She was adopted by Gus and Sarah while they did missionary work in Korea for the Catholic Church. She recalled her parents telling her about how they came to do the Church's work in Alicia's native land. After working their ranch and building it up for eighteen years, they were approached by the local priest, who asked if they were interested in missionary work in a foreign country. After a period of thought, both Gus and Sarah told the priest they would agree to volunteer after they made arrangements for someone they could trust to run the ranch for them. Gus and Sarah decided they would approach Moses as he had been with them for many years. They considered him a part of the family and trusted him completely. After these arrangements had been made, they coordinated with the church for their one-year-long mission trip to Korea.

It was a long shipboard journey but one in which they had some time to reconnect with each other. They had worked and built up their ranch for the last eighteen years, which meant hard back-breaking work of sixteen-hour days except for church worship on Sundays. It was hard to carve out any time together during those eighteen years. However, they had one standing rule that Sarah insisted upon. It was to have lunch together every Sunday at Mary's Café after Mass. They could at least have some time together during the two-hour ride to town, the lunch, and the two-hour trip back. However, this was different since they were taking a full year off away from the ranch.

Gus and Sarah were very well-liked by everyone in Cheyenne as they would pitch in anytime their neighbors needed help whether it was to participate in a barn raising or help anyone in need financially. If a friend was sick, they would make sure the family would have enough food not to go hungry. If a neighbor was injured, Gus would help with the work on the ranch to make sure the friend would not lose their place to the bank because their cattle had not gotten to market or their crop could not be harvested. So when the priest announced that Gus and Sarah were going to do some missionary work in Korea for a year and might need some help with their ranch operation, there was an outpouring of support from the parish members, which brought tears to Sarah's eyes although she would never admit to it. She claimed it was from getting dust in her eyes during the two-hour ride to church that morning. Gus and Sarah truly appreciated the offer of help and explained how Moses would be in charge along with their ranch foreman. Everyone knew Moses from all the years he had been with Gus and Sarah and respected him. They overlooked the fact his skin was black.

After their journey by sea, Gus and Sarah disembarked on the eastern seaboard of Korea where they were met by a Catholic priest, who made travel arrangements for their overland trip to their final destination in Seoul Korea. When they arrived in Seoul, they were provided a small four-room building for their quarters containing one room for sleeping, a small kitchen in an adjoining room to prepare their meals, another for receiving guests and conducting their missionary work, and a spare bedroom for any overnight guests. Their primary goal was to help spread the word of Catholicism and provide humanitarian aid to the local population in any way they could. They both found it very hard to be accepted in an Asian community, which was very suspicious of their work and their attempts to spread the Catholic faith.

Anytime Gus would offer to help a local family, he was always refused no matter how desperate the family's needs might be. They had a limited amount of medical supplies to treat minor injuries, colds, and viruses, and it was Sarah's idea to put up a sign indicating they would treat ill people at any time, day or night. The sign was printed in Korean by a shopkeeper whom they had befriended from down the street, who felt sorry for these new people whose only aim was to help his fellow Korean people. Gus and Sarah were very appreciative and bought all their supplies from this shopkeeper, whom they eventually became good friends with over time.

One day, the shopkeeper came to them and asked if they could treat his nephew, who had stepped on a piece of sharp metal but was not getting any better. The shopkeeper asked if they could come to his shop and treat the boy since he could not be seen bringing his nephew to them—his customers would not approve of him befriending these foreign missionaries. Sarah agreed to help and told Gus what she was going to do. He approved immediately. She made her way to the back of their friend's shop and entered through the back door as the shopkeeper had requested. She bowed a greeting to Mr. Woo, the shopkeeper, and he invited her into the back of his shop where his nephew was lying down on a bed. She immediately noticed the boy's foot was well taken care of and wrapped with a fresh, clean bandage. She approached the nephew, and Mr. Woo spoke to the boy, who nodded his head probably understanding this lady was going to look at his injury. He then stepped back and motioned with his hand for Sarah to step forward and examine the boy. She set her bag down, which contained the medicine and her limited supply of medical instruments. She removed the bandage and immediately saw the wound had become infected and swollen with poison. Sarah knew she would have to lance the wound and then treat it with the antiseptic medicine she had on hand. She hoped this would prevent the injury from turning into blood poisoning. She turned to Mr. Woo and motioned for him to bring some hot water into the room. He understood and within minutes brought the requested water to her. She placed the water basin on the bed and bent the boy's leg so she could get his foot into the basin to soak it. After several minutes, Sarah removed the foot from the basin and stretched the leg out flat. She turned to Mr. Woo and motioned for him to come over to the bed. She tried her best to explain that this part of the procedure would be painful. He would have to hold down his nephew's leg while she lanced the infected area of the foot to drain the pus. Mr. Woo spoke to his nephew and apparently explained—from the look of the nephew's face—there was going to be pain involved in this procedure. The boy looked at her and smiled slightly as if to say it was all right.

As Mr. Woo held down his nephew's leg, she got to work lancing the infected area and draining the wound. The boy never made a sound while she lanced the area and squeezed out the poison, continuing until she saw blood come out without pus. She then applied the antiseptic she brought and put clean bandages on the foot. She explained the best she could to Mr. Woo how to take care of his nephew after she left. She then packed up her medicines and medical instruments, standing to leave. Mr. Woo motioned her into the other room and offered her some tea, which she accepted, and sat with him for a few minutes. Sarah knew very little Korean and Mr. Woo very little English, but they were able to communicate with each other enough to know that Mr. Woo was very grateful to her for helping his nephew. She left after finishing her tea and returned to Gus. She explained what she had done and that Mr. Woo was very grateful for the help.

For the next three days, she went to Mr. Woo's shop through his back entrance and treated his nephew with medicine until she could see he was out of danger. She again explained the best she could to Mr. Woo what he had to do until his nephew was completely healed.

She and Gus continued their missionary work the best they could although with the same limited results as before. About a week after Sarah told Mr. Woo his nephew had made a complete recovery, there was a knock on Gus and Sarah's front door. Gus answered the door and before him stood a Korean monk in his traditional robe. The monk started to speak in perfect English asking if this was where the woman who had healed Mr. Woo's nephew lived. Gus was surprised to hear spoken English from a Korean and especially a monk to boot. The monk had arrived just after Gus and Sarah had eaten breakfast, and Sarah was in the kitchen finishing up the dishes. Gus invited the monk in and asked him to sit down while he went to get her. He went to the kitchen and found Sarah at the sink drying the last couple of dishes.

"Sarah, you're never gonna believe who is paying us a call."

"I have no idea who would be calling on us. The only person that comes to mind would be that nice Mr. Woo. If not him, then I don't know who."

"Well, we have a Korean monk calling on us, who speaks English better than I do," said Gus.

"Let's not keep him waiting. I wonder what he could possibly want and why he is paying us a visit?" asked Sarah.

They walked to the front room where Gus had left the monk. The monk had picked the only chair in the room that was wooden with a straight back, making him sit in an uncomfortably rigid, upright position. As Sarah entered the room, the monk got up and bowed to her, extending his hand in greeting. She returned the bow and also extended her hand. "It is a pleasure to meet the lady who healed Mr. Woo's nephew," said the monk.

"We are here to give assistance whether it is spiritual or physical help. It is our mission to attend to all the needs of the Korean people we can help, which includes medicine, food, and financial help when we can, as well as spreading the word of God. I am only glad Mr. Woo's nephew recovered so nicely," replied Sarah.

"I have heard that you have been telling the people about your religion and spreading the word of your God. My heart is glad that there are unselfish people like you in the world, who only wish to help their fellow man. I am a Buddhist monk, and my religion is much different than yours, although I have read about your Catholic faith and understand some of the philosophy behind it. I have two brothers. You have already helped one of them by healing our nephew. When my brother Mr. Woo called you for assistance to treat our nephew, you did so willingly and without hesitation. My other brother lost his wife in a tragic accident but serves in the military and has been away for a long time. Mr. Woo volunteered to take care of his son while he was away in the army. That is why you see the boy in his shop working beside him. I am here to thank you and invite both of you to my brother monks and my monastery. The monastery is located in the hills above the village, and our mission, similar to yours, is to help the poor, meditate, study philosophy and religion, and train in the ancient martial art of tae kwon do. I would personally like you to visit us so I may learn more about your religion and what you are trying to accomplish for my people. Please do come up for a visit, and we can sit and discuss religion over tea," said the monk.

They looked at each other and then Sarah turned to the monk and said, "Thank you for the compliments. We would be delighted to come to your monastery for a visit. We have not been very successful in attracting members to join our religion as most are suspicious. It would be nice if some of the people would come by for a visit and just talk to us. We could also help them if they are sick or injured as we have a small supply of medicine. Since we are not very busy, we will come to the monastery this weekend if that would be convenient."

"That would be fine. I will see you when it is convenient for you to visit us this weekend. May Buddha smile on you and grant you eternal peace and tranquility." At that, the monk stood and started for the front door at the same time thanking them for their generous hospitality. They both walked him to the door where they said their good-byes.

They walked back to the kitchen area and Sarah made some tea while Gus sat down at the kitchen table. As the water was heating on the stove, she sat down with him at the table, and they discussed the visit from the monk. "That was certainly interesting. What did you think of the visit?" asked Sarah.

"Well, I think he was very sincere and came to see who we were out of curiosity but also to thank you for helping his nephew. He seemed impressed that foreigners would offer assistance to one of his people without requiring something in return. It will be very interesting to go to the monastery and see how the monks live. It sounds like they are very well respected by the people here in the village. If we are seen to accept the monks as friends and not afraid to show people we respect their religion, an invitation from the monks might help us in our missionary work and allow us to spread the word of God and Catholicism," replied Gus.

"I agree with everything you say, and I think it would prove very interesting to visit the monastery and see their religious culture. We can plan on going up to the monastery this Saturday to return the visit. I will contact Mr. Woo and see if he can get word to his brother to let him know we will be arriving this Saturday, so he knows exactly when to expect us."

The next day, Sarah contacted Mr. Woo and let him know of their plans to visit his brother at the monastery. He was so grateful to her for helping his nephew, he arranged for a small wagon with a horse for them to use on their trip up the mountain road to the monastery.

Gus and Sarah were up by seven o'clock on Saturday morning eating a large breakfast and then cleaning up the kitchen's dirty dishes. Just as they finished up, Mr. Woo was at the door to let them know he had brought the horse and wagon for their trip. They gathered up a few things to take with them and then set off on their way. The monastery was located in the mountains at a high altitude, which required a slow journey up a narrow switchback mountain road. The monastery looked magnificent in the distance as they approached the complex. The buildings were constructed in ancient times out of solid rock formed and cut by master stonemasons, forming a circle around a large courtyard. The final road to the monastery was tree-lined and solemn with the branches extending a leafy canopy over the road. The entrance was a large, curved archway with thick double doors which fit perfectly. They stopped their wagon on the side of the road and tied the horse to the tree nearest the entrance.

As they approached the entrance, one of the large double doors opened slowly and Brother Lee stepped out to greet them. They all said hello and walked through the entrance into the courtyard together. Impressive was the word that came to Gus as he took in the immense courtyard area. It had to be at least three hundred feet in diameter with the grounds covered in solid marble. Fountains were spread intermittently around the outside perimeter of the circular courtyard. The buildings contained everything the monks needed for their daily living including a kitchen, housing, medical facilities, and a large area used for meditation, reflection, and worship. The monks were also proficient in the martial art of tae kwon do, which they practiced daily for two hours in the courtyard area. Gus and Sarah had arrived just before ten o'clock, which was when the monks practiced their daily martial arts routine.

This was the first time they would see their future daughter and son. There were approximately forty monks who filed out into the courtyard from the surrounding buildings. Then a little girl and older boy walked out into the courtyard from one of the other buildings and took their place in the last row. Sarah was not sure why such a little girl was permitted to participate in what looked like some sort of physical training. There were four rows with ten monks in a row and one person in front who yelled commands, which caused everyone to kick or punch in unison at the sound of each command.

Brother Lee explained to them what was going on and asked if they would like to watch the workout session. Sarah immediately agreed to watch as she was intrigued by the little girl and boy who were being permitted to participate in an activity which was clearly adult-oriented. She was intrigued that a female—and a tiny girl at that—was permitted to take part in what appeared to be a male-dominated activity, especially considering the Asian philosophy toward women not having any sort of value or decision-making ability in this male-dominated society.

"Brother Lee, who is that beautiful little girl standing in the last row with your fellow monks?" asked Sarah.

"Her name is Young Lee, and I met her on one of my walks through the country," answered Brother Lee.

"I understand that, but why is she here and not with her mother and father?" asked Sarah.

"Young Lee and her brother Eun Lee are two children who met with an unfortunate tragedy. Their parents were killed by bandits at their rice farm while being robbed. The bandits had come upon her family while they were working in the rice fields to take what they could. I had just walked out of the mountain trail, which opened up on their parents' farm, and I could see about ten mounted horsemen screaming at the children's father, who was shaking his head to whatever they were asking him. All of a sudden, the lead horseman drew his sword with lightning speed and killed her father instantly with one strike. The children's mother had been working about fifty yards away but had stopped to see who the strangers were and screamed as she saw her husband killed. I could see Young Lee and Eun Lee about twenty feet away from their mother, standing in the rice paddy and staring at their mother in fright after hearing her scream. Young Lee's mother instinctively ran to her son and daughter, picking up Young Lee and making Eun Lee stand behind her, hoping to protect both children from these bandits. The ten men rode their horses over to the mother and started screaming loudly at her, demanding money, or they would kill her and her family. I started to run toward them after seeing what they did to the father and yelled at them to stop. But the short exchange between Young Lee's mother and the bandits did not look good, and she did not appear to be pleading for her life but the life of her children. The lead bandit looked at her, and she defiantly returned his stare. The children's mother must have known what was about to happen because she put Young Lee down behind her next to Eun Lee and picked up a wooden rake she had with her when she had first run over to her children. She swung the rake at the lead bandit and landed the teeth of the rake into his leg. This caused him to yank back on his horse. The horse bucked and threw the bandit to the ground. He sprang up from the muddy field and drew his sword. He stepped toward Young Lee's mother, who had extended the rake in a thrusting motion. The bandit swung his sword at an angle, cutting the rake handle in half and leaving a sharp point at the end of the handle. The bandit then took one more step, brought his sword back, and swung to kill Young Lee's mother. Just as the sword was about to strike her, she thrust the rake handle as hard as she could into the bandit's chest, killing him, but not before his swinging sword struck and killed her at the same time. By that time, I was only a few feet away from the fight. The other bandits looked at the carnage and the second in charge leaped from his horse and found his leader to be dead. He then turned and checked on the mother to make sure she was dead. He finally walked over to the stunned children, who were crying, and took his sword out to kill them. That is when I instinctively yelled at him to stop as there would be no more killing. He turned to me and said the children were his to kill in revenge as he did not want these children to grow up and take revenge on him some twenty years from now. I told him I would not permit him to kill these helpless children and put myself in between them and the bandit. I told him I would guarantee the children be brought up with love and not revenge. I also told him he would have to kill me even though I would not raise a hand against him or defend myself, but he would have to be willing to kill a holy man. As mad as he was, he knew it would not be to his benefit to kill me. So he told me I could have the children as long as I would make sure they were raised as I promised. I agreed, and he got back on his horse and he and his men rode away into the mountains. I brought the children back here to the monastery and related the story to my brothers, who reluctantly agreed to allow them to remain under our care as long as I would try to locate a family willing to take them both. Unfortunately, I have not been able to find anyone who wants a female child, and in our society, female children are not of any value. Only the male child is. So, I have not been successful in placing Young Lee and her brother with a local family. That is our dilemma. However, Young Lee has such a joyful personality and is so friendly and kind she has melted the hearts of all my fellow brother monks. Eun Lee has also brought much joy to my brothers as he is kind and sensitive but also a hard worker happily doing any chore we ask of him. I think it will be a sad day for all when they leave this place," replied Brother Lee.

"I am sorry for these two children, but why do you allow them to practice fighting? Doesn't that violate your promise to the bandit you stopped from killing them?" asked Sarah.

"I do not think it does. You see, they are being taught tae kwon do, whose sole purpose is to allow them to defend themselves. So, they are being taught to defend themselves from attack and not to attack someone first," answered Brother Lee.

"How is it the brothers have allowed these two to join them in their practice?" asked Sarah.

"You have to get to know these little children with their infectious smiles and good natures. They would come out in the courtyard and not being invited into the group, would stand a little bit away from the monks and try to imitate their movements. They would come out every day, trying to duplicate the brothers' moves when finally the Grand Master Instructor came over to them and asked if they would like to join them. After that, the entire class welcomed them and showed them all the moves and techniques they were practicing. I have never seen the brothers take to anyone so quickly or be manipulated by children who have yet to reach their fourth and eighth birthday," replied Brother Lee.

After he finished explaining about the children, he asked them if they would like a tour of the monastery. Both nodded yes, and he escorted them across the courtyard and into one of the buildings. He decided to show them the kitchen first. Sarah was impressed with how clean and well-kept the kitchen facility was. There was not a dirty dish or utensil in sight and every dish, pot, or pan was clean and in its appropriate place.

The tour continued into the other buildings, which were just as clean, neat and tidy as the kitchen. They were impressed with the worship and meditation area, where they lingered for some time asking Brother Lee many questions about Buddhism and the method they used to worship. By the time the tour was close to completion, Sarah noticed through a window the monks in the courtyard bowing to the Grand Master Instructor, who then dismissed the class.

Sarah turned to Brother Lee and asked, "Brother Lee, would it be possible for us to meet these children and talk to them?"

"Yes, I would be pleased for you to meet them later. However, right now, it is time for lunch, and I hope you will join us and share our meager meal."

They both agreed it would be their pleasure to share a meal with the brothers and the children. They accompanied Brother Lee to the eating area and had a meal of rice, vegetables, and delicious soup. There was no meat served as all the vegetables were grown in the monks' garden, and the local population would donate the rice staple to the monks on a weekly basis.

The monks lived an austere life and had very few worldly possessions. Sarah and Gus both had the same thought at the same time but did not want to say anything to Brother Lee. They could not imagine a life for two little children in such a restricted environment, where they had no one their age to play or interact with.

After lunch, Brother Lee looked at Gus and Sarah asking, "Would you like to come out to the courtyard where we can continue our conversation with some tea?"

"That would be fine, and can we meet the children out there?" asked Sarah.

"I don't see them here, so they might already be outside somewhere. Let's go out and see," replied Brother Lee.

The three of them walked out into the courtyard and located a couple of benches under a shade tree near one of the fountains. As they were getting settled, Brother Lee spotted Young Lee chasing a butterfly on the other side of the courtyard. He called out to Young Lee, waving to her to come over at the same time. Young Lee looked over and waved back excitedly while running over to where the three of them sat.

"Good afternoon, Young Lee, did you catch a butterfly today?" asked Brother Lee.

She stood about two feet tall and couldn't weigh more than twenty pounds. She was dressed in a monk-like robe that looked as though it had been cut down from an adult robe. The monks did a good job, but it was so plain and drab that Sarah thought what a difference it would make if this toddler could have a dress. Young Lee turned her face up to look back at Brother Lee. "No, the butterflies are always faster than I am, but it is always fun to try to catch them," replied Young Lee.

"Tell me what you would do if you caught one of the butterflies," said Brother Lee.

"Oh, Brother Lee, I would let the butterfly go as they are too pretty to catch, and you told me they would bring much joy to people if they were free to fly. So I would never keep them or hurt them since they are so helpless," Young Lee said, with eyes that had grown wide as they could be.

"Young Lee, do you know where your brother is? I wanted to speak to him and introduce him to our visitors."

"I saw him go with one of the brothers to the garden. Would you like me to go get him?"

"No, little one, we will watch for him when he returns from his chores. Our visitors have come to us from a faraway place. This is Mr. and Mrs. Prentiss. Can you say hello to these two nice people?"

Young Lee turned toward Gus and Sarah and bowed to them saying, "It is nice to have you here. Brother Lee, the lady is very pretty. Where do they stay? Are they going back to their faraway place today?"

Brother Lee smiled a knowing smile and looked at Gus and Sarah. "Please forgive the child as she is a very curious one, who seems to ask questions many times a day. She still asks questions to one of our brothers who had taken a vow of silence. At first, he was upset at her for bothering him until Young Lee climbed into his lap one day, pretending not to talk, and just sat with the brother until she fell asleep. The humor, of course, was the brother could not call for help, and so he sat there for two hours while Young Lee took her afternoon nap. She was so small and light, and so beautiful sleeping in his lap that he developed a deep fondness for Young Lee, and they are always together now. The interesting thing about this is that they have developed their own unique sign language, which is only understood them."

"Sir! Sir! Are these people going to stay with us?" asked Young Lee.

"I don't think so, little one. I asked them to come here and visit with us because they have been helping people in the village."

Young Lee then turned toward Gus and Sarah with an inquisitive look. Gus looked down at this tiny, sweet-looking delicate girl. "You look like you would like to ask a question, Young Lee," said Gus.

"Yes, sir. How do you help the people in the village?"

"Well, we will feed them if they are hungry, and we will try to help them get better if they are sick. We also talk to them about worshiping God and becoming something we call a Christian," replied Gus.

Young Lee then turned toward Brother Lee. "Sir, what's a Christian? Do they know Buddha?"

"Young Lee, we believe in a different God than Buddha. Our God thinks all people should be treated equally with love, and no one person is better than anyone else," replied Sarah.

"Brother Lee, that sounds like what you have been teaching us. Aren't we supposed to love everyone and help all those who need help?" asked Young Lee.

"Yes, Young Lee. Our visitors are not as familiar with our beliefs as they are strangers to our land, and you must be patient with them."

The rest of the afternoon was spent talking to Brother Lee and learning about the things they were doing at the monastery and asking questions regarding Buddhism. Young Lee also sat with them during this time and asked questions about where they were from and how people lived in America. Her inquisitiveness, courtesy, and friendly personality impressed and endeared her to both of them.

As afternoon turned toward evening, Brother Lee asked Gus and Sarah if they would like to join them for dinner. They thanked

Brother Lee for the dinner invitation, but politely refused as they had a long journey down the mountain to the village and did not want to start after dark. Young Lee then whispered something to Brother Lee and then scampered off after excusing herself and saying she would be right back.

"May I walk with you to your wagon? I will then say good-bye to you there. I wish Eun Lee had come back so you could meet him and talk to him," said Brother Lee.

Both Sarah and Gus nodded as they stood up to start walking toward the front gate. "Brother Lee, Young Lee is such an adorable little girl. Would it be possible for us to bring both her and Eun Lee to our home and stay with us for a day? I would love to have them visit us, and I could explain more fully what we are doing in your country along with meeting and getting to know her brother," asked Sarah.

Brother Lee paused for a moment before replying and then said, "Why don't you ask her yourself? I see her coming across the courtyard now."

Young Lee was running toward them with a couple of small bundles in her arms. As she stopped in front of Gus and Sarah, she held out the packages to them. "Brother Lee said it was all right for me to go to the kitchen and get some bread and cheese for you to eat on your way back to the village. I hope you like bread and cheese."

"We both like bread and cheese. Thank you for being so kind. We were both wondering if you and your brother would like to come and visit us in the village for a day?" asked Sarah.

"I would like that very much. Would it be all right, Brother Lee?"

"I have already given my permission to our visitors who asked if you could go and see them, little one. I will let you ask your brother, and the two of you can decide for yourselves."

"Then yes, I would like to go for a visit, and I am sure my brother would like to go, too. When can we go?" asked Young Lee.

"I will make arrangements for you to go very soon. I will be visiting my cousin next week on Tuesday. The only difficulty is that I normally go out into the countryside to help our people in need and do not get back until Thursday. Would you be able to take the children back to the monastery at the end of the day if their visit is convenient for you?" asked Brother Lee.

"That would be fine with us. But we could keep them until Thursday and then take them back to the monastery. We promise to take excellent care of them. If they want to go back earlier, we will take them back," offered Sarah.

Brother Lee turned to Young Lee, "Would you and your brother like to stay with our visitors overnight for two nights?" asked Brother Lee.

Young Lee nodded her head excitedly, and it was settled. She, along with her brother, would stay with Gus and Sarah for two days.

They returned to the village and dropped the wagon off to Mr. Woo, thanking him for arranging the visit to his brother's monastery.

For the next several days, Gus and Sarah continued their regular routine of providing help to the local people until the Tuesday of the children's scheduled arrival. There was a small extra room in their living quarters, which Sarah had modified into a small bedroom for Young Lee and Eun Lee.

Brother Lee arrived with both kids midmorning and visited for about a half hour. He introduced Eun Lee, making him comfortable with Gus and Sarah and making sure they were settled in. Sarah thanked Brother Lee for the trust he placed in them to keep the children since they had only known each other a short time. Brother Lee told them he was a very good judge of character and knew they were good religious people, who were selfless in their endeavor to help people they had never met before. He also told them he would be spreading the word it was all right to seek help from these foreigners, but he would not encourage anyone to stray from the Buddhist religion. Sarah, Gus, and the children waved to Brother Lee as he departed on his walk into the countryside to visit with the people he had always helped over the years.

Gus and Sarah spent the next two days doting on the children, taking them out to the market and buying clothes for them. There was also an open-air theater, which they attended. Although Gus and Sarah's Korean was not good enough for them to really understand what was going on, the play they chose was a children's show, which must have been funny as Young Lee and Eun Lee laughed during much of the entertainment.

When Brother Lee returned from his travels and stopped to see how they were doing, he found a little girl sleeping in Sarah's lap in their small living area and a little boy playing chess with Gus, who had taught him the game over the last two days.

Sarah gently woke up Young Lee and whispered in her ear that Brother Lee had come to take her back to the monastery. Young Lee put her arms around Sarah's neck and held her tightly, asking if she could stay a little more. She explained as best she could Young Lee would have to go back with Brother Lee as he would take care of her and provide her with a loving and caring home. Eun Lee also asked to stay a day or two longer as he was having a very enjoyable time with Gus and Sarah.

Brother Lee understood these children had established a strong attachment to these two foreigners in a very short time and thanked both Gus and Sarah for opening their home to them. He explained to Young Lee and Eun Lee that Gus and Sarah could come visit them at the monastery any time they wanted. They thanked Brother Lee and promised the children they would visit them as often as possible. They also extended an offer to have Young Lee and Eun Lee stay with them each month when Brother Lee made his trip to the countryside if that would be convenient.

CHAPTER 4

사랑

During the rest of the time Gus and Sarah were in Korea, they concentrated on doing their missionary work to assist the local peasantry in improving their living conditions and develop better farming techniques. At first, their efforts had little success as the peasants traditionally did not trust strangers. They had an even harder time to convince the rural peasants to use their methods. Not only were they strangers, but they were also foreigners who were white and only spoke a smattering of Korean.

Brother Lee learned of Gus and Sarah's efforts through his travels among the peasants and interceded on their behalf, convincing the peasantry to try some of the methods suggested by these two missionaries. Through Brother Lee's influence, many peasants agreed to try their farming methods, and the results were almost immediate, increasing the yields for those peasant farmers who allowed Gus and Sarah to alter their farming techniques. With the increased yields, peasant farmers could sell more crops from working the same amount of land and raise their income.

Eventually, the wealthy landowners who leased the land to the peasants, along with local public officials, increased the rent and taxes on farm crops resulting in the peasants having to work longer hours even with the improved farming techniques they had taught the farmers.

In 1862, while Gus and Sarah continued to work hard to improve the peasants' well-being, a group of farmers in Chinyu, Kyongsang Do province banded together and rose up against the aggressive local officials and the wealthy landowners. The uprising was a direct result of a newly appointed military commander, Paek Nak-Shin, who had authority over the western half of Kyonyang province. Paek Nak-Shin was responsible, along with other corrupt local officials, for the exploitation of destitute farmers through higher crop taxes and forced free labor on the peasants.

One farmer, by the name of Yu Kye-Chin, was a regular visitor to the monastery, where he practiced Buddhism with the monks. Gus and Sarah took an immediate liking to Yu Kye-Chin and had serious in-depth discussions—Brother Lee interpreting—as to what was happening to the local communities. Yu Kye-Chin would elaborate on the peasants' plight to Gus and Sarah, who tried to explain they were there to offer help to the local peasantry to improve their lives and not get involved with politics. They explained they were trying to demonstrate to the peasant farmers there were new ways to farm by planting other crops besides rice. Gus and Sarah also explained they provided medicine for the sick and comforted the elderly.

However, there was an intense unrest among the peasant farmers, and Yu Kye-Chin arose to become a leader for the people. Gus and Sarah discussed many of the economic issues related to the peasantry, counseling Yu Kye-Chin to resolve their differences without violence. However, it became apparent to them that Yu Kye-Chin was determined to force changes even if it meant violence.

By 1862, Yu Kye-Chin had organized the peasantry into a force, which rebelled against Paek Nak Shin and the corrupt officials in the local government. Some of the local officials were killed and several government buildings were burned down. The Seoul government was surprised by the rebellion and quickly dispatched an investigator, who recommended reforms be instituted.

During the visits Gus and Sarah had with Brother Lee at the monastery and the discussions with Yu Kye-Chin, there were periods of time when Yu Kye-Chin would walk out to the courtyard and watch the monks practice their tae kwon do techniques. Yu Kye-Chin marveled at Young Lee and Eun Lee's mastery of this Korean martial art at such a young age, sometimes talking to them after the training sessions. He would talk to them as if they were adults and not children. Young Lee had been present in the same room when Gus, Sarah, and Yu Kye-Chin would discuss the issues most important to the peasantry. So even as a child, Young Lee asked Yu Kye-Chin simple but straightforward questions only a child would ask.

Once, while speaking to Yu Kye-Chin in the monastery courtyard, she asked, "Why do you want to hurt people?"

"I do not wish to hurt anyone, but some people are bad, and it is the only way I have to help the farmers," said Yu Kye-Chin.

"What do the people look like who are bad? Can I tell if a stranger is evil if he looks a certain way?" asked Young Lee.

"No, you can't tell if someone is bad by the way they look or the way they walk or how they speak. If they hurt my people, then they are bad, little one," replied Yu Kye-Chin.

Gus and Sarah developed an excellent relationship with Yu Kye-Chin and became close friends. Unfortunately, about a year after Gus and Sarah returned to their ranch, they received a letter from Brother Lee informing them Yu Kye-Chin had been arrested and executed for leading his insurrection against the unfair government and landowners who increased taxes and rents.

On Brother Lee's next trip to the countryside, he stopped at Gus and Sarah's house to drop off the kids for their usual two-day stay. Gus asked Brother Lee if he had a few minutes to go for a walk. Brother Lee agreed, and they both went for their walk after goodbyes were said to Sarah and the children. As they walked down the lane, Brother Lee sensed Gus had something important to discuss but was unsure of how to start the conversation.

"Gus, we have known each other for almost a year, and it is quite obvious you want to speak to me about something important. I consider you a close friend, and close friends should be able to talk about anything. So please, tell me what is concerning you."

"Sarah and I have been talking about Young Lee and her brother. Over the last few months, we have grown to love these two children and would like to adopt them, eventually taking them with us back to America. If you would look favorably on our request, we would still need your help as we do not know how to arrange an adoption."

"I have been impressed with the love you and Sarah have shown these two children. I thought this may come up, and I have made some inquiries as to how difficult it would be for a foreigner to adopt Korean children. Unfortunately, I have been told it is almost impossible for an adoption to proceed for any of our children to foreigners. However, a corrupt official by the name of Pak Nak Shin has made it clear he may approve a foreign adoption if he were to receive monetary compensation to offset his administrative expenses in preparing the necessary documents."

"Let's make it simple, Brother Lee. This man wants Sarah and me to give him a bribe. Is that correct?"

"Unless you and Sarah give this man money, he will not allow you to adopt the children, let alone take them to America."

"Sarah will never agree to buy another human being. Isn't there any other way we can take both children with us?"

"The children have been made legal wards to myself and the rest of my fellow monks, and there are no restrictions about who we place the children with. When we have placed orphans in the past, we have only been required to notify the local court by letter. No one has ever said this procedure was not acceptable. I believe the court would question us when they see your American names on the letter. My brothers and I have seen how both you and Sarah love and care for Young Lee and Eun Lee. It would give us great pleasure to see the children live with you and Sarah. There is a way for the children to go with you, but I will need to speak with my fellow monks to make sure they are in agreement. I will speak with them and if they agree, I will tell you of my plan. If they do not agree, there will be no help I can give you. Will you agree with that?"

"Brother Lee, you and your fellow monks have become very good friends, and I think you will be fair in your decision. We will wait anxiously for you to let us know the results of your discussion with your fellow monks."

"Gus, I do not want to impose upon you and Sarah but if you can keep Young Lee and Eun Lee for one more day, I will go directly to my monastery and discuss this with my brothers rather than picking the children up in two days after my trip to the countryside. I will come to your house and give you and Sarah our decision."

"We would love to keep the children for another day. If the brothers agree, Sarah and I will have to get busy making arrangements as our time here ends this month, and we must leave for America by boat in a few days."

"I will be as swift as possible, Gus, and return with our decision tomorrow."

With that, Gus and Brother Lee parted and went their separate ways.

Brother Lee continued his usual walk through the countryside, providing spiritual guidance and help to his fellow countrymen. He gave a great deal of thought to what he and Gus had discussed concerning the adoption of the children. He decided his plan would be to meet with the head of their province and attempt to get approval for a foreign adoption.

His trip through the provincial countryside was routine and uneventful and when he finished, he returned to the monastery to speak with the brothers. He met with all his fellow monks in the courtyard and discussed the request for adoption Gus and Sarah had made. Although a few of the monks voiced some concerns, they were all in agreement Gus and Sarah's love for the children far outweighed their desire to raise them at the monastery. All the monks agreed to help arrange the children's adoption, understanding they would most likely never see them again. It was decided Brother Lee would approach Pak Nak Shin at his palace office as he had personally met this official at a few local village festivals.

Brother Lee made his way down the mountain road to the village where Gus and Sarah lived and softly knocked on their door. Both Gus and Sarah opened the door together, standing there with concerned looks on their faces.

"Please come in, Brother Lee, and make yourself comfortable. Can I get you some tea?" asked Sarah.

"That would be very nice, Sarah, if it is not too much trouble."

Sarah went to the kitchen and poured tea for all of them and brought it back into the room where all three sat. "Brother Lee, I am on pins and needles as they say in America. Can you please tell us what decision you and your fellow monks have come to regarding the children?"

"Sarah, all of us have decided to help you and Gus any way we can for you two to adopt the children. We have decided I will arrange a meeting with Pak Nak Shin, who as you know is the leader of our province. We have to get his permission and approval for you to adopt the children. I do not think it will be hard to get permission for Young Lee as she is a female child and not highly valued in our culture. The boy, however, will be difficult as he is a male and considered to be highly valued even though he is an orphan. I have already arranged a meeting with Pak Nak Shin for tomorrow and will ask him to grant us permission for the adoption. You may keep the children here for one more day if you would like. I will be staying with my brother down the street to visit with him as we have not seen each other for quite some time."

"Sarah and I will be glad to have the children stay with us another day. Please stop by after your appointment with Pak Nak Shin and let us know if we will be able to get permission to adopt them." They continued their conversation for another half an hour and then said their good-byes as Brother Lee left for his brother's store.

The next day, Brother Lee made his way to Pak Nak Shin's office where he was asked to wait in an outer room. After a while, an aide to Pak Nak Shin came out and told Brother Lee he could be seen now. Brother Lee was escorted into a room where Pak Nak Shin sat in a large chair behind an enormous desk in an opulent room decorated with many gold statues, fine furnishings, and several paintings hanging on the walls.

"Brother Lee, I am honored you have graced me with a visit. You and your fellow monks provide invaluable spiritual guidance to our people. Are the brothers in need of my help in some area?"

"It is I who am honored you have granted me an audience with our illustrious leader. I hope all is well with your family, and you are at peace within yourself. My brothers and I pay high regards to any person who gives unselfishly to further the well-being of the people. Sometimes, one must make a difficult and hard decision, which requires us to make personal sacrifices for the well-being of the people. Great leaders always put their people first, and I believe you to be one of our great leaders."

"Brother Lee, I am honored with your compliments and expressions of gratitude. I am also in agreement everyone must make sacrifices and allowances for the benefit of our citizens. May I offer you some tea while we talk?"

"Yes, that would be very gracious of you, my Lord. I am sure my Lord knows my fellow monks and I have been looking after two orphans at our monastery since bandits killed their parents. We have been searching for a suitable family to take this boy and girl but have not been successful until just recently. We have found a childless couple, who would provide these children with a loving home and wishes to adopt them for their own. The brothers and I know we cannot turn over these children without my Lord's approval, and we would humbly request your permission to place these children with this couple."

"Brother Lee, I am always interested in the welfare of all the people, including the children. How well do you know this husband and wife? Will they be able to take care of these children and will they live in this province?"

"My Lord, I have known this husband and wife long enough to assure you they would make excellent parents for these two orphans. They live in a house in the village, and that is where I would take the children. Their love for these children knows no bounds, and they will always be cared for."

"I dislike bringing this subject up, but I have to ask if these parents have money to pay for the papers to go through the Minister of Justice. I would like to give you permission, but we have to collect the fees to pay for the adoption papers and the use of my royal stamp."

"I understand the government must collect compensation to help them rule and enforce the laws of our country. However, I ask his Lordship to be merciful and charitable by giving permission for this adoption and show the villagers how benevolent a leader you are. If you approve the adoption, all the brother monks in the monastery would look upon your sacrifice as a great goodwill gesture and praise you to their religious followers about your glorious deed."

Pak Nak Shin studied the monk and thought about how he could use this adoption to his advantage. He knew he was not well liked because he had raised the taxes to increase his wealth. If he could get these monks to sing his praises to the peasants, maybe it would be in his best interest to grant the adoption and not collect a fee. After all, these were two orphans and had no value to him.

"Brother Lee, you have convinced me to approve the adoption for the sake of these poor orphans. My assistant will take you personally to my Minister of Justice, who will give you a paper approving this adoption." Pak Nak Shin turned to his assistant and ordered him to take Brother Lee across the street and have the minister issue a formal adoption decree. He also told the assistant to take his royal stamp along so the decree could be formally sealed by the minister for Brother Lee's convenience.

Brother Lee and the assistant took their leave and crossed the street, entering the ministry where they located the clerk who normally processed adoption requests. The assistant explained to the clerk why they were there as the clerk looked on, disinterested in the explanation. The clerk located the proper decree and started the process of completing it while asking for the information to write in the decree. After he listed the children's names and ages, he asked for the adoptive parents' names. Brother Lee paused for a moment, looked at the clerk, and then explained he did not have the exact spelling and would be happy to take the stamped form with him, fill the names in, and return the form.

"Brother Lee, I am not allowed to do that. The form must be completely and accurately filled out before I can issue and seal it with the royal stamp. You can go back to the parents and get the exact spelling, bring it to me, and I will then send the form across the street for the stamp as I am sure the assistant will take it with him. His Lordship can then look the decree over, have it stamped, and it will be ready for you in a few days. I will personally deliver the decree to you when I receive it back."

"Most honorable sir, I understand you have rules, which you are required to abide by. That is certainly satisfactory to me. We will go back to his Lordship and let him know you are unable to do what he has ordered due to your office rules."

Brother Lee turned to the assistant and motioned him to leave. When they both turned and started for the door, the clerk called out to him.

"Brother Lee, if his Lordship ordered this paper to be issued then I feel obligated to do that as long as you bring the form back with the proper names on it."

"Is this not the official form the parents would keep when completed and stamped?"

"Yes, Brother Lee, but I do need the parents' names to put in the official village census and check the form to make sure it is correct."

"Just show me where the names are entered, and I will make sure we put them in the appropriate place. Will that be satisfactory?"

The clerk hesitated and then said, "As you are a religious monk, I will trust you. Here is the form with the royal seal."

"Thank you, sir, and may Buddha smile upon you and grant you peace."

Brother Lee bid the assistant good day and asked him to thank their Lordship for granting the adoption as he hurried down the street to Gus and Sarah's house. After Brother Lee knocked on the door, it was just a matter of seconds until it opened with Sarah standing in the doorway with an apprehensive look.

"Sarah, I have very good news for all four of you. May I come in?"

"Oh forgive me, Brother Lee, I didn't mean for you to stand there. Please come in and have a seat. I will get Gus for you." She went into the kitchen where Gus had been helping her with the dishes.

"Who was it, Sarah?"

"It is Brother Lee, and he said he has good news for us."

"Well, let's go in and talk to him."

They brought some tea into the other room with them and sat down across from Brother Lee.

"Gus and Sarah, you are going to be parents. I have the adoption decree here and need to put your names into the proper spaces. However, when I put your names down and return the form, the clerk will look at it and see the adoption is for foreigners and may try to reverse the decision. When will your boat be ready for you to leave for America?"

"Why would you need to know when Sarah and I will be leaving?"

"I need to know for two reasons. As I said, when I put your names in the decree, the clerk will know you are foreigners and report this to Pak Nak Shin. When he finds out who you are, he will be furious and stop the adoption. He may even resort to violence as you are not only foreigners but Christians, whom he has nothing but hatred for. Your lives will be in jeopardy once he discovers who you are and your intention to take these children with you to America. That is why I would like to know when you are scheduled to leave Korea."

"Brother Lee, we are scheduled to travel in four days, however, there is another carriage we can hire tomorrow and take an earlier boat given the circumstances. That should put us on the coast one day before our ship sails."

"You will need to take that carriage tomorrow as I must return the form tomorrow."

"If it means our and the children's safety, I will arrange for all of us to leave tomorrow," replied Gus.

"Gus and Sarah, I wish to express my fondness for you both and thank you for all the kindness you have shown me, my fellow monks, and the children. I have enjoyed our many meetings and discussions this past year. I will say my good-byes now as I will not see you tomorrow."

Brother Lee stood up, stepped toward Gus and Sarah, and gave them each a hug good-bye. The gesture was very unconventional for Brother Lee as it was the first time Sarah had seen him display this kind of affection in the year they had known him.

Their eyes filled with tears when the children realized Brother Lee was saying good-bye forever, and they would not see him again. The three adults resisted crying as they explained to the children what was going to happen and how this would be a great benefit to them. Brother Lee also took the time to ask the children if they wanted Gus and Sarah for their parents and if they loved these two kind people. Neither child hesitated as both said yes at the same time through their tears. As Brother Lee turned and walked out the door and down the street toward his brother's shop, Gus, Sarah, and the children waved one final time when he looked back and returned the gesture. They then walked back inside and started to pack for their journey overland to the Korean east coast.

Brother Lee spent the night with his brother and in the morning, decided to go back to the monastery. That same morning, Gus and Sarah entered the names on the adoption decree and then took the children with their bags, boarded the carriage they had hired and left for the east coast.

Brother Lee took back streets to avoid walking in front of the Palace to the trail that led up the mountain to the monastery. He hoped the clerk would not remember about the decree he left with Gus and Sarah, proving they had adopted the children. He also hoped not returning the decree to the clerk on time, would give them two or three days to reach the coast, board their ship, and embark for America.

Brother Lee arrived safely to his monastery where he gathered his fellow monks and explained to them what he had done. There was silence for a few moments and then the monks' somber faces turned to smiles as they offered words of support and encouragement even though they knew Pak Nak Shin might punish them.

The clerk in the administrative office was going through his normal paperwork, approving and declining various requests from the local population. One of the documents that crossed his desk was an adoption decree he had approved for a local couple. This reminded him of the decree Brother Lee was supposed to return yesterday with the names of the husband and wife who were adopting those two children. He looked through the several stacks of papers on his desk to make sure the monk had not dropped the decree off while he was at lunch or dinner yesterday.

After sorting through all his papers, he was unable to locate the decree Brother Lee had promised to return. He knew Brother Lee stayed with his brother, who owned a shop in the village, so he decided to walk over to the shop and see if he could meet with Brother Lee and get the decree for his records. He went down to the shop and walked in to speak with the owner. The owner approached the clerk, and they bowed to each other in the traditional greeting.

"May I help you select something from my store?"

"No sir, I have not come to buy anything. You are the brother to a monk who lives in the monastery in the hills. Is that correct?"

"That is correct, most honorable sir. Do you have some spiritual matters to discuss with my brother?"

"No, I have nothing spiritual to discuss with him. Your brother was supposed to return an official document to me yesterday, and he failed to return it. I know he usually stays with you when he comes to the village. Is he here?"

"No, honorable sir, he left yesterday and returned to his monastery."

"Thank you, sir, for the information. I know it is a long trip to the monastery, but I need to get that decree for my office. I will arrange for a carriage to take me there and retrieve the decree. Thank you for your help, you have been most kind."

"May Buddha grant you a safe journey to my brother's monastery."

After they bid each other good-bye, the clerk returned to his office and made arrangements for a carriage.

Gus, Sarah, Colin, and Alicia were well on their way to the east coast where they would board the ship taking them back to America. Gus was confident they had a good head start in case Pak Nak Shin decided to pursue them when he found out foreigners were adopting the two children.

By evening, their carriage stopped at an inn in a small village where they spent the night. The next morning, they continued their cross-country trip, arriving at the port city where they would board their ship in the morning.

The clerk arrived at the monastery that afternoon and requested an audience with Brother Lee. As the two of them sat down, Brother Lee knew what he was going to be asked about. After the exchange of some pleasantries, the clerk asked Brother Lee why he had not returned the decree.

"I did not return the decree because I gave it to the new parents. They were going on a trip, and they might need to prove they have adopted the children."

"I don't understand, Brother Lee. Why would they ever have to prove they are the parents of these children? Please tell me what their names are."

"The parents' names are Gus and Sarah Prentiss."

The clerk sat with a stunned look on his face for about ten seconds before he could speak. "Do you mean the Catholic missionaries the Lordship graciously allowed to stay and work in the village?"

"That is correct. These two people grew to care and love these two children when no one else would step forward to adopt them. I tried to place these two children with the people I visit on my walks through the country to promote Buddhism, and no one was interested when they found out a female would also have to be adopted with the boy."

"Brother Lee, I think his Lordship is going to be very upset about this as you did not volunteer the names of the parents. Lord Pak Nak Shin is completely against foreign adoptions. I must leave now and immediately report this to his Lordship. Before I leave, you said the parents needed to be able to prove the children were theirs because they were going on a trip. Where are the parents taking these children?"

"They left early this morning to travel east to the coast where they will board a ship to America in two days."

"I am leaving immediately and cannot tell you what actions his Lordship will take."

As the clerk started to walk toward the door to leave, Brother Lee stood up and wished him a safe journey with peace and tranquility.

When the clerk arrived back to his office, it was early evening but he crossed the street to the Palace and requested an audience with Pak Nak Shin. A half hour later, his Lordship entered the room and sat down plainly irritated.

"Why are you asking to see me at such a late hour?"

"My Lord, I received a decree yesterday authorizing an adoption Brother Lee had arranged."

"Yes, yes, I am fully aware of it. Is there a problem with the adoption?"

"My Lord, I have just discovered these children were adopted by the missionary foreigners from America."

The clerk saw the information sink in, and his Lordship's face turn into intense anger. "Brother Lee has deceived me by not telling me who these parents were when he came to my Palace with his request. Where are these people now?"

"My Lord, I have also just found out they hired a carriage to take them east to the coast where they will board a ship taking them and these children to America."

His Lordship looked at the clerk and then turned to one of his assistants saying loudly, "Order a squad of mounted guards immediately. They are to ride cross-country to the coast and retrieve these children before they board this ship. If the missionaries resist, kill them and take the children. They are to ride without sleep and when they need new mounts, they will commandeer them from the nearest village. Give the order now."

Pak Nak Shin then turned back to his clerk. "Brother Lee did not directly lie to me so I cannot punish him. But if he comes to you with another request, you are to defer it to me. He is very popular with the villagers and if I were to overtly punish him, I would lose the people's respect, which is far more dangerous."

On the third morning, Gus and Sarah woke up to a beautiful day with bright sunshine.

They cleaned up, dressed and headed out to the ship they were to take to America. The carriage took them to the dock where they boarded an American flagship, which also had a passenger section. Gus showed the deck officer his four tickets and adoption decree, which the officer acknowledged and welcomed them aboard. The officer turned to a steward and asked him to show the passengers to their cabin.

Gus asked the officer when the ship would leave port and was informed the ship was leaving within an hour, at ten o'clock. Gus and his family were getting settled in when there was a knock on their cabin door. It was the first officer, who asked Gus to accompany him to the bridge to see the captain. Gus asked why, but the officer only explained the captain would answer all his questions.

When Gus arrived on the bridge, he noticed there was a Korean soldier there. The first officer made all the introductions and then the Captain turned to Gus.

"Mr. Prentiss, this officer of the Korean army has alleged you have kidnapped two Korean children, and he is authorized to either remove them or stop us from leaving the dock. Can you explain to me what he is talking about?"

"Yes, sir, my wife and I have adopted these two children and showed the adoption decree to the deck officer when we boarded this morning. This document has the official royal seal and would be accepted by anyone."

"Lieutenant Kwon, please explain to me why you believe this is an illegal adoption?"

"Lord Pak Nak Shin has voided this adoption and ordered myself and my men to remove these two children and return them to their village where they will be cared for."

"Lieutenant, do you have a written order from Lord Shin voiding this adoption and giving you the authority to take these children."

"No Captain, I do not have a written order as we left immediately and did not have time to wait for a written order."

"Then, lieutenant, you give me no choice but to refuse your request to remove these children from their legally adopted parents. You will need to rejoin your soldiers on the dock as we will be disembarking in seven minutes."

"Captain, my orders are not to allow your ship to leave with these two children on board."

"First Officer, escort Lieutenant Kwon to the dock and make ready to get underway."

"Captain, I know this is an American flagship and should be treated as if it were on American soil. I will not board your ship, but I will also prevent any of your crew members to come to our dock and release the lines holding you here."

"Lieutenant, you do what you must, and I will do what I must. First Officer, return to the bridge after you have escorted Lieutenant Kwon ashore."

"Aye, aye, sir," the first officer said as he escorted Lieutenant Kwon from the bridge down to the dock. He then returned within a couple minutes to where Gus and the captain had been talking.

"First Officer, are we ready to get underway?"

"We are, sir, except the ship is still tied to the dock, and we all heard what Kwon said if we attempt to go on the dock and release the tethers."

"First Officer, we have a crew of thirty on board. I want you to arm ten of them and Mr. Prentiss, as he has consented to defend the ship if necessary. I want you to position two armed men on the stern lines and two men on the bow lines. Also, position three armed men mid ship on both the port and starboard sides. Equip two more unarmed crew members with axes and send one to the stern line and the other to the bow line. These men will chop through the rope tethers while being covered by our crewmen. Make sure you make it clear to the crewmembers they are not to fire their weapons first. They can only fire if Kwon's soldiers fire first. If we fire first, we will cause an international incident, and we cannot afford to do that."

"Aye, aye, sir. Please follow me, Mr. Prentiss."

The two of them went down to the deck and equipped the crew with arms and axes as the captain had directed. The armed men took up their positions, and the two sailors with axes started chopping at the lines holding the ship to the dock.

Lieutenant Kwon ordered his soldiers to take aim at the sailors cutting the lines, and at the same time, the first officer ordered his men to take aim at Kwon and his soldiers. Neither side wanted to fire first and as the ship's tethers were severed, it started to drift out to sea, and eventually, out of range of Kwon's soldiers.

The rest of the trip was uneventful. They returned to San Francisco and then took an overland stage back to Wyoming, where they returned to their ranch and the life they had left before their missionary work in Korea.

Gus and Sarah took great pains to integrate the kids into the western lifestyle, helping them get to know their friends and neighbors. The townsfolk, with very few exceptions, accepted the kids into the community, treating them like any other children. Gus and Sarah also made sure the kids kept practicing the martial art of tae kwon do.

There was a loud rapping on Alicia's compartment door, startling her from her deep sleep. "Miss, this is the conductor. We are pulling into Chicago Union Station in about five minutes. You'll need to transfer trains for your trip to Wyoming. Let us know if you need help with your baggage," said the conductor.

"Thank you, but I've only got one bag so I won't need any assistance," she replied, loud enough for the conductor to hear her through the compartment door.

As the train pulled into the station, she grabbed her bag, exited the compartment, and headed down the passageway toward the end of the car. She exited onto the station platform, heading for the main lobby area to confirm her departure time and track number.

In the main area of Union Station, she located the schedule and track number, which showed the train for Cheyenne Wyoming leaving in thirty minutes. Since the train was already in the station and allowing passengers to board, she walked out to the platform and stepped in the car with the sleeper compartments. She was greeted by the porter, who checked her ticket and then escorted her to her assigned compartment. She entered her quarters and noticed the compartment was identical to the one she had just occupied from Pittsburgh. She set her bag down and sat in the window chair, waiting for the train to depart for Wyoming.

O'Malley stopped by his office, picked up his medical bag, and after hitching up his horse to the buggy, he climbed in and snapped the reins to begin his trip to Gus and Sarah's ranch.

The two-hour ride to their place gave O'Malley time to rehearse what he would say to Sarah if the worst had happened and Gus had died during the night. He had a feeling though that Gus would pull through due to his exceptionally strong will and just plain old stubbornness. He then leaned back in his buggy and recalled his second encounter with Gus shortly after he had arrived in Cheyenne.

CHAPTER 5

사랑

It was about six weeks after his altercation with Stu and Whitey when O'Malley next saw Gus. He had found a house to buy on the south side of town and converted part of it into an office area. He then hung his doctor's shingle from the eaves over the front porch steps. Gus had let it be known around town the new doctor was a friend of his, which resulted in many of the townsfolk seeking treatment from O'Malley if they were ill or needed medical treatment due to injuries.

The word spread quickly this new doctor was good and knew what he was doing, so the rest of the townsfolk, including rural ranchers alike, decided if Gus thought the new doctor was fine, then they would also give him a chance. So he started to see his patient load increase from only one or two patients the first week to several each day by the end of the fifth week, plus a full patient load on Saturdays.

Early on, he decided to open his office on Saturdays so he could treat the rural farmers and ranchers that were unable to get into town except on Saturdays. On the day O'Malley saw Gus, he had just finished up an especially busy Saturday treating patients until six o'clock in the evening. He washed up and changed his clothes then decided to walk over to Mary's Café for dinner. It was a typical Saturday night with the ranch hands in town starting their drinking at the Grizzly Saloon. Just as he was approaching Mary's, he heard someone call to him. "Hey, Doc! Heyyy, Doc!"

O'Malley turned and recognized Gus from down the street. "Well hello, Gus. You're in town kind of late. Shouldn't you be on your way back to the ranch by now?"

"Yeah, I should've been on the road about an hour ago, but Jake, over at the livery stable, didn't get my buckboard wheel fixed and said it will be another hour before it's done. So I figured I'd just come over to Mary's and get some supper. I hoped by the time I got done eatin', Jake should have the repairs done, and I can get headed back home. Doc, I don't know if you know it, but it's past supper time, and I'm hungry and you look hungry. Why don't you come on in here to Mary's with me, and I'll buy you supper."

"Gus, I was already on my way to Mary's for dinner, but I insist on buying your meal. You spread the word around town to your friends to come see the new doctor in town if they need medical treatment. Everyone respects you and by spreading the word, I now have a full patient load thanks to you. So, I would feel honored to buy supper for the first friend I made after arriving in Cheyenne."

"Okay, Doc. Let's stop wastin' time. Come on in and buy me a steak and potato dinner."

For the next hour, they ate their steak dinners, talking about their different childhoods and the reasons why each of them had come west. They wrapped up their dinner by seven o'clock, paid Mary, and walked out of the café, making their way down the boardwalk toward the livery stable while continuing the conversation they had started in the café.

As they walked toward the livery still engrossed in their conversation, they passed by the Grizzly Saloon just as the doors burst open and two drunken cowboys barreled through them, colliding with Gus and O'Malley and sending all four of them sprawling into the street.

"Don't you two watch where you're going?" shouted one of the cowboys at Gus and O'Malley.

"Boys, the Doc and I were walking down the boardwalk minding our own business. I think you two cowboys should have been the ones watching where you were goin'," said Gus.

"Well, looky here, Whitey. If it isn't the dude and his keeper. Dude, you afraid to walk around town without Gus to protect ya?" said Stu.

"I think you two have been drinkin' too much. Gus is just a friend of mine, and I don't need anyone to protect me. Why don't you just get your horses and run back out to the Double X where you can go and sleep it off," replied O'Malley.

"If Gus wasn't here, maybe we could settle this man to man unless you're too afraid," replied Stu.

"I'll handle this, Doc," interrupted Gus as he turned and took a step toward Stu and Whitey.

Before Gus could move any closer, he felt a hand on his shoulder holding him back. "Just a minute, Gus. I think you should go on down to the livery and pick up your wagon before it gets too late. Sarah will be worried as you're already late by two hours. I'm sure the boys and I can discuss our problems and work them out."

"I don't like it, Doc. I wouldn't trust either of these cowboys if they were the last people on earth," said Gus.

"Well, Doc, it just don't seem like we're gonna settle this. But I'm sure we'll see ya around without your protector," said Stu.

"Gus, if you're going to stay, you will have to give me your word you won't interfere with Stu, Whitey, and me. Otherwise, you're going to have to leave and let me work this out with these boys."

"Okay, Doc. But I'm gonna stay to make sure this is a fair fight if that's what you got in mind." Gus then turned to Stu and Whitey and said, "First thing, boys, is you're gonna take your guns off one at a time. You understand that Stu...Whitey?" asked Gus.

"Sure thing, Gus. Whitey, get your gun off and set it on the hitchin' post with mine," said Stu.

"Gus, would you mind holding my coat?" O'Malley asked as he held it out for Gus to take.

"Doc, are you sure about this?"

"Yes, Gus," Doc said softly but sternly as he turned his attention to Stu and Whitey. "Boys, I don't want to settle this here on the main street of Cheyenne. Stu, Whitey, if you want to settle this thing, I am going to insist we go down the alley and behind the general store where that open field is. That way, we keep this between ourselves and no one else will see us."

"Okay, Doc, let's get goin' down the alley and get to it. That field's wide open and will suit us just fine," said Stu.

"I want you both to know it's not too late for us to forget this altercation and then you and Whitey will not need to go through with this. What I mean is it's not too early to call it off."

"Doc, I just hope you can fix yourself up after I get through with ya," said Stu as he and Whitey started to walk toward the alley. As the four of them exited the alley and walked out behind the general store, it opened up into a large vacant field, which was level and absent of any vegetation except for some patches of grass here and there.

"Okay, Whitey, I get to go first. You can have him next if there's anything left, and he's still able to stand up after I get through with him," said Stu.

"Stu, you and Doc stand over here. Now, this is gonna be a fair fight. There won't be any eye gouging, kicking, choking, or wrestling on the ground. I'm gonna referee and if I see either one of you doin' that, I'll stop the fight. When you're both ready, I'll yell fight and you can start. Do you both understand?" asked Gus.

"Yeah," said Stu.

"Yes," said O'Malley.

Stu and O'Malley walked over to where Gus was standing. They both squared off from each other, with Stu holding clenched fists in front of his torso just below his chest. O'Malley, on the other hand, assumed a position with his left arm bent at a ninety-degree angle with clenched fist and knuckles directed straight toward Stu at eye level. O'Malley's right arm duplicated his left about ten inches lower and about half the distance from his body that his left arm was. The knuckles of his clenched right fist also faced his opponent.

Stu chuckled and said, "Hey Whitey, look at the dude! This ain't gonna take me long so don't get comfortable. In fact, why don't ya go order us a beer? By the time it's poured, I should be there to drink it."

"Naw, I think I'll hang around and watch the fun, Stu," replied Whitey.

"Okay, you two. Ready? Fight!" yelled Gus.

Stu stepped with his right foot throwing a right cross, which missed by inches as O'Malley slid his feet back. Then Stu threw a left hook, which missed again as O'Malley slid back again. Stu tried several more punches, but O'Malley either backed away or sidestepped to avoid the punches. Finally, O'Malley saw the opening he was waiting for. Stu dropped his left hand and brought his right fist back to throw another right cross at him, as he had been trying to do throughout the fight. O'Malley understood the pattern, which gave him the opportunity he was looking for. Before Stu could start the forward motion of his fist, O'Malley landed three short, powerful jabs with his left hand to Stu's face, snapping his head back with each thrust. After the third jab, Doc threw a straight right hand into Stu's face while shifting his weight and throwing his shoulder and hip into the blow, sending Stu stumbling straight back into the wall of the building where he stood momentarily before slowly sliding down to the ground in an unconscious heap.

"My God, Doc. I've never seen anything like that. Where'd you learn to fight like that?" Gus asked.

O'Malley looked at him grinning, "Did I forget to tell you I was on the Harvard College School boxing team back east? I haven't boxed for several years, but I guess you don't forget something that you train in for several years. I don't like to hurt anyone but as I told you, Gus, I can handle my own fights."

"Well, Doc, you sure proved it to me. I sure don't want to tangle with you after seeing this fight." Gus then turned toward Whitey. "Okay, Whitey, it's your turn. You want some of Doc's medicine?" asked Gus.

"N-N-No! I changed my mind, Doc. I'll get some water for Stu to wake him up and then we'll get outta here," said Whitey.

As Gus and Doc talked a bit more about the fight, Whitey had run back down the alley and used his hat to dip it into the nearest horse trough, returning with a hat full of water. As Whitey approached Stu, he noticed the color had gone out of his face, and he seemed almost as white as a sheet. Whitey threw the water on Stu's head, figuring it would bring him to, but the only result was a faint low moan that came out of his bloody mouth. Whitey got scared and turned toward Gus and O'Malley, who were still talking. "Doc, Doc! Doc! Stu's not wakin' up! I just threw a whole hatful of water on his head and he just groaned so low I could hardly hear him."

O'Malley quickly ran the twenty-five feet or so over to where Whitey stood and looked down at Stu. He bent down and checked Stu for broken bones or a neck injury. He quickly ruled out tissue or bone injury and gently slid Stu from his half-sitting position against the building wall to flat on his back on the ground. As he moved Stu, he noticed blood on the building wall and carefully moved him to his side where he saw a long deep laceration to the back of his head. He carefully rolled him onto his back and looked up at Gus and Whitey. "Stu's hurt bad, Gus. I need you and Whitey to go over to the livery, pick up your wagon, and bring it back here. We need to move Stu over to my office, but we need to be real careful until I can thoroughly examine him."

O'Malley took his coat and laid it over Stu to keep him warm. Gus and Whitey both hurried off for the livery stable and returned ten minutes later with the wagon. Gus grabbed Stu's feet while Whitey supported the back, and Doc held Stu's shoulders and neck. The three men lifted Stu at the same time under Doc's direction and gently placed him in the wagon bed. Doc picked up his suit jacket and rolled it up placing it under Stu's head for support. "Whitey, would you please get in the wagon with Stu and try to keep him as still as possible for the short ride to my office. Gus and I will go up front and get this rig rolling," said O'Malley.

"Gotcha, Doc! I'll keep Stu real quiet," replied Whitey.

Gus and Doc hopped up and started the horses on a slow walk so the ride would be as gentle as possible. Gus took the reins and drove the wagon slowly through the alley turning onto the street directly for O'Malley's office. They pulled up in front of the doctor's house where Gus, Whitey, and O'Malley hopped off the wagon and went to its rear. Just as they loaded Stu into the wagon, the three men took the same position after O'Malley had unlocked and opened his front door. They carried Stu through the door and to the doctor's office where they placed him on the examining table.

"Doc, are you going to be able to help Stu? He looks real bad off," said Whitey.

"I think he has a severe concussion, Whitey. I'm going to clean and sew up the cut on the back of his head to stop the bleeding and then treat him for the concussion. I need you to help me roll him over so I can clean and sew up this cut," said O'Malley.

Gus and Whitey rolled him over onto his stomach as they had been directed while Doc washed his hands, got his instruments out, and went to work on Stu. He finished sewing him up in about twenty minutes and then looked up at everyone. "Okay boys, now help me turn him over so I can finish my exam." After he was turned over onto his back, O'Malley checked him closely and confirmed his initial diagnosis as a severe concussion. He walked into the next room where Gus and Whitey had withdrawn while he worked on Stu. As he approached, both of them stood up from the chairs they had been sitting in to talk to him.

"Well, Stu has a very bad concussion, and he's going to have to stay here for at least a couple days. Whitey, let's just keep this between the three of us and say he slipped and hit his head on the wagon wheel. I don't think he will want the boys back at the ranch to hear the town doctor beat him in a fight. What do you think, Whitey?"

"Yeah, Doc! I'm much obliged. I'll let the ramrod know he's laid up here at your place for a few days. I think your idea about his slipping and hitting his head on the wagon wheel is a good one.

You're right that Stu wouldn't be allowed to forget about losin' a fight to the dude. No offense, Doc."

"No offense taken, Whitey. Gus, can we count on you to go along?" asked O'Malley.

"If that's how you want it, Doc, I'll go along with it. Your secret's safe with me."

"Okay, you two, you may as well go home. There won't be any change for a day or two. I'll get word to the ranch as soon as Stu is able to travel," said O'Malley.

"Okay, Doc, you better get some rest yourself. Thanks for lookin' after Stu. That's nice of you seein' how bad we treated you," said Whitey.

O'Malley saw that he was only about another mile or so from Gus and Sarah's ranch. He always enjoyed this last part of the trip although he could have enjoyed it more if this were a social call. As he continued on his way, he admired the tall mountains on either side of the valley jutting into the clear blue sky. Water ran the length of the valley through a fifty-foot wide stream, which helped the grass flourish on the range. This was extremely important to support the cattle ranch Gus and Sarah had built up over the years. He had already begun to see part of the herd of cattle grazing on the range a short distance from the stream. Gus and Sarah had built up the herd to several thousand and would normally sell about twenty percent of the herd each fall. Newborn calves in the spring would normally replenish the number sold in the fall.

As he came over the small rise in his buggy, he spotted the ranch house with smoke coming from the chimney. As he approached the house, he noticed no one was about, which may be a good sign. All seemed normal, with the ranch hands tending the herd and the other hands attending to chores. He reined in his horse and stopped in front of the house, set the brake and climbed down out of the buggy. He reached back into the buggy and grabbed his medical bag along with the telegram Joe Hicks had asked him to deliver to Sarah. He slipped the telegram in his inside suit coat pocket and walked up the few steps across the porch to the front door.

He knocked lightly and waited a few moments before knocking a little harder. After what seemed like a long pause, he was just about to knock again when Sarah opened the door. He immediately saw she looked haggard and drawn as if she had not slept all night. "Hi, Sarah, how's our patient doing this morning? I can tell you've been up all night with him."

"You're right, Doc. I have been up all night just as you suspect and must look a sight. The good part is Gus has been asleep all night. He hasn't stirred or opened his eyes once last night or this morning. Is that bad, Doc?" she asked with a worried look.

"No Sarah, that's probably normal with the injury he sustained. It took me a long time to get the bullet out, so his body is probably just trying to heal itself by keeping Gus quiet. I'll know more when I examine him and change the bandages."

He walked into the house and went straight into the bedroom where he had treated Gus just hours before. He had been in their house but never had the occasion to be in this room until last night when he attended to Gus. It was daylight now, and the sunlight streamed through the window facing the mountains on the east side of the house. O'Malley was struck with the magnificent view of the mountains situated about a quarter mile from the house. A wide north-south stream ran about a hundred feet outside between the house and mountains. Green pasture grew between the house and stream continuing up to the mountains. The mountains appeared to be about a thousand feet tall with a red hue to them. By this time in the morning, the sun illuminated the red rock and green pastures in a duet of color contrasting with the blue stream, dividing the pasture in half. O'Malley could only think how spectacular it would be to start each morning seeing such beauty through the window of his bedroom. He looked to the right where Gus lay in bed. He was still unconscious but noticed his color had improved although he was still slightly pale.

O'Malley walked over and sat down on the side of the bed to examine him. He was amazed to find Gus seemed normal in most aspects considering the shape he was in last night. He unwrapped the bandages, cleaned the wound, and put new bandages on. "Well, Gus, you're doing well. Get some rest, and I'll be out tomorrow to look in on you." He knew Gus was still unconscious but felt like he needed to say something to his good friend. As he stood up to walk toward the living room, he thought he heard a low soft sound like the wind softly blowing through a window, which was opened just a crack.

"Dooooc!"

He quickly turned back to Gus and saw his eyes flutter with some slight movement. "Gus, Gus, can you hear me?" he asked as he sat back down on the side of the bed. But Gus had shut his eyes and appeared to have lapsed back into unconsciousness.

O'Malley got back up and walked out into the living room where Sarah had been waiting for news on her husband's condition. "Well, how's he doin'?" asked Sarah.

"Sarah, he's doing better than I thought he would. He even called my name and then went back to sleep. I think you might see him come to off and on for short periods of time during the coming days."

CHAPTER 6

사랑

The train slowly edged out of Chicago's Union Station, beginning the second and final leg of Alicia's trip to Cheyenne Wyoming. The train stopped at several small cities where passengers exited and entered the train. After a while, the stops became more infrequent until the train continued on its way without stopping except for water or wood. Since this train would be a direct route to Cheyenne with no further connections there, was a club car which offered the passengers meals at certain times of the day. Alicia had not eaten anything since she had boarded the train in Pittsburgh so she left her compartment and made her way down the hall through the next two cars into the club car, where she was met by a waiter.

The waiter asked if he could help her. "Yes, I would like a table and something to eat." She had seen the look the waiter was giving her—the one assuming Asians were low-class people and did not deserve to socialize with the white race. Many in this category felt Asians could only hold the most menial of jobs and are not able to rise above that level. This kind of discrimination was common, and Alicia knew how to deal with it.

The waiter led her down the length of the club car past several empty tables with pleasant views of the rolling countryside to a table at the back of the car in a little windowless alcove separated from the other passengers. Turning toward Alicia, the waiter said with a smirk on his face. "Here you are, Miss, this table should suit you."

"You are mistaken, sir. This table is entirely unacceptable, and I will not take my meal here. You have several unoccupied tables in the main part of this car, which would be suitable. So you either seat me at one of the other tables with a window or get me the conductor immediately, and then you can explain your attitude toward first-class passengers," Alicia said, with a look so serious it scared the waiter.

She noticed the smirk quickly disappear from his face as she rebuked him. This waiter knew a complaint lodged against him by a first-class passenger could result in his being fired no matter what the passenger's nationality or race was. Shakily, the waiter said "M-m-my apologies, Miss. Please step this way so I can show you to a better table."

The waiter led her back to the main section of the car where he showed her a table with a window seat. After she was seated, the waiter remarked, "Can I get you anything else?"

"Just a menu so I can order something to eat," Alicia curtly replied.

From that time on, she was treated exceedingly well after word had circulated among the train employees to treat this first class Asian passenger with care and respect or face the consequences.

For the next three days, she spent most of the time in her compartment, reading and watching the scenery through her window. As the train continued on its westward journey toward Cheyenne, she noticed the gradual change in the country from the congested city outskirts of Chicago to the smaller towns and villages. The train did stop occasionally to replenish the water in the locomotive and restock its wood pile as it continued on its journey. The country slowly turned into farmland, which seemed to go on forever. Eventually, the land turned into prairies and fields stretching for miles. She slept soundly the last night of her trip and woke the next morning fully rested. The train finally entered the Wyoming territory, and she could now clearly see her familiar mountains. The trip continued on for the rest of the day, approaching the end of its journey for her as it neared the Cheyenne train station late that afternoon.

O'Malley could see the relief on Sarah's face as his words describing Gus's medical condition sank in. "Doc, thanks for everything you did. I don't know what I would have done without that ornery old cuss."

"Sarah, I'm so glad he's starting to heal up. I think you can look forward to his improving each day. I cleaned his wound and changed the bandage this morning. I didn't see any sign of infection, and he is sleeping comfortably, which is the best thing for him right now. Also, I wanted to let you know that everyone in town has been asking about Gus and you. Some of your friends want to pay you a visit right away although I'm going to suggest they wait a few days to let you two rest up after the ordeal you have been through. Oh, that reminds me. I almost forgot Joe Hicks asked me to give you this telegram that came in for you," said O'Malley as he handed the envelope to her.

Sarah tore open the telegram and looked at O'Malley saying, "It's from Alicia, and she says she is leaving immediately and will be arriving in Cheyenne the day after tomorrow. We haven't seen her in such a long time. I can't wait until she gets home. Thank you so much for bringing the news out," remarked Sarah.

After three days of constant train travel, Alicia recognized the mountains and land that were familiar to her before moving out east. The train finally arrived in Cheyenne at 6:15 p.m. She had packed her bag about an hour before its arrival at the station so she could disembark as soon as possible without delay. After three days of being cooped up, she was anxious to get off the train, where she was either in her compartment reading or in the club car.

During the trip, the porter had also befriended her, making her trip as comfortable as possible. His name was Carl and before she left the train, she made sure she found him to tell him how much she appreciated his help by giving him a five-dollar tip. Carl was very appreciative and tried to give the tip back, saying it was his pleasure to help her. She insisted he kept the tip and told him she considered it a gift to a friend. "Well, I wish you luck, Miss, and I hope you have a good visit," said Carl.

"I will, Carl, and thank you for everything you did," Alicia replied as he helped her step out of the train and onto the station platform. She walked through the train depot and out the front entranceway across the street and started walking down the city boardwalk. She noticed almost immediately all the new buildings in town that had been built while she was out of town. Since the railroad arrived in Cheyenne, many new businesses had started up resulting in new construction and a significant population increase.

As she continued to walk down the boardwalk passing townsfolk, she noticed the typical stares and glances people were making toward this well-dressed Asian. It was simply out of place to see an oriental person, not connected with the local laundry or railroad being, well-dressed in the west. As she continued walking, she passed by Mary's Café and continued down the street.

When she had gotten about ten feet past the café, she heard someone calling her name. "Alicia! Alicia! Alicia, is that you?" Mary yelled out.

She turned and recognized Mary standing just outside her café door. She walked back up to Mary and stood a few feet from her. Mary looked at her and then moved forward the few steps, taking Alicia into her arms and giving her a big bear hug saying, "Alicia, I heard you were coming to town. I'm really glad to see you although

I wish it were under different circumstances. Just let me look at you, girl. It has just been too long since you have been home," said Mary as she released her from her hug and stepped back to get a better look.

"Mary, you don't look any different than when I left town five years ago. How's the café going for you?"

"Business has grown a lot with all the new people that have moved here since the railroad got here. But child, you look skinnier than when you left town. Come on in here so I can get you something to eat and start puttin' some weight on that little body."

"Well, I just got off the train, and I was heading for the hotel to get a room for the night so I can get an early start in the morning for the ranch."

"Alicia, your folks would never forgive me if I let you stay overnight in the hotel especially since I have a spare room upstairs over the café. So you come in here, get something to eat, and then I'll take you upstairs and get you settled for the night. It will also give me a chance to let you know what's been going on here in Cheyenne over the last five years."

"Well, Mary, when could I ever say no to you? How about putting my bag in the kitchen, and then we can sit down and have something to eat. Remember, I always loved sitting in the café kitchen with you when Mom and Dad brought me to town with them. I always loved the fresh bakery smells and your food, which tasted so good."

"Well, let's get on in, little girl," said Mary as she led her through the door and into the kitchen.

This was now the third day O'Malley had been out to the ranch to check on Gus's condition. He was still weak from the large amount of blood loss but was conscious off and on a lot more frequently than the first twenty-four hours following the shooting. This morning, O'Malley had sat on Gus's bed after cleaning his wound and changing the bandage when Gus stirred, opened his eyes, and saw him at his side.

"Doc, where's Sarah and how'd I get back to the ranch?" he asked in a raspy voice.

O'Malley leaned over and in a soft voice said, "All I know is you were shot out on the trail and must have somehow managed to stay on your horse or if you fell off your horse, you were able to get back in the saddle and come here, where you rode in slumped over your saddle. The boys saw you ride in, pulled you off your horse, and got you into the house. I don't know anything more than that. Do you know who shot you?"

"It's really fuzzy, Doc. I remember bits and pieces of riding back to the ranch and then waking up here with you this morning," Gus muttered as he dozed off again.

O'Malley saw Gus had lapsed back into sleep and knew he would not get anything more out of him for the time being. He got up and walked into the parlor where Sarah was waiting. "Sarah, I think Gus is going to pull through just fine. He's just going to need rest and care for a few weeks. Not much more I can do here, so I'm going to head back to town."

"I don't know what to say except thanks, Doc, for all your work. You gave me Gus back, and I just don't have the words in me except thanks," Sarah said as she put her arms around him and gave him a heartfelt hug.

It was still early afternoon when he started back to town, and he thought he would arrive between three and four o'clock in the afternoon. That would give him enough time to take care of his horse, get cleaned up, and head for Mary's Café to get some dinner. For the last three days, O'Malley had been making the trip to Gus and Sarah's ranch to make sure his wound was properly cleaned to prevent infection and apply new bandages. Upon leaving the ranch, he told Sarah that Gus was healing nicely, and he wouldn't need to come back for three or four days to check on him. He showed her again how to properly clean the wound and change the bandages on a daily basis to make sure it fully healed before he left.

On the ride back, O'Malley started to think about this situation and was troubled by it. He still had great difficulty in trying to determine who had reason to shoot Gus. The only person Gus had any problems with was Jason Long, who had moved to Cheyenne Wyoming about five years ago. No one really knew anything about Jason other than he had moved out here from the east and then started buying up property in Cheyenne, including the ranches surrounding it.

Gus and Sarah's ranch controlled the water to the rest of the area ranches; however, they never impeded the flow of this lifeblood to any of their neighbors, including the ranches owned by Jason. It was obvious to him that Jason's intention was to accumulate as much land through acquisition of all the ranches in the valley.

Shortly after Jason arrived and acquired his first ranch, O'Malley noticed the new ranch hands Jason hired all carried their guns similar to the style of a gunslinger. Before Jason arrived, Cheyenne had been a quiet town with the occasional saloon fight and minor pranks by kids. However, after his arrival and the employment of his so-called ranch hands, it was not uncommon for saloon fights to result in a gunfight where the victim was almost always one of the local ranchers, who had been goaded into a fight by one of these gun hands.

O'Malley started treating more and more gunshot wounds as these fights escalated to an alarming degree. He spoke to the marshal constantly about the fights and gunplay, but the marshal told him all the witnesses claimed they were fair fights, and he couldn't arrest a gunfighter if he didn't draw first. The marshal also knew these fights always started after he had made his rounds since he was never present at the fights. He tried varying the times of his rounds, but that did not help either. O'Malley had always known the marshal to be honest and fair to all of Cheyenne's citizens, but the marshal had his hands tied since he only had one deputy to help patrol and enforce the law in Cheyenne and the surrounding territory. That's all the city government would allow the marshal, and the town council—headed by Jason Long—would not approve any more deputies for him.

As soon as Jason got elected to the town council, he did everything in his power to reduce the marshal's efforts at enforcing the law. When Jason had come to town, the marshal had convinced the town council to pass an ordinance banning guns within the city limits. Six months after Jason had moved to Cheyenne, he was elected to the town council and with his money and power influenced the council to repeal the ordinance, allowing folks to once again carry firearms within the city limits. This played right into his hands, and he wasted no time with his plan to buy up as many businesses and surrounding ranches to develop his own little empire.

As time went on, he bought up most of the businesses in town and many of the surrounding ranches either through intimidation, violence, or purchase. However, he was never successful in convincing Gus and Sarah to sell. He tried every way he could to convince them to accept an offer to sell the ranch, but Gus was known to be the toughest man in the territory with both his fists and gun and when he said no, that was the end of the conversation. He earned this tough reputation early in life when he was one of the first settlers in the territory, claiming his land and defending against hostiles and outlaws. It was extremely hard work and long hours that enabled Gus and Sarah to fight the elements and build their ranch over many years.

As other settlers moved into the territory, Gus tried to help them establish their ranches so the territory could develop for the good of all. Gus met Jason shortly after his arrival in the territory. He was a very good judge of character and even though he wanted to give everyone a chance, he had a bad feeling about Jason that he could not shake. He could tell Jason was here to look after his own best interests and no one else's. So, when Jason offered him double what his ranch was worth, Gus in no uncertain terms told Jason he didn't have enough money to buy his land, his soul, and his family roots. He would never let him buy his ranch as it would give Jason absolute power over the other ranchers who have not yet sold out.

CHAPTER 7

사랑

It was 5:30 p.m. by the time O'Malley arrived back into town. He was tired and needed to clean up. He pulled up in front of his house, unhitched Dollar, and led her back to the barn where he gave her a quick brush down and some oats. He then went into the house and started a small fire in the cook stove, where he heated up some water for his washbasin and then cleaned up, washing the trail dust off his arms, face, and neck. After he emptied the basin, he refilled it with clean water and then washed his hair, feeling it going from a dirty stiffness to soft and pliable in his hands. Then taking the last of the warm water, he poured it over his head and into the basin giving his hair a final rinse. After towel drying his hair, he went into the bedroom and put on a clean shirt. Walking into the kitchen, he realized how famished he was but did not feel like cooking as he was nearly exhausted from the day's activities. He knew Mary's was open and decided to get some supper as it would be a lot easier than having to wait until he could cook something for himself at home.

He put his suit coat on, grabbed his wallet, left the house, and started walking to Mary's. It was a cloudless evening and still quite warm for 6:30 p.m. with a gentle breeze out of the west. The sun would not be setting for a couple hours and its rays reflected off the mountains and trees to the east, displaying different shades of various colors, brighter than during the middle of the day. It was only a five-minute walk to the café where he entered and located a table by a window looking out onto Main Street. Sandy, who waited tables for Mary, came right over as soon as she saw O'Malley take a seat.

"How ya doin', Doc? You've been pretty busy with Gus and Sarah I hear tell. Is Gus doin' better now? Can I get you somethin' to drink?" she asked.

He leaned back into his chair. He had forgotten how talkative Sandy could be when she knew someone. "Hi, Sandy, it's nice to see you again. I'm fine but just a little tired. Gus is starting to come around, and I think he'll be up and around in a few weeks. I think I'll have some coffee and what's Mary got for supper in the kitchen?"

"Her special tonight is beef stew, and it's really good if I do say so myself."

"Then make it the stew, Sandy."

"Okay, Doc, let me get you some coffee first and then I'll bring out the stew for you." Sandy returned in just a minute with the coffee, and O'Malley started to relax and began reading the evening newspaper he had picked up on the way to Mary's. Sandy walked back to the kitchen to turn her order in where Mary and Alicia were sitting and talking.

"Mary, Doc just came in and ordered some stew. Do you have any fresh biscuits made up to go along with it?"

"They're warming on the stove under that towel, Sandy. Alicia, you haven't seen anyone else in town to say hello to. When Doc's stew is dished up, let's surprise him and take it out to him together. I know he'll be surprised to see you."

Alicia thought for a moment about seeing O'Malley after five years. She and the doctor had courted and been involved romantically to the point that some folks thought they may be considering marriage. However, she had decided to leave town to go and teach in a private, expensive boarding school before O'Malley and she had discussed marriage. She frequently thought about him, wondering how he was doing.

"Alicia, the stew is ready. Do you want to take it out to Doc or do you want me to take it?" asked Sandy.

"I'll take it out, Sandy. Let me grab the tray and silverware, and I'll take it out right now."

Sandy handed the tray to Alicia, who walked backward through the swinging kitchen doors turning around to face the eating area. She spotted O'Malley, who was seated at the table with his back to the window overlooking Main Street. He was facing the kitchen reading a newspaper, which was held high enough preventing him from seeing her approach. When she got to his table, she said, "It's been a long time, Doc!"

She took the bowl of stew and biscuits off the serving tray and set it before him. At first, he didn't recognize the voice and thought Sandy was joking with him. He lowered the newspaper and was struck by the beautiful Asian girl. He had always thought how beautiful and graceful she was when they were courting before she had decided to leave town. He couldn't take his eyes off her and could see she hadn't changed over the five years she had been gone. Her coal-black hair was still long and silky, appearing to flow down to the middle of her back. Her eyes were coal-black, sensuously looking out from her delicately slanted eyes. Her skin maintained its light olive coloring with an oblong face completely smooth and free of any marks, blemishes, or wrinkles. O'Malley thought to himself, she was still the most beautiful woman he had ever known.

At the same time these thoughts were going through his head, Alicia had her own thoughts about him. O'Malley was four years older than Alicia and stood a tall six feet. She compared him to the picture she still had in her mind of what he looked like when she was last in town. From what she could tell, he had not aged at all and still looked like the handsome man she remembered. He had a square strong jaw and light, sandy hair with blue eyes and always a friendly smile.

O'Malley pushed himself away from the table and stood up to greet her. "I completely forgot your mom told me you were arriving in town today," he said, stepping forward and giving her a welcome home hug.

"She must have gotten my telegram I sent letting her know I would be coming in today."

"I actually took the telegram out to her two days ago, and she opened and read it while I was there. It told her you were coming into town today. She was extremely happy about your coming. Where are you staying tonight?" asked O'Malley.

"More importantly, I want to know how my dad is. Will he be okay? All I know is that Dad was shot but not how bad he was hurt."

"I am pretty sure the worst is over for your dad. I think with a few weeks rest, he should just about be as good as new. If the bullet had been over another inch, it probably would have killed him. Your mom has been caring for him night and day ever since he rode into the ranch slumped over his horse. How he ever made it back to the ranch, I'll never know. I guess he's just too stubborn to die."

"I'm glad to hear he's going to be okay. Mom's telegram never said how it happened. Can you tell me what went on? Do you know who shot him? Did Dad tell you who it was?"

"Your dad doesn't remember anything except riding back to the ranch and then waking up in his own bed. Now, you didn't tell me where you're staying tonight," inquired O'Malley.

"You know Mary. As soon as she saw me walking by the café, she came out and made sure I came in to visit with her. She has insisted I stay in the spare room upstairs tonight before heading out to the ranch. I didn't really expect anyone to meet me because I wasn't sure when I was going to get in, and I didn't give an arrival time in my telegram. So I had intended to get a room at the hotel when, as I said, Mary spotted me walking by the café. I was just going to ask Mary to tell me about all the changes that have occurred these past five years. I certainly see a lot more new people and businesses that were not here when I left. Why don't you tell me what's been going on around here?" said Alicia.

"I have a better idea. Let's take my dinner and move into the kitchen, where Mary is so we can talk about these changes without anyone else around," replied O'Malley.

With that, they picked up the food and coffee and headed to the kitchen. Mary was at the sink washing some dishes that Sandy had brought in from the dining area. O'Malley and Alicia set down the food on the table where Alicia had been sitting just a few minutes ago talking to Mary.

"All right, Doc, Mary, you both need to tell me what's been going on around here. Make sure you don't leave anything out."

They took turns telling her about Jason Long's arrival in town shortly after her departure. They told Alicia the little they really knew about Jason's background and went over the land and business purchases he had been making since his arrival in town. O'Malley also related to Alicia the conversations he had with Gus regarding the many offers Jason had made to buy the ranch.

Gus always refused Jason's offer on the spot and always ended the conversation by telling him he would never sell to him at any price. Jason suspected that Gus was quite wealthy due to the cattle he had raised and sold over the years. O'Malley remembered that about a month ago on a Saturday, he was having lunch with Gus when Jason walked in and asked if he could talk to Gus for a few minutes. He remembered Gus looking up at Jason and asking him if this was about buying his ranch. Jason paused for a moment and then said yes, he would like to know what it would take to buy the ranch. Gus's face slowly turned into a mean, disgusted look, with eyes that seemed to shoot knives through Jason. He then told Jason he had tried to give him the benefit of the doubt, but he could see what he was up to and didn't like it.

Jason tried to explain to him he was just a businessman looking for opportunities and saw the ranch as an investment. Gus told Jason he wouldn't sell and if he tried to threaten him with his hired gunslingers, he would come directly to him to settle things. Jason appeared to be shocked and paused for a moment before remarking to him that what he said seemed to sound like a threat and asked Gus if that was what he meant.

Gus stared back at Jason with a steely look and then told Jason it wasn't a threat but a fact that he could take to his bank. O'Malley remembered Jason had one of his hired guns with him, who stepped forward and asked if that went for him, too. Gus slowly stood up, took a step closer to the gunman, and then quickly reared back and hit the gunslinger so hard he flew back through the café's front door and out into the street—unconscious and with a broken jaw that the doctor treated the gunman for later. Then Gus turned to Jason, looking coldly at him and said, "Now, have you got any questions as to exactly what I mean?" He then sat down and they finished their meal as if nothing had happened.

Alicia absorbed everything they related to her about what had happened during the last five years and how this could be related to her dad's shooting. "Well Doc, Mary, thanks for bringing me up-to-date. Do you think my dad's shooting had anything to do with this land grab Jason or do you think it was just an outlaw trying to rob him?"

"I don't think this was a robbery as your dad only had ten dollars in his pocket at the time of the shooting. That is what was found on him when he got back to the ranch and what your mom said he had with him when he went to town that day. So I think there had to be some other reason other than an outlaw robbery or some random shooting," replied O'Malley.

"Well, I've had a long three days, and I need to get out to the ranch to see Mom and Dad. I'm going down to the livery stable to see if I can get a horse to ride out there."

"Child, it's late, and you need to rest up. I told you I would not allow you to stay at a hotel. You come upstairs with me and get a good night's sleep before taking that long ride. Then in the morning, Doc and I will make sure you get out to the ranch," replied Mary.

"Actually, I'm going out to the ranch tomorrow morning, so you can ride with me. I have to check on your dad to make sure his wound is healing and he's still recovering. If things are going as I suspect, your dad should be awake and talking by now. I'm hoping he can tell the marshal what happened on the trail. Last time I treated him, he was just conscious enough to tell me he couldn't remember anything about the shooting. I know you're anxious to get out there so why don't I come here tomorrow morning at about eight o'clock, and we can get breakfast before heading out to the ranch," offered O'Malley.

"Mary, what time in the morning do you open for breakfast?" asked Alicia.

"I'm down here by five o'clock to prepare for the day's business. We open up for customers at six o'clock, honey."

"Then, Doc, let's meet here at seven, eat, and be on the road by 7:30. I want to get out to the ranch as soon as possible. Is that time okay with you, Doc?"

"From your tone, it sounds like I'm not going to have much of a choice. I just thought you would want to rest a bit longer in the morning after being on a train for three days. But from your look and tone, I think we'll be on the road by 7:30. Mary, your stew tasted great as always. I'll go out front to pay and then head back home so I can be back here at seven o'clock tomorrow morning."

"Doc, the stew is on the house tonight. I'm glad you enjoyed it."

He got up and thanked Mary for dinner, said good night to everyone and left the café for the short walk home. Mary then took Alicia upstairs to the spare room where they said good night to each other. She brought her bag in and decided to get changed into a comfortable nightgown she had packed for the trip. After changing, she sat down on the bed, feeling the fatigue overtake her. The desire to lie down and go to sleep was irresistible and she pulled back the bed clothes and got into bed, covering herself, and immediately dropped off to sleep. Even though she was exhausted, she later woke up and spent a restless night tossing and turning while thinking about her father and mother.

CHAPTER 8

사랑

Alicia woke up at six o'clock upon hearing the customers' voices coming up through the floor of her room and decided to get out of bed and start cleaning up. She got up and poured some water from a pitcher into a washbasin and began to wash. As she cleaned up, she was able to take in the room Mary had insisted she stay in. There was a large window facing west overlooking Main Street. The bed she had slept in was a four-poster bed with a beautifully hand-carved headboard. The bed was quite sturdy as it was constructed from solid oak and had an incredibly comfortable mattress that seemed to softly cradle you like a newborn baby wrapped in a comforter. Mary had decorated the room with soothing light blue paint on the walls and pretty lace curtains on the window. The room was furnished with a tall six-drawer dresser and a separate vanity with a large mirror. She appreciated the mirror as it afforded her the ability to step back a couple of feet and check her hair and dress before venturing out into the public. She finished getting dressed and left the room to go downstairs a few minutes before seven o'clock.

As she left her room and stood at the top of the stairs, she could smell the bacon, potatoes, pancakes, and other breakfast food Mary had been preparing to fill the orders of her customers. When she reached the bottom of the stairs, she saw O'Malley already sitting at the same table they had been at last night in the kitchen.

"Mary, am I late? The clock in my room said it was ten to seven when I left to come down."

"No, honey, Doc came in at 6:30 this morning when I was busy filling orders for the early birds. So I had him come back here where I gave him some coffee. He's been keeping me company while he waited for you to come down. Course, if you ask me, I think he was just anxious to see you again," laughed Mary.

"Aw, Mary, that's not entirely true, although I am looking forward to Alicia's company on the long ride out to the ranch. I just love your company, Mary, and I thought if I came in early, I could get an extra cup or two of the best coffee in the west."

Mary looked at O'Malley with a smile as she shook her head in disbelief. "Honey, sit down at the table with Doc, and you can have some of this breakfast I've fixed for you two."

She sat down across from O'Malley while Mary brought her some tea and then fixed them each a plate of food. "Mary, I appreciate you remembering I prefer tea rather than coffee."

"Why, it was no problem at all as I keep tea to serve some of the ladies in town when they come in to eat. I'll get out the teapot and put the rest of the hot water in it along with some more tea. I'll sit down for a few minutes to have some with you as long as it doesn't get too crazy around here. Now, I've put together this breakfast, and I want to see clean plates when you're both done. I've made eggs, bacon, ham, and potatoes, along with my homemade biscuits," said Mary.

O'Malley and Alicia looked at each other and said together, "That's great!" The next half hour was spent eating their breakfast and passing the time with some idle chat about the weather and local politics with Mary joining in the conversation between cooking up orders for her regular customers. After they had finished breakfast, Doc asked Mary what he owed for the two of them.

"Doc's not paying for my breakfast, Mary. I'll pay for both of ours. How much is it?" asked Alicia.

"I wasn't trying to upset you, Alicia. I was just trying to be nice and offer to buy breakfast for a lady. I guess you had better split the bill up, Mary. What do I owe for my meal, Mary?" asked O'Malley.

"I can't believe you two. You've seen each other twice in five years and can't even agree on who is going to pay for breakfast. I'm going to settle this my way. First, this breakfast is on the house. Now, Alicia, you go upstairs and bring your bag down, and Doc will take it and put it in his buggy for you like the gentleman I know him to be. I know you both want to get out to the ranch as fast as you can for your own reasons. So let's get moving since I can see you both have finished eating and want to get on the road. And I don't want any backtalk about this," Mary said as she picked up their dishes from the table and took them over to the wash tub.

O'Malley and Alicia looked at each other and smiled. "I'm sorry, Alicia. I was really just trying to show you some hospitality," said O'Malley.

"No, Doc, it wasn't your fault. I'm just tired and worried. I should have been gracious and accepted your offer. It was rude of me to refuse. But we had better get out of here before Mary puts us to work washing and cooking. I'll run upstairs and get my bag. Be back in a minute."

"That's fine. I'll wait for you right here."

Alicia went upstairs, closed up her bag and was back downstairs within two minutes. They thanked Mary for their breakfast, said their good-byes and Doc took Alicia's bag out to his buggy and put it in the open area behind the seat. He took her hand, helped her into the buggy, and then started their long ride out to the ranch.

Sarah had spent another night in her rocking chair wrapped in a soft, comfortable quilt. It was an uncomfortable night, but she was so exhausted from the last three stressful days she was able to sleep until seven o'clock when she heard Gus call out to her from the bedroom. She got up and quickly walked over to the bedroom, opening the door to see Gus propped up slightly with his shoulders leaning against the headboard.

"Gus! You're awake! How long have you been up? I was so worried about you," Sarah said as she walked around the bed and sat down next to Gus, leaning over to give him a light kiss. Then it hit her. After three days of tension and intense stress and worry, she could hold it in no longer and put her arms around Gus, breaking down into tears. He slowly put his arms around her and gently stroked her hair as he let her cry her eyes out.

"Sarah, Sarah, Sarah. We've been through tougher times than this. Everything's going to be okay," he said.

She collected herself after a few minutes and sat up looking at him, wiping away her tears. "Do you feel like having something to eat?" she asked.

"That's one thing that I am and it's hungry. But for now, I'd just like some coffee and one of your homemade biscuits," replied Gus.

She leaned over and kissed him again, then got up from the bed. "I love you, dear," she said as she walked toward the bedroom door.

"I love you, too," replied Gus.

"I'll be back in just a few minutes with your coffee and biscuits," she said as she left the bedroom and walked into the kitchen. She put some kindling on the stove and lit a fire to heat the water in the coffee pot. She had baked some biscuits the previous day and took a couple out to reheat on the stove for a few minutes after the coffee was done. When the coffee and biscuits were ready, she took two cups out along with the warm biscuits and put everything on a tray including the coffee pot and took it to Gus. She brought the tray in and set it on the dresser next to the bed and then poured two cups of coffee, handing one to him along with a biscuit, which she had cut open and put some honey on.

He took the cup from her carefully not to spill any hot coffee on himself or the bed. As he gingerly sipped the hot coffee, Sarah handed him a biscuit. He took a bite and remembered how good a cook she was as the biscuit melted in his mouth and he tasted the honey she had put in it. "Sarah, what's been going on since I've been out?"

"Well, the hands have all pitched in and made sure the cattle and ranch kept going as normal as possible in your absence. Doc was out as soon as he found out you had been shot and dug the bullet out of your chest. He tried to paint as good a picture about your chances as he could, but I made him tell me straight so I could deal with it. Folks in town sent out food with Doc every day and they all sent their best wishes. We owe a lot to Doc. He has come out every day to check on you and make sure you pull through. Oh my God, I just remembered. Doc brought out a telegram from Alicia saying she was coming out, and she should have arrived on the train yesterday if I am reading the telegram right. I wonder where she stayed last night."

"She probably checked into the hotel and made arrangements to get out to the ranch today if I know anything about our daughter," said Gus.

"I can tell you one thing and that is if my baby is not out here by noon, I'll make sure you're okay by making some soup up for you and then I'm leaving to go to town and find out what is what," replied Sarah.

"I'm feeling pretty good, honey, so you don't need to worry about me. You go ahead after lunch and bring our daughter back to the ranch with you."

They continued to talk for another half hour until it was obvious he needed to rest. She leaned over, gently kissed him, and told him he needed to get some sleep. "I'll be just outside in the parlor or kitchen. I'm going to bake some bread and do a little cleaning so I can get everything done in case I need to head out to Cheyenne this afternoon."

But he had already fallen asleep before she had finished talking. She went back to the kitchen and started fixing the soup and kneaded some bread for baking. By half past eleven, she had straightened up the house, baked two loaves of bread, and finished the pot of soup for lunch, hoping Gus would be awake and hungry.

She went in to check on him and found him still asleep. She wasn't sure whether to wake him but thought it best so he could have something to eat. She went over, sat down on the side of the bed, and slightly jiggled his arm, which was on top of the bed covers. Gus jumped slightly and opened his eyes, taking a second or two before he realized where he was and at whom he was looking.

"Gus, I have some soup in the kitchen and thought you might like some. It's almost noon. Would you like me to bring in a bowl for you?" she whispered.

"That's fine. Can you also bring me some of that bread I smell along with a cup of coffee? I may be tired, but I sure am hungry."

"Let's try to prop you up with an extra pillow. You'll be more comfortable sitting up to eat." She leaned over and put her hands under Gus's arm to help him sit up. She could tell from the look on his face it was painful for him to sit up, but he made no complaint, which was normal for him. He never complained when he was sick or hurt. He just kept going. When she got him settled, she went back out to get the soup, bread, and coffee on a tray and brought it to him where she set it on his lap.

"This looks great, Sarah. Are you goin' to have anything to eat?"

"I had a small bowl of soup and some bread before I woke you up. I'm gonna clean up the kitchen and get ready to head into town and see about Alicia."

"That's fine. I think I'll eat and then get some more rest. I'll get up later today. I've got to try and start getting around and back on my feet," said Gus.

"Not if I have anything to say about it, you won't. Doc'll tell you when you can get up," said Sarah.

O'Malley and Alicia started out for the ranch as planned at 7:30 a.m. It was a cloudless day with a crystal-clear blue sky and a slight breeze from the west, which made it cool for the start of the ride. O'Malley knew that although the morning air was chilly, the morning sun would quickly heat the air and turn the day into a hot one. He could tell Alicia was chilled but knew from memory she would never complain. If nothing else, she had definitely learned that trait from her folks. He pulled up, set the brake and got out to go in the back of his buggy where there was a small storage area, which kept his medical bag and other assorted things.

"Doc, what are you doing back there?" Alicia asked.

"Just a minute and I'll be right there. I'm just getting something to make the trip a bit more comfortable."

He found what he was looking for and closed the lid to the storage area, walked around the buggy, and climbed into the seat next to her. "I was getting chilled, and so I thought we could put this blanket on our laps and keep the wind and cool air out."

"Well if you're cold, Doc, I guess this is the best thing to do."

He leaned over to spread the blanket over her lap and as he leaned back, he detected the scent of cherry blossoms, which reminded him of the perfume she had worn when they courted. They began to talk about the past and how they used to ride together out into the mountains to have picnic lunches. They would sit on top of a knoll under a tree, relaxing with their shoes off and enjoying the grass while looking over the valley. They fit together almost as if they were twin brother and sister. They laughed at the memory of their talking for hours and hours and how they would instinctively finish each other's sentences. They remembered how their relationship grew from friendship into a trusting relationship until one day they both realized their feelings for each other had grown into something much more than friendship.

As they continued their conversation on the way to the ranch, he pulled over to the side of the trail and stopped the buggy. By this time, they had been riding for almost two hours and O'Malley thought they might need a break.

"Doc, why are you stopping?"

"Oh, I thought we would stop for a few minutes to stretch our legs and rest the horses," replied O'Malley.

"I suppose you're right about letting the horses have a little rest. Let's just make it a quick stop. I really want to get to the ranch as soon as possible. I see you picked an interesting spot to stop," said Alicia as she looked up a grassy hill with a shade tree on it along a small running stream.

It had not dawned on O'Malley where he was until she had made her remark. Then he realized what she had been talking about. O'Malley recalled it was about six months before she had left town. He had gone to church with her on this particular Sunday and then after church, they had ridden out to this very spot to have a picnic. The day was quite similar to this one, without a cloud in the sky and the sun warming the early June weather. O'Malley had enlisted the help of Mary to fix a fried chicken picnic basket. He had strapped on the basket behind his saddle for the trip out here and remembered they had walked up this very hill, which had wildflowers in full bloom accentuating the rich green grass. Halfway up the hill, O'Malley gently took Alicia's hand, intertwining his fingers in hers. At first, she was surprised then looked at him, smiled, and gave his hand a soft squeeze acknowledging she felt the same. It took another few minutes to reach the top of the hill where O'Malley released her hand. He set down the picnic basket and took the blanket off his shoulder, spreading it on the ground for them to sit on.

Suddenly, he heard his name. "Doc, Doc! What are you thinking about? You look like you're daydreaming. Are you ready to go? We've been here for fifteen minutes already."

"Sorry, Alicia. To tell you the truth, I was thinking about your remark regarding this spot and the picnic we had here. I'm a little surprised you remember that afternoon," said O'Malley.

"I've always remembered that afternoon. It was one of the happiest days of my life. We had a marvelous time together, and I remember sitting close to you toward late afternoon after enjoying our food and conversation. But what I remember most is when we were putting our leftovers back in the basket, standing up, and then bumping our heads together when we bent over at the same time to pick up the blanket. We stood up, and I immediately brushed your hair back from your face to see if you were hurt. It was then our eyes met, gazing at each other while moving slowly together, our lips finding each other's and kissing passionately for what seemed to be the most pleasurable experience I ever had. I remember you holding me close in your strong arms as we continued to kiss each other repeatedly and passionately. As we kissed over and over, we slowly lowered ourselves back down onto the blanket, lying there and embracing each other until dusk had turned into night. I remember telling you I had deep feelings for you, but I knew we needed to stop before we lost control and things went too far. I could tell from the look on your face you did not want to stop, but I knew you would respect my wishes. As I recall, we got up slowly, finished packing, then rode back to the ranch. It took a while to get back to the ranch, and we talked about what the future might bring as our courtship continued. I also expressed to you I didn't want to settle down until I got out of Cheyenne to see a different part of the country and live on my own," replied Alicia.

"Well, let's get back in the buggy so we can get to the ranch before it gets any later. We can continue our conversation as we still have a little while longer to go," replied O'Malley.

As they continued their ride to the ranch, they spoke about the feelings they had for each other before Alicia had left town. Both of them were surprised neither had formed a lasting relationship with anyone else over the last five years. They talked about the different people they had seen during their time apart.

O'Malley had gone out for an occasional dinner. He explained to Alicia that in the small town of Cheyenne, anytime he took a lady to dinner more than once, the gossip in town would talk about him courting someone and how serious they thought it might be. Since he had not met anyone that stirred deep feelings, he would only occasionally see an eligible lady in Cheyenne for an evening out. However, O'Malley attended most of the church socials and holiday festivals the local organizations sponsored.

Alicia discussed her experience living in a large city. There were so many more people in the city that she could see gentlemen as many times as she wanted without fear of listening to idle gossip or worrying about her reputation. She also confessed to O'Malley she had not met anyone who could keep her interest more than a few dates. Alicia intimated she longed for the Wyoming territory, which included the surrounding mountains, valleys, pastures, and down-to-earth people, who don't pretend to be something other than what they were.

As they continued their trip toward the ranch, they reconnected with each other and talked about the last several years until they both recognized the last rise they had to cross before arriving at the ranch.

"Doc, pull up here at the top of the rise for a minute. I just want to take a look at the valley before we ride down to see my folks."

"I have always liked to see this land from here with the mountains, grass, and the river running through the valley. Even though I've seen this view several times in the last week, I never get tired of the beauty," observed O'Malley.

After a few minutes, he snapped the reins, and the buggy moved forward down the rise to the ranch. As they entered the gate, O'Malley noticed Sarah coming out the front door and walking toward a buggy that was hitched to a horse. She was so intent and focused on walking toward her buggy she didn't hear or notice the approach of O'Malley's rig.

Alicia couldn't contain herself any longer. "Mom, Mom!" she yelled out.

Sarah stopped immediately and turned quickly to her right. It took her a second to focus on O'Malley's buggy with the two occupants. She immediately recognized her daughter. "Alicia! Alicia!" exclaimed Sarah as she started running in the direction of the buggy.

Alicia quickly jumped out of the buggy before O'Malley could stop and ran toward her mother. Within seconds, mother and daughter were hugging each other.

"I can't believe this. I was just leaving for the town to see if you had arrived. We would have met on the trail if I had left a little earlier. Well, let's get in the house. Your dad's just as anxious to see you as I am. Forgive me, Doc, I didn't mean to be rude. I was just so surprised to see Alicia with you. Do you have a bag, sweetheart."

"My bag's in the buggy, Mom. Let's go in and see Dad first, and then I'll come out and get the bag later."

"No problem, ladies. I'll get her bag and bring it in for you. I imagine you want some time alone with your dad, Alicia."

"I think we'll take you up on that offer, Doc. Just come on in and make yourself comfortable in the parlor," said Sarah.

The ladies walked up the short gravel walkway to the porch and on into the house.

"Your dad said he might try to get some sleep. Let me look in and see if he's awake." Sarah opened the bedroom door a crack, peeked in, and saw Gus was sound asleep. She softly closed the door and told Alicia her father was asleep and suggested they go into the kitchen for some tea.

Jason Long sat behind the desk in the private office at his bank. He had opened this financial institution shortly after his arrival in Cheyenne almost five years ago. Almost immediately, he began lending money to local ranchers, who secured the loans with mortgages on their ranches through his bank. At the same time he was lending money, he was buying up as many of the businesses in Cheyenne as fast as he could. He also paid a fair price, or a little more, than the current value of the business he was purchasing. It was quite obvious he was attempting to purchase as many of the buildings and businesses that he could.

The few businesses that held out were the livery stable, the general store, and Mary's Café. Jason either owned the rest of the businesses in town or owned a majority interest in those he did not own outright. Over time, he would acquire ranches through foreclosure when the mortgages could not be repaid, and he refused to extend the note. All mortgages Jason put in effect carried a lump sum payment provision due at the end of the loan term. When the term was coming to an end, strange things would happen, such as the rancher's cattle being rustled or a mysterious fire destroying equipment, buildings, or stock. This prevented the cattle from being sold at market and the rancher defaulting on his mortgage with Jason assuming ownership.

He looked at the map that hung on the wall next to his desk. This large map designated all the ranches within a fifty-mile radius of Cheyenne. He now owned most of the ranches of importance in regard to acreage and fertile pasture grass. There were some holdouts that he had been unable to buy out or as he put it, "persuade" to sell out.

However, the biggest thorn in his side was the ranch owned by Gus and Sarah. Their ranch controlled the water that flowed to the rest of the ranches, providing needed moisture for the range grass and water for the cattle. If he owned Gus and Sarah's ranch, he would control the water to all the ranches refusing to sell out. He realized their ranch had always been the key to consolidate his holdings and control the valley extending from Gus and Sarah's property south to Cheyenne and most of the town.

"Vic, I heard about Gus being shot a few days ago, and it sounds like he's going to live. When I told you last week we needed to do something about Gus, I didn't mean for you to shoot him. If I wanted him dead, I would have told you."

"Boss, I've been with you for the last four years and when you say something like that, we all know what you mean. How else did you think this problem was going to be taken care of?"

He just looked at Vic and shook his head. "Vic, haven't you figured this out yet? I'm a legitimate businessman. I can't afford violence to get what I want. You see this map here with all the green pins in it? What do you think it means?"

"Well...I guess you're keeping track of all the land you own. Why else would you have it?"

"Vic, do you play chess?"

"No, ain't never learned how to play that game."

"Well, Vic, if you understood chess, you could probably figure out this map would be my chessboard and the pins would be my chess pieces. The object of this game, just like any game, is to win. Not by violence but by letting the law work for us like the foreclosure process or the outright purchase of some of the ranches. We start killing people illegally it will get back to the law, which will bring unwanted attention. However, if someone dies in a fair gunfight, we cannot be held responsible. So, I don't want to hear about something like this again. I need Gus's ranch to complete this map and give me total control of the valley and Cheyenne. His ranch is the key to this game because his ranch controls the water to all the other cattle ranches and farmland. If I can't get his ranch, I can't complete my plan and all I've got is a large area of land with some cattle and crops and someone else controlling the water rights. That would be completely unacceptable. But if I get his ranch, I own it all and can charge whatever price I want to the cattle buyers in Cheyenne. Now, do you understand what I am doing with this map?"

"Well, yeah! I see what you're tryin' to do, boss. But I don't see how you're gonna do it without takin' care of Gus."

"You just leave Gus to me and do what I tell you to do, Vic."

"Sure, boss, I always follow your orders."

"Now, why don't you clear out of here? I've got some thinking and planning to do."

"No problem, boss. I'll be over at the saloon if you need me."

Jason sat back down behind his desk and looked at the map, calculating what his next step was going to be.

Alicia and Sarah went into the kitchen, and Sarah put some water on the stove to brew some tea. She wanted to hear all about Pittsburgh, where Alicia had been living since leaving the ranch. But first, Alicia wanted her mom to tell her about what she knew concerning the shooting of her father.

"Mom, tell me what you think happened to Dad other than the obvious. All I got was a telegram delivered to the school that said Dad was shot. I spent last night in Cheyenne at Mary's in her spare bedroom she had upstairs. I got in from the train yesterday evening at six o'clock and was walking toward the hotel when Mary spotted me and insisted I come into the café for something to eat. So I accepted her invitation and then Doc came into the café for dinner, which we all had together. So, Doc and Mary filled me in with as much as they knew including what someone by the name of Jason Long has been up to around here for the last five years. Doc said Dad was shot somewhere on the trail between here and Cheyenne but either managed to stay on his horse or was able to get back on his horse after being shot and made it back here. What else can you tell me about it, Mom?"

"Well, dear, it sounds like you know as much as I do about what happened to Dad. He's only come around a couple of times and can't remember anything about being shot. He recalls coming home on the trail from town and then the next thing he knows is waking up here in bed all bandaged up. I'm not even sure if at first he even knew he had been shot. So there's really nothing more I can add to what you already know."

"Well, Mom, we need to find out what happened and have whoever did this to Dad arrested and sent to jail!"

"Sarah, I know Gus is sleeping but have you talked to him today? I was wondering how he was doing from the last time I saw him?" asked O'Malley.

"I think he's doing very well considering being shot in the chest. I changed the bandage like you showed me and didn't see anything that looked infected. We talked a little while, and he ate some soup and bread then went back to sleep just a little while ago. I didn't want to wake him up, but I'd like you to look him over, Doc, before you leave today to make sure he's doin' okay."

"That's one of the reasons I came out, Sarah. The other one was to bring Alicia out."

They continued their conversation for a while longer until Sarah thought she heard Gus stirring in the bedroom. "Excuse me, I think I hear Alicia's Dad. I'll check and see if he's awake. You two sit here for a few minutes." She walked out of the kitchen to the bedroom door and opened it slightly.

"Sarah?" he said in a raspy voice. "I thought you said you were heading' into town to see if Alicia got in?"

"Gus, I've got the best news. I was walking out to the buggy just as Alicia and Doc rode into the ranch. Doc was going to come out to check on you so he gave Alicia a ride out to the ranch. She spent the night in town just like you thought she would."

"Well, what're you waiting for? Bring her in so I can see her."

She turned and opened the door, raising her voice to call out to Alicia and O'Malley that Gus was awake. Alicia quickly got up and bolted out of the kitchen into her parents' bedroom. She saw her dad lying in bed and felt the tears welling up in her eyes as she went to her father, putting her arms around his neck and giving him a hug as she broke down into a good cry. As she hugged her father, she let go of the emotions that she had pent up for the last several days. "Dad, Dad, Dad! I've been so scared and worried about you ever since I got the telegram from Mom. Doc says you are going to be okay," she said as she released her grip from around her father's neck and sat up on the bed beside him, wiping away her tears.

"You ought to know it would take more than a bullet to kill your father. Besides, your mom claims I'm just too stubborn to die. It's just great to see you. I'm so glad you came out, Alicia. Your mom and I have missed you a lot. How long can you stay with us?"

"I'll be staying here for quite a while, Dad. I plan on helping Mom run the ranch and making sure you behave yourself and get back up on your feet."

"That's just fine, Alicia, but I plan on being up in the next day or two. I got work to do around here, and I can't be lying in bed all day while everyone else is working."

O'Malley had come in during their conversation and gave a worried glance toward Sarah as he heard what Gus had just said.

"Gus, you aren't doing anything until Doc says you can. I will tie you down if I have to," said Sarah.

"Honey, I just can't lie here day after day when there's work to be done. So don't be surprised if I'm up and around in a day or two," Gus replied to Sarah.

"I'm afraid you're not going to be able to do that, Gus. If you try to get out of that bed in less than a week, you'll end up tearing all those stitches I put in your chest. If you don't bleed to death, you'll probably get an infection, which could very likely kill you. So what will it be, Gus? Stay in bed for another week and get well or get out of bed early and get so sick you might just not get well at all?"

"Doc, this husband of mine is gonna stay here in bed for the next week even if I've got to go out and get five or six of the hands to tie him down to this bed."

"Well, I sure can't fight you all so I'll give you all one week. But after that one week, I'm getting' up to take care of business. Now, you all get out of here so I can get some rest. Alicia, I want to hear about everything you have been doing a little later."

"Okay, Dad, you get some sleep, and I'll be by later to talk." She leaned over and gave Gus a kiss on his forehead and then got up and walked out of the bedroom with O'Malley and Sarah.

"Well, Dad hasn't changed. He's just as stubborn as I remember him," she remarked as they all walked back to the kitchen to sit down and finish their conversation. Sarah poured everyone some tea and put out some homemade cookies she had baked. All three sat at the kitchen table where Sarah and Alicia talked about the past few years and caught each other up on past events. Alicia thought about everything that had happened over the last couple of days and decided something must be done. "Mom, I intend to find out who did this to Dad and make sure they are made to answer. I know the marshal is not involved from what you and Doc tell me, and it sounds like he isn't going to be able to help us much. So, I'm going to get to the bottom of this and make them pay."

"Alicia, I really don't need you to get involved in this and get hurt. I don't need another family member shot."

"Mom, I'm not going to get shot. But we're also not going to sit by and let someone get away with shooting one of us. Let's face it, we all know when Dad gets well, he's going after the person he thinks is behind this. My bet would be he will have a serious talk with Jason if you know what I mean. Dad knows Jason had the motive to get rid of him and then try to run you off the land. So tomorrow I'm going back to town to see the marshal and ask some questions."

"Well, ladies, I'm going to check on Gus and make sure his wound is healing properly and then head back to town." O'Malley got up and walked out of the kitchen and into the bedroom. In a soft voice, he called his name until he stirred awake. "Hi Gus, I just wanted to check your bandages and make sure there is no sign of infection. I'm going to clean your wound up if it needs it and put some clean bandages back on. If everything looks good, then I'll be heading back to town."

Gus's voice was still raspy as he replied. "No problem, Doc. I want to thank you for what you did patchin' me up and takin' care of me."

"I was glad to help, but I sure didn't like to see you shot. I think your daughter has the idea of finding out on her own who did this to you. She's pretty mad about it and intends on going into town tomorrow to ask some questions."

"Thanks, Doc, for tellin' me. I will make sure I talk to her first. I don't want her going into town alone. Although I don't think anything would happen to her since she doesn't really have anything to do with the ranch. If she insists on goin' into town, I'm gonna ask her to stop by your place first, Doc. I'll tell her the reason is to let you know I'm still doin' okay. I will talk to her and see if I can convince her to stick around here for a few days, but we both know when she gets something in her mind it is almost impossible to convince her otherwise."

"Okay, but I don't think it'll do any good. From talking to her last night and on the ride out here this morning, I think you can count on her being as stubborn as she was before she left town. I'll make sure I stay at my office tomorrow. I need to be there anyway as I think I'll have several folks coming in since I wasn't there today."

"I appreciate all the time you've been out here, Doc, but the next time I see you will be when I'm able to ride into town on my own."

"Okay, Gus, I hope that's the case. I'm all done here, so I'll be heading back to town now. You are healing quite nicely. I'll let Sarah know she can send for me if you start feeling poorly or if she sees signs of infection."

During this brief conversation, he could tell Gus was exhausted and noticed him drifting in and out of consciousness as they talked. He allowed him to drop off and then gathered up his medical supplies he brought and packed up his medical bag. He decided to leave the extra bandages he had brought so Sarah would not have to make up new ones. After packing his medical bag, he looked over at Gus, who was sound asleep and appeared to be resting comfortably. He opened the bedroom door and gently closed it behind him so as not to wake him up. He then walked out to the kitchen where Alicia and Sarah were still sitting and talking.

"Gus looks just fine, Sarah. I can see you have been cleaning the wound and putting clean bandages on every day so I think it is safe for me to stay in town for a few days. If he takes a turn for the worse, just send one of the hands into town to get me, and I'll come right out. I'm going to start back to town now. You two have a good afternoon and get caught up on everything," said O'Malley.

"Mom, I'm going to walk Doc out. Why don't you relax here, and I'll be right back."

They walked out the front door, down the step, and out to his buggy. He put his medical bag in the front seat and climbed in beside it. Alicia stood next to the buggy as he picked up the reins to urge Dollar on.

"Doc, I wanted to thank you again for taking care of Dad. I'm sure if it wasn't for you, he would be dead." She put her foot up on the buggy step slowly, leaned in, and kissed Doc on his left cheek.

She then leaned back, stepping off the buggy and onto the ground. They looked at each other with longing for several seconds.

"Alicia, I want to see you again soon. I am coming out next week to check up on your dad. How would you like to go on a picnic like we used to? I can pack a basket of food and bring it with me when I come out to see your dad. We could then ride out from the ranch into the country and enjoy a quiet afternoon together."

"I think I would like that a lot. I haven't been on a picnic since I went on one with you five years ago. But instead of waiting for next week, why don't we go this Sunday? Mom and I will be in for church, and you and I can go on the picnic after services are over. That is, as long as you are willing to give me a ride back to the ranch."

"That sounds great, Alicia. When I get you back to the ranch, I'll check on your dad and see how he is doing. I'll be at church also, so unless you have any objections, I'll sit with you and your mother."

"That's fine, Doc. I'm going to especially look forward to this Sunday. You have a safe trip back to town, and we'll see you on Sunday," replied Alicia as she turned and walked back to the house.

He snapped the reins once and turned the buggy around to start his trip back to town. The way back was uneventful, and he made it back to town within two hours. Upon arrival at his house, he unharnessed Dollar, gave him some oats, and then headed into town to get some dinner at Mary's. When he arrived at the café to order his dinner, he ate in the kitchen and brought Mary up-to-date on how Gus was doing.

When Alicia walked back into the house after seeing O'Malley off, she sat with her mom, and they talked for the rest of the afternoon. It was dinnertime before they knew it, and they started to prepare the evening meal. With both of them working together, dinner was ready in no time.

Alicia had forgotten what a good cook her mom was. They had decided on steak—it was a cattle ranch after all—along with potatoes and mixed green vegetables from the root cellar. There was a small table in the parlor, and Alicia convinced her mom to move it into the bedroom where her dad was so they could all eat together on her first night at home.

Gus had woken up to the delicious smell of the dinner being prepared and was surprised and delighted when Sarah and Alicia came in with a plate of food for him and themselves. They put the plates down on his bed and then went out and brought the small table in from the parlor. Gus's appetite had returned, and he was famished after eating only small portions of food over the last several days. This was one of the best meals they had eaten in a long time, and they enjoyed excellent dinner conversation. This was also the first time Sarah, Alicia, and Gus had truly relaxed since the shooting and enjoyed a meal together as a family. After dinner, the three of them sat around with Sarah and Alicia updating Gus on what they had talked about all afternoon.

CHAPTER 9

사랑

To own and operate a cattle ranch required long hours and grueling work. The ranch had its own cook, who prepared the meals for the ranch hands—they slept in a separate bunkhouse. When Gus and Sarah built the ranch, it became quite apparent a cook was needed to prepare the meals for the increasing number of hands they had hired over the years to help run the ranch.

One day, a visitor stopped by the ranch on his way south to Cheyenne looking for work. It was a hot day, and Gus invited the stranger to climb down from his horse and refill his canteen, which was empty. Gus introduced himself to the stranger and extended him an invitation to eat the noon meal with them. The stranger introduced himself as Moses Washington and gladly accepted the invitation to eat with Gus and Sarah.

During lunch, the conversation turned to the reasons Moses was going to Cheyenne. He said he had been drifting for several months and was looking for steady work. Gus asked him if he had ever considered being a ranch hand to which he replied that he had never done manual labor and would not be very good at it, but if Gus had an opening for a cook on a trail drive or at the ranch, he said he was his man.

It was the middle of August, and Gus always drove his cattle to the railhead at this time of year. Since he did need to hire a cook, he asked him what his experience was on short cattle drives. Moses gave him the names of several ranches he had worked at as a trail cook and then quickly gave him the recipe for an apple pie, asking Sarah if that was right. She nodded in agreement and then turned to Gus, telling him he had found himself a cook.

That was the beginning of a long relationship, which lasted to this day. After the first cattle drive with Moses, Gus hired him on the spot to be the permanent ranch cook for the hands and any future cattle drives. When Gus introduced him to the hands, there were some of them who did not believe a black man would be good for anything. Gus made sure the hands understood Moses would be treated like anyone else on the ranch and be expected to pull his own weight. Disbelief by the hands disappeared after Moses prepared their first breakfast of eggs, potatoes, pancakes, bacon, sausage, and light-as-air biscuits, which melted in the mouth. After that breakfast, Moses became one of the most appreciated workers on the ranch.

Moses was up every morning by 4:30 a.m. to start up the stove and prepare breakfast for the ranch hands, serve it, and then clean up after the morning meal. He would then have a couple of hours to himself to do as he pleased before starting preparation for the noon meal. Sometimes, he would take his horse out for a ride to enjoy the valley and surrounding mountains between meals.

Gus would often find him sitting under a shade tree reading. When Gus asked what he was reading, he was surprised to learn that Moses enjoyed reading Shakespeare and poetry. He could tell Moses was educated from the way he talked, but he never gave the impression he was better than anyone else. He always made it a point to talk on the same level of everyone else and treated them as an equal.

After the noon meal, he would clean up and once again have a couple of hours to himself before preparing dinner. He kept this routine all year round although he confined his reading to the bunkhouse during the cold winter months.

One spring day, Moses was finishing cleaning up breakfast dishes after the ranch hands had finished eating and noticed Sarah marking off a plot of land down by the river with stakes and twine. Curious, he walked over to where Sarah was tying the twine to the last stake.

"Well, Sarah, it looks like you're going to do some work. May I ask what you're planning?"

"I decided it's time we had a garden. So I'm marking off the area I intend to grow our vegetables in," replied Sarah.

"Well, I see you've picked a nice sunny spot by the river, which should make it easier to haul the water over to the garden. Now, I know a little bit about gardening because my mother always had a garden every year and part of my chores was to tend it. I think you have picked a great place and I don't want to tell you what to do, but I would suggest you may want to look down the river fifty yards to locate your garden plot," said Moses.

"I don't see the difference, Moses. Why would that ground be better than this area? In fact, I would have to walk up a slight slope to get the water for the garden."

"That's just it, Sarah. We could put a pipe with a shutoff in the side of the bank to the river and irrigate the garden whenever you want."

"I see your point, Moses. That's a great idea. It sure is better than hauling buckets of water from the river every day to water the garden. It sounds like you enjoy gardening, Moses. If that's the case, I'd love to have you help me but only if you'd like. I'm not trying to force you to do something you might not want to do on your time off. But I'd take any help you would like to give. Why don't you think it over while I take these stakes out and put them back over there where you suggested."

"Sarah, I don't need to think it over. Let me help you remove these stakes and set them up over there, where we will start the garden. After we set them up, I'll get a couple shovels, rakes, and a hoe so we can turn the earth over, break it up, and rake out the rocks. Do you have the seed to plant after we get the ground prepared?" asked Moses.

"I sure do. I bought some from the feed and seed store in Cheyenne. I've got seed for tomatoes, green beans, corn, peas, carrots, radishes, onions, and potatoes. We're also going to plant some herbs like mint and basil plus a couple others. We can use them to season the food," replied Sarah.

"Time's a wastin'. Let's get this garden started. I'll go get those garden tools if you can start staking out the plot of land for the garden," said Moses.

That was the start of an annual ritual between Sarah and Moses. They both loved to garden and every spring, they would plan what they wanted to grow, preparing the land, planting the vegetables, and tending the garden throughout the growing season. Moses would work in the garden during the free time he had between preparing and serving meals, and Sarah would normally join him during these times. Their combined efforts resulted in a huge bounty of produce throughout the summer. They used this produce to prepare their meals—Sarah for her family and Moses for the ranch hands.

During the hot summer days when temperatures would rise into the nineties, Sarah would wear a light airy sundress, allowing her to work and remain cool in the heat of the day. Unlike the rest of the ranch hands, who would remove their shirts to stay cool in the summer heat while working around the ranch, Sarah never saw Moses without his long-sleeved shirt.

One hot windy afternoon, Sarah made some lemonade and brought it out to the garden to share with Moses. They stood under a tree close to the garden sipping their drinks and talking about how large they thought the watermelons were getting. He leaned over to pick up the lemonade pitcher from the ground when a sudden breeze came up and blew his untucked shirt halfway up his back. Sarah gave a slight gasp when she saw the scars on his bare skin. He heard Sarah and turning toward her, noticed the look of concern on her face.

"Are you okay, Sarah?" asked Moses.

"I-I'm sorry Moses, I saw the marks on your back and thought you were hurt. I know it's none of my business but those look like whipping scars."

"You're right, Sarah. Many years ago when I was a young man, the daughter of a ranch owner I worked for was teaching me how to read and write. She was the local schoolteacher, and I picked up reading very quickly. I had gone into town one Saturday night and was walking by an alley and heard the muffled screams of a woman. I went into the alley and found the rancher's daughter being held against a building wall by three cowboys. It was obvious what they wanted to do. One of the men was pressed up against her with his hand covering her mouth while the other two men were on each side of her, pinning an arm against the side of the building. Something had to be done and there was no time to get help so I ran toward the three, screaming my head off at them to stop. My yelling seemed to unnerve the man who had his hand over her mouth and he turned to face me. He removed his hand from her mouth, bringing it down to his side where he had his gun. Before he had a chance to get his gun out of his holster, I leaped at him and drove my shoulder into his side, crashing him into the man behind him and knocking them both to the ground. The third man came up behind me and struck me on the back of my head with his pistol gun barrel. That blow really stunned me, and the three were getting ready to either kill me or beat me within an inch of my life. But because of the ruckus I made, there were people gathering at the alley entrance and walking toward us. The three attackers fled down the alley but not before the one I knocked down turned and yelled at me, 'Just wait, Darkie. We'll get you for this.' They took off and escaped through the other end of the alley. When the girl and I explained what had happened, the townsfolk couldn't be kinder to me. They congratulated me and took me to the local restaurant where they bought a nice dinner for me.

"After dinner, the sheriff spoke to me and said he was not able to catch the three attackers but would keep looking for them. It was late by the time we finished dinner, so I got my horse and started my ride back to the ranch. About a mile out of town, there was a small forest area the trail went through and as I entered the forest, the three attackers saw me from where they had been hiding and jumped me. Instead of killing me, they spread-eagled me between two trees on the side of the trail. The man I knocked down in the alley approached me and said, 'This is what we do to darkies who get in our way.' He then took a bull whip off his horse and whipped me until I lost consciousness. They left me to die like that, but I had the good luck that one of the other hands from another ranch was riding by and saw my horse standing on the side of the trail. As soon as he saw me spread out between the trees, he jumped off his horse, took his knife out, and cut me down. This ranch hand then removed the bedroll from his horse, spread it out, and laid me on top of it. He told me he thought I was dead when he cut me down until he heard a moan. He brought me around by putting some water on his bandana and applying it to my forehead.

"Later, the ranch hand told me he had recognized me from the excitement in town and related how he had found me. After seeing my back, he knew he had to get me back to town to see the doctor. That was the way I found out what really happened to me after passing out from the whipping. This ranch hand's name was Luke, he told me while helping me get up on my horse. He apologized for the pain he was causing to lift me up on the horse but explained it was either a ride back to town together, or he would have to get help, which would take quite a while for him to return. Luke didn't want to leave me because of my injuries, and he was afraid the attackers might return to finish the job. He securely tied me to my horse so I would not fall off and then took the reins and led me back to town where the doctor treated my wounds.

"Because I saved the girl from those hooligans, the town went all out to help me get well, and the law eventually caught the men in a town about twenty miles south of where I was recuperating. However, they were arrested in the county where their family had lived for fifty years and were very powerful. The local authorities insisted on bringing them to trial in front of their local judges and citizens. The trial found the attackers guilty, and they were fined twenty-five dollars without any jail time. It was then I learned my first lesson on how the law works for my kind versus the white man. When I got well, I worked on the ranch through the winter and continued my education with the assistance of the ranch owner's daughter.

"After that winter, I left in the spring and have been on the road by myself hiring out as a ranch cook for cattle drives. Over time, I acquired a well-known reputation as a cook and received many requests from local cattle ranchers to sign on for their drives. Then I arrived here from the south and after Gus gave me the cattle drive cook job, I could tell he and you were good people with whom I felt right at home.

"So, that pretty well outlines most of my life. We're about done here, Sarah, and I've gotta get cooking for the boys."

"My, Moses, I don't think I've heard you talk as much as this in all the years I've known you. That is the most incredible life history I have ever heard of anyone. It must have been very difficult for you, and I want you to know we appreciate all you have done around here and have always thought of you as one of our family. Anyway, I've also got to get dinner ready for Gus. He should be coming in from the range within the hour. We both better get in and start getting dinner ready."

Sunday came and Sarah and Alicia left early in the morning, taking a buggy out to Cheyenne. Church was at eleven o'clock, and they met O'Malley at the church where they attended Mass together. On the way to church, Alicia had explained to her mom she would be going on a picnic with O'Malley after Mass.

When church was over, Sarah decided to go over to Mary's Café to have lunch and say hello to Mary. Her plan was to have something to eat and then head back to the ranch. O'Malley explained to Alicia he needed to stop at his house to change clothes and pick up his medical bag as he wanted to check on Gus when he drove her home after their picnic. So Sarah went on directly to Mary's, and Alicia walked with O'Malley to his house. She had brought a change of clothes with her, which she changed into at O'Malley's house while he also changed into jeans and a comfortable shirt.

While Alicia was changing her clothes in another room, O'Malley was thinking they would have to drop by Mary's Café as he had asked her to prepare some of her famous fried chicken that she was so well-known for throughout the territory.

"Well, Doc, how do I look?"

He turned and looked at Alicia, who had put on a light, airy sundress. It was a white dress with a flower print and two thin straps over her bare shoulders. "You look very pretty, Alicia. That dress looks like it was made just for you. As you know, I am not a very good cook so I bought a picnic lunch for us from Mary. She always opens for lunch after church so we can go over and say a quick hello to your mom and Mary, and then head out for our picnic. How's that sound?"

"That's great! To be perfectly honest with you, I was hoping your cooking had either improved or you were going to make arrangements with someone to prepare our meal. I don't mean to complain, Doc, but as I recall, you could hardly stand to eat your own cooking."

"I can't dispute that fact since I almost always eat at Mary's. Shall we get started on our way to the café?" asked O'Malley.

❀ ❀ ❀

Sarah walked to Mary's Café after leaving Alicia at O'Malley's house to change clothes. She entered the café and immediately was greeted with a hearty hello and hug from Mary after she had put some plates of food on a table she had been waiting on.

"Sarah! How are you? I've heard Gus is going to be all right, thank God. Let me get you some tea, and we can talk while you think about what you want for lunch."

Mary went out to the kitchen and while she was gone, Vic came into the café and sat a few tables apart from Sarah. He had been out late from Saturday night into early Sunday morning drinking with the boys. He had come into the café to get himself some coffee and lunch, hoping this would help lessen the pain he was feeling from his long night of drinking. He looked up and motioned to Sandy to come over from behind the counter where she was working. Sandy walked over to his table and took out an order pad.

"What can I get for you, sir?" she asked.

"Coffee, I need coffee as soon as you can. Then I'll order some lunch so when you finally get back here with the coffee, bring me a menu," barked Vic.

"No need to wait for a menu. I brought one with me just in case. Why don't you look it over and order when I get back? That way you won't waste your time waiting to decide."

Sandy brought the coffee back within two minutes. Vic had a reputation as a mean and vicious bully when he was drunk, who had no regard for anyone's safety. Sandy had always been afraid of him as he had bullied and started fighting with many men she knew in town, who were peaceful but easy to pick on. When drunk, he started fights for any reason and always with someone he thought he could easily beat up. Sandy waited patiently with an order book in hand to take his lunch order. He had his elbows on the table, holding his head between his hands and looking down at the menu. He then reached for his coffee, putting it up to his mouth and noisily slurping some of the brew. As he put the coffee down on the table, he looked around and noticed Sarah sitting at her table on the other side of the café.

Sandy finally asked Vic, "Do you know what you would like for lunch?"

"How's the beef stew?" asked Vic.

"Mary makes the best stew in town. I don't think you can go wrong with it," replied Sandy.

"Okay, okay, I'll go with the beef stew. Bring some biscuits with it, too," snarled Vic.

"No problem. We'll have it up for you in just a minute," Sandy said as she wrote down the order while walking back to the kitchen.

Mary returned to Sarah's table with some tea but did not sit down. "Sarah, I've got to prepare the food back in the kitchen for the normal rush of church people that usually get here in a few minutes. You can come back to the kitchen and we can talk or if you want some peace and quiet after all the excitement you've been through, you can sit here, and I'll be out in a little bit to talk. Right now, you can enjoy your tea and relax for a little bit. When I deal with the lunch rush, I can bring out some lunch for the two of us, and we can sit and talk."

"You know, Mary, I think I'll just stay out here and enjoy a quiet lunch. I know you have some of that great tasting stew out there. Can you bring me a bowl with some bread and butter? I think I'd like a glass of lemonade as well as the tea to go along with it."

"That's fine, Sarah. I'll send Sandy right away with your lunch. Like I said, we'll talk later."

Sandy brought out the lunch for Vic, putting it in front of him. Vic looked up at Sandy and muttered, "Bout time." He then grabbed a spoon, holding it in his fist, and ate his lunch noisily without regard for anyone he might be disturbing. He wolfed down his food like he hadn't eaten in a week, leaned back in his chair, wiped his mouth on his sleeve, and let out a loud belch. He got up and glanced over at Sarah, who had turned her head toward Vic and gave him a disgusted look while shaking her head with a grimace and turning back to her meal. He pushed himself back from the table, got up, and walked over to where she was sitting. "You gotta problem lady?"

"Well, young man, since you brought it up, I think you could use a lesson in manners. If you want to eat like a farm animal maybe you should consider living with them," she retorted.

"Maybe I oughta teach *you* some manners, lady. You don't scare me, and I know your old man is bad sick and sure as heck can't come to your rescue now," he snarled.

"Young man, I don't need my husband to fight my battles with some lowlife bully like you. Why don't you go outside? I saw some small children with their mothers at church you could beat up.

Maybe you can go pick a fight with some of them. I'm not sure, but they might be afraid of you," she said.

"If you were a man, I'd teach you somethin' lady," growled Vic.

Alicia and O'Malley were on their way to the café to pick up their picnic lunch Mary had prepared. Alicia also wanted to drop off her church clothes so her mom could take them back to the ranch. As they approached the café, they noticed Sarah through the window talking to a large man, who seemed to be either very angry or agitated about something. "Doc, do you see that man talking to my mom? Do you know who that is?"

"That's Vic. One of Jason's hired guns, and he sure doesn't look very happy. Let's go through the side door and see what's going on."

"No, Doc. I have a better idea. I'm going to go through the front door because Vic has never seen me before and won't think I have anything to do with my mom. This way, I might hear something that could be of use. Do me a favor, Doc, and go through the side door into the kitchen and just listen through the café kitchen door. You can always come in if you think Mom and I are in trouble and need help."

"Okay, Alicia, have it your way, but I will be in there to help if I see any sign of trouble."

She continued to walk down the boardwalk in front of Mary's Café, making her way to the front entrance. She looked in the windows of the restaurant as she approached the front entrance seeing only one other couple in the café, who were approaching the front door indicating they had finished their lunch. She thought there would be more people, but maybe the church parishioners had not yet shown up. As she reached out to pull the front door open, it moved toward her as the couple who were in the restaurant came through the door almost running into her. The three looked at each other, muttered an excuse me and moved on.

Vic had noticed the man and wife pay their bill, get up, and head for the door to leave. He turned back to Sarah to reply to her last remark and never noticed Alicia slip into the café as the couple left. As she softly walked into the dining area, she put her finger to her lips and shook her head back and forth as she met her mother's eyes. Sarah was puzzled as to why Alicia did not want her presence known. Whatever the reason, she made no sign or movement to let Vic know another person was in the café.

"Knowing you, Vic, beating up women should come naturally to the likes of you. So don't let me being a woman change your mind. Just remember we are in town and not on some deserted road where an ambush can take place. Cheyenne also has an honest marshal who can deal with your kind. Or is shooting people on a lonely road who can't see you more your style?" asked Sarah.

"Yeah, I heard your old man is doin' okay. Maybe next time, Gus won't be so lucky. There are a lot of bad men out there and maybe Gus ought to think about sellin' to Jason and move on. It might just be safer and healthier for him and you," snapped Vic.

"I can see why you would be worried about whether Gus remembers who shot him. Or do you think it might have been a cowardly bushwhacker who was afraid to face him? Maybe the marshal ought to talk to you, Vic. I hear you like to fight with people weaker than you or who you can take advantage of. Like I said before, if you hurry, you can still find some of the kids outside from the church service to beat up. Bullies like you delight in picking on women and children. But mind you, Vic, this is one woman who is not afraid of the likes of you. So, why don't you crawl out of here and let me eat my meal in peace? Our conversation is over, Vic."

As Sarah dressed down Vic, his face started to get flushed and his eyes narrowed as the anger began to build and visibly show in his glare at Sarah. After she had made this last remark, he straightened up and looked down at Sarah. He stared hard at her for a moment and then said, "Your old man needs to beat you some, lady. I think I'll help him out since he's sick in bed."

Vic slightly stepped back with his right foot and quickly raised his open right hand in order to slap Sarah across the face. Sarah saw what Vic was about to do and raised both hands in an attempt to defend herself. Alicia, seeing what was about to happen, took two silent steps toward Vic and reached up with her right hand, grasping and squeezing a certain part of Vic's neck, which resulted in freezing Vic's position with his hand still in midair. She moved slightly to her left to see where her mom was.

"Mom, are you okay?"

"I'm just fine, honey. What are you doing to Vic?"

"It's a pressure point hold, Mom. As long as I keep the pressure on, he can't move his body. Why don't you go on home, and I'll deal with your friend here. I don't think he'll bother you anymore."

"Are you sure, dear? I can go into the kitchen and get Mary to send for the marshal."

"No, Mom, don't do that, but Doc's in the kitchen, and you could send him out to help me with Vic. On the way over here, I dropped my church clothes into the buggy, so let Doc and me take care of this problem and you can head back to the ranch."

Just as Sarah started to get up, Doc was already coming through the kitchen's swinging doors into the dining area. He had been watching Vic through the kitchen doors, which had small windows in each door so waitresses could see if someone was going in or out of the kitchen. As he approached, he had heard the exchange between Alicia and Sarah.

Alicia turned to O'Malley and said, "Doc, as soon as Mom gets in the buggy and takes off, I'm going to let Vic go. He's going to have a sore neck and a headache to boot."

"That's okay with me, Alicia. There goes your mom now. Let him go and step back. I'm sure he's not going to be in a very good mood," replied O'Malley.

Alicia released her hold, and Vic dropped his raised arm to his side. He then grabbed the right side of his neck. "Jeez, what the heck did you do to my neck and who are you? Some Chinese cook the railroad brought in," snapped Vic.

"No, sir I'm Gus and Sarah's daughter. I came in from back east after learning about my father being shot, and I intend on finding out who did it."

"Yeah, I heard about you. Some Chinese kid Gus and Sarah picked up to raise. So, you think you're gonna find out who shot Gus, are you? That might be pretty dangerous for a little lady like you. You could get hurt poking your nose into places it doesn't belong. Besides, I've been out here four years, and I ain't ever seen you here before. So all of a sudden, Gus gets shot and you hightail it home? What did you come back for? You think you might get some money if Gus dies?" asked Vic.

"Hold it, Vic. I've been standing here listening to your garbage, and I'm not going to let you talk to her like one of your saloon girls. I think you either get out of here, or I'll help you to the door."

"Doc, I don't need you to fight my battles. And Vic, I'm here to visit my family and help take care of my dad. Anything else I do here is none of your business. But let me make this clear enough so even you understand it. You ever threaten one of my family or attack them in any way, you'll be dealing with me. If you think that little pain in your neck is bad, that hold I had on your neck is just a sample of what I could have done."

Vic stepped back and slowly lowered his right hand to the gun in his holster.

"You better think about it, Vic. Neither of us is armed, and Mary and Sandy are watching from the kitchen door. What are you going to do, shoot all of us and claim self-defense? The marshal will make sure you hang. There are too many folks on the street, which means witnesses seeing you come out of the café," retorted O'Malley.

Vic's face had turned red with anger, his gun hand trembling by his holster. After a few seconds, but what seemed like eternity to O'Malley, Vic turned and walked to the front door, opened it, and stared back at O'Malley and Alicia. "You both got your way today, but I wouldn't always count on comin' out on top every time," said Vic as he walked out the door and started for Jason's office.

O'Malley and Alicia looked at each other for a few seconds. "Doc, when you asked me out for a picnic, I had no idea it would be this exciting. Why don't we grab the basket and head out."

"Alicia, I always try to put a little excitement in the lives of those I like. Now, let's get that basket and head out."

They headed out for their afternoon picnic after going into the kitchen to pick up their basket. When the ruckus had started with Vic, Mary had to be held back by O'Malley as he explained to her in a soft voice that Alicia wanted them to stay in the kitchen and not make any noise. O'Malley and Alicia said their good-byes and headed out for his buggy and an afternoon of fun.

They enjoyed a pleasant ride to a meadow with a small stream running through it. O'Malley pulled the buggy off the side of the trail, got out, and went to Alicia's side, extending his hand to help her down. After she got out of the buggy, he went to the rear and took out the picnic basket and blanket they were going to spread out on the ground. She took the blanket from O'Malley, and they walked toward the stream while talking and continuing to catch up with each other. They spread the blanket under a shade tree by the stream and took out the food to eat.

O'Malley had picked a beautiful setting for their picnic. They sat under a large sprawling shade tree situated about twenty-five feet from a small slow-moving stream. There was a clear view of the mountains on either side of the valley, and the grass was as green as an emerald and as lush and soft as a new, thick rug. They ate their fill of the picnic goodies Mary had prepared for them and then relaxed on the blanket they had spread out.

"Alicia, I've always wondered what possessed you to leave your folks' ranch and go out east to teach. I thought we were beginning to enjoy each other's company."

"To be quite honest, Doc, I was beginning to have feelings for you, but I had never been away from the ranch except when we lived in Korea before Mom and Dad adopted me. I wanted to see more of this country and meet people who were different from a ranching community. I'm not saying the people here are inferior.

All I'm saying is that I wanted to meet and know a lot of different people. Even though I've been back just a short while, I am glad to be here, and I am especially glad to see you are still here," replied Alicia.

"I can't tell you how thrilled I was to see you at Mary's Café when you first returned to town. It brought back so many pleasant memories from the past that I had hidden away when you had left. I turned to my work, putting all my effort and energy into my medical practice to keep my mind off you. It took me a very long time to accept the fact you might not return to Cheyenne. I was overwhelmed with emotion when I first saw you in the café but dared not show it as I was not sure if or how long you were going to stay. I'm still not sure how long you intend to stay, but I hope you will be here for a long time."

As he poured out his feelings, he slowly moved closer to Alicia. Her hand was lying slightly away from her body as she lay on the blanket with her head propped up by her right hand. As O'Malley edged closer, his hand brushed against hers and he pulled it back slightly. But Alicia slowly reached out and gently took his hand in hers and raised it to her face, caressing it softly. He moved his hand to her hair and brushed it back from her face, moving his hand behind her head and moving slowly toward her, kissing her forehead, then caressing her eyes and moving slowly down to her lips, hesitating briefly before he pulled her into a tender embrace, which developed into a long, passionate kiss arousing a deep need for each other.

O'Malley's hand moved slowly to Alicia's sundress and slowly began to slide the straps off her shoulders. She gently pushed him back and looked at him with half-closed eyes that clearly and silently said, *I want you*.

"John, nothing would give me more pleasure than to make love to you out here, right now. I just don't think this is the right time or place with what is going on in my life. I know after coming back home and seeing you again, I realized what else I had come back for besides the tragedy that happened to my father. John, I love you, and I want us to be together, but not like this on some hillside. If you love me, you will understand and not be hurt because I want to wait," whispered Alicia.

O'Malley hugged her and then leaned back on his right elbow, supporting his head as it rested in his right hand. "Alicia, I would never do anything to hurt or upset you. I loved you even before you left town. When you told me you were going, my heart sank for two reasons. The first was I could not bear to tell you my true feelings because I did not know if it would change your mind and end up staying here and resenting me for it later. I didn't want you to hold that against me in later years and feel that you stayed here because of me, losing your opportunity to see other parts of this country. The second reason was my heart was broken, fearing that you would meet someone else back east, get married and settle down. I'm so glad you came back although I wish it was not due to your dad being shot. Alicia, I can truly say I feel the same way you do. I have always been in love with you from the very first time I met you. I also understand why you wish to wait, and I respect your wishes. But when things settle down, we are going to talk about marriage and settling down."

"John, this makes my day one of the best I have had in the last five years. I know we will be happy together, and I wish I had come back a lot sooner. Since you mentioned my dad, I want you to know I intend on finding the person who shot him. I hope you can understand and accept that."

"I completely understand it, but you're going to need help, and I will be happy to give you a hand. I hope this will clean up this town and get rid of the likes of Jason Long."

They reached out to one another and hugged tightly for a long time, neither wanting to let the other go. After a while, they slowly released each other and decided to clean up the picnic area, fold the blanket, and start back to the buggy. As they walked toward the buggy, they discussed the strategy they would adopt in locating the person who shot Gus and left him for dead. O'Malley loaded up the picnic basket and blanket into the back of his buggy. Once seated in the buggy, they started on their ride to the ranch.

"Doc, I appreciate you wanting to help me finding who shot my dad. Tomorrow's Monday, and I am going to come into town to talk to the marshal and ask him some questions. There are still a lot of people in town who were there before I left town. I'll stop by your place tomorrow before I head into town to nose around."

"You had better stop by. I won't lose you again, and I want to make sure you stay safe. It's about a two-hour horseback ride to my place so why don't we get together at ten o'clock?"

"Doc, you must hold banker's hours. I'll be out there by nine o'clock at the latest. I get up early, and you might as well start getting used to it if you know what I'm hinting at."

They got in the buggy and rode back to the ranch, arriving shortly after five o'clock in the evening. As they approached the ranch, she turned to him and said, "John, let's not say anything to my folks about this afternoon. They have enough to worry about right now and if we told them about our feelings and plans for one another, it would just be one more thing they would worry about. So I'd like what we said to stay between the two of us until Dad gets back on his feet. Is that okay with you?"

"I have to be honest with you, I'm so happy for us that I'm just crazy to tell someone. But if that's how you feel, I will respect your wishes," replied O'Malley.

Sarah was in the kitchen making supper when she heard the buggy approaching the house. She set the steaks she was frying to the side and walked out to the front porch.

"Well, I didn't expect you two back from your picnic until later this evening."

"We had a great time, Mom, but Doc's got a long ride back to town and has some early patients coming in tomorrow morning."

"Well, I'm making supper right now. Doc, you can join us if you have a mind to."

"That sounds great, Sarah. I'd be glad to join you for dinner. I have my medical bag with me so let me bring it in and I'll check on Gus while I'm here. How's he doing today by the way?"

"Well, he hasn't been the best patient. Every day he gets more cantankerous and ornery. He's also getting a lot stronger and this afternoon, he got out of bed and walked to the front porch where I found him dozing in the rocking chair when I returned from church. Now, you two come on in. Alicia, I want you to tell me what you were thinking when you came into the café this mornin'."

They entered the house, and Alicia went with her mom into the kitchen to help with dinner while O'Malley walked over to the bedroom where he found Gus resting in bed.

"Good afternoon, Gus. I see you've been up and around a little today. That's good. I think you're starting to get better faster than I thought. Let me check you out and see how well you really are."

As he was examining his patient, Gus said he felt quite well this morning and wanted some fresh air so he walked to the front porch and sat down in the rocking chair, exhausted.

"Gus, I think you're making a good recovery so far. But it's only been a week, and I told you not to start moving around for two weeks. I know it's hard for you to lay low, but you're going to make yourself so sick you'll be in bed for a month. I'm pretty sure Sarah will make you stay in bed this coming week after I speak with her. However, I do think it is a good idea you walk a little each day, but with someone around in case you trip or stumble. I don't want you walking any further than the front porch or to the table for meals this first week. That will help you to start recovering your strength and building up your stamina."

"Okay, okay, I'll stay in bed. We don't need to involve Sarah, Doc. I'll make sure I don't do more than what you want me to. But I need to get out there as soon as possible. I'm gonna find out who shot me and deal with it," replied Gus.

"I think you need to concentrate on gettin' well first then worry about the other later. Come on, let's go to dinner. Alicia's here, and she's in the kitchen with Sarah, helping her make dinner for the four of us."

O'Malley put out a hand to help him out of bed, but Gus brushed it aside and told him he didn't need any help to get out of bed. After he got up and started to walk toward the kitchen, O'Malley fell in behind him and slowly they made their way to the dinner table and sat down to begin their meal. Just as they sat down, Sarah and Alicia put the bowls of food on the table. Sarah had made a large meal when she learned Doc and Alicia were going to join them. She had fried steak with mashed potatoes and gravy along with fresh carrots, green beans, and corn from the garden. Earlier that day, she had also baked a cherry pie for dessert.

The four of them sat down and Sarah said grace, thanking God for Gus's recovery and O'Malley for attending to the gunshot wound and healing Gus. She then thanked the Lord for Alicia's safe trip to Cheyenne from back east and the big help she has been around the ranch and house. After grace, they dug in, passing the bowls around and eating their fill. They were all amazed at the seconds Gus took, and everyone laughed as he filled his plate. When he asked what they were laughing at, he justified the quantity he took by the fact he had eaten little during the last week and had to make up for it.

After the laughter died down, Sarah sat back in her chair and said how having everyone at the dinner table together meant so much to her. She remarked the only thing that would add to the happiness she felt right now was if Colin were at the table with them. However, she let everyone know that Colin's teacher had sent them a letter a few days before Gus had been shot, informing them Colin would be coming home on the train this coming weekend. Alicia had not brought up the subject of her brother since she had returned to Cheyenne but was now curious as to how he was doing.

CHAPTER 10

사랑

Alicia had fond memories of her older brother, who always looked out for her and protected her from older kids that made fun of them because they were Asian. Colin was four years older than Alicia and one day as they were walking to his horse, which they used to ride back and forth from school, three older boys approached them and started calling them names. Colin told her to pay them no mind and that names couldn't hurt them. He told her boys who called them names were people they should feel sorry for as they were ignorant.

Alicia, at the tender age of nine, was not sure what Colin was talking about but decided to continue to walk with him toward his horse. However, the boys heard Colin's remark and one of them picked up a rock and threw it at them. The rock struck Alicia in the back, knocking the wind out of her and bringing her to her knees gasping for air. Colin quickly kneeled down next to his sister, making sure she was not seriously hurt. When he knew she would be okay, he turned toward the boys. Colin told her to stay put, and he would be right back. She nodded her head, still trying to get her breath back, as her brother stood up and turned to face the boys. She watched Colin as he approached the boys. She could not clearly hear the words exchanged between Colin and the boys; however, she could see their angry faces and hear some of the insults they taunted him with.

Finally, the boy in the middle of the group stepped forward and attempted to push Colin down. As the boy straightened his arms out to push, Colin stepped to his left and grabbed the boy's right forearm, pulling the boy forward. As the boy started to go forward, Colin used his left leg and kicked high, striking the back of the boy's head and sending him sprawling to the ground. The other two boys rushed forward, and Colin side kicked with his right foot into the midsection of the attacker on his right. At the same time, he landed a punch to the solar plexus of the boy who was attacking him from the left, doubling him over and dropping him to his knees. Colin looked to his right and saw the other boy sitting on the ground. He continued to keep an eye on both boys as he started to slowly back up.

However, he forgot the first boy who had attacked him. The boy had recovered enough from the fight and as Colin came near, the boy grabbed a rock, sprang up behind him, and struck him as hard as he could to the right side of his head. He collapsed to the ground, completely still and bleeding profusely from the head wound. The three boys stared at him for a moment and then ran away, scared of what they had done.

Alicia struggled to her feet and staggered over to where her brother lay sprawled on the ground. He was seriously hurt, and she realized he needed immediate help. She got up and ran around the corner of the street, down two blocks to the old doctor's office that was upstairs over the general store. She climbed the stairs two at a time and banged on Doc Williams's door as hard as she could. She heard his footsteps and then he opened the door.

"Well, Alicia!" Doc began.

"Doctor, my brother's hurt! Please, come quickly!" she exclaimed.

"Where is he?"

"Down Street," Alicia half-yelled with tears streaming down her face.

"Just a minute, let me grab my bag." He turned around and picked up his bag from the table in his office then followed her down the stairs. They walked and half-ran as quickly as possible down the street and around the corner to where Colin lay on the ground. He quickly examined him as Colin lay on his stomach before gently turning him over onto his back. The doctor took the small supply of bandages he always kept in his bag for emergencies. He applied them to his head with direct pressure then he wrapped the head with some cloth strips and tied the bandages. "His head wound is serious. I need to get him to my office as soon as possible."

When some townsfolk had seen the doctor running down the street, their curiosity got the best of them and some of them followed behind him and around the corner to where Colin lay. Doc Williams saw there were some men among the crowd and motioned them over. "Please, help me get this boy to my office. He's hurt bad."

Some of the men picked Colin up and started for the doctor's office. Doc Williams told them to slow down as he wanted them to carry Colin with as little movement and bouncing as possible due to his head wound. The men carrying him slowed to a normal walking speed and carried him carefully with as little movement as possible.

It had taken the doctor and Alicia only a minute to get to Colin when Alicia first reported the injury. It took nearly ten minutes for the men to slowly carry Colin back to the doctor's office to prevent his condition from getting any worse. The men climbed the stairs to his office, where he opened the door and told them to put Colin on his examining table. After Doc Williams positioned Colin the way he wanted on his table, he sent one of the men who had helped out to the ranch to fetch Gus and Sarah as Colin's injuries were quite serious.

Doc Williams then went to work on Colin, who was still unconscious from the head injury. He took off the temporary bandages he had applied to his head when he initially treated him in the street and then removed the hair from the wound, cleaned it, and began stitching it up. Just before he put the first stitch in, he noticed something unusual. He used his magnifying glass to take a closer look at the wound and through the glass he could see small bone fragments protruding from the wound. He removed all the fragments he could detect and then proceeded to stitch the wound closed taking fifteen stitches to close the laceration.

Colin never stirred or even moved during the entire procedure. After he finished treating him, the doctor once again solicited the help of some adults to carry him from the exam table to a bed in an adjoining room, which would be quiet for Colin to sleep and recover.

Alicia was waiting in the doctor's office, which adjoined the exam room where he had treated Colin. After he got him settled, he went into his office to ask Alicia if she needed anything. The doctor found Alicia distraught and crying her eyes out; he suspected she had been in this state since she had come in with her brother. Alicia related how she had been struck in the back with a rock, thrown by one of the three boys and how Colin confronted the three boys while she was on the ground. She told the doctor how Colin defended himself against the three without a single blow being landed by the attacking boys and how the first boy to attack her brother came up behind him and struck him with a rock in the head as hard as he could. The doctor was silent for a moment and then said he needed to contact the marshal and report the incident. Alicia told the doctor that these were older boys, whom she had never seen around town before.

The doctor was getting tired of treating Asian minorities, who were getting beaten up for sport by cowboys who thought it was fun on a Saturday night. He told Alicia that something had to be done as the violence and hatred continued to grow. Instead of appreciating what the Asians have done in building their railroads, they were targets of violence, hatred, and injustice simply because they came from a different culture and had different religion and looks. He reported the incident to the marshal, who investigated the attack, but later told the doctor he was unable to identify the attackers as they were strangers and no one in town knew anything about them.

As he was walking across the street after talking to the marshal, he glanced south and saw Gus and Sarah coming into town with their buckboard at full gallop. He raised his hands and motioned for them to pull over in front of the stairs leading up to his office. They jumped out of their wagon, and the three of them hurriedly climbed the stairs up to the office. Alicia recalled the commotion as her parents entered the office asking Doc Williams how bad Colin and Alicia were hurt.

"Doc, how bad off are the kids? When can we see them and what can we do?" asked Gus.

"Folks, I treated Colin as he had gotten the worst of it. He's in the next room sleeping quietly. His injury is quite serious. It looks like his skull was fractured by the blow from the rock he was hit with. The question isn't when he will wake up. The question is how he will be when he wakes up. I know enough about the brain to understand that an injury like this could result in him not being the same as before," replied Doc Williams.

"What do you mean when you say he might not be the same? What do we have to look forward to?" asked Sarah.

"We'll just have to wait until he wakes up. In the meantime, Alicia is in the other room over there. Why don't you two go in and comfort her? She was hit in the back with a rock pretty hard but other than a large bruise, she will be fine physically. You have to understand she's pretty upset seeing her brother attacked viciously without being able to help him."

"My God, Doc, we didn't mean to ignore her. You wait here, Gus, and let me go in alone to talk to her first," replied Sarah.

She walked over to the room and slowly opened the door. There in a chair with her knees pulled up to her chest and her arms wrapped around her legs sat Alicia. Her head was face down on her knees, and Sarah could tell she was sobbing quietly. She approached her and gently put her hand out to brush her hair away from her face.

Alicia had not heard Sarah enter the room and jumped at the touch of her hand and looked up at her. She immediately held up her arms to Sarah, who bent down and hugged her tightly. They stayed that way with Alicia now openly crying into her mom's shoulder. She stroked her daughter's head softly and comforted her, telling her everything would be all right and how happy she was that she had not been seriously hurt by the boys who had attacked them.

Alicia remembered sobbing into her mother's shoulder as they held each other tightly. She also remembered the words of comfort her mother said, trying to calm her down while reassuring her everything would be all right. She told her mother between sobs how the rock that hit her brought her to her knees, making it impossible to breathe. She continued to explain that she could hardly move and when Colin had come over to help her, he asked if she was okay, and she was not able to speak but shook her head yes. That was when she saw Colin's face turn from concern to anger as he stood up and walked toward the three boys. She continued telling her mother about the fight and how Colin received the blow to his head that caused his injury. She also told her mom she thought it was her fault that Colin got hurt. She remembered telling her if she could have just gotten up and warned her brother that the boy with the rock was behind him, he could have avoided being hit. Alicia insisted it was her fault if Colin doesn't get better, and she remembered her mom gently pushing away and lowering herself to one knee so she was at eye-level with her.

She looked at Alicia with loving concern and said, "Alicia, I know your big brother was just trying to protect his little sister from those boys. Even though he doesn't always show it, Colin can fight and argue with you, but if anyone else threatens and fights with you, he would be the first one to come to your aid and defense. Now, you need to understand, the boys who caused the injury to your brother were at fault. Not you. You were on the ground with the breath knocked out of you, and you couldn't talk and hardly move. I don't see how you could have warned him about the attack. We're all gonna pray and hope Colin comes out of this okay, but whatever happens, I want you to promise me you will not blame yourself."

Alicia looked back at her mom shaking her head yes and saying okay between sobs. Sarah then took a small hanky out of her pocket and wiped the tears from her face. She then stood Alicia up from where she was sitting and sat down in the same chair. She pulled Alicia to her and put her on her lap with Alicia's head resting on her shoulder and started rubbing her back.

After a few minutes, Alicia heard the door open, and her dad quietly came in to see how things were going. He walked over to them and talking softly, he leaned down slightly and stroked Alicia's head.

"How's my little girl doin'?" asked Gus.

"Okay," Alicia sobbed.

"She blames herself for Colin getting hurt. She thinks if she could have warned him about the boy getting up behind him, he would have avoided being hit," said Sarah.

"Alicia, you can't blame yourself for this. The only ones who are at fault are the three boys who attacked you and your brother. You are not to blame for anything that happened today."

"That's what I told her too, and Alicia promised me she would not blame herself," whispered Sarah.

"Well, that's good. Doc told me Colin is asleep and will most likely stay that way all night. He suggested I take everyone over to the hotel and get a room for the night. He said he would be staying up in a chair with Colin all night in case there was a change. I told him we would do as he suggested and to come and get us immediately if there was any change in Colin no matter what time it was." said Gus.

They left the doctor's office and walked across the street to the hotel where they checked in and rented a suite large enough for the three of them. Sarah helped Alicia get ready for bed although there wasn't much to do since none of them had a change of clothes. After putting her in bed, Sarah and Gus lay down in their clothes on the second large bed that was in the suite.

After Alicia's stress-filled day and the fact it was midnight, she fell into a deep restless sleep. Neither Gus nor Sarah could get to sleep as they were both worried sick about Colin. Finally, after a few hours, they both dropped off into an uneasy sleep.

They both woke by six o'clock with the sunlight streaming in through the window and were unable to get back to sleep. After quietly cleaning up in the wash basin, Gus went out to get some coffee and rolls from Mary's Café and bring the food back to the room.

When Mary saw Gus come into the café, she asked him about Colin. Gus told her Colin was asleep in the doctor's office, and they were going to go over as soon as he got some rolls to take back to the room. She then told Gus to go back to his hotel room, and she would bring breakfast over. He tried to tell her he would wait for the food and take it over to their room himself, but Mary would have none of that and told him if he didn't go back to his family right now, she'd never let him eat another slice of her homemade cherry pie, which was his favorite. Gus knew he was up against a determined and stubborn woman so he decided an orderly retreat was better than standing his ground.

He went back to the hotel and explained to Sarah that Mary was delivering their breakfast. Sarah remarked it was just like Mary as she was always helping those who had fallen on hard times. About a half hour later, Mary came over to their room with a large pot of coffee, scrambled eggs, biscuits, butter, bacon, and fried potatoes, including a pitcher of cold milk for Alicia.

When Gus answered the door and Mary came in with breakfast, Alicia woke up to the smell of the delicious food Mary had brought to their room. Mary stayed and had a small bite to eat while Sarah and Gus brought her up-to-date on what had happened to Colin and his present condition. Mary suggested that Sarah and Alicia stay with her in the spare room in the café if they had to spend another night so that Gus could get back to the ranch and make sure everything was all right. Gus didn't want to leave while Colin was still unconscious, but Sarah told him he needed to go back even if it was for just a couple of hours to make sure the ranch was doing well and ask Moses to take over the day-to-day operations.

By this time, Moses was no longer just a hired cook but also a friend and confidant. Gus often discussed the ranch operations with Moses over the last few years. Sarah also asked him to pick up some clothes for them since they had not brought anything with them yesterday. Reluctantly, Gus agreed to go back to the ranch after they checked in with the doctor to see if there was any change in Colin's condition. Mary left to go back to the café and shortly after, Gus, Sarah, and Alicia finished their breakfast and went downstairs to check out of the hotel.

The three of them walked across the street, returning the tray and dishes Mary had brought over and then headed for the doctor's office. They climbed up the stairs to his office, and Sarah knocked gently on the door. When the door opened, a bleary-eyed, disheveled doctor appeared.

"Come on in, folks. Have a seat." He went into the other room, picked up a chair and brought it out to the office area so there were enough chairs for everyone. They took a seat and the doctor sat on the front edge of his desk, looking at them.

"The only pleasure I have in my job is when I can give good news to people. I detest it when I can't help someone who is sick or hurt. Even after all these years, I still don't know how to give bad news."

"Doc, if it's about Colin, just say it right out. We're a strong family and can take just about anything," exclaimed Gus.

"Colin is in a coma, and I can't say when or if he will wake up. He suffered a very serious head injury to his brain. If he wakes up, I can't say what condition he will be in. The next forty-eight hours will tell us one way or the other. I'll tell you one thing, Alicia. Colin loved you enough to protect you from those three boys without any regard for his own safety. He is a very brave young man. At this time, I can't forecast how long you will need to stay in town. It could be a day or a week. Where did you folks decide to stay yesterday?"

"Last night we stayed at the hotel, but tonight, Sarah and Alicia are going to stay with Mary. I'm headin' back to the ranch to get a change of clothes for everyone," replied Gus.

"Would you like to see Colin? I have him in the back room where he's sleeping comfortably. Just so you know I have his head in a bandage, which is pretty large and looks worse than what it is. C'mon with me and let's go back and see him. Remember, he is asleep and won't wake up, but you can still talk to him."

The doctor took them to Colin where they stayed for a while. Each one of them told Colin, in their own way, to get better and how much they missed him. Just as they were leaving the room, Alicia told her folks she needed to go back alone to whisper something to her brother. Gus and Sarah both told her to go ahead, and they would wait for her in the doctor's office.

She went back into Colin's room, walked over to his bed, and bent down so her mouth was close to his left ear. "Colin! This is your little sister Alicia. Please! Please! Get well soon as I don't know what I will do without my big brother. And thanks for stopping those boys from hurting me. I'm so sorry I couldn't warn you about the boy who came up behind you. Please forgive me because if I could have shouted a warning, you would have not gotten hurt. You're my only big brother, and I need you back to help me. So come back to us as soon as you can," she whispered. She kissed Colin on his forehead and then went out to where her folks were waiting in the doctor's office.

They said their good-byes to Doc Williams after thanking him for taking care of Colin and then went down to the street and walked silently toward Mary's Café, lost in their own thoughts. Just as they reached the café, the marshal came out the front door.

"Sarah, I want to talk to the marshal for a minute. You and Alicia go in and get settled, and I'll be in directly."

"Okay, Gus. But I want to know what he's doing about the attack on Colin. Then you can go back to the ranch to get some things for us."

He agreed and then called out to the marshal, who stopped and waved from the front entrance of the café. Gus had Sarah and Alicia walk along the building to the side entrance to go in. He then quickly walked over to the marshal.

"Tom, have you got a minute to talk?"

"Sure, Gus. How's Colin? I know he's been hurt pretty bad, and I would like to talk to both Alicia and Colin when he gets well."

"Colin's over at Doc's, and he is still unconscious. Doc's doing everything he can to help him, and he told us the next forty-eight hours will tell. Tom, do you know anything about the three boys who attacked them?"

"Well, the problem I'm running into is that no one saw what happened and all I've got is there were three boys, whom no one saw, without any description. I asked around town, and no one saw or heard anything. But three horses disappeared, and I suspect those boys stole them. I was going to ride out this morning and see if I could pick up a trail and track them down. Did you want to come along?"

"No, Tom. I've got to go out to the ranch and bring some things for the three of us. I'm also gonna check on the ranch to make sure Moses doesn't need anything. Sarah and Alicia are going to stay in Mary's spare room in case Colin wakes up. When I get back, I'll make sure Alicia talks to you this afternoon about the boys that attacked them."

"Okay, Gus. I'll ride out this mornin' and see if I can turn anything up. I'll make sure I get back to talk to Alicia this afternoon. Give my best to them and let them know I'm thinking about Colin."

Gus said good-bye to Tom. He walked over to his buggy and took off for the ranch. When he arrived, he let Moses know about Colin's condition and briefly discussed what needed to be done and how things were going at the ranch. He then went to the house and packed some clothes and miscellaneous items he thought the women might need. After packing, he quickly walked out to the buggy, threw a bag in, and took off for the town.

Meanwhile, Mary showed Alicia and Sarah into the kitchen where Sarah brought Mary up-to-date on Colin's condition. Mary made some tea for Sarah and gave Alicia a sarsaparilla. She then told Sarah she could stay down in the kitchen area and chat while she prepared for the lunch hour. Sarah asked Alicia if she would like to go upstairs, but Alicia said she would rather stay with the two of them.

Gus ran the two horses as fast as he dared since he wanted to get back to town as soon as possible. When he got into town, he pulled up in front of the café and ran over to the side entrance into the kitchen.

"Any news about Colin?" he asked half out of breath.

They both shook their heads. "We haven't heard anything more than when you left," replied Sarah.

"I think I'll go up to Doc's and just check on him," said Gus.

Sarah and Alicia both insisted on going with him. They went up and just as before, the doctor told them there was no change with Colin. He let them sit in the room where they talked to each other and to Colin as if he were conscious, relating to him the chores he was going to get behind on at the ranch and the lessons he was going to miss at school each day.

After a couple of hours, they went back to Mary's where they took their belongings upstairs, unpacked, and got settled in the spare room. Mary had an extra bed brought up to the room for Alicia so that everyone had their own bed.

The next morning, they were woken by loud banging on their door. It was five a.m. and still dark as Gus, sleepy-eyed, stumbled to the door and opened it. There stood Mary in her bathrobe with an excited look in her eyes.

"Gus! Come quickly! Doc was just here! He said that Colin was waking up. He knew you would want to know immediately. Doc's already gone back to his office and wants all three of you to come as quick as you can!"

"Thanks, Mary. I'll get Sarah and Alicia, and we'll be there in no time."

Sarah and Alicia had overheard the conversation and were already up, hurriedly throwing on some clothes behind a dressing screen. As soon as they were done, Gus grabbed his clothes and changed behind the screen, and they flew down the stairs and out the restaurant side door, running directly to the doctor's office.

Gus didn't even bother knocking on the doctor's door. He walked right into the office calling his name. Doc Williams entered the room with a look of concern on his face.

"Doc, is Colin okay? Mary said you came by to let us know he was waking up. Can we go in and talk to him?"

"It's best that we talk for a couple of minutes before you go in to see him. You're right that Colin has woken up. But he's not himself. His speech is slurred and sometimes he stutters. He also has a hard time putting into words what he wants to say. That injury he took to his head may have caused permanent damage to his brain. I will need to keep him for another day or two, and then you should be able to take him home and care for him there. We will have to wait and see if time heals that head injury. Well, I don't want to delay your going in any longer. Just don't stay too long as he needs his rest," instructed the doctor.

They walked into Colin's room and saw he was resting comfortably. Sarah gently gave him a hug, careful not to disturb his bandage. Colin weakly put his arms around Sarah's neck, returning the hug. Alicia then moved forward and sat down at the foot of the bed. Gus walked over beside Sarah.

"Colin, Colin, Colin! We've been so worried about you. How do you feel, dear?" asked Sarah.

"Fa-fa-fa-fa-fine," Colin replied, in a soft whispering stutter that took all three of them aback.

Gus took a step closer, lightly patting Colin's shoulder. "Son, do you remember what happened to you?"

Colin turned his head slightly and looked at Gus. "N-n-n-no, Dad."

"Let me help you try to remember. There were some boys you were defending your sister from. She told us you fought three boys and knocked them all down. But one of them came up from behind you and struck your head with a rock. You protected your little sister and made us aware of the man you are becoming. We're proud of you, son. Doc says we can take you home in a couple of days. So you rest and get well soon. Doc said we should only stay a little bit, so we're going to leave and let you get some rest. We will come back a little later this morning to visit," said Gus.

Sarah got up, and Alicia slid over to give her big brother a hug. She hugged him and got close to his ear. "Colin, I'm really happy you're going to be all right. I don't know what I would have done without my big brother to protect me. Get well soon because I need my big brother to lean on and depend on."

She stood up from the bed and joined her parents. They went into the outer office where Doc Williams discussed Colin's condition.

"Well, Doc, we will wait to take him home in a couple of days. Mary is generously letting us use her spare room while we wait to take him back to the ranch. What do you think of his speech and the way he answers questions, Doc?" asked Sarah.

"I just don't rightly know. We just don't know a lot how the brain works. He was hit real hard, and I think he suffered a brain injury. Sometimes, these things get worse and, sometimes, these things get better or there is no change at all. As I had said before, time will tell if his condition improves or not. You'll be able to take him home the day after tomorrow. I think he'll be okay from his physical wounds. I'll come out in a couple of days after you take him back to the ranch and see how he's doing."

Two days later, Sarah and Alicia borrowed several blankets from Mary and made a nice comfortable bed for Colin in the back of a buckboard Gus had retrieved from the ranch to take Colin home. They slowly helped him down the stairs from the doctor's second-floor office and into the buckboard, where they made him as comfortable as possible.

It was a slow ride home, taking twice as long as usual. Gus drove as slowly as possible to avoid causing discomfort to his son. When they arrived at the ranch, all the hands came round to greet

Colin and tell him how brave he was in protecting his little sister and also praised Alicia for her swift action in getting help for her brother. Several remarked if Alicia had not been as quick to get the doctor as she was, Colin might have been worse off than he is right now. Within a few minutes, the hands noticed how silent the usually talkative Colin was. It was even more pronounced when several of the hands asked him how he was doing, and he could only manage a one-word answer of "fine."

Everyone pitched in and gently lifted him out of the buckboard and into his bed. Colin slept throughout the rest of the day as he was exhausted.

Doc Williams was a man of his word and always on time. He came out two days after Colin was back at the ranch just like he said he would. Colin had gotten up on his feet and walked short distances several times. However, Alicia noticed he walked off center, with his left foot angled out at a forty-five-degree angle. His arms did not sway back and forth by his side like they used to. Instead, his arms were bent at his elbows, straight out in front of him like he was running except he was walking. The doctor spent about a half hour that day examining Colin in his room and then emerged with a look of deep concern on his face.

Doc Williams called Gus and Sarah to the kitchen table to talk about his condition. Sarah also called Alicia to the table explaining to Gus and Doc she'd been involved in this situation from day one, which entitled her to see it all the way through.

"Well, folks, the good news is he's recovering from his head injury—physically—and should be well within about two weeks. However, the bad news is the injury to his brain. His speech has been significantly affected along with his balance and coordination. I don't believe he will get any better after his head wound heals. We will have to watch over him the next few weeks to see if he improves with his speech and balance."

"We appreciate everything you've done for him, Doc. Is there anything we can do to help him get better?" asked Sarah.

"Nothing more than what you are doing for him at this time. For now, just look after him and keep him comfortable. Get him up more often so he can walk and use his legs. Let him rest when you see him getting tired so he doesn't overdo it. If he starts to get worse, get word to me, and I'll come right out. That's about all we can do right now. It's gonna be a wait-and-see situation."

"Doctor, can I ask you a question?" asked Alicia.

"Sure, little lady, what would you like to ask me?"

"Well, what do we do if Colin doesn't get any better? I mean how can Mom and Dad and I help him?"

"Well, now that's a very good question, Alicia. But I think we should see if he gets any better over the next couple of weeks. Now if he doesn't get any better, there are some special schools that I know of that help people who have the kind of injury your brother has. But before we get into that area, let's see how he does. Then we will see what we can do that will be best for him. I hope that answers all your questions for now, folks. I've got to get back to town but plan on coming back to check on our little man in about two weeks." Then, Doc Williams said his good-byes and headed back to town.

For the next two weeks, everyone on the ranch pitched in to help with Colin. Before he was attacked, he had worked the ranch doing chores before school started and after school. Sarah did put her foot down before his injury, making him do his schoolwork when he came home with Alicia from school before he was permitted to take his horse out and work on the ranch.

All the ranch hands respected Colin for his hard work and not because he was the boss's son. For his age, he worked harder than anyone else and would pitch in if another hand needed help. So, with the help of the ranch hands and Moses pitching in between meals, Colin quickly regained his strength, sooner than anyone thought was possible. Everyone wanted to keep him walking and took turns helping him with the exercises the doctor had left for him to do twice daily. However, his swift physical recovery did not result in the hoped for mental improvement.

Unfortunately, Colin's speech, balance, and coordination remained the same. Doc Williams came out two weeks later and then once a week for the next four weeks. On his last visit, he decided it was necessary to sit down with Gus, Sarah, and Alicia. At that meeting, he told them he could do nothing more and recommended a special doctor and school in Colorado Springs for Colin.

After the doctor had left for town, they discussed what was in Colin's best interest. Alicia voted to keep Colin on the ranch where they could take care of him and try to help him get back to normal. She didn't feel they should put his care in the hands of strangers. Gus and Sarah took their time to explain to Alicia how her brother needed special help that none of them would be able to provide. Only experts could give him the best chance of improving his condition. They went on to explain to Alicia that the four of them would take a trip to this special school in Colorado Springs. Alicia reluctantly agreed to at least go with her parents to the school and take a look at what it had to offer.

By this time, Moses was almost a part of the family, and Gus trusted him enough to ask if he would take over the ranch operations for the two weeks the round trip to Colorado would take. So, the four of them made the trip and visited the school for several days. They took the time to speak to the administrators and teachers and observed how the kids were taught and treated. The school also offered dormitory accommodations with plenty of staff to help the students with their daily needs. The school's staff lived with the students in the dormitory, which made it convenient and easy for them to respond to the children's needs. Everyone seemed pleasant, and Colin instantly liked several teachers he met, who warmed up to his sensitive and gentle demeanor.

So, it was decided to send Colin away to school with the hope they could develop his abilities to their greatest potential. That first year, Colin spent around nine months at the school, coming home on holidays and for about two months of the summer. There were several areas the school focused on for kids with special needs. The staff was exceptional in the chosen teaching methods, and each class had one main instructor, who taught the students in areas that would help them to live independently. There were several aides who assisted the teacher and gave the students individual attention, and there were no report cards or grades. Instead, students would have goals set at the beginning of the year and their progress would be reviewed every three months with a letter sent to the families outlining the progress achieved. The teachers and aides were extremely patient and disciplining a student was extremely rare. The school policy forbade the admittance of any student who exhibited behavior of a violent nature. These types of students would be sent to other institutions.

Colin fit into the program exceedingly well and developed a close relationship with the main teacher in his classroom. The teacher's name was Connie, and she was the same age as Sarah. Connie could see from the start that Colin would be a very good student. He was helpful in the classroom and sensitive to the other children's needs. He could also read at a lower level, which was exceptional as no other student in her class could read more than a few words. He stayed in a dormitory that was supervised by handpicked staff. Colin was in a class of fifteen students, which because of its size, allowed an almost one-to-one teacher-to-student ratio. Connie took a special interest in Colin as she could see he would be a student who would learn and progress at a higher level and faster pace. Another part of the program was to teach the students job skills they could use in the local community with the hope they could eventually live independently. Students were taught farming skills, ranching work, clerical and office work.

Colin was always trying his best to read the newspaper, which came to the school office every day. He also loved music and always joined in the singing during music class. Connie took note of this and spoke to the local Catholic priest, who wholeheartedly endorsed him joining the church choir. She then paid a visit to the local newspaper and convinced them to give Colin the opportunity to learn typesetting, at which he became proficient after a few years.

At the time Gus was shot, Colin was well on his way to developing his individual independence.

"Mom, we haven't spoken about Colin. How is he getting along at school?"

"Well, he actually graduated from the school, but they have another program that will continue to improve his skills. He is supposed to return home on Wednesday so you can judge for yourself how he's doing. He's grown a lot bigger since you last saw him. He's taller than me but a little shorter than your father."

"That sounds pretty good, Mom. I have taken an indefinite leave of absence from teaching at my school. Since we don't have classes during the summer, I am planning on being here until the fall at the very least. I also plan on working really hard to find out who shot Dad."

"Alicia, I'm getting better and better every day. I'll be back to my old self in no time, and I'll find out who did this to me. I don't want anyone else to get hurt. I've got my own ideas on who is behind this, and I intend to help the marshal get to the bottom of it."

"Well, Dad, I think the more we work together, the quicker we will find out who shot you and get justice."

"Okay, I've heard enough about who's going to do what about Dad's gunshot wound. I didn't put this meal together to hear about our problems. Let's just be thankful Dad is recovering very nicely and by Wednesday, all the family will be home once again." exclaimed Sarah.

It was obvious to everyone Sarah was not going to put up with any further discussion regarding who shot Gus and how they were going to identify the gunman who was responsible. Sarah discussed how the ranch was doing with Moses taking over the day-to-day operations and then turned the conversation to general topics including reminiscences about better times in the past.

When dinner was over, O'Malley and Alicia volunteered to clean up and wash the dishes, giving Sarah and Gus the opportunity to relax on the front porch by themselves. Gus was still fatigued but slowly walked with Sarah to the porch where they sat together on the porch swing. Meanwhile, Alicia and O'Malley attended to the dirty dishes with Alicia taking the lead.

"Doc, tomorrow I'm riding into town, and I have some questions for this Jason Long Dad has been having trouble with. I want to meet this man and see what kind of person we are dealing with."

"Alicia, I would like you to do me a big favor and stop by my office when you come in tomorrow. Jason Long is a powerful man in town, and I think it may be wise if the two of us go see him together."

"I appreciate the offer, but I want to see Jason alone to size him up."

"Okay, I won't argue with you as long as you promise you'll come to my office and let me know when you have gotten into town."

Alicia saw the serious look O'Malley gave her and decided it was better to agree than argue. "All right, Doc. I will stop by if it makes you happy. Now, let's go out on the porch and visit with Mom and Dad for a while before you have to go home."

They finished up the dishes and headed to the porch where they were joined by Moses. He filled in Gus on the daily ranch operations and visited with everyone for a while.

"Sarah, I've got to go into town tomorrow to pick up supplies. I'll be taking the buckboard with me. Do you want anything special besides the food supplies on this list?" asked Moses.

"I don't need anything other than what is on the list. Alicia is riding into town tomorrow, too. Why don't you two ride in together?"

"Mom, I'm sure Moses has his own schedule, and I don't know how long I'm going to be. I think we need to go into town separately."

Moses looked up at Alicia with a sly smirk on his face. "I think you just don't want to be seen riding into town with an old man like me."

"Now Moses, you know I think of you like a second father. You're one of the family. I'd never feel awkward riding anywhere with you. Why don't we make a deal? How about I tie my horse in the back of the buckboard, and we ride into town together? That way, we can catch up over the last five years."

"That's the best offer I've had all day. I'll take you up on that. How about we leave around eight o'clock tomorrow morning after I've made sure all the hands are fed and out to work?"

"That's fine with me. I'll be out front at eight."

CHAPTER 11

사랑

The next morning, Alicia was up early. She had some breakfast and went out to the barn where she saddled her horse. She then brought out the horse to the hitching rail in front of the house and tied it up. It was almost eight o'clock, and Alicia was just about to go look for Moses when she saw him coming with the buckboard to pick her up. It then occurred to her there never was a time that she could remember Moses ever being late for anything. *At least some things never change*, she thought.

"Well, Alicia, I see you're ready to go. Just let me tie your horse to the buckboard, and we can be on our way."

While Moses tied up the horse, she climbed up on the bench seat and after Moses got in, he snapped the reins to start their trip into town. The ride into Cheyenne was a pleasant one. The conversation between them was relaxed as they recounted the events in their lives over the last five years. After about an hour, Alicia asked Moses about Jason Long. What he told her about Jason reinforced what she had heard from everyone else she had talked to. Moses confirmed that Jason had moved into the territory shortly after she had left town and began buying several businesses in town, including any land or ranches surrounding the town that he could get his hands on. It was also suspicious that shortly after Jason made an offer to buy someone's ranch and was refused, buildings would mysteriously catch fire or the owners would be beaten up by unknown assailants. In a few die hard cases when the owner would not give in after the burnings or beatings, he would be found on a deserted trail shot to death with no witnesses or clues to the murderers. Jason would then buy the ranch from the widow at a rock bottom price.

By the time she and Moses were wrapping up their discussion, they arrived in Cheyenne. Alicia asked Moses to stop at O'Malley's house as she had promised to let him know when she got into town. He rolled up to the house and stopped the buckboard. He got out and walked around in front of the horses to help her down from the wagon. By the time he got to the other side though, she had already jumped down and started toward her horse to unleash him from the wagon.

"Alicia, in all the time you spent back east, didn't you learn any manners? Didn't you know I was coming around to help you down from the wagon?"

"I was just trying to help with my horse but if you need me back in my seat so you can help me down, I'll just hop up like this to make you feel better."

Before he could say anything, Alicia was back in the buckboard seat waiting for him to help her down.

"Okay, smarty pants, let me help you down and then I'll untie the horse for you."

Moses helped her down, and they went to the back of the wagon, untied her horse, and then tied it to the hitching post in front of the house.

"Moses, I really enjoyed the ride and our conversation."

"Well, young lady, I want you to promise me that you're going to be careful. I know you're going to ask questions in town, but there are some dangerous people here who aren't going to like the questions you ask."

"I know and rest assured I will be careful, but I have to start somewhere," said Alicia.

Moses and Alicia said their good-byes and while he drove off to the general store for supplies, Alicia opened the entrance gate to O'Malley's house, walked up the front porch steps, and knocked on the door. She heard O'Malley's footsteps approaching and then he opened the door.

"Alicia! Come on in."

She walked through the front door and turned toward O'Malley as he closed it. He looked at Alicia for a moment, taking in her beautiful features. They took a small step toward each other and embraced with a passionate kiss that still lingered on their lips after they parted.

Alicia took a step back and said, "Now, Doc, although this was very pleasant and enjoyable, I'm not here for you to court me or for romance. You know I'm here to go into town and speak with Marshal Jackson and Jason Long. I want to see what information the marshal has about my dad and what he is doing about it. I stopped here for two reasons. One was because you asked me to and the other is because I wanted to see you again. I would certainly like to stay, but I need to get into town and get the information I came for."

"I understand. I've got some patients to go see this morning but when I'm done, I will see you in town," replied O'Malley.

"I've got a better idea. Instead of you walking all over town looking for me, let's meet at Mary's Café and you can buy me lunch."

"That's fine with me. That should work out good. Mary's at noon."

Alicia leaned forward and gave O'Malley a kiss, and then they walked to the front door where she gave him one more kiss and a hug before she opened the front door and went down the steps and left through the front gate. She turned and started walking down the street toward town. It took her about ten minutes to get to the marshal's office.

She walked in to see Marshal Jackson sitting behind his desk doing some paperwork. He had not changed one bit. He was dressed the same way he was five years ago. He wore a cotton long-sleeved shirt with an unbuttoned leather vest. Marshal Jackson stood up, and she could see he still wore jeans, but without his gun and holster. These were hung up on a peg behind his desk within easy reach.

It took a few seconds but then the marshal recognized Alicia and came around the desk, extending his hand in greeting. "I heard you had come back to town. It's sure good to see you after so many years. I just wish it was under better circumstances."

"I'm glad to see you too, Marshal. It's been five years, but you haven't changed one bit. So how are things going for you?"

"Well, if you don't think I've changed, I wonder where all these gray hairs have come from. As far as the town goes, everything is going fairly well. How's your dad doing? I hear he's up and around. Knowing Gus he'll want to get up and start running the ranch as if nothin' ever happened."

"You're sure right about Dad. Within a couple of days, he wanted to get up and back to it, but Mom put her foot down and even Dad wasn't about to tell her no. So he's been resting, and we expect he'll be up and around in another week or so. You probably have guessed why I'm here. I would like you to tell me everything you know about the shooting and anything else you can think of that might have led to his attempted murder."

"Whoever did this was very careful. I spoke briefly to your dad on the morning of the third day after he had been shot. When I rode out to the ranch the morning after he had been shot, I found where the blood trail had started—by a stream that had a lone shade tree about ten or twenty yards from the stream bank. I followed that blood trail all the way back to the ranch. There looked like a lot of blood on the ground where he was first shot, which tells me he was shot clean off his horse and may have lain on the ground bleeding for a while before he came to. I have no idea how he ever got back on his horse, but if he hadn't, I think he would have died out there. When I got to the ranch, I wasn't able to talk to your dad that day as he was in a coma but on my way back to town, I stopped where he was shot to look around and found one rifle shell casing under that shade tree. I believe it came from a Henry rifle and with the exception of some ranchers who hunt large game, there just ain't a whole lot of Henrys in the area. I've talked to the owners of these rifles but so far all of them could explain where they were and had witnesses who swore to their whereabouts. To tell you the truth, I would have been surprised if any of the local ranchers had shot your dad as he is well liked by everyone. During the last two weeks, I have eliminated from suspicion everyone that I know who owns a Henry. Also, let me show you something on this shell casing that might interest you."

The marshal walked around behind his desk where he opened a drawer and pulled out the shell casing. He then walked back toward Alicia and handed her the casing.

"Do you see anything unusual about this shell casing?"

She took it and examined both ends and then looked at the sides of the casing. "I'm not comfortable with guns. This just looks like a spent shell casing."

"Well, it isn't really obvious. Come over to the window where the light is better." The marshal took the casing and stepped over to the window as she followed. "You can see a lot better over here although this isn't the best light. Can you see the faint scratch that goes along the length of the shell?"

"You're right! I can see it in this light. But it's such a faint scratch. Is it important?" asked Alicia.

"I think so. You see, when this shell was loaded, there must have been a slight defect in the rifle that caused this scratch. This was a fresh shell, and I'm certain the bullet that came from this casing was the one Doc took out of your dad's chest. Whoever owns this rifle is also the person who shot your father. We just need to find the rifle and the person who owns it."

"How do we know the owner fired the shot? What if the rifle was stolen? What if someone borrowed it?"

"Alicia, you've been away for several years and wouldn't know the value a Henry rifle has to its owner. A Henry rifle costs quite a bit of money so you're not going to lend it out, and you're going to make sure it's kept in a very safe place. There is a remote possibility the rifle was stolen, but I doubt it because whoever it was stolen from would have reported it to me. We should focus on finding that rifle and who has it now. The only problem is I'm out of people who own that kind of rifle. I have questioned everyone I know who owns a Henry and have come up empty. At this point, I really don't know anyone else who has a Henry that I have not checked. If you have a way for us to identify the owner of the Henry rifle in question, I would appreciate any suggestions."

"I can't think of anything off the top of my head, Marshal. But thanks for the information. At least it's more than I had before. Thanks for all your help and time, Marshal. I appreciate it."

She turned and started for the door. As she grabbed the door handle, she hesitated and turned back toward the marshal. "Doesn't Cheyenne have an upcoming city celebration?"

"You mean the annual Cattlemen's Association celebration?"

"Yes, isn't it coming up in about a week? I saw posters in the merchants store windows on my way over to your office. They were advertising a sharpshooting contest as one of the events. Do you think there will be a lot of contestants?"

"We always have a pretty good turnout every year. This year, we should have more contestants than we have ever had because this year the first prize is a brand new Winchester rifle. That's going to draw contestants from all over the territory."

"Marshal, do you think the association would consider a second event added to the contest?"

"Well, I'm sure it depends on what it is. What do you have in mind?"

"I think I can convince my father to put up one of our best horses for the prize. The contest will be for the best three-shot grouping with a Henry rifle. That way when word gets around, we'll not only get people from town but folks from the surrounding ranches and possibly even strangers. I have an idea on how to get a spent shell casing from each rifle, which we can check for the scratch. The person who shot my father probably thinks he got away with it since he has not been arrested yet. As you say, no person in his right mind would throw a Henry rifle away knowing how expensive it is. Who else knows about the scratch on the casing?"

"Just us, I haven't told anyone else."

"Good, let's keep it that way. The fewer people who know about it, the better chance it will not get out. Let me know what you find out about adding the second sharpshooting event as soon as you can. I'm going over to see Jason Long to ask a few questions and see if I can get some information."

"You make sure you're careful, young lady. Jason has surrounded himself with several mean gunslingers. He isn't dumb enough to start a fight or even get into a fight. No, Jason's the kind of man who hires other people to do his fighting for him," warned the marshal.

"I appreciate the warning, but I'm not looking for a fight either. I need to meet this Jason and talk to him to see what kind of person I'm dealing with."

"Well, he's just down the street at the bank. Would you like me to walk down and introduce you?"

Alicia turned and started toward the door. She looked back over her shoulder and said, "No thanks, I'll go down and introduce myself."

She walked out of the marshal's office and turned left toward the bank. The bank wasn't hard to locate. It was a large two-story red brick structure, which looked like it had just been built in the last two or three years. Then it dawned on her the bank stood where a dress shop had been. The dress shop had been run by a widow in her sixties. She had lost her husband years before in an Indian raid and wasn't able to run their small ranch without him. She sold the ranch and bought a building in town where she made dresses. It must have been one of the many businesses Jason bought and then tore down to build his bank. Alicia wondered if the old woman was offered a fair price or if there was some friendly persuasion to convince her to sell. Well, that was another matter the marshal might want to look into at another time. Right now, she knew she needed to confront Jason Long.

She walked up the two stairs to the bank's front entrance where she opened the door and walked into the lobby. She briefly looked around the large room and noticed six teller windows along the wall on the left. Straight ahead, was a three-foot railing that had three desks behind it where three employees sat. The rest of the lobby area was taken up by small round table stands about four feet tall used by customers to complete deposit and withdrawal slips.

She walked up to the railing where one of the bank employees looked up from his desk. It was the same hateful look she had seen people give her when she took the train to Cheyenne. The same look she saw when she walked down Cheyenne's main street for the first time in five years.

"Well, what can I do for you?" said the clerk in a half-surly tone.

"I'd like to see Mr. Jason Long, please."

"Do you have an appointment? Is Mr. Long expecting you? He's a very busy man and doesn't see anyone without an appointment," said the clerk.

"I think he might see me without an appointment. Would you tell him Gus and Sarah's daughter from the Double Bar X Ranch would like to speak with him?"

The clerk continued his disrespectful smirk and said, "He's in a meeting right now. You might be able to see him after lunch. Why don't you try then?"

Just then, a slightly overweight man with thinning hair, standing at five foot six and around thirty pounds overweight came out of the back office and started to talk to one of the tellers to the left of where Alicia was standing. She could hear the teller answer the question and then ask if Mr. Long needed anything else. She turned to her left and walked briskly over to the teller window where Jason Long was finishing his conversation. He looked up and saw her approaching the window.

"Mr. Long, could I have a few moments of your time?"

Jason looked at the clerk Alicia had been talking to and who had followed her when he saw her approaching Jason.

"Mr. Long, I'm sorry for this interruption, but I told this...this lady you were very busy, and she said she did not have an appointment."

Jason raised his hand with the palm out and gave the clerk an icy stare, abruptly stopping him from saying anything further. Looking back at Alicia, he asked, "What can I do for you, young lady?"

"My parents own the Double Bar X Ranch. I believe you know them, Gus and Sarah."

"Everyone knows your folks. They own the largest ranch in Southern Wyoming. Why don't you come back to my office, and I'll make time to talk to you right now."

He turned to the teller advising him to have a report finished and on his desk by close of business today. Jason then turned back to Alicia and asked her to follow him to his office. They went through a door that had a sign on it reading "Employees Only" and continued down a long hall with offices on the right, to a door at the end of the hall with a sign that read "Private." Jason opened the door and gestured with his left hand extended toward the office saying, "After you."

"Thank you," Alicia answered, and stepped into Jason's office.

She was impressed with the décor. The wall to the right had a massive solid oak bookcase, and she noticed many of the books on the shelves were Wyoming law books. She also noticed books on Shakespeare plays and Caesars commentaries along with books on world and Roman history and also a biography of Napoleon Bonaparte. The rear wall of the office had two large windows that were arched at the top, letting in a large amount of natural light. Jason's desk was located in front of these two windows. It was a large desk and appeared to be made out of cherry wood stained and polished to a glossy hue. The wall to the left had a solid four-by-six-foot window with one oil painting on each side of it depicting sailing ships on an ocean. Finally, she noticed the floor. The floor was solid oak planks sanded to a smooth finish with a polished stain.

"Mr. Long, I am very impressed with your office."

"Thank you, I put a lot of thought into designing it. My desk and these overstuffed chairs I ordered handmade from Boston Massachusetts, and the windows were special ordered from New York City. In fact, most of the office furnishings, including the artwork, were ordered from back east. Why don't you have a seat, and we can talk, which reminds me, I don't think I have the pleasure of knowing your name."

"My name is Alicia, and I am here visiting my mom and dad for a while."

"I was very sorry to hear about your father. How is he coming along?"

"He's getting stronger every day and should be completely healed in about two weeks. Thank you for asking. Mr. Long, I was curious about a few things involving my father."

"Well, I don't know what I can help you with but go ahead and ask your questions, and I'll do my best to answer them."

"I've heard a lot of rumors around town about your involvement with ranchers, who have either died or sold their ranches to you. It seemed coincidental my father had an argument with you at the café the same day he was shot. I'd like to find out your side of these rumors."

As Alicia was speaking, Jason's face turned serious. After she had finished, there was a ten-second pause before Jason cleared his throat and then said, "Miss, I am sure you have heard these rumors. It never fails to amaze me that when someone becomes very successful, envy by others always results in a breeding ground for vicious rumors and gossip. Just because I have been quite successful in land and business purchases, does not give anyone the right to start unfounded and unsubstantiated rumors. If there were any truth to these rumors, don't you think the marshal would have placed me under arrest? You're correct I had a disagreement with your father at the café. It's well-known I want to buy your parents' ranch so it doesn't make any sense for me to shoot your father on the same day he and I had words. I don't shoot someone because I disagree with them. When you approached me at the teller's cage in the lobby, I was having words with the teller who failed to give me an accurate report on time. Did you see me take out a gun and shoot him? No! I learned a long time ago it's much better to negotiate a fair price and acquire property through legal means. As I've been trying to explain, I'm not a violent man nor would I like to see anyone hurt. But a man in my position must protect himself when necessary," replied Jason.

"Is that why you have hired men who are fast with a gun? Seems to me you could run a legitimate business without hiring violent men."

"Well, Miss, I know you haven't been here for several years and a lot of changes have occurred during that time. With all due respect, I don't think I have to justify how I conduct my business operations to you or anyone else. Now, I'm a busy man. I'd love to talk more, but I need to get back to work. Let me walk you out and if you have further questions, I'm sure we can make an appointment to meet again."

"I think I can find my way out on my own, Mr. Long. I appreciate your time, but I want to make sure you and everyone else in town understand I will find out who shot my father. Please don't get up, and I believe we will talk again at a later date."

"Good day, Miss. I wish you good fortune."

Alicia stood up and opened the office door, proceeding down the hall and through the second door into the bank lobby where she exited the building into the bright sunlight. Alicia looked to the right and saw Mary's Café on the opposite side of the street down about a hundred yards. It was 11:45 a.m., and she could already tell the day would turn into a blistering hot one as she started to walk down the street on the wooden plank boardwalk every store had out in front, which substituted as sidewalks.

As she passed the Bear Claw Saloon, she heard the swinging doors open, followed by the footsteps of an emerging cowboy. "Hey, chink! Ain't you that chink daughter of Gus and Sarah?" shouted the cowboy.

Alicia slowed her pace, hesitated, and then decided it wasn't worth her time to confront this imbecile and continued to walk.

"Chink, I'm talkin' to ya! Don't ya dare walk away from me! Woman or no woman, nobody turns their back on me! If I have to come after you, you're going to be very sorry."

As the cowboy continued to yell at her, she stopped walking and slowly turned to face her antagonist.

"Well, that's a good little chink! Just stay there. I'll be there in two shakes so we can have a little talk," said the cowboy, slurring his words.

She instantly recognized Vic as he approached and recalled how he was going to strike her mother before she stopped him with a paralyzing grip on a pressure point in his neck. He stopped in front of her, and she could tell he had been doing a lot of drinking even though it was before noon. He reeked of beer, which she could smell from a distance of five feet, and she noticed he was walking unsteadily, which meant the effects of alcohol had also slowed his balance, coordination, and reflexes.

As Vic moved closer, he started to talk. "Well, Miss Chink, how's your daddy doin'? I heard he's getting better. Oh well, maybe he won't be so lucky if whoever shot him tries again. I think you outta try to convince him to sell out to my boss and move on. Don't you think that'd be the smart thing to do, Miss Chink?"

"I think, for once, I'll lower myself to your level and talk to your kind. First of all, my father's health is none of your concern. Second of all, don't ever call one of us Orientals by the word *chink*. If you do it again, I will make sure you understand the consequences of your behavior and teach you some manners like I did in the café.."

Vic's eyes doubled in size as Alicia spoke. He couldn't believe his ears that some chink was telling him how to act or talk.

"One more important thing for you to remember is my father will never sell his ranch. Even if he did, he would never sell it to Jason Long. He knows what Jason's up to, and he isn't going to help him put a stranglehold on his friends. Now, I have more important things to do than talk to you."

Vic was furious and as Alicia turned to go on her way, he reached out and grabbed her right shoulder to turn her around and teach her a lesson. She felt his right hand on her shoulder jerking her around and instinctively used this force against her opponent as the monks had taught her. As she turned toward Vic, she brought her right forearm up and knocked Vic's right arm sideways off her shoulder. At the same time, she stepped forward with her left foot and using her left hand struck Vic on the right side of his throat with a controlled knife-hand strike. He collapsed onto his left knee, grabbing his neck with his right hand. Alicia looked down at Vic with an icy stare.

"Don't you ever put your filthy hands on me again, or I may have to give you a further lesson in manners," Alicia coldly remarked.

He rubbed his neck hard to lessen the pain as Alicia scolded him. As the pain started to subside, Vic's temper boiled over. As he stood up, he drew his Colt 45 from his holster.

Alicia had not taken her eyes off Vic, treating him as one would an enemy. When she had struck him by stepping forward with her left foot, she had kept her right foot back. When she saw him drawing his gun, she timed her next move perfectly. Just as he pulled his gun out of his holster and leveled it at her, she brought her right foot in a semicircle to the left, crossing it over and striking Vic's gun hand with the instep of her right foot, dislodging the weapon out of his hand. She allowed her right foot to continue its path and turning her body to the left, she completed the turn, planting her right foot on the boardwalk. Bringing her left foot up, she struck him squarely in the nose, sending him flat on his back, unconscious with blood pouring out from his broken nose.

As soon as she had delivered the kick to Vic's nose, one of the townsfolk who had witnessed everything saw the marshal coming out of his office and yelled for him to come down where they were. Alicia heard them calling the marshal and decided to stay where she was. The marshal arrived and looked at Vic and then Alicia.

"What the devil happened here?" he asked.

"Vic decided he wanted to talk to me so he stopped me and said, among other things, that he thought my father should sell out to Jason. He also called me a chink, and I told him to never use that word again when talking to an Oriental and that my father would never sell his ranch to Jason Long. I then told him I had more important things to do and started to walk away. That's when he grabbed me. I reacted, and this was the result," replied Alicia.

"That's right, Marshal. I saw the whole thing and that's exactly what happened," said one of the townsfolk.

"Well, Alicia, what do you want to do? I can put Vic in jail for assault if you want to press charges."

"No, I don't think I want to press charges. I hope he has learned some manners from our little meeting here."

"Well, it looks like he's starting to come around. I'll make sure he gets over to Doc's if he needs him."

"Doc's meeting me at Mary's, so if you need him, that's where he will be."

She said good-bye to the marshal then turned and started walking toward Mary's to meet O'Malley for lunch. The altercation with Vic had made her about fifteen minutes late so she hurried her pace to meet him as soon as possible.

She arrived at the café and walked to the front door where she looked for O'Malley. She saw him sitting at a table by the window. He had seen her through the window walking quickly toward the café and waved at her when she came through the door. She nodded back at him and walked over to his table where she sat down. They exchanged warm greetings and then he said, "Looks like there was some commotion up the street. I saw several people head in that direction and form a crowd. I couldn't see what was going on from here, and I didn't want to go see as I thought I might miss meeting up with you if I left. You were walking here from that direction; did you see what was going on up there?

"Well, Doc, now I don't want you to get mad."

"Uh-oh! I don't like the start of this conversation," interrupted O'Malley.

"Well, I'll make it quick. After I had my talk with Jason, I had a slight misunderstanding with Vic. He confronted me on my way here and among other things called me a chink. I told him to never call me that again. He also told me my dad should sell the ranch to Jason and move on. That's when I told him dad would never sell the ranch to Jason, no matter what his offer was. I then told him I had more important things to do and continued on my way here. That's when he grabbed my shoulder, and I instinctively whirled and hit Vic a couple times, and he may have suffered a broken nose. The marshal arrived right after this little scrape, and I explained what had happened and that I was on my way to meet you at Mary's. I told him to send someone here if Vic needed a doctor. So now you know why I was late."

"Did Vic hurt you? Are you all right?"

"He never laid a hand on me, Doc. I think his physical injuries will heal a lot faster than the hurt to his pride when it gets around town that a little girl like me beat him up."

"Tell me about your conversation with the marshal. Was he able to help you any?"

"Yeah, he was very helpful. He showed me the shell casing of the bullet he thought Dad was shot with. It had a mark, like a faint scratch, that could only be made by a slight defect in the gun that fired it. So the marshal is going to try and set up a second sharpshooting contest for Henry rifles during the upcoming city celebrations. Since he was sure the shell casing came from a Henry rifle, we thought we could identify the owner by checking shell casings during the contest. The owner and the person who shot my father may be one and the same. We will have two contestants shoot at the targets at the same time. I will have children pick up the spent shells and bring them back to me to examine and hopefully identify the owner," said Alicia.

"Even if you identify the owner, it doesn't mean you have the person who shot your father. He could claim he bought it from someone or even found it on the prairie. How are you going to get him to admit he did the shooting?"

"I've got some ideas about that but before I go into them, I think we should see if the first part of my plan works."

"Well, it sure sounds interesting. I'll be more than happy to help with anything I can do for you," said O'Malley.

They continued talking as they ate lunch. The two of them talked so much they didn't notice the time until O'Malley took out his watch and saw it was already two o'clock. They had been talking for almost two hours without stopping.

They finished their lunch, and O'Malley walked Alicia back to his house where she got onto her horse and headed back to the ranch. On the ride back, she caught up with Moses, who had left earlier and was on his way back after picking up the supplies. Moses stopped and convinced her to tie her horse to the back of the buckboard and ride the rest of the way with him back to the ranch.

Upon their return, she helped Moses unpack the supplies and put them away. She was so certain the marshal would arrange for the additional sharpshooting contest she spent the rest of the day designing a poster announcing the additional event at the Cattleman's Association celebration.

The next morning, she rode the two hours into town and stopped at the marshal's office with the posters she had prepared. He looked over her design and let her know he had received approval from the Cattleman's Association to add the additional contest. She gave the marshal money to have the posters printed and distributed to the local merchants to post in their windows. They both thought it wise for the marshal to arrange the printing and distribution of the posters as he was in charge of all sharpshooting contests, and no one would suspect this additional contest would be used to identify the person who shot her father.

True to his word, the marshal had the poster printed and distributed in every store window he could find. He also hired some of the kids in town to post the flyers on vacant posts in town and hand out the posters to cowboys or ranch hands, making sure the posters got out to the surrounding ranches.

CHAPTER 12

사랑

That week, Alicia stayed on the ranch and helped out with the work any way she could. Only a few ranch hands knew her from before she had left the ranch. It was customary back then for cowboys to move from one ranch to another or even drift to another state thinking they could make more money. Another reason for cowboys to move on was simply a lack of work. If the ranch owners had to cut back, the ranch hands would be laid off, and they would be forced to find work at another ranch or move completely out of the territory to seek a job. So when Alicia decided to put her work clothes on and pitch in, many of the ranch hands suspected that this small lady didn't have the stamina or muscle to do the long and hard hours of ranch work.

It didn't take her long to disprove the ranch hands that had doubts about her abilities. She was up every morning before the other hands had gotten out of their bunks. Moses was usually in the middle of making breakfast for the hands when she would come in and get a couple biscuits, which he sliced and put a fried egg and a slice of ham in between. She would wolf down the biscuits and have her usual glass of milk, which Moses always set aside for her each morning. She had never liked the strong coffee the hands seemed to live on as she preferred tea, like her mother, for all meals except breakfast.

She took about fifteen minutes to eat her breakfast while chatting with Moses as he prepared the usual fried potatoes, bacon, eggs, and ham, along with several pots of strong coffee. At around the time she finished eating and was ready to start her day, the hands would be filing in to get their breakfasts.

One day, she rode out to the main herd where they had started to brand the mature calves. The herd was located about a mile from the ranch where a large stream cut through the property. The source of the stream was a large body of spring fed water located on the north side of the ranch, which continued on through the neighboring ranches to the south. Green pasture with sweet grass was on both sides of the stream, and the cattle did not wander very far from the water and their food source.

As she approached the herd, she saw the night rider ranch hand. Hank Rice was tired. He had been riding night herd since midnight when he took over from Joe Wright, who rode the herd from six o'clock in the evening until midnight. Hank was bent over his saddle, whistling softly to the cattle to keep them calm. He was tired but knew if he fell asleep, he would certainly fall off his horse, which might result in his getting a busted head. Even if he didn't get hurt, he would have a hard time living it down in the bunkhouse if another hand saw him. So he whistled to calm the cattle and make sure he stayed awake.

Just as he was about to doze off, he heard a horse approaching, and he snapped straight up in the saddle. There was always the possibility of rustlers although Hank wasn't sure what he could do as a band of rustlers may have ten or twelve men against just him. He looked off in the distance and breathed a sigh of relief when he saw a lone rider on a horse in the distance. As the rider drew near, he recognized Alicia on her favorite horse. As she continued to get closer, he thought what a hard worker she was. She pitched in on any job no matter what it was and treated everyone as an equal, ignoring the fact she was the owner's daughter. He never saw her try to shirk whatever job the foreman assigned her. He remembered when she first rode in and all the hands, including himself, took one look at the small oriental woman and wondered what she was doing on a working ranch. Then she approached the foreman and asked him what he would like her to do. The foreman gave a little chuckle and asked her the same question. What indeed could she do? Her face was serious as she told the foreman she had worked every job on this ranch before she moved east and could do them as well or better than the foreman or any hand on the ranch. So he assigned her the job of rounding up the strays that had wandered off. She walked over to her horse, threw her right leg up over the saddle, and seated herself squarely on the horse. She slipped her feet into the stirrups and took off for the hills to start her own personal roundup.

She worked from dawn to dusk for three days, never stopping or resting and single-handedly brought in the strays that were out there. After her first task, the foreman assigned her to help with the branding and for the next two days, she showed them she could handle the branding iron as well as any of the hands.

She rode up and stopped her horse a few feet from Hank. "Hi, Hank, how were the cattle last night? You had any problems with them?"

"They were pretty quiet for the first couple of hours. Then the coyotes started up. There must be a pack of them cuz I could sure hear several off in the distance. Their yellin' stirred up the cattle and made 'em uneasy so I started some whistlin' and that seemed to calm 'em down as I rode around them on the outside of the herd. The coyotes finally stopped their howling a couple of hours ago, and the cattle have been quiet ever since. So, why are you out here so early?" asked Hank.

"Oh, I thought I'd get an early start and get the branding iron fires started so we'd be all set to start when the rest of the hands get out here. Let me get the fires started and then if the men aren't out, I can take over the watch so you can get back to the bunkhouse and get some sleep."

"I appreciate that, but I think I'll stay out here until the boys get here. If I head in early, I'm sure I'll catch some ribbin' from them. Let me know if you need any help with the fires."

Alicia thanked Hank for his offer and then rode over to the clearing where they had been branding yesterday. She got down off her horse and saw the coals were still hot. She piled some kindling on the fires and blew on them until they caught fire after which she put more wood on each fire to get them going. By the time she had the fires just right, it was daybreak and the ranch hands rode up to start another day of branding. She had put the branding irons in the fires so they would be ready to use as soon as the hands arrived. With a few words of good morning between the hands and Alicia, everyone started their job. The hands brought the cattle in one by one and tied their feet. Alicia did the branding. They worked all day long with a lunch break and then headed back to the ranch for supper. This routine went on day after day until they finished—the day before the Cattleman's Association celebration was to start in Cheyenne.

The previous weekend, Alicia had ridden into town and laid out her plans to O'Malley, asking him to arrange some things that were integral to their success. He readily agreed to help her.

By the time the celebration came around, Gus had almost completely recovered from his gunshot wound. He was now up and around riding his horse out to check on the branding and all the other ranch work being done.

That evening, the family sat in the kitchen enjoying their dinner and talking about the upcoming events. Alicia brought up the topic of the Henry sharpshooter contest. She had already convinced her dad to put up one of his finest horses for first prize.

"Well, Dad, are you going to the celebration tomorrow?" she asked.

"I was thinking about going since I haven't been to town for quite some time. As you know, your mom has made me slow down for the last few weeks."

Alicia and her mom looked at each other and smiled at the understatement.

"Well then, we can ride in together, Gus. I want to go into town, too. You're not the only one who hasn't been to town for a while. Maybe the next time you get shot it'll be in your arm or leg. That way I can patch you up without getting Doc out here and having to spend so much time in the house to make sure you stay in bed and get well. I swear, Gus, you're the worst patient for anyone to look after," said Sarah.

"But, Sarah, you can't say you haven't been to town in a long while. You were just there Wednesday to pick up Colin from the train," remarked Gus.

"Yes, and Colin will want to go into town with us also, right, Colin?" said Sarah.

"Y-y-yes," Colin replied, with a stutter.

Alicia chimed in, "I think you have a good idea, Dad. You, Mom, and Colin can take the two-seat buckboard in and tie up the bay behind you so we can get it in for the prize at the Henry sharpshooting contest. I'll take my horse and ride along with you and Mom on the way in," said Alicia.

"Okay, okay, I guess I know I'm beaten when the two strong-willed women in my life gang up on me. So, let's just say I'll be happy to drive the buggy in and deliver the horse for first prize. I'm still not sure why you want to do this but if I ask, I don't think you are going to tell me, so I'll just go along with it for now."

"Dad, are you thinking of competing in the contest?" asked Alicia.

"I was thinking about it since I'm pretty good with my Henry. But if I won, some people might think the contest wasn't honest since I'd end up winning the prize we put up. So no, I think I'll let the others try their luck, and I'll just sit back and watch."

"That sounds fine, dear. I think it'll do us a world of good to go into town for some fun. Lord knows we all deserve it," offered Sarah.

After they finished eating, Gus went out to the porch with Colin to enjoy the cool evening as they looked over the range. Sarah and Alicia stayed in the kitchen and cleaned up the dinner dishes, giving them an opportunity to talk without anyone else around.

"Okay, Alicia, it's just you and me here. I don't know how you convinced your dad to put the horse up for first prize, but I suspect you're up to something, and I want to know if there's any chance anyone will get hurt."

"Mom, I really don't want to say anything right now. But I can tell you nobody is in danger and what I've got planned may help us find out who shot Dad."

Sarah looked sternly at Alicia and said, "You make sure your plan works and does not cause any harm to anyone. I don't want you or anyone else to be in danger."

"I plan on being very careful, Mom. Well, that's the last dish. Let's go out to the porch and sit with Dad and Colin before we go to bed."

Sarah readily agreed, and they walked out to the porch to join them. They spent the rest of the evening in pleasant conversation.

The next morning, they were up by seven o'clock and ate breakfast together. Afterward, Alicia went out and helped her dad hitch up the wagon, tying up the horse they were putting up for first prize to the back of the buggy.

They set off by eight o'clock with Gus and Sarah in the front seat and Colin in the back seat, Alicia riding her horse alongside it. It was a sunny and sweltering day. It looked and felt like it was going to be ninety by noon. The early morning ride into town was pleasant enough before the heat had a chance to rise to an intolerable level.

When they arrived into town, they rode directly to the marshal's office where they turned the prize horse over to him. They talked for a few minutes and then the marshal took charge of the horse and took it over to the livery stable.

The celebration was just starting with street vendors setting out their wares and the barbecue fires being started for the noon celebration. Gus, Sarah, Colin, and Alicia walked down the main street of Cheyenne toward the south side of town where the sharpshooting contests were being set up. Picnic tables had been set up in an adjacent field where folks could sit and enjoy their barbecue lunches with room for the kids to play.

At around one o'clock in the afternoon, the first group had gathered to participate in the sharpshooting event that was originally planned. This event took about an hour to complete and the Winchester rifle went to a local ranch hand. By 2:15 p.m., contestants were gathered to start the Henry sharpshooting competition. Three targets had been set up one hundred yards from the firing line. There were twenty-four contestants and after each round, the targets would be examined and scored by the marshal.

The contest went on for about an hour until it had been narrowed down to two contestants whose groupings were almost identical. These last two repeatedly tied with groupings spaced so close in their individual targets that the marshal could not determine a winner. The marshal decided to move the targets back another fifty yards. Both contestants agreed, and the targets were relocated. Once again, the contestants fired their Henrys, but the marshal still could not declare a winner.

The marshal was determined to come up with something that could determine who was the best shot. So he had the targets put back another fifty yards and gave the shooters only two bullets apiece, hoping the spread would be enough to determine the winner. The marshal also decided to have each contestant shoot individually and not together as before. The order was determined by the flip of a coin. The first shooter stepped up to the firing line and carefully aimed and fired his two shots. His target was removed and replaced with a fresh target for the next contestant. The second shooter stepped up and fired his two rounds after taking careful aim. Both targets were returned to the marshal, who decided to announce the first shooter as the winner. The second shooter shook his head and asked the marshal to reexamine his target. The marshal looked again and said there was only one bullet hole in the target, which meant the second shooter had missed the entire target with either his first or second shot. The second shooter remarked he hadn't missed. He just made the mistake of shooting right through the first bullet hole. This brought laughter from the contestants and the spectators. Who could ever imagine anyone having the ability to put his second shot through his first bullet hole? When the laughter died down, the shooter stunned everyone when he offered to do it a second time, with the agreement he would take first place and no one else would be permitted to shoot if he was successful. The marshal asked the other shooter if that was agreeable to him.

Both parties agreed, and the marshal said they would put another clean piece of paper behind the target after the first shot was taken to verify the location of the second shot. Everyone settled down, and the shooter took careful aim and fired. His first shot hit the target dead center. The second sheet of paper was then placed behind the original target, and the shooter once again took careful aim and fired his second shot. The target was quickly brought up to the marshal for his official review. Sure enough, the shooter had put his second bullet through the first bullet hole as the paper behind the target verified the shot. Everyone was ecstatic and rushed over to see who the unknown contestant was.

The shooter was at least six foot two and weighing about 170 pounds. He was the average cowboy, dressed in jeans and a blue cotton work shirt. He had the typical cowboy hat all cowpunchers wore and cowboy boots, which were well worn and beat up from working cattle on the range for the last several months. He had a handsome face with a strong square jaw and black hair protruding from under his hat. A crowd had gathered around him mostly asking how he learned to shoot like that and where he was from.

The marshal made his way through the crowd, approaching the shooter. "Folks, folks! Let's give this stranger some room. Well, young man, you certainly taught us something about the fine art of shooting tonight. I know you're a stranger in town so why don't you tell us your name."

"My name's Thad Greenway. I just got into town yesterday. I was one of the men bringing in a herd to the railroad. I heard you folks had a Henry rifle shooting contest so I thought I'd try my luck, Marshal."

"Well, Thad, that's as fine a shootin' as I've ever seen. Let's bring in your prize. Alicia, are you around? Someone go find her and let's get the horse from the livery for this young man," said the marshal.

In a few minutes, Alicia appeared with the horse and moved up to where the marshal and Thad were standing together. Prior to the contest, Alicia had arranged for two local town boys to retrieve one shell casing from each contestant and bring them back to her, telling her who they came from. The boys then returned to the shooting line and collected shell casings from the next contestants. They repeat these trips throughout the competition. When the boys delivered the shells, Alicia placed them in separate bags with the contestants' names on them. Finally, the boys came back for the last time, advising Alicia there was a stranger who signed up at the last minute, and no one knew his name. She placed those casings in an unnamed bag and then went down to the livery stable and brought the horse up the street. She tied the horse to a railing about one hundred feet from the ongoing contest so the noise of the rifle shots would not spook the horse.

One of the spectators came down and told her the contest was over and it was time to give the horse away to the winner. She untied the mare and started walking toward the shooting line where the marshal was with the winning contestant.

As soon as the marshal saw her, he yelled out above the din of the crowd. "Here she is, folks, with one of the best horses in the territory. Alicia, would you do the honors? I want you to meet Thad Greenway. Thad, this is Alicia. Alicia's family was generous enough to donate this fine horse," said the marshal.

"Thank you, Marshal. On behalf of the festival committee and the City of Cheyenne, I would like to present you with what we believe to be the finest mare in the territory. Congratulations on your marksmanship," remarked Alicia as she handed over the reins to Thad.

"Well, thank you, Miss. This is a fine-looking horse," Thad said as he handed the reins back to Alicia so he could walk around the horse, inspecting his prize. When he completed his inspection, Alicia handed the reins back to him.

Since the contest was over, the townsfolk had started to disperse to other festival activities the city had planned. The marshal walked over to Thad and Alicia and said, "Thad, you did a great job winning this mare. You said you came in with the cattle drive. What are your plans now that the drive is over?"

"I haven't given much thought about it. I've been on the drive for about three months and just got paid. I'm tired of being on the move and eatin' trail dust all day long. Seems like you've got a nice town with friendly folks, so I may just see if any of the ranches around here need an extra hand."

"Well, young man, you might be in luck. I overheard what you just said," Jason Long remarked as he approached the three of them. "I'd like to talk to you about this fine horse you just won. Yes, this is an excellent horse you have here. I can't think of anyone who wouldn't want to own such an animal. Would you consider taking three hundred dollars for her?" Jason said as he walked around the mare, admiring her.

"Well, sir, I'm sure that is more than I've ever had offered me for any horse I've ever owned. But if it's that valuable of a horse, I think I'll just keep her while I'm in town. But if I decide to sell her, I'll keep your offer in mind."

"Well, that's fine, son. I'd still like to talk to you about coming to work for me. Can we sit down in my office to discuss it?"

"I just rode into town after spending ninety days on a cattle drive. Right now, looking for a job is not something I want to think about. So, just like my horse, when I get to looking for work, I'll keep you in mind."

"Okay, young man, but I think you're making a mistake. By the way, we haven't been introduced. I'm Jason Long. When you're ready to go to work, ask anyone in town and they can tell you where to find me," Jason replied.

Thad stuck his hand out and Jason shook his hand. He then walked back to his office.

"Well, I'll be dogged," Thad said as he watched Jason walk away.

"Why do you say that?" asked Alicia.

"I'll tell ya why. I don't think I've ever ridden into a town and been offered a job without lookin' around for one. Who is that man? I know his name but who is he, really?"

Alicia and the marshal looked at each other and smiled.

"Did I say somethin' funny?" asked Thad.

"No, no, no, it's just a long story. Alicia, if you'll excuse us, maybe Thad will join me for a drink and I can answer his question."

"I'll leave him in your capable hands, Marshal. Thad, congratulations on winning the mare, and I hope you enjoy her. I'm going to find my family and then head back home before it gets too late."

"I forgot to tell you, Alicia. I saw your dad this afternoon, and he looks pretty good for being near dead a month ago. When do you think he'll be back full-time on the ranch?" asked the marshal.

"If it was up to him, he would already be working the ranch full time. But Mom put her foot down, and you know what that means. Knowing Dad, I expect he'll be back full time in another week or so even though at this time he has already been working many hours a day. Now, you two go have your drink so you can answer Thad's questions about Jason Long. Thad, I hope to see you around town and, Marshal, I'll see you the next time I'm in town."

"Well, Thad, grab your horse and let's go get that drink. Say hello to your folks and Colin for me, Alicia."

"I sure will, Marshal," she replied as the marshal and Thad started to walk down the street to the nearest saloon.

She walked back to the general store where she had left her individual bags of spent shell casings from the shooting contest. She went into the back room and folded the top of each bag so none of the casings would fall out and placed the small bags in a satchel. She then picked up the satchel and headed out of the store in search of her parents. She went past several stores and as she passed Mary's Café, she glanced in and saw the four of them through the window, sitting at the lunch counter having some coffee.

As she opened the front door and went in, she noticed her parents and Mary seemed to stop their conversation midsentence. The three of them had serious expressions on their faces.

"Hi folks, did I interrupt something?"

"Not really, sweetheart. We were just talking about the things we saw and did today. I know you were involved with the rifle contest so your dad and I talked for a few minutes with the marshal and then walked around town for a bit. We decided to come over to Mary's for some of her homemade lemonade and a sarsaparilla for Colin," answered her mom.

"Sarah, that's not all that's happened. Why don't you tell her the rest of it?" said Mary.

"Okay, Mom...Dad, I'm not a little girl anymore. Tell me what's going on."

"Jason Long stopped in while you were down at the contest. Said he wanted to talk to me about a deal to sell the ranch. Said he was sorry to hear I had been shot and hoped I would keep getting better. He had his gunman Vic with him. Anyway, he said it's a tough life out there running a ranch and hopes no other accidents come to my family or me," replied Gus.

"That's when your dad got out of his chair and walked a couple of steps over to Jason. He stood about six inches from his face and said something to him very quietly that none of us heard. Whatever your father said, he wiped Jason's confident look off his face, and Vic took a step forward. Jason outstretched his hand to stop Vic and then turned and left the café with Vic not saying a word," said Mary.

"I can just imagine what Dad said to Jason. Do you want to tell us about it, Dad?" asked Alicia.

"I just made it very clear to Jason that if anything, such as an accident, hurt my family or any of the ranch hands workin' my spread, I would go straight to him whether or not he had Vic with him for protection. Jason didn't have anything to say. He just turned and left. When he was outside, I saw him say somethin' to Vic. Jason then started walkin' toward the shootin' contest, and

Vic got on his horse and rode out of town. The next thing we knew, you walked in," said Gus.

"Well, it's getting late in the day. Don't you think it's about time we started back to the ranch?" asked Alicia.

"Not until you four sit down and have a piece of fresh apple pie I just finished baking in the kitchen," said Mary.

"That sounds great, but then we have to get back to the ranch," replied Sarah.

It was about an hour later when they started back for home. The ride was uneventful until they were down the road from where Alicia and O'Malley had their picnic. Just then a shot rang out, kicking up the dirt in front of the buckboard horses, which took off at a dead run. The horses galloped at full speed down the trail.

Alicia immediately kicked her horse into a full run and went after the buckboard. The wagon had a thirty-yard start by the time Alicia had gotten her horse into full pursuit. As the buckboard passed the tree, several more shots rang out, but the bullets missed all four of them. Meanwhile, Gus tried hard to rein in the horses.

Alicia looked to her left and saw a figure lying down on the grass behind the tree where O'Malley and Alicia had their picnic. She was unable to recognize the figure and what was also strange was the absence of a horse.

The buckboard was wildly out of control, and Alicia realized that the only way to stop it was to leap onto one of the buckboard's horses. She urged her horse to go faster, and she rapidly gained on the buckboard. As she approached the rear of the wagon, she decided to go around to the left side. She got alongside the wagon and saw Colin holding onto the front seat as tight as he could so he would not fall out. As she passed by her parents, she caught her dad's attention. She pointed to herself and then at the horses letting him know she was going to leap onto the horse closest to her and rein it in. She saw her dad look back at her, yelling something and shaking his head.

Gus couldn't believe his eyes. Alicia was going to jump on one of the buckboard horses and attempt to stop the wagon. He knew there was a left-hand bend in the road a short distance ahead and if she jumped when the wagon went to the left, she would misjudge her leap and wind up in the middle of the two horses, falling between them and to the ground where she would go under the wagon and be seriously hurt or killed.

As the wagon drew nearer to the bend, Gus saw Alicia edge her horse closer to the racing horses he kept trying to rein in. It seemed to him Alicia had gotten so close that she was practically touching one of the wagon horses. All of a sudden, he saw her stand up in the stirrups. She removed her left foot from the stirrup and bending her left leg, placed it on top of the saddle. He could see Alicia slightly crouch and prepare to jump. They were no more than a hundred feet from the bend when Gus yelled at the top of his lungs warning her not to leap. But she couldn't hear the warning and jumped just as the wagon pulled to the left.

She had focused her attention on the horse she was going to leap onto and had not seen the bend in the trail. As she leaped, the wagon horse veered left into her horse, making her miss the horse's back. Her left knee hit the horse's back and she started to slide down the right side of the horse toward the ground. She realized that if she continued her slide, she would fall between the horses and under the wagon.

She felt the horse's harness under her left arm and realized she had one chance to grab it before falling to her death. She made a desperate grab and caught the horse's harness in her grasp, stopping her fall. Her left leg was still on top of the horse's back and her right leg dangled down between the two horses. She tightened her grip on the harness as hard as she could and although it seemed forever, it took only a few seconds to pull herself up on top of the runaway horse.

Once she was upright, she was able to pull back the horse, gradually slowing it down to a walk and then a complete stop. When she stopped the horses, she jumped off and ran back to the wagon.

"Mom, Dad! Are you two all right? How about you, Colin? I was so scared you were going to have an accident and get hurt, or worse," she said.

"Daughter, what in the heck were you thinking? You could have been killed. Didn't you see me screaming at you and shaking my head so you wouldn't do such a foolish thing?"

"Dad, it took me about a half mile to catch up with you. It sure looked to me the horses were completely out of control and help was needed before an accident happened."

Sarah quickly put her hand on Gus's knee just as he was about to reply. "Sweetheart, I think your dad was going to thank you for the help, but he was afraid you were going to be hurt. Isn't that right, Gus?"

She could see Gus's face soften as he turned his head toward Alicia. "Mom's right, Alicia. I was having trouble getting the horses under control, and I appreciate the helping hand cuz my chest sure hurt from pulling back on the reins. But all be told, I think I would have had 'em reined in pretty quick without your help."

"Dad, I'm sure you would have stopped them, but I thought I'd help before you and the horses got to California," replied Alicia.

Sarah smiled and then started to giggle, which turned into a hard laugh. Gus, Colin, and Alicia looked at her and then at each other and joined in the laughter. After a few seconds, all of them were laughing uncontrollably until tears started coming out of their eyes.

When things eventually calmed down, Alicia looked at her family. "I love you all so much. Now, why don't you keep heading back to the ranch? I'm going to ride back to where we were shot at and look around."

"Alicia, we love you just as much, but I don't think it's a very good idea for you to go back there alone," replied Gus.

"I'll be all right, Dad. I'll be careful, but I don't think whoever shot at us is going to hang around for someone to come back. I know the country so I'll approach that spot from behind and be very careful."

"You're too old for me to order you not to go. So you better be real careful about goin' back. If you're not back to the ranch in an hour, I'm gittin' some of the boys and come lookin' for you," said Gus.

Alicia glanced down the trail and spotted her horse, which had stopped running about a hundred yards up the trail from where she had stopped the wagon horses. Her mare was just off the side of the trail, grazing on some grass as if she had just been on a gentle walk instead of a full speed mile-long run. She walked up to the mare and stroked her neck several times, finishing with a few gentle pats. She then mounted the mare and took off down the trail back to where she thought the shot had come from.

After riding for about a half mile, she headed off the main trail and circled around, coming up by the stream. She dismounted and slowly walked toward the area by the tree from where she thought the shot had come from. She immediately saw signs telling her someone had been there. The grass was matted down as if someone had been lying there waiting for some time. As she was looking around, a metal reflection from the sun caught her eye. She bent down and picked up a shell casing from the ground. She held it up and inspected it closely, stepping into the sun and slowly turning the casing around. She saw a minute scratch identical to the one the marshal had showed her. It certainly appeared to her that whoever was after her dad was not going to stop until he was dead or driven off his ranch.

She continued to look around and noticed the grass was bent by someone who walked or ran through it toward the stream. She followed the trail to the stream and continued for about a hundred yards until she came upon an area where a horse had been tethered. The area was far enough from the road where it could not be seen. It was apparent the shooter had made his escape using this area to hide his horse and then coming here after taking his shots to make his escape.

She found nothing else, so she made her way back to her horse and started for the ranch. She kept a watchful eye for anyone lurking off the trail but saw no one, which meant she was either being watched by a shooter who was very careful or he had left for now.

When she got back to the ranch, Gus asked her what she had found. She said she did not see anyone but knew someone was there from the matted grass under the tree.

After dinner that evening, she brought in the saddlebags from her horse and after everyone went to bed, she removed the bags of casings and examined them all very carefully before she turned into bed. Unfortunately, none of the shell casings had any scratches on them.

The next morning, she was up helping Sarah prepare breakfast. Gus came in and sat down at the head of the table, watching his wife and daughter cooking eggs and bacon. Colin then came in and sat down beside Gus.

"It's good to see my family all home at the same time and sitting together for a meal. I hope everyone's hungry. Alicia and I cooked plenty of food for everyone," said Sarah.

"This morning, I felt good enough to get up and join everyone for breakfast at the table. In fact, I think I'll get out of the house and get back to work finally," said Gus.

"Gus, you're not going out and doing anything until Doc gives you a final okay," Sarah declared with a stern look that could melt ice in the middle of winter.

Alicia chimed in. "I'm riding into town this morning to report yesterday's shooting. After I report the shooting to the marshal, I'll stop by Doc's to see if he can come out and make a call."

CHAPTER 13

사랑

After Alicia had left to go back to the ranch, O'Malley returned to his office where there were a few townsfolk waiting to see him about some routine ailments. There was Jennifer, who came in with a severe stomachache. At first look, he thought she might have appendicitis until she said she had eaten a large Mexican meal topping it off with a dozen jalapeño peppers.

"Now, Jennifer, you know these peppers have never agreed with you before. You have come to me with this same complaint at least five or six times before, and I keep telling you not to eat those peppers. All I can do for you is give you some stomach powder, which you will need to take with milk, and then you will just have to wait until you get better."

"Aw I'm sorry, Doc, but you know I jus luv them peppers. I'll try to lay off 'em, but I ain't promising anything. If I get a hankerin', you know I'll give in and eat 'em again."

"Okay, Jennifer, then you come and see me next time, and I'll give you some more medicine," O'Malley said as he walked her to the front door.

The next patient was Ike, the local smithy, who had burned his hand while working in his shop. He applied some burn ointment, bandaged his hand and sent him on his way.

Doc walked out of the exam room after making some notes in Jennifer's and Ike's files to see if there was anyone else in the waiting room. There was a man standing in the waiting room, looking out the front window. O'Malley walked into the room, stepping up behind the man.

"Can I help you?"

When the man turned around, O'Malley instantly recognized him. It was Vic, one of Jason's men. He had a bandana tied around his head, which covered his right eye.

"Doc, I got somethin' in my eye, and it hurts just awful."

"Well, come on back here so I can take a look at that eye."

As Vic followed him back to the exam room, O'Malley remarked, "If I'm going to help, you need to tell me how you hurt your eye."

"I really ain't sure, Doc. I was out on the prairie when I got somethin' in it."

"Lie down on this exam table so I can get a good look at your eye."

As he got on the table, Doc strapped on a mirror around his forehead to better reflect the light. He then lifted the bandana off Vic's eye and saw what appeared to be a small sliver of metal. Doc gently widened Vic's eye with his fingers and examined the eye thoroughly with the aid of the reflector. He got a much better look at the object that was causing the discomfort to Vic. It had always amazed O'Malley how a tiny cinder or speck of dust could cause a person such pain. He had experienced the same thing when he had got a cinder in his own eye from being out on the dusty plains. When the obstruction was removed, he was surprised at how small it was.

However, O'Malley noticed this tiny object seemed to be embedded in Vic's eye with some force. It was also shiny. His tweezers were needed to extract this one. O'Malley removed his fingers from Vic's eye and covered it back with the bandana.

"Vic, I can see the trouble. I can get it out, but it will be painful when I remove it. The pain should last for about five or ten seconds. Or you can leave it as is, and it will probably work itself out in about a week or ten days. However, that means you will have to put up with the discomfort for that time. I always give my patients their choices when they have them. How do you want to handle this?"

"It hurts like blazes, Doc, so I'd just as soon have a little more pain now as long as it will stop."

"Okay, Vic, relax for a minute while I get things ready. When I go in there, you will have to stay completely still so I don't injure your eye with the tweezers."

O'Malley opened his black bag and took out a small pair of metal tweezers. He then turned back to Vic and pressed down slightly on the skin under Vic's eye, using the fingers on his left hand. He reflected the light into Vic's eye, telling him to look up, which gave him an excellent view of the foreign object. Slowly and carefully, he positioned the tweezers so he could get hold of the object. O'Malley squeezed the tweezers together and was able to get hold of the obstruction.

He felt Vic's body tense as soon as he had touched what looked like a small flake. He told Vic to stay still and carefully removed the foreign object out of Vic's eye, making sure he got all of it. It took about four or five seconds and immediately after he got it out, he felt Vic's body relax.

"All right, Vic, that should do it. You did really good staying still. How do you feel now?"

"It hurt like heck when you were getting' it out, but it sure feels great now," answered Vic.

"I think you'll be okay now. You won't need any medicine, and you can go back to work immediately."

"Yeah, Doc, I'll be doin' that. How much do I owe ya?"

"This wasn't very complicated so how's fifty cents sound to you?"

He reached into his jeans pocket and handed Doc a silver dollar.

"Here ya go, Doc, take the whole dollar. It was worth it."

Doc followed Vic to the front door where they said good-bye, and Doc went back to his exam room. Something bothered him about the speck of material he had extracted from Vic's eye. He walked into the exam room and looked at the small tray on the stand next to the exam table. Doc took out his tweezers and picked up the speck, looking at it carefully. It definitely was not a cinder or a grain of sand. He placed the speck in one of his empty glass vials and labeled it, noting the time.

It was already six o'clock in the evening so he decided to clean up the exam room and get dinner at Mary's Café. He walked out into the street and started on his way to the café. On his way, he noticed Jason in bank's lobby, which was odd since the bank had closed at five o'clock.

The next morning, Alicia helped her mom clean up the kitchen and wash the dishes after breakfast. She then said good-bye to everyone and got on her horse, heading out to Cheyenne.

It was another beautiful day. The sun was starting its climb into a cloudless blue sky. She could tell it was going to be another hot day as it was already getting steamy, and it was only eight o'clock in the morning. It was a long ten-mile ride into town, but she greatly enjoyed it as she had time to think about the recent events.

About five miles into her trip, she spotted a lone rider coming toward her in the distance. As the rider got closer, she didn't recognize him, but she knew the horse. It was the mare her father had put up as first prize in the Henry rifle shooting contest. As the rider got closer, she finally recognized him as Thad Greenway. They stopped their horses when they were side by side.

"Hello, Miss. I'm surprised to see you out here. Are you out for a morning ride?"

"No, I'm heading into town to take care of some business. I might ask you the same thing. What brings you way out here from town?"

"The marshal told me a couple ranch hands quit the Double Bar X, and he thought I might get hired. He told me about how your pa got shot, and I'm sure sorry about that. After thinking it over last night, I know my money won't last forever and after talking to the marshal, I sure don't want to work for Jason. I was hoping your pa might hire me. Do you know if he's looking for an extra hand?"

"I don't know, Thad. Pa runs the ranch as he sees fit. But he's fair. If he needs more hands and he likes your look, you will have just as good a chance as anyone. Well, it was nice to see you, Thad. I wish you luck, but I need to get into town."

"Nice to see you too, Miss. I'll go to the ranch and talk to your pa. Have a nice day, Miss."

Alicia and Thad rode off in their respective directions. It took another hour and a half before she reached the outskirts of Cheyenne. It was eleven o'clock, and she decided to go directly to the marshal's office. She rode up to his office, dismounted, and tied her horse to the rail.

Upon entering the marshal's office, she saw him sitting behind his desk doing some paperwork as usual. As she entered, he looked up and walked around from behind his desk to greet her.

"Good morning, Alicia. What brings you into town today?"

"Morning, Marshal. We had an incident yesterday, on the way home from the celebration. I'm sure you remember the tree on the trail where you found that shell casing you showed me. Yesterday, someone shot at us while we were heading back to the ranch in the buckboard. The horses took off and ran wild for about a mile before we got them reined in. After that, Ma, Pa, and Colin drove back to the ranch, and I went back to the tree where I found this shell casing."

She took the casing out of her jeans pocket and handed it to the marshal. He took the casing and walked over to the window and slowly rolled it in his fingers until he spotted what he was looking for. A long thin scratch ran the length of the casing.

"Alicia, this looks identical to the shell casing I found at the same place. I guess this would mean the person who tried to kill your father is still around."

"I think you're right, Marshal. We need to put our heads together and make a plan to catch whoever it is. I've got another idea that I think may work if you are willing to go along with it," she said with a sly smile.

She began to explain her plan to the marshal, who listened intently.

"Well, Alicia, that sounds like a very good idea. We just have to figure out how to work it out. One way is to arrest Rory on damage charges he owes to one of the saloons, where he started a fight. He promised to pay the damages but has not made good on his promise. Once I get him in jail, we can add the other charge and see if Jason reacts the way we think he will."

"That's fine, Marshal. When do you want to make the arrest? Do you need any help besides your deputy?"

"Nope, I won't need Chet to help me on this arrest. Rory's a loudmouth and bully, but he doesn't pick a fight he can't win. He knows he can't win with me so I don't expect there will be any trouble. Are you headin' back to the ranch or do you have some other business in town? I'm askin' because you want to be careful here. I've heard some talk that Jason and his men are pretty mad about you tryin' to find out who shot your pa."

"The only other thing I was going to do was to see if Doc would give Colin an exam on Saturday. Doc has the most recent medical information, and Colin has not been examined since his injury years ago."

"I'd offer to walk you over to Doc's, but I know what you'd say. So just do me a favor, stay safe and out of trouble."

"No problem, Marshal! Get me word when you arrest Rory. I'll be back in town on Saturday with Colin. See you then," Alicia replied as she walked out of the marshal's office onto the boardwalk. She untied her horse and started for O'Malley's house.

As she rode through the main street of Cheyenne, she was pleasantly surprised to see a lot more people had moved out west to start new lives. She passed the bank where Jason was but did not see him in the building. As she continued down the street, she passed by Mary, who waved at her from the front window where she was serving lunch to some customers. She saw O'Malley down the street, walking toward her on the boardwalk. He saw her at about the same time, and they both waved at each other.

"Alicia, I didn't expect to see you in town today. I'm on my way to have lunch at Mary's. Can I buy you some lunch?"

"I'd love to, Doc. I was on my way to see you, anyway."

"I hope you're not sick or injured."

"Nothing like that, Doc. I just wanted to discuss something with you. Let's get to Mary's and see if we can get a table away from everyone else to talk."

They walked into Mary's Café together and found a corner table away from the other customers. Mary came out from the kitchen, said hello, and took their orders. When she turned away and went back to the kitchen, O'Malley turned his attention to Alicia.

"Now, would you like to tell me what's on your mind?"

"I just left the marshal's office where I spoke to him about another plan to catch the person who shot my father. He seemed to think it was a good idea and is going to move forward with it." She explained her plan to O'Malley, and he listened intently.

"That sounds like a well thought-out plan. When does the marshal think he will make his move?"

"He plans on arresting Rory the next time he shows up in town. I told the marshal I was coming back to town this Saturday with Colin. You're up-to-date with all the latest medical information, and Colin has not been examined to any extent since he was first injured. Would you do me a favor and give him a complete exam to see if there is anything you can do for him?"

"I'd be happy to. But you need to realize the medical profession does not know a lot about how the human brain works. I can fix broken bones, remove bullets, and even do surgery, such as taking someone's appendix out to save her life. An injury to the brain is way out of my knowledge and training. Medical schools are still starting to understand how the human brain works and whether we can help or cure people through surgery. I have some medical books on the brain that I can review before you get back to town with Colin. Like I said, I'd be happy to examine Colin and see if there is anything I can do."

"That's all I ask, Doc. Would eleven o'clock on Saturday morning be okay?"

"That's fine. I'll make sure that is my last appointment for the day. After my examination is complete, I am going to take you and Colin out to lunch at Mary's if you have the time."

"Both of us will look forward to it, Doc. I think Colin has only seen Mary once since he has been back in town. He has always liked her like a second mom."

"Good. Then I will see you both on Saturday. I'm looking forward to spending the afternoon with the two of you and have some fun."

"Okay, Doc. I'm going to head back to the ranch because it's getting late. Even with Pa nearly mended, there's still work to be done. So, we will see you Saturday, Doc."

Alicia left Cheyenne at around half past one in the afternoon. The morning had turned into a gorgeous afternoon. The sky didn't have a cloud in sight and although it was hot, there was little humidity so it was still comfortable. This was the first time she wasn't in a hurry to be somewhere at a certain time. So she decided to keep her horse at a walk and enjoy the ride back to the ranch.

As she continued down the trail, she noticed the green and lush pasture grass rolling and swaying from a gentle breeze blowing down the valley. The sun reflected on the mountainsides, giving the rock a reddish hue. There were few trees in the valley since most of it was open range for the remaining ranchers—those who had not given in to Jason Long's pressure to sell or quit. She remembered how much she enjoyed this ride in the past especially when she had taken a leisurely ride with O'Malley.

It was about half an hour into her ride when she noticed the silhouette of a rider coming toward her in the distance. After a few minutes, she once again recognized Thad, probably returning to town after seeing her dad about a job. As they rode up to each other, Thad smiled and said, "Howdy, Miss, I wasn't sure if I'd see ya on the trail. I knew ya hadn't come back to the ranch but wasn't sure how long you'd be in town. I hope ya got everything done that ya wanted."

"I didn't think you'd be at the ranch this long, Thad. I was able to get everything done in town. How about you, Thad? Were you able to talk to my pa about a job?"

"Well, I got to the ranch at about eleven o'clock this morning and met your ma first thing. She told me your pa had ridden out on the range for a few minutes but was comin' in for lunch shortly. Your ma let me sit on the porch to wait and even brought me out some lemonade to drink. Your ma's a real nice and friendly lady. After she brought the lemonade, it was only a few more minutes until your pa rode up. Your ma then let your pa know right off I had come to see if he had room for another hand. He said hello to me and asked your ma if she had any more lemonade. She went into the house to get your pa a glass and then he turned to me and came right to the point. He asked me for my experience with cattle and who I worked for. I told him this last cattle drive I'd been on was also my first. I also added that I was a fast learner and that I had learned a lot on this drive."

"Let me guess, Thad. After you told my pa you were a fast learner, he paused, looked at you with an icy stare and said something like, 'I ain't got any use for ya son if you don't learn fast.'"

"Miss, that's about word for word what he said. Then he told me to go and get some lunch over at the cook's house before I headed back to town."

"Well, Thad, that means he sized you up from your brief conversation and decided he likes you. Did you get the job?"

"Yep, he told me he could use another good hand and the job was mine if I wanted it."

"When do you move out to the ranch and start work?"

"I start work tomorrow. I'm headin' back to town to get my gear together and ride back out early in the morning. Your pa told me to store my gear in the bunkhouse when I get out tomorrow and then go out and help with the branding. Once we get the brandin' done, he said something about getting the herd ready to drive into the railhead as the buyers will be in town."

"Thad, I'm glad you landed the job. I'll be out on the range working with the cattle tomorrow so I'm sure I'll see you then."

"I'd say so, Miss. You have a nice ride back to the ranch."

Alicia rode into the ranch late in the afternoon, washed up, and then pitched in to help her ma prepare dinner. After dinner, Alicia and her ma cleaned up the dinner dishes, washed them, and put them back in the cabinet. Later, they went out to the front porch and sat with Gus and Colin for the rest of the evening until it was time to go to bed.

CHAPTER 14

사랑

Thad must have gotten an early start because he rode into the ranch at about eight o'clock the next morning. Alicia had finished helping her ma in the kitchen. She had just put on her work clothes when she saw him ride up from the parlor window. She walked out onto the front porch and yelled hi to him.

"Howdy, Miss. Looks like all the hands are out already. Can you tell me where I can store my gear and point me in the direction of where your pa's at?"

"Sure thing, the bunkhouse is that long building over there. Have you had anything to eat this morning?"

"I ate some jerky I had in my saddlebags on the way out here. That'll do me until the noon meal."

"Come along with me, Thad. You can unload your gear in the bunkhouse on any of the empty beds. After you unload your gear, let's walk over and see Moses, our cook. I'm sure he will have some coffee on the stove and maybe even some leftovers from breakfast."

"That suits me fine, Miss, just lead the way."

Thad dropped his gear on the first empty bunk he spotted in the bunkhouse and then went out and joined Alicia. They made their way to the cookhouse where Moses was cleaning up from breakfast.

"Moses, Moses? Are you here?" Alicia called out as she opened the door.

"Well, how's the prettiest Asian girl I've ever known?" Moses said as he walked out from the kitchen into the eating area where the ranch hands had finished breakfast just a while ago.

"Oh, I didn't know you had someone with you. I'm Moses, and you are?" Moses asked as he reached out to shake hands.

"My name's Thad, and I'm the new ranch hand. I was just hired. Gus brought me over here yesterday and fixed me something to eat late in the morning while you had taken the noon meal out to the hands. I'm pleased to meet you, Moses."

"I thought someone had been here, and it doesn't surprise me it was Gus. Whenever he makes something, he never cleans up after himself."

"Moses, Thad rode out here this morning and hasn't had anything to eat except some jerky he had in his saddlebags. I know everyone else has eaten and it's past breakfast time but could you fix him something to eat?" asked Alicia, giving Moses her best sad puppy look.

"Well, Thad, take it from me, when Miss Alicia gives you that look, there's not much you can do other than give in to what she wants. I haven't cleaned the dishes or pots and pans. I've got eggs, bacon, potatoes, and some biscuits left. Why don't you sit down, and I'll rustle up some grub."

"Much obliged, sir. I guess I could eat a little."

"Young man, if we're going to get along, you'll drop the sir and just call me Moses like everyone else on the ranch."

"Sure thing, Moses. I sure don't want to get on the wrong foot with the man who feeds me."

Moses chuckled at this and then said, "You'll get along just fine, Thad."

Moses cooked up some breakfast, and the three of them sat down. While Thad ate, Moses had some coffee and Alicia some tea, which he had brewed specifically for her.

After Thad had finished eating, everyone pitched in and cleaned up the dishes. Afterward, Alicia took him out to the horses, and they rode out to see Gus. As soon as they spotted Gus, they rode up to him. He welcomed Thad and told him to begin his work with the rest of the ranch hands. Alicia rode over to where a group of hands were still branding cattle and got to work.

She took some good-natured ribbing from the hands because taking care of Thad had delayed her by an hour. She gave as well as she got and told the boys she could start an hour late and still do as much work as they did in a day. Everyone laughed and then got back to work for the rest of the day.

By the end of the day, Alicia and the group of hands she was working with had gotten the rest of the cattle branded. They cooled off the branding irons, put out the fires, and headed back to get the grub they knew Moses would have ready for them.

Upon returning to the ranch, the hands went to the bunkhouse to wash up as they had learned long ago Moses does not serve food to smelly cowhands. Alicia went to the barn, took the saddle off the mare, and gave her to Colin for a rubdown before getting cleaned up. She then went to the main house where her ma had prepared dinner for the four of them. Gus arrived at the same time but as usual had insisted on taking care of his own horse.

When the four of them sat down to dinner, there was some light conversation about the day's activities. Alicia turned to Colin and asked if he'd like to go into town tomorrow.

"Y-y-y-yeah," replied Colin.

Gus and Sarah looked at each other.

"Ma...Pa, I'd like to take Colin with me to have Doc O'Malley give him an examination. I thought it might be good to see if his opinion was different from when the accident had happened."

"But dear, Colin saw Dr. Williams many times until he retired. He also saw the doctors at the facility he stays at when he's at school," replied Sarah.

"Dr. O'Malley is from one of the finest medical schools back east, and he keeps up with all the medical changes and new information. I'd like you to trust me on this. Living back east for the last five years has shown me the difference between a western doctor and a doctor trained back east. It couldn't hurt to have Dr. O'Malley look at Colin," said Alicia.

"How about you, Colin? Would you like to go into town and visit Dr. O'Malley?" asked Gus.

"O-o-o-okay, that's fine," replied Colin.

"All right, brother of mine, we'll get up early and take the buckboard in. After we see the doctor, we can go over and have lunch at Mary's. I think she's only seen you once since you've been back, and I know she'd love to visit with you."

"Okay, sister, w-w-we need to go to bed early."

"Okay, Alicia. Tomorrow's Saturday, and I don't see any reason why Colin can't go into town for the day with his sister. Just be careful for both of you as we all know there could be some trouble."

"Don't worry, Pa. I plan on going to Dr. O'Malley first as he has set his last appointment to see Colin just before lunch. Then it's over to Mary's for lunch and after we eat, I'm going to stop by the marshal's office to find out if there's anything new."

"Alicia, why don't you let the marshal do his job? I'm sure if there was anything new, he'd come out and let us know."

"I know, Pa, but I might as well stop by his office to see if he has anything to say."

"Okay, okay. Like I said, just be careful," said Gus.

"Gus, why don't you take Colin and relax on the porch. Alicia and I can take care of cleaning up the kitchen," said Sarah.

With that, Gus and Colin got up and took their plates, placing them in the sink. They then headed out to the porch to wait for Sarah and Alicia to join them. "Ma, don't you think Pa and Colin should help us clean up the kitchen and wash the dishes?"

"Sweetheart, I tried that once and by the time your pa and Colin got through, I think I had half the dishes broken and the other half still dirty. So since that episode, I decided the dishes would be cleaner and less expensive if I did them. I really don't mind washing the dishes. Your pa is back out on the ranch full time now and is teaching Colin how to feed the animals and brush down the horses for the ranch hands as part of his chores. So, we silently have an understanding that I'll take care of the house and your pa takes care of the ranch. As the years of marriage continue, husbands and wives accept each other's strengths and weaknesses along with their different feelings without having to talk about them. That's what marriage is about. But the most important part of marriage is love and friendship. I truly like your pa and love him with all my heart, and I know he feels the same about me. I think I may have given you the long answer as to why I don't mind doing the dishes. I hope when you find the right man, you will be blessed with the same loving relationship your pa and I have. Now, let's finish up these dishes and join the boys."

On Saturday morning, O'Malley was up bright and early in anticipation of his routine patient visits. He was also looking forward to Alicia's visit with Colin. It was not a busy morning and by ten o'clock, O'Malley had dispensed with the last patient. As he was closing the front door, he saw Jason Long riding up. Curious, he remained at the front door and opened it as Jason was crossing the porch.

"Hello, Doctor. I was wondering if I could see you this morning."

"Certainly, Mr. Long. My services are available to everyone in town. Please come in, and I'll see if I can help you."

As they both walked into the waiting room, Jason turned toward O'Malley. "I'm concerned about your friend Alicia. I think she is getting into things she shouldn't. Last night, the marshal arrested Vic's brother over a minor altercation, which occurred a week ago regarding some damages to a saloon. The marshal made this arrest after your friend visited him. Anyone who caused damages while fighting was always allowed to pay for it on payday in the past. I don't want anyone to get hurt, so I ask you what you know about this."

"Mr. Long, I am sure you must understand that what goes on between the marshal and another individual is between them. I would suggest instead of wasting your time here, you go talk to the marshal. Now, unless you have an ailment I can treat you for, I bid you good-bye and please avail yourself to leave by the front door."

"Very well, Doctor, but I suggest you take me seriously. I will not tolerate any interference involving my business operations from anyone. Good day to you, Doctor." Jason then opened the door and walked out to his horse.

O'Malley walked back to his exam room and cleaned up the area in preparation for Colin's visit. By eleven o'clock, O'Malley had everything in order and as he walked out to the waiting room, he saw Alicia and Colin pulling up in their buckboard through the front door. He walked out to greet them.

Alicia had already gotten down and was helping Colin get out of the wagon. When O'Malley asked if he could help, Alicia said she could handle it. After Colin got down, O'Malley stepped toward him and offered to shake his hand.

"Hello, Colin, do you remember me? I'm Doc O'Malley. How are you doing today?"

Colin looked at O'Malley, hesitating for a moment and then shook his hand with a smile crossing his face. Colin glanced at the ground and softly replied, "F-f-f-fine."

"Well, why don't you and your sister come in, and we'll talk awhile. Maybe we can go see Mary and have a bite to eat for lunch afterward. Would you like that, Colin?"

Colin's eyes brightened and with a big smile he blurted, "Yes!" He then turned to Alicia and said, "Alicia! We go see Mary and eat lunch, honey?" asked Colin.

"That's the most he has said all the way out here from the ranch. Yes, Colin, after you and Doc talk, we will eat at Mary's. But first, Doc's going to look at your eyes, ears, and throat and check you over to make sure you're good and strong. It won't take a long time. So, let's go into the house."

They walked into the house and stood for a moment inside the door. "Doc, should we take Colin back to your exam room?"

"Sure. C'mon, Colin, we'll leave your sister out here in the waiting room, and you and I can go back here so I can take a good look at you."

Colin walked with O'Malley to the exam room, and Alicia took a seat to wait. O'Malley had him sit up on the exam table and began to examine him to see if there was anything that he could do to improve his condition.

Alicia took a seat in the front room, which also served as a patient waiting room during office hours and a parlor at all other times. She looked around the room and could see O'Malley had tried to decorate but lacked the ability to make it look like a family home instead of a doctor's waiting room. There were a couple of upholstered chairs in two corners and lining the wall across from the front window, were six straight back wooden chairs she assumed were set up for patients. The walls were decorated with a few general scenery pictures and a few hanging knickknacks. There was a couch against the wall between two upholstered chairs and between each chair and the couch was an end table. She thought the room could really use some attention as the best word she could use to describe it would be plain.

As she continued to look around the room, she noticed a newspaper lying on one of the end tables. She walked over and picked it up, noticing it was today's paper. Either O'Malley had purchased it or it was left behind by one of his morning patients. She picked up the paper and looked at the front page. As she glanced over it, an article jumped out at her. It read, "Saloon Brawler Arrested." The article went on to say how Marshal Jackson arrested Rory Mason for a brawl that occurred last week. The other man involved in the fight did not press charges. However, there remained fifty dollars worth of property damage to the saloon. Eyewitnesses reported Rory going into the saloon at approximately 7:00 p.m. and spending his weekly wages on liquor. At around 8:00 p.m., Marshal Jackson entered the saloon while making his usual rounds. Rory was at the bar with his back toward the front entrance. One of the saloon patrons said the marshal recognized Rory. Walking right up to him, he removed Rory's gun from his holster and informed him in a quiet but commanding voice that he was under arrest. Rory Mason turned around with a surprised and angry look toward the marshal, asking why he was being arrested. The marshal informed Mr. Mason he had not paid the saloon owner for the damage he had caused a week ago. Rory must have decided to go along peacefully as the article did not mention Rory resisting arrest.

So, the marshal was successful as he had predicted. Alicia gave the article some thought and decided to call on the marshal after they had lunch at Mary's. While she was lost in thought, O'Malley and Colin appeared in the parlor.

"It took longer than I thought, but Colin and I wanted to make sure everything was working and in good order. How about it, Colin? Did we have some fun listening to your heart and checking your reflexes with that little hammer?"

"S-s-s-sister, I had fun with Doc. I-I-I could hear my heart with that thing he put on my chest and the two things he put in my ears. C-c-c-can we go to Mary's and eat?"

"Sure we can, Colin. Doc, why don't we walk down to Mary's? It's just a short walk, and I could certainly use it to stretch my legs after that long ride in from the ranch."

"Sure, Alicia. You can leave the buckboard out front and come back after lunch."

"That sounds good. Let's get going to lunch."

They left for the walk down to Mary's. When Mary saw Colin come through the front door, she ran out from behind the counter and called his name several times as she ran toward him with arms outstretched to envelop him in a huge bear hug.

"Colin, how is my favorite man doing?" Mary asked as she stepped back, with her hands still on his shoulders.

His grin filled his face, and he stepped forward and gently hugged Mary without saying a word.

"Well, folks, come on in and have a seat. I hope you're all here for lunch," said Mary.

"I knew you'd want to see my brother, Mary, knowing how much he adores you."

"You're right. Colin and I always got along fine. Have a seat here at the counter. The specials are written on the board behind the counter and here's a menu with the rest of your choices. Colin, I know just what you would like. It's that special fried hamburger sandwich with melted cheese on top. Would that be okay for you to eat?"

"Sure, M-M-Mary. That's fine. I'm hungry now!" exclaimed Colin.

"You all heard my man. Now, what would you two like to order?"

"Mary, I'll take the stew but only if it comes with some of your homemade biscuits," replied Alicia.

"Honey, I always include a couple of biscuits with the stew so I'll put you down for the stew. Now how about you, Doc?"

"Mary, I'm pretty hungry so I think I'll have one of your thick steaks with potatoes."

"Sounds good, Doc. I'll get those orders cooked up and be back in a few minutes." Mary walked through the swinging doors to the kitchen.

Doc looked at Alicia after Mary had entered the kitchen. "I had a visitor this morning who dropped by and was not sick or injured. He just wanted me to give you a message about the questions you're asking around town."

"Are you telling me Jason stopped by to see you?"

"He sure did, and he was a bit upset over you trying to find out who shot your pa. Jason intimated it would be better for you to drop the subject altogether. He also wanted to know why the marshal had arrested Rory last night on a petty property damage charge. If this is part of your plan, it certainly has gotten under Jason's skin. Why do you think Jason's so mad?"

"Doc, I think after we eat, I'll go over and have a talk with the marshal about his arresting Rory."

Mary came out of the kitchen carrying three plates of food, including drinks, to their table. "Here you go, folks, the best food in the west if I do say so myself!"

"As usual, Mary, the food looks good and smells great," replied O'Malley.

Mary thanked him for the compliment and then went back to the kitchen to continue cooking for the other customers. She came out a few minutes later to see if everything was all right and if they needed anything. Nothing more was needed, and Mary walked over to the other side of the restaurant to take an order from some folks who had come in for lunch.

"Alicia, I need to drive out to the Stimsons this afternoon to see how she is doing. She's due to have a baby in just a few days and Mr. Stimson is extremely nervous since this is their first. So if you'd like me to go over to the marshal's office with you, we'll have to do it right after we finish here so I'll still have time to see her."

"I won't need you to come with me, Doc. I don't plan on being long. Colin and I will make it a short visit. I just want to see what he plans on doing regarding Rory. Let's finish our meal, and we can both go about our business."

O'Malley was taken aback by the abruptness of Alicia's reply but decided not to make an issue of it. Instead, he changed the subject to Colin's exam results. From a physical standpoint, Colin was slender with hardly an ounce of fat on him. His biceps were not pronounced but tough and strong as iron. His leg and abdominal muscles were just as strong. The injury to his head had left a scar, which was not visible unless the hair is pulled back. Colin's physical condition was excellent. The damage to the head had caused some sort of injury to the brain causing his current condition.

"Unfortunately, I have little information, which would identify a treatment to help you, Colin. Maybe, the future will hold a cure to help you, but right now, there is nothing we can do to improve your condition," said O'Malley.

Colin looked at Alicia and said, "What did he say?"

"Doc said you're as strong and healthy as any man in town. So, big brother, you're still my hero."

They returned to their lunch, talking about things that were going on around town. O'Malley asked Colin what he did at the ranch during the day. Colin explained that his father had put him in charge of the barn where he took care of the horses and made sure the stalls were kept clean. He also explained how he brushed down the horses for the ranch hands after they took off the saddles for him.

Colin would talk to the horses as he rubbed them down and brushed them. All the hands noticed how well he treated their horses and provided them the best care they had ever received. Alicia knew about this as the ranch hands had expressed this to her and had also told her how surprised they were considering Colin's condition. The hands told Alicia it was as if the horses sensed Colin was different, and they acted very calm and patient with him.

The rest of the lunch touched on routine topics while they continued eating. When they had finished, O'Malley offered to pay, but Alicia insisted on buying lunch. However, when Mary came out, she told them the lunch was on the house since they had brought Colin with them. They thanked her for her generosity and then got up to leave.

They stopped outside the front door of Mary's Café to say good-bye and go on their separate ways.

"Alicia, I know we haven't had much time to be alone, but I think things are going to come to a head shortly, and I hope I can start seeing more of you. In fact, there's an ice cream social coming up next Sunday, and I was wondering if I could take you. It would be right after Mass and since you're going to be in town anyway—"

"Doc, I'd love to go with you," Alicia interrupted him before he could finish his sentence.

"That's great! I'll see you next week, and we can have a relaxing day," replied O'Malley.

"Actually, you'll see me tomorrow unless you're not going to attend Mass."

"You're right. I will see you tomorrow since it will be Sunday. Well, I've got to head out to the Stimsons. You two be careful in town, and Colin, take good care of your sister."

"I w-w-w-will, Doc," Colin replied.

Alicia stepped toward O'Malley, lifted herself on her toes, and kissed him on his left cheek. "You take care of yourself too, Doc. I look forward to seeing you tomorrow and at the ice cream social next week."

As they parted, Doc walked back to his office to get his buggy, and Alicia and Colin walked to the marshal's office. As they made their way to the marshal's, she noticed Colin still walked with an uneasy left-sided limp, which was slight but noticeable. It reminded Alicia he had walked this way ever since his injury. They stepped onto the boardwalk and walked the short distance to the marshal's office.

When they arrived, Alicia asked Colin if he'd mind sitting in one of the straight-backed wooden chairs next to the front door. He said his usual "fine" and sat down in the chair as Alicia walked into the office.

Marshal Jackson was in his usual chair doing paperwork at his desk. "Well, hello, Alicia. I was wondering when you would stop by. Have you heard the news about Rory's arrest?"

"Colin and I came in late this morning to see Doc, and then the three of us had lunch at Mary's. I read about the arrest in the paper while I was at Doc's office this morning. So how are we going to do this, Marshal?"

"Well, Rory's sober now and locked up in the cell in the back. Alicia, you leave it to me, and we'll see if this works. I hear Vic is coming over this afternoon to post bail. When he comes in, I'll let him know there will not be bail for Rory since I'm charging him with attempted murder. Then we just sit back and wait to see what happens."

"Have you told Rory you're going to charge him with attempted murder?"

"Not yet, Alicia, I thought I'd wait until Vic got here and then spring it on him to see what his reaction will be."

"Marshal, I think you should let Rory know about the new charge now. Then he can talk to Vic when he visits, and he'll find out what has happened."

"That might be a good idea."

The marshal moved from behind his desk and opened the door leading to the cells. It was a short walk to the cell where Rory was being held. The jail was small with one cell on each side of the corridor and one cell at the back where Marshal Jackson had placed him. Rory was lying on the cell cot. He stepped to the bars when he saw the marshal walk toward him. "Ain't it about time you let me outta here?"

"Rory, I think you got more to worry about than you think since I'm charging you with the attempted murder of Gus."

"You're what? You can't put that on me. I ain't done nothin' to Gus. You get Vic and Jason real quick. I want to talk to them now."

"I'm sure you do, Rory, but I think you ought to see a lawyer first."

"You just get Vic and Jason over here."

"Rory, I ain't your errand boy. Besides, I heard Vic is coming over to see you this afternoon. So you can wait until he shows up."

"Marshal, you can't hold me for attempted murder. You don't have any evidence against me."

"Sorry, Rory, but I found the evidence I need to hold you. We found the rifle that was used to shoot Gus, and we can track it back to you."

"You're crazy, Marshal! I don't even own a Henry rifle."

"How'd you know it was a Henry? I only said we found the rifle that was used to shoot Gus."

Rory's eyes got wider as he stammered, "You just get my brother in here. I'm not answering any more questions."

"That's just fine, Rory. I'll send Vic in as soon as he gets here."

The marshal then walked back to his office, closing the door to the cells behind him. "I figure you must have heard what went on back there. You think he's a bit nervous?"

"I'd say he got really nervous when you told him you hadn't mentioned what type of rifle it was. I think you hit a raw nerve."

Just then, the door opened and Jason Long, followed by Vic, walked into the marshal's office.

"Good afternoon, Marshal, Miss Alicia. I hear you have arrested Vic's brother Rory for that scuffle he had at the saloon. I hear you're holding him because he hasn't paid the damages. I'm here to pay those damages and get Rory released. I understand the damages amounted to about fifty dollars. Here you go, I brought cash. Now, I'd like you to release Rory to us."

"You are correct, Jason. That is the amount of the damages. But I think you may want to speak to your brother, Vic. He has something to tell you. Follow me back to the cells, Vic." Marshal Jackson got the cell door keys and took Vic back to Rory's cell.

Jason looked at Alicia. "I'm surprised to see you in town, young lady. More so, that you're here in the marshal's office. I explained to your doctor friend how things happen to people that don't mind their own business."

"Mr. Long, I made it clear I intend to find the scum who shot my pa. So if you know anything, you better speak up," retorted Alicia.

Vic came from the back after talking to Rory with a worried look on his face. "Jason, they're charging Rory with attempted murder. They said they found the rifle and can trace it back to him."

"That's right, Vic. Maybe my pa will finally get justice."

"Miss, you remember what I just said a minute ago. Unpleasant things do happen to people who don't mind their business."

"You also remember what I said, Mr. Long. I will find the lowlifes that shot my pa."

Vic took a step forward toward Alicia and with a snarl said, "Hey lady, you better watch what you're sayin'. You give Mr. Long some respect."

"You're the one who better simmer down. This conversation is between your boss and Alicia. You make any threats in my office, and you'll be keeping your brother company in the same cell he's in," interrupted the marshal as he returned from the cells.

"All right, all right, let's just settle down. I apologize if I upset you, Miss. It surely won't happen again. I'm certain I speak for Vic also, isn't that right, Vic?" Jason asked.

Vic looked a bit surprised and then looked at Alicia and blurted out, "Yeah, okay."

"All right, Marshal. You have my money, and I take it you're going to drop the property damage charge against Rory. So I'd like to leave now if that's acceptable to you?" asked Jason.

"That's fine, Jason. Of course, we may be very close to finding out who shot Gus."

"Marshal, did I just hear you right? You said you're very close to finding the person who shot Gus. I didn't think the shooter could be identified."

"Not yet, but we think we know where the rifle is, and we can identify the shooter through the rifle," replied the marshal.

"So you don't have the rifle yet?"

"No, Jason, but we got a tip this morning and after you folks leave, I'm goin' down to the livery, get my horse, and head out to pick it up."

"C'mon, Jason, let's get outta here. We got things to do," said Vic.

With that, Jason said good-bye, and both of them left the office. Jason and Vic crossed the street and stopped on the other side where they stood talking. Then abruptly, they went their separate ways with Vic walking directly toward his horse. He quickly mounted and took off at a fast run out of town.

"Marshal, aren't you going after Vic? Won't he lead you right to the rifle we're after?" asked Alicia.

"That's just what I was countin' on. Chet's been in the alley right next to the jail here, and I'm sure he's already on Vic's trail as we speak. As soon as Vic gets to the rifle, I told Chet to arrest him and bring him back with the Henry."

"Are you sure, Marshal? Vic's pretty good with his gun. Is Chet going to bring him in alone?"

"Alicia, I made sure he took a double-barreled shotgun and told him to pick his place really careful and get the drop on Vic. Chet's an excellent hunter and tracker. He'll bring Vic in. I have no doubt about it."

"I sure hope it works out, Marshal. Get word to me when he brings him in. I think I'll get Colin and head back to the ranch."

"Well, I'll walk out with you and say hello to that young man."

CHAPTER 15

사랑

Vic rode north out of Cheyenne as fast as his horse would carry him for about twenty minutes and then slowed to a walk. He looked around him to make sure there was no one in sight. Then he headed off to the right, down a valley that was a few hundred feet wide with hills on either side, ending in a box canyon. About a hundred yards in at the end of the canyon was an dilapidated old shack. He rode up to it, dismounted and approached the front door. He pushed against the door. At first, it wouldn't open. So, he put his shoulder into it and pushed harder. The door was out of level and as it started to open, the bottom of the door scraped across the wood floor, making a screeching sound.

He walked into the one-room shack and looked around. It didn't look like anything had been disturbed since he was here a couple of days ago. Of course, he had no idea how he would know if someone had been there or not. There was no glass in the two windows on opposite walls, and the wind and dust flowed freely through them. He walked toward the wall on the right, took his pistol out, and lightly tapped the barrel against the vertical wooden planks nailed to the wall until he came across one that was loose. He returned the pistol to his holster and took out his pocket knife. He worked it in the groove of the loose board and pried the board out so he could get a hold of it with his left hand. He pulled the board away from the wall and dropped it on the floor.

There in the wall, he could see the oilskin container that held what he was looking for. He reached into the wall cavity and pulled it out, carrying it over to an old, rickety table that had been left behind when the shack had been abandoned by its last occupants.

Placing the oilskin on the table, he unwrapped it and found the Henry rifle. If the marshal somehow knew where this was, it had to be moved to a different location right now.

Chet stopped his horse at the beginning of the valley and tied it to a small tree to the right of the valley entrance. He started up the valley on the right side, walking up the twenty-five-yard slope of the hill. He had a plain view of the valley and the dilapidated shack at the end of the box canyon where he saw Vic's horse tied to a railing. He slowly edged his way toward the end of the canyon, keeping an eye on the shack. About twenty yards from the shack, he saw an outcropping of rock, which he used to take cover behind. He had brought his shotgun along like the marshal instructed and decided to wait and see if Vic would come out.

After about ten minutes, the door opened and out came Vic carrying what looked like a long package. As he approached his horse, Chet stood up from behind the rock and yelled, "Hold it right where you are, Vic. I got a double-barreled shotgun aimed right at your head. From this range, it won't be very pretty if you force me to fire."

"Okay, Chet, I see ya. What's this all about? I was just out for a ride and stopped at the shack to give my horse a rest."

"Put your hands up, Vic. You're trespassing on private property. Didn't you see the 'No Trespassing' sign at the entrance to this place?"

"Ah c'mon, Chet, ya mean ya followed me all the way out here to arrest me for trespassing? This place has been abandoned for at least five years. I don't think anyone even knows who owns it anymore."

"Gee, Vic, I thought you'd recognize the place. This was part of the small ranch owned by the widow Mrs. Schultz, the dressmaker who now has a small shop in town. This was a separate piece of land she and her late husband had. Jason didn't take it after her husband was gunned down on the trail because it was worthless to him. It couldn't be used for grazing or raising cattle, so as far as Jason was concerned, he didn't need it. The widow has kept it all these years for sentimental reasons. So she still owns it, which means you're trespassing. I'm only going to ask you one more time to raise your hands. Put the parcel down and get the hands up."

Vic looked at Chet and wondered if he was quick enough to draw and shoot before Chet could open fire. He decided it was far better to raise his hands. Chet stepped to the side and went around the rock. He slowly started down the slope while keeping the shotgun trained on Vic.

Vic watched him intently to see if he would slip up and give him a chance to take his gun away and overpower him or draw quick enough to shoot him before the deputy could fire his shotgun. Chet walked down the slope carefully. He didn't want to give Vic a chance to draw. When he got down the slope, there were about ten yards of flat open ground between them.

"Vic, I want you to take your left hand and reach down and unbuckle your gun belt. Then drop it to the ground."

As Chet got near, Vic started to unbuckle his gun belt. By the time Chet had reached Vic, the gun belt had been loosened, and it started to fall to the ground. However, Vic had not released it from his grasp. He held on to the tongue part of the belt, which was the belt's right side.

As the left side of the belt slid toward the ground, Vic whipped the belt around, striking Chet on the left side of his head. At the same time, he grabbed the shotgun by its barrel and forced it up into the air. He pushed him backward until he tripped, and both of them fell back on the ground with Vic on top. They hit the ground hard, and Chet lost his grip on the shotgun, which landed about ten feet from them. Chet grabbed him and twisted to his left, rolling Vic in the same direction. He got on top of him and reared back, hitting him with a right cross.

Vic was stunned but quickly realized he needed to get Chet off him. He reached up with his right hand and grabbed a handful of Chet's hair, yanking hard to the right and pulling Chet in the same direction on the ground. Chet also knew he had to get the upper hand in this fight and then remembered he still had his sidearm in the holster.

Vic rolled over on his right side and struck him full in the face with his left fist. He pulled back his left fist to strike again, but Chet saw it coming and rolled to his right, causing Vic to hit the dirt with his left fist. Chet rolled back to his left toward Vic and landed a punch on his face with his right hand. At that point, they grabbed each other and struggled to their feet, each trying to gain the advantage.

As they stood up, Vic grabbed Chet's sidearm with his left hand. Instinctively, Chet grabbed Vic's left wrist with both hands and brought it straight up in the air, pointing the gun at the sky as both men struggled for its control. As they moved around, they moved the gun from side to side, ending up with the gun between them at midsection. Suddenly, a shot rang out and a look of astonishment appeared on each man's face.

"Colin, do you remember Marshal Jackson?" asked Alicia.

"Y-y-yes, Alicia," replied Colin.

"Hello, young man. I haven't seen you in a long time. I think it was last year in the summer when you were back for a visit. How are you doing?"

"F-f-fine, Marshal Jackson."

"Did you like school, Colin?"

"Yes!"

"Colin, your sister told me you take good care of the horses out at the ranch. Do you like horses?"

"They're nice."

"Can you do me a favor, Colin?"

"Yes."

"Your sister told me you and she will be going back to the ranch. I want you to make sure you take real good care of her since you're her big brother," said the marshal.

A big smile crossed Colin's face, and he stepped over to Alicia, spreading his arms and gently hugging his sister while clearly saying, "I will."

They said their good-byes, and Colin and Alicia started walking down the street to O'Malley's house where their buggy had been tied up since their arrival this morning. As they walked back to O'Malley's house, Alicia wondered how Chet was doing going after Vic. She and Colin got to their buckboard. Colin climbed up into the seat while she unhooked the heavy anchor she had put out and untied the horse from the rail. She picked up the anchor, put it away under the seat, and climbed up to sit down. She then took the reins into her hands and released the brake lever, snapping the reins to start the horses and started on their way. About twenty minutes into her ride, she heard a horse coming up at what seemed a full-out run behind them.

The shocked look of astonishment drained from Chet's face as he fell away backward from Vic. He hit the ground hard on his back and rolled over onto his stomach unconscious with blood spreading out from a wound to his midsection. Vic stepped forward with the pistol cocked and aimed it at Chet's head. He kicked Chet's boots and when there was no reaction, he assumed he was dead. He didn't want to shoot again in case the gunshot could be heard by someone. Vic had a sinister smile on his face as he stepped across Chet's body toward his horse.

"I guess I handled that pretty good. Jason sure can't be mad at me about this. After all, he was the one who sent me out here. They might find Chet if the buzzards don't get him first," Vic muttered to himself.

He walked over to his horse and picked up his gun belt, strapping it back on. He then retrieved the oblong oilskin package and used the tie-downs to secure it to the bedroll behind his saddle. He mounted his horse and rode out of the canyon, spotting Chet's horse tied to a small tree. He rode over, untied the horse from the tree, and then slapped its backside as hard as he could. However, instead of running away from the canyon as Vic thought, the horse turned and galloped into the canyon toward the shack.

"That's okay, boy. You're just gonna find your dead owner down there," he said to himself. With that, he galloped off toward Jason's ranch.

A searing burning pain flooded through the lower half of Chet's body as he regained consciousness. He rolled onto his side and immediately doubled up in pain again. He'd never felt such an intense pain in his life. It was even worse than the pain he had experienced when he had broken his left arm and the bone had protruded through the skin. He grabbed his bandana from around his neck and balled it up, pressing it hard against the bullet wound under his left rib cage. After a minute or two, the pain subsided somewhat and he could finally relax the muscles in his abdomen.

Chet slowly propped himself up on his right elbow, but he became immediately dizzy and lay back down. Just then, he saw his horse walking toward him. Chet had named his horse Socks for the four white feet the horse had. He urged Socks to come closer, and the horse slowly kept inching forward until it stood right beside him. He knew he had to get up into the saddle no matter how hard or how painful it was. This was his only chance to save his life before he bled to death.

Well, there was no time like the present, he thought to himself. He rose up again on his right elbow and reached for the stirrup with his left hand. He put his hand in the stirrup, working his arm down until he had slid it all the way to his elbow. He reached up with his right hand and grasped his left wrist. Chet talked to Socks, urging him to walk forward to see if Socks could drag him over to the horse railing. Socks hesitated but with Chet's urging, his horse slowly walked forward.

For Chet, it seemed like eternity before Socks dragged him over to the horse rail. He slipped his left arm out but grasped the stirrup with his right hand to keep Socks from moving. He lay back on his left side to rest, relieving the pain for a few moments. Then he reached up and grasped the horse rail. With both hands, he slowly pulled himself up until he could get his feet under him. He slowly rose up and moved his right hand up, grabbing his saddle horn. He then moved his left hand from the horse rail, also grabbing the saddle horn. Keeping both hands on the horn, Chet leaned his body against the left side of Socks to regain his strength, knowing what he would have to endure next.

Chet knew he needed to act fast as his bleeding had started up again, and he was feeling lightheaded. He leaned back from Socks, lifted his left foot into the stirrup and summoning all his strength lifted himself up, swinging his right leg over the saddle and on the other side of Socks. Chet screamed out from the excruciating pain, which struck him immediately as he settled down in the saddle. Another wave of dizziness came over him, and he slumped forward resting partially on Socks's neck. He reached down with both hands on each side of Socks's neck and grabbed the reins. He tried to sit up but found the pain and dizziness too much to bear so he remained prostrate on Socks's back and neck.

Chet knew he had to get back to Cheyenne as soon as possible, but he also knew he had to go slow to prevent bleeding to death. He managed a slight kick with his heels into Socks's sides and urged him along. The horse started to walk forward while he hung on its neck. Chet hoped he could remain conscious long enough to get back to Cheyenne and Doctor O'Malley.

Alicia looked behind her and saw Marshal Jackson coming up fast at a full run on his horse. She pulled back on the reins and stopped the buckboard, waiting for him to catch up. The marshal pulled back on his horse and stopped next to the buckboard.

"Alicia! Chet just rode in on his horse shot up pretty bad and unconscious. I need to get Doc back to town as soon as I can. I stopped at his office, but he was gone. Do you know where he is?"

"He's on his way to check on Mrs. Stimpson. Would you like me to go after him, Marshal?"

"Na, I know where the Stimpsons live. My horse is faster than your buckboard. I'll get Doc, but I'd sure appreciate it if you'd go back and help look after Chet. Mary's with him now. Doc never locks his door so I put Chet on the bed in the exam room. See if you can help Mary."

"Sure, Marshal, I'll turn around right now and head back."

"Thanks, Alicia. I know a shortcut I can take to cut off Doc." With that, the marshal turned his horse and sped away to go after O'Malley.

Alicia turned the wagon around and snapped the reins, urging the horses into a fast run.

"Hold on, Colin! This might be a little bumpy, but we need to get back to town fast to help Chet."

Colin said nothing but held on tight with the understanding they had to give their friend Chet some help. Within ten minutes, they arrived at O'Malley's and pulled up in front of his house.

Alicia jumped off the wagon in one leap and then turned to face Colin. "Can you get down off the wagon by yourself or do you need a hand?"

"I-I'm fine," replied Colin.

"Okay, Colin. As soon as you get down from there, come into Doc's house and wait in the front room, okay?"

"Okay, Alicia."

She ran into the house where she quickly walked to the exam room in the back. There she found Chet lying on his back unconscious. Mary was leaning over him applying a cool cloth to his forehead and had also removed his shirt and cleaned the wound. However, after applying the cloth to his forehead, Mary went right back to cleaning the wound, trying to stop the bleeding. Each time she wiped the blood away more would come out. Alicia knew they had to do something to stop the blood loss as quickly as possible. Chet's breathing was labored and raspy.

"Honey, I don't know what to do. He's bleedin' awful bad, and I can't get it stopped!" said Mary.

"Let me take a look, Mary, and see if we can come up with something."

Mary gestured for her to come over quickly. She took a couple of steps closer and then saw what the problem was. Chet had a gaping hole in his midsection from a gunshot. She knew they had to do something quickly so she looked around the room and spotted some bandages in a glass cabinet. Alicia stepped over to the cabinet but when she tried to open the door, her hand slid right off the handle.

O'Malley had locked this cabinet because it contained his drugs and medicines. For a second, Alicia laughed to herself. Someone who is so concerned about locking up his medicines forgets to lock the front door to his house. *Oh well, I'll take care of this little problem*, she thought. She stepped back, brought her right knee up, and with a quick front snap kick broke the glass in the cabinet with her shoe. She then reached in carefully, unlocked the door, and retrieved several boxes of gauze, bandages, and tape. She brought the supplies over to where Chet lay.

"Mary, there's so much blood. Do you know if the bullet is still in Chet or did it come out through his back?"

"I don't know, honey. Chet was here flat on his back when I got here from the café."

"Okay, Mary. Hand me that towel next to you and help me roll him a little bit on his side so I can see if the bullet passed through his body and out his back."

They rolled Chet onto his side while Alicia wiped the blood off his lower back. There was no hole in the back, which meant the bullet was still in him. They eased him slowly over onto his back.

Alicia looked at Mary. "Chet is in very bad shape, Mary. That bullet has to come out quick, or I don't think he's going to make it."

"I've helped with broken legs and arms and bandaged cuts and wounds, but I've never dug a bullet out of anyone," replied Mary.

"Neither have I, Mary. I wish my mom was here. She's taken bullets out of ranch hands, my dad's leg when he was accidently shot while hunting, and even an Indian who had been beaten up, shot, and left to die on our ranch. We have two choices. We can pack the wound and bandage it in hopes that Doc will return in time to remove the bullet, or we can try to remove it, bandage the wound, and hope for the best. I don't think Chet will make it if we wait for Doc to get back without taking that bullet out. I saw his surgical instruments in the cabinet that I broke into to get the bandages. What do you think we should do?"

"If you don't think he will live until Doc gets back, then we have to try and help him. You get the stuff you need out of Doc's cabinet and let's go to work."

Alicia turned to the cabinet, opened the door, and looked at all the surgical instruments lying on the shelf. After deciding what she would need, she reached in and removed those instruments she thought she would use to work on Chet. At the same time, Mary brought over a table next to where Chet lay for Alicia to put the instruments on. She placed a towel on the table and then laid out the instruments.

She remembered O'Malley telling her he had to use a long metal probe to locate the bullet and determine how far in the body it was. Alicia saw the instrument she was looking for, picked it up, and stepped over to the table.

"Mary, I'm not sure if this will work, but I intend to put this into the bullet hole and try to locate the slug that is in Chet. He's unconscious so I don't think he will move, but I'd like you to hold down his legs just to make sure he doesn't move."

Mary moved to where she could grasp the legs just above the knees. Alicia looked at the bullet wound and while Mary put pressure on the legs, she slowly inserted the metal probe deeper and deeper until it finally met an obstruction. When the probe hit the obstruction, she realized the probe had met with the bullet. She kept the probe still and looked at the rest of the instruments and spied what looked like a pair of scissors that was flat on the inside. She instinctively knew this long-necked, clamp-type instrument would be exactly what she needed in her attempt to remove the bullet.

"Mary, I think I have found the bullet. I'm going to put this instrument into the wound and try to get hold of it. Keep holding down his legs because I don't want to make it worse if he jerks while I'm in there."

"You go ahead, honey. Chet's not breathing very well so we need to be quick about it."

Alicia picked up the clamp device and slowly inserted it next to the probe to get a hold of the slug.

Marshal Jackson was running his horse at full speed without regard for his safety or that of the horse. He was right to take the shortcut he knew because as he came over the top of a small hill, he could see a horse-drawn buggy on a trail that looked to be about a mile ahead. He kept his horse galloping at full speed down the other side of the hill and straight toward O'Malley. He thought about taking his .44 Colt out of his holster and firing it to alert O'Malley, but he was afraid it might make him whip his horses into a full gallop, thinking there was an outlaw after him. So the marshal spurred his horse to go even faster and was able to pull up behind O'Malley's buggy in just a couple of minutes.

"Doc, Doc! Hold up! It's Tom, and I need to talk to you."

O'Malley pulled back on the reins, stopping the buggy. He leaned out to talk to the marshal. "Tom, what's this all about?"

"Doc, I need you to turn around and head back to your office right now. Chet came back into town slumped over his horse. He's been shot, and his saddle and horse are covered in blood. Me and some other men got him down and carried him over to your house. The house was unlocked, so we took him in and put him in the back room where you do your surgery. Doc, let's get your rig turned around and get back pronto."

"Okay, Tom. You lead the way, and I'll go as fast as I can."

"Doc, you need to go it alone. I've had this horse running at full speed to catch up with you. I've got to give her some grain and a little rest before we go another foot."

With that, O'Malley snapped the reins and turned his buggy around, heading back to town as fast as he could.

"Mary! I think I can feel the bullet against the clamp. I'm going to open the clamp and see if I can get a hold of it and bring it out."

Mary looked up, smiled slightly and said, "I know you can do it, honey. Get it out of there and then let's get him bandaged up."

Alicia opened the clamp and moved it slightly down then closed it on what she thought was the slug and started to pull back. She assumed the bullet would slide out easily, but it appeared to be stuck just like a boot stuck in swamp mud. Trying to pull the boot out with sudden force, the foot would come out, but the boot would remain. However, slowly wiggling it back and forth, sideways, and twisting it while pulling at the same time, the boot comes out gradually.

Alicia tried this method, with her clamp tightly clasped around the bullet. She wiggled the bullet in all directions while pulling with a firm, constant pressure. Just like the boot in the swamp, she could feel the bullet starting to come out. Suddenly, as if the bullet had become tired of the fight, it came free all at once. Alicia held the bullet at the end of the clamp. She had removed the probe when the clamp had closed on the bullet so it would not be in the way. She placed the clamp, still holding the bullet, on the table next to the rest of the medical instruments. Blood was still coming out of the wound but at a much-reduced flow.

"Mary, the only other thing I know to do is to pack the wound and bandage it tightly. That may stop or slow down the bleeding."

"Let's get to it, Alicia. We need to get this done as soon as possible."

They packed the bullet hole and wrapped bandages around Chet's body.

O'Malley kept snapping the reins and yelling at Dollar to go faster. Dollar was running as fast as she could, and O'Malley knew it. If Chet was bleeding as bad as Marshal Jackson had indicated, he'd be lucky to reach him while he was still alive. It was about a thirty-minute wild drive back to town, but Dollar kept up at full speed until reaching his house.

He fiercely yanked back on the reins, almost causing Dollar to stumble as she and the buggy came to an abrupt halt. He grabbed his bag as he leaped out of the buggy and ran toward the front door, pushing the door open. He ran straight down the hall into the exam room where he found Mary and Alicia cleaning up the room.

What a sight it was. There was blood on the floor along with gauze and bandage remnants. Chet was on his back bandaged up, and his surgical tools lay on the table next to him. There were glass shards on the floor, and he noticed the broken cabinet door where his supplies and surgical instruments were kept.

"Alicia! Mary! What's going on here?"

"Chet was in real bad shape, Doc. Alicia and I did our best, but he kept getting worse and worse so we decided to try and take the bullet out ourselves. I should say, Alicia took the bullet out, and I held Chet down to make sure he didn't move. She worked real hard and careful not to make him worse. All her hard work seemed to pay off because she was able to pull that slug out. Then we packed the bullet hole up and bandaged him as tight as we could."

O'Malley walked over to the table and set his bag down next to his surgical instruments. "Let's get these bandages off so I can take a look at your handiwork, ladies."

They helped to cut off and remove the bandages, and O'Malley removed the gauze packing Mary and Alicia had inserted in the wound to stem the flow of blood. O'Malley examined the wound and could see the bleeding had stopped completely. He turned to the table and looked at the bullet closely. The slug was in one piece, which meant there were no fragments to remove.

O'Malley looked up and said, "Ladies, this was fine work. I don't think I could have done any better. All he needs is some stitches now, which will protect the wound from infection and start the healing process. I'll get the stitches and finish this up. As soon as I get him sewn up, I'll check him to see if there is anything else that needs attention."

It took about ten minutes for O'Malley to sew up Chet. Then he listened to his heart and examined the rest of him for any other injuries.

"The only wound Chet has is the gunshot wound, but he's in awful shape from the loss of blood. We'll keep him here for at least a week."

"Do you want me to stay here tonight and help with Chet?"

"No, Mary, I'll sit up with him tonight so I can attend to him if he takes a turn for the worse. You can go back to the café and Alicia can get back to the ranch with Colin."

"Oh my goodness, I forgot Colin is in the front room," said Alicia.

"When I ran into the house a few minutes ago, I noticed Colin out of the corner of my eye. I think he was sitting quietly in one of the chairs."

"No need for you and Colin to stay. I'll help Doc clean up the mess in the back room. You get started, Alicia. You have a two-hour ride back to the ranch and if you don't get started, your folks are goin' to be worried," said Mary.

"All right, you two, Colin and I will get started for the ranch. Doc, I'll see you at church tomorrow, and you can let me know how Chet is doing."

Alicia and Colin said their good-byes and went out to the buckboard where they climbed up, took their seat, and headed back to the ranch.

After they were out of town, Colin looked at Alicia and said, "I-I-Is Chet sick, sister?"

"Some person shot Chet with a gun, and he is very sick. Doc is going to do everything he can to make Chet get well."

"I-I-I hope Doc can make Chet better."

Marshal Jackson allowed his horse to rest for an hour, giving it some grain he always carried in his saddlebags along with some water he poured into his hat from his canteen. The marshal had learned many years ago from tracking outlaws to carry extra grain for his horse in case they wound up in an area that had no grazing grass.

After the hour was up, the marshal mounted up and headed back to town. He knew there wasn't anything he could do for Chet that O'Malley wasn't already doing. He started the horse at a normal walk back to town. It took him an hour and a half to get back to O'Malley's house.

He tied up his horse on the rail in front of O'Malley's house and knocked on the front door. O'Malley opened the door.

"Doc, how's Chet? I just got in and came straight here."

"He's unconscious, Tom. He's in a very serious condition. Only time will tell. I give him a slight chance if he makes it through the night. His major problem is the large amount of blood loss. If Alicia had not gotten that bullet out, I suspect he would have been dead before I got back into town."

"Wait a minute, Doc. What do you mean Alicia got the bullet out?"

"That's right, Tom. Alicia took out the bullet with Mary's help. Apparently, they were getting worried as time went on and I had not returned. I asked Mary why they had decided to take the bullet out on their own, and she said he was bleeding and they couldn't stop it. She also said his breathing was raspy and every breath was a struggle. So as time went by and Chet kept getting worse, Alicia told Mary she thought he would die unless they removed the bullet. So she broke into my cabinet, got my medical instruments out, and removed the bullet. She and Mary then packed the wound with gauze and bandaged him up. I'm going to sit up with him tonight in case he takes a turn for the worse."

"Doc, was he ever conscious enough to say who did this to him?"

"No, Tom. He hasn't come to as long as I've been here, and Mary and Alicia told me he was unconscious when they brought him to my office. So, no, he hasn't said a word about how he got shot."

"Doc, when he wakes up, I want you to get a hold of me right away so I can find out who shot him. I suspect it was Vic since that's who Chet went after."

"Tom, I can't promise he'll wake up. As I said before, he's seriously wounded. I'll let you know how he is tomorrow morning."

"Okay, Doc. Let me know how he's doing either way first thing in the morning. I'm headin' back to my office, and I'll be there all night. So if Chet wakes up during the night, let me know so I can talk to him."

"Sure thing, Tom, but I wouldn't count on him waking up tonight. He might be unconscious for a couple of days."

"Okay, Doc, I'll see you sometime tomorrow."

The marshal left and went back to his office. O'Malley returned to sit up with Chet.

❁ ❁ ❁

Vic rode back to Jason Long's ranch with his package. It was midafternoon, and he knew Jason wouldn't be returning from the bank for a couple of hours, so he went to the bunkhouse where he stashed the long parcel under the mattress in his bunk. He then went back outside and sat down in one of the chairs outside the bunkhouse to wait for Jason.

As soon as Jason heard the commotion outside, he went to investigate what the excitement was all about. When he found out Chet had been shot but was still alive, he returned to the bank to think about what his next move would be. He also wanted to be there in case Vic was stupid enough to come back to town. He sat at his desk, wondering what possessed Vic to shoot Chet.

He assumed Vic had shot Chet. Although he wouldn't know for sure until he talked to Vic. After a while, he was sure Vic wasn't coming into town so he closed up his office, left the bank, and started riding back to his ranch.

Jason's ranch was only a mile out of town so he came in sight of his house in less than twenty minutes. As he got closer, he recognized Vic's horse tied to the rail in front of the house. He rode his horse up beside Vic's, dismounted, and tied his reins to the same rail. When he started walking toward his house, he heard someone call his name. He turned in the direction of the voice and saw Vic sitting in a chair in front of the bunkhouse across the yard.

"Mr. Long! Over here!" Vic said as he gestured toward Jason to come over to him.

Jason walked across the gravel yard toward Vic, hearing the crunch of gravel under his shoes. "Vic! What happened to you and where have you been?"

"You sent me out to that shack to pick up the Henry. I got out there and picked it up when Chet showed up with a double-barreled shotgun on me."

"So you shot him? That was smart."

"Boss, you gotta believe me, I had no choice. I know he's dead. He was gut shot from close up and bleedin' like a fast flowin' stream. If I knew he was alive, I would have finished him off."

"Well Vic, that just might turn into a major problem. Chet's unconscious, and Doc says he may or may not make it through the night. If he lives through the night, the marshal will be looking for you after he talks to Chet. If that's the case, there isn't a thing I can do for you, Vic."

"Don't worry, boss. I know how to handle this."

"Vic, I don't want to know anything about it. You just make sure this problem is taken care of."

"Don't worry, like I said, I know exactly what to do, boss."

CHAPTER 16

사랑

O'Malley fetched some blankets from a hall closet and then moved a chair into the exam room where he was going to spend the night. He looked at Chet and put a blanket over him to make sure he was comfortable after checking his vital signs. He seemed to be sleeping comfortably and his breathing was improving. The color in his face was markedly better. He was starting to feel hopeful that Chet would recover from his wound, but he knew he had to check on him a couple of times during the night to make sure he was stable.

He dimmed the lamp so he could still see in the dark and went back to his chair. He settled down and spread a blanket over him, knowing he would have a fitful night of sleep. It was uncomfortable at first, but he eventually got used to the chair and started to nod off.

It was about one o'clock in the morning when O'Malley seemed to sense someone outside. He was not fully awake. He was more in a dreamlike state—too tired to wake himself up. All of a sudden, there was a breaking of glass and the sound of three pistol shots rang out in quick succession. O'Malley woke from his stupor and saw the bullets hitting the blanket on the exam table.

❁ ❁ ❁

The marshal sat up with a start, throwing his legs onto the floor on the edge of the bed. He shook his head from side to side to clear it. He then stood up and got dressed quickly. He could have sworn he heard shots fired. He got up, strapped on his gun belt and walked to the door. But before he opened it, a thought occurred to him. He turned and walked over to the gun rack, unlocked it, and removed one of the 8-gauge shotguns. If he ran into any trouble, he'd have plenty of firepower to deal with it. He walked back to the door, opened it, and slowly stepped out onto the boardwalk.

He looked both ways down the street but saw no activity. Then he saw a light coming out of a house as the front door opened and someone came running out into the street toward him. As the runner approached, Marshal Jackson recognized him as O'Malley. That's when he realized the shots must have come from the doctor's house where Chet was. He ran toward O'Malley until they met up.

"Marshal, Come quick! Someone just shot through the exam room window."

"What about Chet, Doc? Is he okay?"

"Come with me, Tom. I'll explain on the way back to my house."

They quickly walked toward the house while O'Malley explained what had happened. They reached the house and went straight back to the exam room where O'Malley went in first followed by the marshal. Tom stopped and looked around the room. The room was a mess with the feathers from the down quilt everywhere.

"Doc, you could have been killed tonight. What were you thinking sitting up in this room?"

"Tom, I needed to stay up in case Chet needed me. If I went to bed, I might not have heard him. How do you want to handle this, Tom?"

"Well, Chet didn't have any family so I won't need to notify anyone of his death. Can you prepare a death certificate that I can pick up?"

"Sure, Tom. I can have one first thing in the morning."

"That's fine, Doc. How about I give you a hand so you won't have to take care of this by yourself?"

"Thanks, Tom. But I'm not going to be able to go to sleep for a while so I'll take care of this tonight. You go back to your office, and we'll get together in the morning. I'll also take care of arranging for Chet's coffin and grave tomorrow just like we discussed out in the street. I'm sure sorry about this, Tom. I never thought they'd try something like this."

"There's nothing you can do about it, Doc. I'm headin' back to the office. I'll see ya in the morning."

The marshal left O'Malley's house and returned to his office. He removed his gun belt and took the gun out of his holster, placing it on the floor next to his cot just in case he needed it.

O'Malley stayed up for the next hour cleaning up the room and attended to Chet. It was 3:30 a.m. by the time he had everything organized the way he liked it. He then got ready for bed and went to sleep for the night.

Gus, Sarah, Colin, and Alicia boarded their buckboard at 8:30 a.m. for the two-hour ride into Cheyenne. Sarah always made Gus leave by half past eight to be sure they would be on time for the 11:00 a.m. mass.

Alicia told her folks she was going to tie her horse to the back of the wagon with a change of clothes in her saddlebags. Her pa asked why she was taking her horse if they were all riding in together. Sarah explained to Gus there was an ice cream social after church and O'Malley was going to take her there. Her parents were also going but would probably leave before Alicia was ready to go.

Gus looked at Sarah, and they both smiled a knowing smile at each other. Both liked O'Malley and hoped things would continue to grow between him and Alicia. The ride into Cheyenne was uneventful, and Alicia was a little apprehensive as they approached and passed the tree where they had been ambushed. However, nothing happened as they continued into town.

They pulled up at the church, and the four climbed down from the buckboard. O'Malley had been waiting for them by the church steps and waved at them with a worried look on his face.

"Doc, you look exhausted. Did things go bad with Chet?" asked Alicia.

"It could not have gone worse. I was sitting up last night in the exam room when a gunman shot through the window and hit the exam table," replied Doc.

"But what about Chet?" asked Gus. Alicia and Colin had told Gus and Sarah what had happened when they returned to the ranch last night.

"That's where Chet was when I stitched up the bullet hole. Need I say more other than I gave the marshal Chet's death certificate and made funeral arrangements with the undertaker," replied O'Malley.

"How horrible! Does anyone know who did it?" asked Sarah.

"No, the marshal suspects someone, but I don't know who it is. I took care of Chet last night and made arrangements for the undertaker to bring the coffin to my office. I also made an appointment to meet the undertaker after church so I may be a little delayed before I get to the ice cream social. But I will be there if you are still going," said O'Malley.

"We all had planned on going to the social so if you get done with the arrangements before it's over, please come by and join us," replied Alicia.

O'Malley walked into church with Alicia and her family for Mass. After the church service, he went back to his house where he waited for about ten minutes until the undertaker arrived. O'Malley had the coffin brought in and asked the undertaker's helpers to set it up in the exam room.

"Doc, do you need any help to get Chet into the coffin?" asked the men delivering the coffin.

"No, I'm fine. I've had plenty of experience with this sort of thing. Even though Chet was not Catholic, I am going to ask our priest to conduct a memorial service for him tomorrow at 1:00 p.m. So when you go back to the undertaker's office, please put in your schedule to come by and pick up the coffin so we can get it to the church on time for the service. I will let you know if the plans or time change. If you do not hear from me, you can count on the day and time I told you."

The workers promised him they would be on time. After they had left, Doc spent the next half hour getting everything ready for tomorrow. After finishing up, he left the house and headed for the ice cream social.

When he got there, he spotted Alicia and sat down with her family. The mood at the social was a somber one as everyone discussed the latest events surrounding the death of Chet.

O'Malley excused himself for a few minutes to go and discuss the memorial service with the priest. Alicia watched from across the yard as he explained to the priest how he wanted the memorial service conducted. At first, Alicia saw the priest nodding his head in agreement but then stopped abruptly with a surprised look on his face. As O'Malley continued to talk, the priest again nodded in agreement as a look of understanding came over his face. O'Malley walked back to the table where he sat down next to Alicia.

"Doc, what was that all about? Father Luke seemed confused when you were talking to him. Didn't he want to do the memorial service for Chet?" asked Alicia.

"There was no problem. I wanted to make sure he was comfortable doing a service for a non-Catholic," replied O'Malley.

The rest of the afternoon was spent reminiscing about Chet. The five of them also discussed the weather, the ranch operations, and the current situation in town. Alicia eventually turned the subject back to Chet's death and the shooting of her father. She wanted to know what everyone thought should be done about Chet's shooting.

Gus took up the issue and addressed it bluntly. "Alicia, you need to let the marshal handle this. You've thrown yourself in the middle of this, and I'm afraid you're going to end up just like Chet. That would devastate all of us here. So, I want you to promise me to stay out of it. You're done, and I don't want to hear about it anymore."

Alicia looked at O'Malley, Colin, and then at Sarah, who just shook her head slightly indicating it was best not to argue with her father. Alicia collected her thoughts for a few seconds and then looked at her father. "Pa, I have the greatest respect and admiration for you. You're asking me to ignore someone who has attacked our family. I can't just sit by and let this person or persons get away with it. When I grew up, you and Ma made sure we all knew our family was the most important thing in our lives and if one of us was hurt by an outsider, then all of us were hurt. How can you reasonably expect me not to do everything I can to find out who did this to our family? I'm sorry, Pa, but I can't promise you I won't keep trying to find the person who shot you."

"Doc, maybe you can convince her to stop before she gets hurt. I know there is no proof Chet's death had anything to do with my shooting. But I admit, we don't know that for sure, and I want to make sure nothing happens to Alicia," said Gus.

"Gus, I've tried to caution her to go slowly and be careful. I think she's done a pretty good job of it. I think we all need to work together at this point and do whatever we can with the marshal to find out who did these things to you and Chet," replied O'Malley.

After that exchange, Gus knew Alicia was determined to continue her search for the person who shot him regardless of what he said. The rest of the ice cream social was spent talking about the best way to support and help the marshal in his investigation.

The next day, O'Malley woke early to a clap of thunder. It was seven o'clock. He climbed out of bed and went to the window. Drawing the drapes back, he looked out over a cloudy, dreary landscape. It looked like it had been raining, but he couldn't tell if it had stopped yet. He squinted hard and realized it wasn't raining. Instead, there was light mist that was coming down. *Well, it figures*, he thought, *a whole month of dry weather and on the day of Chet's memorial it turns into lousy weather*.

In honor of the memorial service he had closed his office for all except emergencies. He got cleaned up and went down to Mary's for a quick breakfast. Afterward, he returned to his office to wait for the undertaker's helpers to collect the coffin.

At 11:30 a.m., there was a knock on the front door. He thought it was a bit early for the undertaker, but maybe they needed some extra time to load the coffin and get it to church on time. Doc opened the door and there stood Alicia.

"Morning, Doc. My parents and Colin went over to the church to put some flowers on the altar for the service. I thought I'd come over and join you in the procession to the church. A lot of people are already starting to line the streets to pay their respects."

There was another knock on the door.

"I'm glad you came by, Alicia," Doc said as he walked toward the door and opened it. He recognized the two men who had come by yesterday and dropped off the coffin.

"Hi, Doc. Mr. Peterson sent us over to pick up Chet. He said you were going to have everything taken care of."

"Yes, everything's ready. I have it back in the exam room where you put it yesterday. You can go ahead and take it out to the hearse. I've already nailed the lid on it."

"Well thanks, Doc. We usually put the lid on and nail it ourselves. But if you've already gone to the trouble, we'll go ahead and get it in the hearse."

"Thanks, boys. Alicia and I will head downtown for the memorial service."

"Doc, it will be a long funeral procession. I think everyone in town is going to walk Chet to the cemetery after the service."

O'Malley thanked the men and walked out with them as they carried the coffin. He and Alicia then started to walk down to the church. When they got to the church, it was nearly filled to its capacity and the service was not due to begin for another half hour. The marshal had arrived early and set aside seats for O'Malley and Gus and his family so they could sit together during the service.

❁ ❁ ❁

Jason sat in his office and leaned back in his chair, closing his eyes to think. *How could Vic be so stupid,* Jason thought. He didn't have to kill Chet. Jason had the mayor of Cheyenne in his pocket and all Vic had to do was let Chet arrest him. He would have had court convened the next day with the mayor presiding since he also held the office of justice of the peace.

Vic had managed to kill a deputy marshal and probably succeeded in turning the town against him and making him put his plans for the territory on hold. As he sat there behind his desk, he heard the faint beat of a drum every five or six seconds that seemed to be getting louder and louder. Jason got up from his desk and walked out to the lobby area. There were no customers in the bank, and his employees were looking out the windows to the street. The clock in the bank chimed twice, and Jason realized the memorial service must be over and the drummer was leading the funeral procession down Main Street.

Jason decided not to admonish his employees to get back to work. Instead, he walked out on the boardwalk in front of the bank. As the funeral procession approached, he put his right hand over his heart to show sympathy while edging closer toward the front of the boardwalk. As the townspeople noticed Jason, they moved over to give him room to stand in the front. The folks looked disgustedly in his direction. He knew they blamed him for Chet's death, and he already suspected the town was starting to turn against him. They weren't ready to voice their feelings out loud at this time, but that sure could change quickly. He had to act fast and put his plan in place.

It took about ten minutes for the funeral procession to pass by and then the townsfolk fell in line behind the hearse, following it down the street to the cemetery. However, Jason turned around and walked back into the bank. When he went back to his office, there stood Vic partially sitting on his desk.

"Vic! What do you think you're doing? All I need is for the marshal to find you here. How'd you get into my office?"

"You gotta back door to your office right over there, and it was unlocked. Let's get right down to it, Jason. I gotta get outta here, and I need some money to do it. I figure five thousand oughta be about right. Otherwise, if I get caught, you won't like what I'd say."

"No, Vic. I'm not going to pay you off. You need to go back to the ranch right now. I've decided what I'm going to do, and I'm going to need you and all the gun hands at the ranch. So, leave by the same way you came and head back now before the townsfolk get back from the cemetery and see you."

"All right, Jason, but I'm gonna need to know what you want to do by nightfall."

"You'll know, Vic. Now get out of here and get the boys together. We'll have a meeting tonight at the ranch, and I'll fill you and everyone else in on what I plan to do."

"All right, Jason, but make sure you have a plan." Vic then walked out the back door.

Jason walked over to the window and watched him ride out in the direction of his ranch. He then went back to his desk and sat down to determine the best course of action.

Gus and his family thought the memorial service for Chet was extremely well done. Father Luke did an extremely good job. They were now at the cemetery, and Father Luke was finishing up his graveside service with a final prayer. Afterward, the crowd of mourners said a final Amen. Some of them started to leave while others gathered around in small groups to chat. Most of them spoke about the tragedy that had befallen Chet. Many remembered the times Chet would help his friends without even being asked. He was also somewhat of a practical joker, but he never played a mean or vicious joke on anyone. Many times, the jokes were just silly, and everyone would have a good laugh.

Eventually, everyone left the cemetery and walked back to the town where they tried to get back to their normal routines. Gus and his family walked back with O'Malley to their buckboard for the trip back to the ranch. O'Malley motioned Alicia to step to the side and talk to him privately.

"Alicia, I wish we could have taken some time by ourselves to visit. It obviously has not been a very good time, and I'd like to come out and see you next Saturday. Would that be all right?"

"I would love it, but you won't need to come out as Pa will be coming into town next Saturday to pick up some things that are coming in at the freight office. Ma and Colin are going to come in to do some shopping, too. I wasn't going to come in, but I might as well. It will save you a trip, and we can finally spend some time together. What do you think, Doc?"

"That's a great idea. We can have lunch and maybe take a ride out in the country. You can come by my office. When do you expect to arrive?"

"By the time we finish our early morning work at the ranch, we will probably get here at around eleven o'clock in the morning. Pa stopped at the general store before they went to the church and found out the supplies he ordered will be in for him to pick up anytime Saturday."

"That's perfect as I should be done with my last patient at about the same time you will be getting in town. Instead of you coming to my office, I'll hitch up my buggy, and we can meet at Mary's for lunch and then go for that ride in the country."

"I'm really looking forward to Saturday, Doc. It will be nice to have a day to ourselves and just relax and enjoy it."

At that, Alicia took O'Malley's head in her hands and pulled him down to give him a kiss. She then returned to her family and left for the ranch.

After doing some thinking, Jason finalized his plan and left the bank early to go back to his ranch and tell the men what they were going to do. When he arrived at the ranch, Vic was waiting outside the bunkhouse. He tied up his horse and walked over to where Vic stood.

"Vic, get the boys together and meet me at the ranch house. We're going to speed up what I thought might take another six to twelve months because of you killing Chet. I think we have about ten gun hands excluding you."

Vic nodded and mounted his horse to go out on the range and bring in the men. It took him about an hour to round up the particular hands Jason wanted. The hands tied their horses in front of the ranch house while Vic walked up to the front door and knocked. Jason answered the door and told Vic to bring the men into the dining room where there would be room for everyone. The men entered the room and Vic motioned them to sit down. Most of the hands sat but a few decided to stand. There were twelve hands excluding Jason. All were hired guns and had worked for men who hired them to stop rustlers or settle personal disputes. Most had experience fighting in range wars and knew their professions quite well. They were professional, hardened gunslingers, who worked for the highest bidder. For the next half hour, Jason laid out his plan and answered any questions his hands asked.

The trip back to the ranch was uneventful and Gus and his family enjoyed a relaxed and casual conversation on the way back. All the previous troubles seemed to have melted away during the ride home that late afternoon.

Alicia's thoughts turned to how things were before she had left to teach back east. *Why can't people just get along*, she thought. It seemed that people always lost their concern for their fellow human beings when money took over and greed entered the picture.

It was dinnertime when they arrived back at the ranch. Everyone went into the house to change out of their dress clothes they wore to Chet's memorial. Sarah and Alicia went to the kitchen to prepare dinner while Gus went out to check on the ranch.

As Alicia and Sarah worked together to prepare a nice dinner for the evening, Alicia looked at her mother. She noticed the lines in her face had gotten a bit deeper. Although she was aging, she was doing so gracefully. She had noticed the same thing about her father, but he now seemed fully recovered and was back to his normal work routine.

"Ma, how is Pa really doing? Is he really healed and back to normal?"

"I think so, sweetheart. He's working his regular hours now and hasn't complained or shown any signs of being tired. Why do you ask?"

"Well, from what I heard in the past, Pa wouldn't have let the marshal find who shot him. He would have gone out and found him on his own. I don't know if his getting shot changed him or if there is some other reason."

"Alicia, your father's a tough, tough man. He's not going after the person he thinks is responsible for two reasons. First, he doesn't have any proof and second, he's worried his family might get hurt if he goes after the person he suspects."

"Ma, he shouldn't be worried about us. We can take care of ourselves and as for Colin, we all look out for him."

"I know, honey, but he's not going to do anything that would put this family in danger. Now, go call your pa and Colin for dinner. I think they're both in the barn taking care of the horses."

Alicia walked out to the front porch and called them to dinner. They both yelled out they would be there in a minute or two. She returned to the kitchen and helped her mom bring the food to the table.

CHAPTER 17

사랑

Jason was seated at the head of the table, answering the questions about how and when they were going to take over the town. Every gun hand in the room had either killed men in range wars or was hired by private individuals to kill in the name of personal feuds.

"Well, boys, that takes care of everything. Each of you will receive a one-hundred-dollar bonus for your work when we take over the town this Saturday. As I said, we will meet in the bank at exactly 11:30 a.m. I'll send all the employees home and close the bank. No one is to ride into town down Main Street. I don't want anyone to see you. Vic knows the exact route to take so you will follow him. Vic, make sure you get the men in without being seen. I'll meet everyone at the back door of the bank. The marshal always eats lunch at Mary's on Saturdays at noon. That's where you'll take him. Once you dispose of the marshal, we'll go have a talk with the mayor. Vic will be appointed as the city sheriff. Since Chet's dead, there won't be a deputy to worry about. I want a show of force so the townsfolk know who is in charge. After we take care of business, the town will be open for you to celebrate."

After the remark about an open town, the hands yelled out various epitaphs in support of what was to come on Saturday. Whitey and Stu joined in but were not as energetic as the rest.

"Okay, okay, boys, calm down. After we get our business done in town, we will have one other job to do. We're going to ride out to Gus's ranch and convince him to sell his spread to me. His ranch hands aren't gunslingers and since it will be Saturday, they will be running a skeleton crew at the ranch. Friday is payday so most of his hands will be in town working up their usual drunk and then sleeping it off on Saturday. I don't want any of you going into town on Friday after you get paid. I need everyone sober for what we're going to do on Saturday. Is that understood?"

Everyone said yes or nodded in agreement. Seeing there was nothing else to discuss, Jason told the men to make sure they cleaned their guns so none of them jam or misfire. He motioned Vic to remain behind as all the other men were clearing out. When they were alone, he turned to Vic with a serious look. "I want this to go as planned. No folks in town are to be harmed unless they pick up guns to fight us. Is that understood, Vic?"

"Sure, Jason. Anything you say, but you know the marshal has a lot of friends. They won't like it when we gun him down."

"You heard me, Vic. I don't want anyone injured unless they try to fight us. Once you take care of the marshal, everyone else should fall in line. Just stay on your toes and be ready."

"You don't have to tell me that, Jason. Me and the boys will be ready for anything that comes up." With that, Vic left and resumed his duties as the ranch ramrod.

Throughout the rest of the week, Vic made sure the boys worked their normal jobs and were given time off to make sure they cleaned and oiled their pistols and rifles. On Friday, Jason handed out the pay envelopes at the end of the day and repeated his instructions to each man to remain at the ranch that night.

That week was also routine at Gus and Sarah's ranch with one exception. Alicia seemed to be running into Thad on a daily basis during her normal workday. As they worked several jobs together and talked, Thad told her where he was from and why he was on his first cattle drive.

He was from Texas, San Antonio to be exact. His family owned a farm along a river just outside of the town's city limits. The weather was scorching hot in the summer, and they often dealt with semi-drought conditions. Things weren't easy for them, but they weren't terribly hard either. His family dealt with the weather and occasional Indian raid, but they always managed to come in with a cash crop.

Over the years, Thad's father continued to purchase more land expanding his operation, hiring more hands, and he continued to increase his profits. But Thad grew tired of the farm life and wanted to get out on his own. His father had paid Thad just like any other farm hand, and Thad saved most of his pay. So at the age of twenty, he sat down with his parents and explained he had decided to go out on his own.

"Neither of my folks was really happy to see me go. My ma didn't want to see her only child leave, and my pa thought I would someday take over the farm. I told him I wasn't going to be gone forever. I just wanted to see what else was out there. My pa made sure I had all the necessary gear I needed, and my ma gave me an extra two hundred dollars to make sure I wouldn't starve. I traveled west for many months, picking up jobs here and there until I hit Las Cruces, New Mexico, about eight months ago. I got a job on a cattle ranch and within about two months, I was on my very first roundup. A month after that, I signed up for the cattle drive. At the end of the drive, I wound up here in Cheyenne. Now you pretty well know all there is to know about me."

"That answers a lot of the questions I had but was too polite to ask. There is one thing that really interests me."

"Well, Miss, go ahead and ask anything you want."

"I was very impressed with your shooting at the rifle contest. How did you become such an expert marksman?"

"That's easy, Miss. My pa bought me my first rifle at the age of seven and started teaching me how to use it. He told me I was a natural although at seven years old I didn't know what that meant. So in no short time, without bragging, I could cut the center of pretty near any target that was put up. That's the story of how I learned to shoot."

"I also see you carry a holstered sidearm, Thad. Are you as good with your six gun as you are with your Henry?"

"I don't have much use for six guns, Miss Alicia. I carry it because I think I'd just feel out of place without one. Mostly, I just use my Henry rifle when I need to shoot."

"You certainly proved you're good with it. Thad, you know it's Friday. Pa should have your pay envelope for you. Are you going to ride into town with the other hands and blow off some steam?"

"Miss Alicia, I don't care for a lot of that drinkin' and carousing, so I will probably just stay in the bunkhouse until tomorrow. Since I got Saturday off, I'm goin' into town to pick up some ammunition for my Henry and also one of my stirrups needs repair so I thought I'd take it to the saddle maker."

"That's a coincidence. My folks, Colin, and I are going into town tomorrow, too. I'm sure they'd be fine with you riding into town with us."

"That'd be fine, Miss Alicia. I'd enjoy the company."

"Then it's agreed, Thad. Let's finish up repairing this fence, and then we can ride in and you can pick up your pay. And Thad, you can call me Alicia. We know each other well enough."

"I'll do it, Miss, I mean, Alicia."

With that, they finished their fence work, packed up the tools, and rode back to the ranch. They were the last two to come in and found the rest of the hands already washing up for a night on the town as they had already collected their pay.

"Hey, Thad!" one of the ranch hands called out.

"Git on over here and wash up quick. We're goin' into town for some fun. Hurry on up! We'll be leavin' in about fifteen minutes."

"You boys go right on in. I'm gonna stay here tonight and ride in tomorrow for some supplies."

"Suit yourself, Thad, but I doubt if we'll be awake if you're comin' in tomorrow morning."

"Well, you boys have fun. Hey! Do you know where Gus is?"

"Yeah, I think he's over at the cookhouse havin' a cup of coffee with Moses."

"Thanks," Thad yelled back and turned to Alicia. "What time are you and your family headin' into town tomorrow mornin'?"

"Usually Pa wants to get going no later than eight o'clock. But why don't you ask him when you collect your pay? I'll see you in the morning, Thad."

Thad tipped his hat to her and started walking toward the cookhouse. He opened the door, walked in, and saw Moses and Gus sitting at the far end of the long table with two cups of coffee.

"Hey, Thad, the boys have already eaten. You're a little late for supper, but I kept some grub on the stove for you. Take a seat, and I'll dish up a plate for you. Hope you like beef stew 'cause that's what we got, with some biscuits and butter," said Moses.

"That'll be just fine. Howdy, Gus, how's the coffee?"

"Just fine, Thad. The stew was really good, too. Have a seat like Moses said. I bet you're looking for this." Gus held out a pay envelope that contained Thad's weekly wages.

"Thanks, Gus. I appreciate it."

"No thanks necessary, Thad, you earned it. You best hurry up and eat so you can get cleaned up and go into town with the rest of the boys."

"There's no hurry, Gus. I'm gonna stay at the ranch and go into town tomorrow. I've got to pick up some rifle ammunition and get the stirrup on my saddle repaired. Miss Alicia invited me to ride in with you folks tomorrow morning but wasn't sure what time you'd be leavin'."

"You'd be welcome to go in with us, Thad. I try to get everyone on the road by eight o'clock in the morning. But sometimes, it just doesn't work out with the women folk. But I never complain about the wait as they all make sure they look very pretty. You know, Thad, it's none of my business, you are one of my hardest working hands but never go into town to blow off any steam. I was just curious as to why you don't leave the ranch?"

"Here you go, Thad, a nice hot plate of stew," interrupted Moses.

"To answer your question, Gus, it's not a long story. I just don't cotton for getting drunk and then have some other drunk pick a fight with me. Some of my friends back in Texas would drink and fight every Friday night, but I just never saw the sense of it. So I'll take a drink or two once in a while, but not enough to lose my senses."

"Thad, that's a right sensible way to think. Now, go ahead and eat that stew before it gets cold," butted in Moses.

He started on the stew and biscuits not realizing how hungry he was until he started eating. Moses got up from the table and went out to the kitchen, returning with the remaining biscuits and stew in the pot, which he spooned onto Thad's plate. Thad ate as Gus and Moses carried on with their conversatión while playing a game of chess they had started just before Thad had come in.

Suddenly, there was a tremendous clap of thunder that shook the cookhouse and startled all three men. Gus got up and went over to the window facing west. He could see dark black clouds that looked like they were filled to the brim with rain. The wind started to pick up and continued to increase in intensity. Gus could see the lightning strike every twenty or thirty seconds. He crossed over to the door of the cookhouse and opened it to look out.

"Well, I sure hope the boys have fast horses. They've only been gone for about ten minutes. That storm's comin' in awful fast. I can see the rain coming down in the distance. Looks like it's comin' down in sheets. Thad, if you're done, you might want to head back to the bunkhouse unless you want to go swimin' in a few minutes. Moses, you might want to clean up the kitchen later so you don't get caught in the rain. I'm headin' back to the house. I'll see you two tomorrow," said Gus.

With that, he went out the cookhouse door and noticed Thad's horse had not been taken to the barn. The horse looked skittish, most likely from the thunder, so Gus trotted over to the mare and stroked its neck to settle it down. The horse calmed down a bit.

Gus heard footsteps coming up behind him. He turned and saw Thad approaching. "Thanks, Gus. I meant to take her into the barn and then we got talking and I forgot."

"No harm done, Thad, but your horse is just as important as the rest of your gear. You need to take as good care of her as you do with your guns. She could just as easily save your life the same as your guns."

"Yep, boss, you're right. I'll take her to the barn and give her a good rubdown." Thad took the reins and led his horse into one of the stalls where he removed the saddle and started the rub down after giving her some oats.

O'Malley was finishing his evening meal at Mary's when he noticed the hands from Gus's ranch ride by and tie up their horses at the rail in front of the saloon. He looked at his watch. It was 7:30 p.m. They were right on time as usual. He glanced at his watch again and thought he could set any timepiece to 7:30 p.m., within a couple minutes either way, every Friday night by the arrival of the hands from Gus's ranch. Well, it may be a long night if the hands get drunk and start fighting with each other. Fortunately, he usually ended up treating minor cuts and bruises or at the worst an occasional cracked rib.

O'Malley paid Mary for his meal and left the café. As he went outside, he noticed dark, ominous clouds rapidly heading toward town, accompanied by a lot of lightning. He hurried home, pretty sure the storm would strike with a vengeance. As he made it to his front gate, he felt the first few raindrops. By the time he got on his porch, the clouds let loose with torrential rainfall, and the wind and lightning kicked in with a force O'Malley had not seen in years. He hurried into the house to avoid the rain and wind and hoped he wouldn't be called out on a night like this, but he'd surely go if he was needed.

He walked to his exam room and made sure his bag was fully supplied. After that, he grabbed a medical journal, which had just arrived, and went into his parlor to relax and do a little reading. The rain and wind were so strong it almost sounded like hail hitting the side of the house. He couldn't remember when he last saw a storm as vicious and furious as this one.

As the evening wore on, he became drowsy from reading and eventually fell asleep in the rocking chair he was sitting in. A loud banging on his front door startled him and woke him from his sleep. He looked at the parlor clock and saw it was ten o'clock. He hoped he wasn't being called to the saloon this early. Usually, he was summoned at two or three in the morning. He put the journal down on the end table next to him and got up to answer the pounding on his door.

"Hold your horses, I'm coming!" O'Malley shouted out as he made his way to the door, still a little groggy from being woken up from a sound sleep. He opened the door, and two cowboys in their rain slickers and hats stepped in. He didn't immediately recognize them until they took their hats off, which had been pulled down to protect their faces from the rain. As soon as they removed their hats, he recognized Stu and Whitey, who still worked for Jason's ranch. They shook the rain off their hats, and Whitey wiped the wet rain from his face with his hands.

"What's going on, boys? You don't look like you're in need of medical attention."

"Naw, Doc, we're leavin town but wanted to stop by and tell you what's goin' on tomorrow."

"What do you mean you're leavin' town?"

"Doc, tomorrow the boys are coming into town to meet Jason at the bank and then go out and kill the marshal. They then have it set to make Vic the city sheriff and go out and make Gus sell his ranch to Jason. If he refuses, they'll kill him and make Sarah sign the ranch over."

"How come you two are telling me this? You work for Jason, and it sounds like you stand to make a lot of money tomorrow. Now, what's really going on and why should I believe you?"

"You're right, Doc. Stu and I have done a lot of bad things for Jason. But Doc, we haven't murdered anyone for him and especially no marshal. So we snuck out tonight, and we're ridin' on. You've always been good to us, Doc. That's why we decided to stop by your place before we headed out. We're tellin' you this so you don't go downtown and get in the way where you might get hurt. We owe you that much at least," said Whitey.

"What time tomorrow is all this going to happen?" asked O'Malley.

"The boys will be at Jason's bank a little bit before noon. They plan on catchin' the marshal eatin' lunch at Mary's, killin' him, and then appointin' Vic to take over as the sheriff. After that, they're goin' out to Gus and Sarah's. We don't want any part of this so we're leavin' town but not before we stopped and warned ya," said Whitey.

"Okay, boys, I appreciate the information. Do you want to stay here until the storm blows over?"

"Naw, Doc, we're gonna ride through this mess and get as far from here as we can tonight. It's a long trail, but we're headin' back to Texas," said Stu.

"All right, you two have a safe trip and thanks for stopping by."

"Watch out for yourself, Doc, and if Stu and me ever git back up this way, we'll stop by and say howdy," said Stu.

They put their hats back on, and O'Malley opened the door for them. They said their good-byes and made their way to their horses where they mounted up and took off south for Texas in a torrential downpour.

O'Malley shook his head in disbelief at what he just heard. *I'll get to the marshal first thing in the morning, and then we can figure out some kind of plan. Gus and the family will also be here, and I can tell them what happened*, thought Doc.

He spent a fitful night trying to sleep, but his restlessness kept him awake all night long. By seven o'clock the next morning, he had enough and got up and dressed. As he was getting ready, he noticed the storm had blown itself out and the sky was blue without a cloud to be seen. He finished dressing and walked out the front door onto his porch to look around. The torrential downpour had soaked everything in sight and made the road into town thoroughly muddy.

O'Malley went back into his house and put on his cowboy boots to replace the shoes he had on. With that, he walked out to the street and started into town. As soon as he got to the store boardwalks, he crossed the street and walked to the marshal's office. He walked in and found Tom behind his desk already doing some paperwork. Tom looked up and waved Doc in, offering him a cup of coffee.

"That sounds real good, Tom. After the night I've had, I could sure use some coffee."

"What do ya mean, Doc? There were no fights that needed your help."

"It's not about that, Tom. Stu and Whitey stopped by my place last night at about ten o'clock to warn me that Jason and his hands are coming to gun you down today."

"What are you talking about, Doc? None of Jason's hands were even in the saloon last night when I made my rounds. The only cowpokes in town came from Gus and Sarah's ranch. I just figured none of Jason's men were gonna brave the storm to make the trip in. So, tell me what Stu and Whitey told you about Jason's plans."

O'Malley related what they had told him, and he and the marshal talked at length how to deal with Jason and his gunslingers. O'Malley let the marshal know that Gus and his family would be in town today. Once Gus understood Jason's plans, O'Malley was sure he would throw in with them. That still meant they were severely outnumbered. The marshal knew the surprise element had now shifted from Jason's advantage to their group. They agreed on a strategy but decided to go over it with Gus when he arrived.

O'Malley left the marshal's office feeling a bit more relieved than before they had met. The street was still filled with soft mud, which made it very hard to get his footing. By the time he got back to his office, he already had one patient waiting for him. He took the local farmer into his office to treat a lacerated hand and after he was done with him, he put a sign on the front door letting everyone know the office would be closing at 10:30 a.m. instead of the usual noon.

Gus was able to convince everyone to get started for Cheyenne by eight o'clock in the morning, which meant he had everyone down in the kitchen eating breakfast by six thirty and finishing up within half an hour. Alicia and Sarah cleaned up the dirty dishes while Gus took Colin out to the barn to hitch up the horses to the buckboard.

As Gus was starting to get the horses in position, Thad came into the barn to get his horse saddled. The three worked together to get the buckboard ready, and then Thad saddled his horse. When they were ready, they led the rig and Thad's horse across the yard in front of the house. The three of them walked up to the porch and sat down in the chairs to wait for Sarah and Alicia.

Gus looked at Thad and Colin. "Well, boys, it's almost eight, and the women will probably be late as usual. I'm sure they're all getting prettied up to go into town, and I'm sure there is a certain doctor Alicia will want to see."

"Yeah, I kinda noticed something was goin' on between those two. Have they been courtin' quite a while?"

"It depends on what you mean, Thad. They were courtin' for about a year, and then she decided she wanted to see what else was in the world. So, she lit out to Pittsburgh, Pennsylvania and taught school for about five years until I got shot. Then Sarah sent her a telegram about my shooting, and she came back to us. Even though they haven't had a whole lot of time together, it sure seems like the spark is still there."

Just then, Sarah and Alicia opened the door and stepped out onto the porch. Sarah had put a pretty blue sundress on with a matching blue bonnet. Alicia, on the other hand, came out dressed in jeans and a long-sleeved cotton shirt with cowboy hat and boots.

"Sarah, you look real pretty today. Is Alicia stayin' behind to work the ranch today?"

"Dad, I'm dressed like this because I'm going to ride in on my horse, so Thad doesn't have to ride alone behind the buckboard."

"Alicia, we didn't saddle your horse, so we'll wait for you to throw a saddle on her."

"Okay, Dad. I'll go saddle her right now and be back in five minutes." She walked quickly to the barn and within five minutes, returned with her horse.

"Okay, everyone, the princess has joined us so we can finally get this parade on the road," Gus remarked loud enough for Alicia to hear.

"Ah, Pa, does the way I look remind you of a princess or a ranch hand. You know you can't have it both ways."

"You got me there, Alicia. But you will always be my princess no matter what you're wearing."

"That's enough, Gus. Stop embarrassing Alicia in front of Thad. Now, get in the buckboard, Gus, and let's get into town," directed Sarah.

"Well, folks, I guess you can tell who the real boss is around here," Alicia said, laughing.

Gus hesitated for a moment as he climbed up on the rig and then looked up and started laughing along with everyone else. After they took their seat, he sat down, picked up the reins, and snapped them, commanding the team of horses to get moving toward Cheyenne.

Marshal Jackson had another cup of coffee after O'Malley left and thought about what he needed to do. He rarely had anything more than coffee in the morning and this morning was no different except after he finished his coffee, he turned back to unlock the gun rack and removed three shotguns, placing them on his desk. He then removed a box of shotgun shells and loaded each double-barreled shotgun. He kept the rest of the shells in his pocket.

After he finished preparing the weapons, it was already nine o'clock. The marshal was as prepared for Jason and his men as he could be. O'Malley had said he would be closing by 10:30 a.m., so the marshal decided to finish up some paperwork he had on his desk and then go see O'Malley to make sure their plan was set and see if Gus had arrived in town.

It was just after ten o'clock when Gus pulled his rig up in front of O'Malley's office. "Let's say hello to Doc, and then we can go into town," said Gus.

"Gus, I'm goin' to ride on into town and drop off my saddle to be repaired. Tell Doc I said hi, and I'll see him later."

"Okay, Thad, we won't be very long. We'll see you in town shortly," replied Gus.

The rest of them walked up and entered O'Malley's house into the foyer. O'Malley came out of the exam room and approached everyone.

"Hello, folks, come on into the parlor and have a seat. We have some very important business to discuss." He then excused himself to get some coffee for everyone.

Alicia followed him into the kitchen to help. He put some water in the coffee pot and set it on the stove to boil. Alicia approached O'Malley, who had his back to her, and gently put her hand on his shoulder. He turned to face her, and their eyes locked for a moment. With a smile on his face, he stepped forward and brushed Alicia's hair back from her face, slowly leaning in and then taking her into his arms, softly kissing her on her forehead, then the eyelids, and slowly moving to her mouth for a long embrace.

As they parted from their embrace, Alicia looked up at O'Malley, who was clearly a good six inches taller than she. "Doc, you seem awfully worried about something. Can you tell me what it's about?"

"After that kiss, I can tell you anything. But let's go out to the parlor, so I can share the information with everyone without having to repeat it."

The water came to a boil and O'Malley finished making the coffee. He carried the pot and cups into the parlor. As they brought in the coffee, the front door opened and Marshal Jackson walked in.

"Come in, Tom. You won't believe this, but Gus and his family just arrived. Come on into the parlor so we can all talk together," said O'Malley. They walked into the parlor, and O'Malley poured some coffee for his guests.

"All right, Doc, Marshal, what the heck is going on? I wasn't born yesterday. I can see you both have something on your mind," said Gus.

"Doc here can probably tell you better what went on yesterday and what we want to do about it," said the marshal.

O'Malley told everyone about Stu and Whitey's late night visit and his discussion concerning Jason's plans for today. He also made sure Gus understood Vic would be appointed as sheriff after they killed the marshal and then went on to tell them that Jason and his men would then ride out to Gus's place to convince him to sell his ranch. If Gus refuses to sell the ranch, Jason's gunslingers were directed to kill him and force Sarah to sign the deed over by force. Jason would then have the water rights, giving him the power to take over the rest of the small ranchers by denying them the water Gus had always freely provided them without a charge. After explaining Stu and Whitey's visit, O'Malley outlined the plan he and the marshal had put together to fight Jason and his men.

Gus looked at O'Malley and Tom and said, "You two put a good plan together except for one thing. You didn't include me. You know I'll be throwing in with you when Jason starts this fracas."

"Dad, I'll also be in on this fight and don't try to tell me I won't. However, I would suggest we send Ma and Colin back to the ranch so they aren't harmed in any way," said Alicia.

"Now just a minute, young lady! I'm your ma and a western woman to boot. I know how to shoot any gun we have and if anyone goes back to the ranch, your pa and I will decide who. I've fought off enough Indians in my time not to worry about a varmint like Jason and his men," said Sarah.

"All right, ladies, if you're going to be involved in this fight, then we are going to change our plans on how we will fight Jason. Our initial plan is fine, but we're going to call Doc's office our last stand if we need it. So when the fight first begins, we should be able to whittle down their numbers by two or three as we will have surprise on our side. Colin, you like Ma Jenkins, don't you? I thought you could stay with her for a while if that would be okay?" asked the marshal.

Colin looked at Sarah, who nodded her head. "O-o-okay, Marshal," replied Colin.

"Folks, it's already eleven o'clock. I'm goin' back to my office and bring back some rifles for Sarah and Alicia," said Marshal Jackson.

The next couple of minutes were spent discussing a few minor changes to their plan with input from Gus and his family. The marshal went back to his office where he gathered the rifles along with an extra pistol and holster fully loaded with ammunition, both in the gun and belt. He took the weapons back to O'Malley's. By this time, it was 11:20 a.m., and the marshal and the boys took off to put their plan in place.

Jason was in the bank's front lobby going over some books with his chief accountant when he noticed Marshall Jackson walk by. He took his watch out of his vest and looked at the time. He realized it was a few minutes past eleven and told the accountant he had some work back at his office he needed to attend to and they could finish this up on Monday. Jason announced to all bank employees he was closing the bank early and everyone could go home. He then went back to his office to wait for Vic and the rest of his hired guns.

As he looked out his back window, he saw Vic and the men ride up to the bank as they had been told to do. He walked to the rear entrance and opened the door, letting everyone into his office. He cautioned the men to sit wherever they could find space, and he went out to the bank lobby to make sure no one could venture back to his office and discover the men.

Alicia and Sarah walked Colin across the street to Mrs. Jenkins and asked if she could keep him with her for an hour or two. Mrs. Jenkins was surprised to see them when she opened the door.

"Sarah, please come on in. You too, Alicia and Colin. I haven't seen you folks in a long time. Can I get you some tea?" asked Mrs. Jenkins.

"No thanks, Clara. We're kind of in a hurry, and I need to ask a big favor of you," replied Sarah.

"Anything I can do for you, Sarah. You and Gus were so kind to me when Ben died. You helped me when no one else in town would or could help a widow. That was because Jason wanted our ranch for his own purposes. After Ben was shot and killed on the prairie, I had to sell, and it turned out Jason was the only buyer. I got a little more than enough to pay my bills when I sold him the ranch, and you and Gus were the only ones to come forward and lend me the money to buy this boarding house. So you tell me what you need, and I'll do it for you if I can," replied Clara.

"Thanks, Clara. There's gonna be some shootin' today, and it might get all the way down to Doc's house. Can you keep Colin over here so he will be out of danger?"

"I'd be glad to but what about you and Alicia? Shouldn't you come over to stay with me and out of danger?"

"Clara, if the fight gets this far, Alicia and I are gonna join in and help our men. Jason has decided to attack us. Attacking our friends is one thing, but he is also attacking my family and when he attacks one of us, he attacks all of us. No one, absolutely no one, does that to my family."

"But Sarah, why not bring your guns over here instead of Doc's house. You know if it gets this far, they will naturally go to Doc's house. Here you can surprise them, and I'll throw in with you. As you know, I can shoot just as well as anybody else. If trouble comes, we can get Colin down to the cellar where he will be safe."

"What do you think, Alicia?" asked Sarah.

"I think it's a good idea, and I think we should do it."

They all agreed. Leaving Colin with Clara, Sarah and Alicia went back to Doc's house and collected their weapons, which they brought across the street to Clara's. Alicia then remembered she had left her small box of items in Mary's spare room and excused herself to go retrieve it. She went through the back alley and through the kitchen door entrance to the café so no one would see her. She explained to Mary she had forgotten a small box in the spare room when she first arrived and needed to retrieve it. Mary told her to go ahead and pick it up and let her know she could stay for tea.

Alicia went up to the spare room and took the item she needed out of the box. She then went down to the kitchen and told Mary to expect a visit from the marshal shortly. Mary asked if there was some trouble, but Alicia told her the marshal would explain everything and left for Clara's house.

By the time Alicia returned to Clara's, there was freshly brewed tea and cookies Clara had prepared for everyone.

CHAPTER

18

사랑

Jason made sure all the employees left the bank by 11:45 a.m. and then walked back to his private office to give the go ahead to his plan. “Okay, Vic, you take a couple of men and head over to Mary’s Café. It shouldn’t take more than three of you to take care of the marshal. I saw him walking toward Mary’s just a little while ago. He always sits at the counter with his back to the front door so all you’ve got to do is open the door and when you tell him to turn around, start shooting immediately. That way no can say he was shot in the back,” said Jason.

Vic turned toward the men and picked two to walk over to Mary’s Café with him. The three of them stood in the street in front of Mary’s and saw the marshal sitting at the counter with his back to the street just like Jason said. “All right, boys, get on up there, open the door and call the marshal out. Remember to shoot when he turns to face you.”

“Wait a minute, Vic. Ain’t you comin’ too?”

“It shouldn’t take more than the two of you to take care of one marshal. That’s what Jason is paying you for. I’ll be out here in case you need some help.”

The two gunslingers shrugged and stepped up on the boardwalk and to the front door. They could see the marshal bent slightly forward over the counter, appearing to eat his lunch just like Jason said he would be. They opened the door, stepped quietly inside, and stood there without closing the door in case they needed to get out fast. Both gunmen drew their Colt .45s from their holsters and yelled for Marshal Jackson to turn around. The marshal slowly stood up and just as slowly turned to face them. When he turned, the two gunmen looked surprised and alarmed at the same time.

"What's wrong, boys? Haven't you ever seen a doctor in cowboy clothes?"

"Doc, you picked the wrong side to be on. C'mon let's get 'em."

The two aimed their guns and were about to fire when Chet stood up from behind the counter and fired both barrels of a double-barreled shotgun at the two gunslingers, hitting them with such force they flew backward out of the café and landed at Vic's feet, dead.

Vic looked up through the door and couldn't believe his eyes. *How was he alive?* He was sure he had killed him at O'Malley's office. Vic only hesitated for a moment. Seeing Chet reloading his shotgun, he recognized he had a direct line of fire at him so he drew and fired, hitting Chet in the shoulder. He went down behind the counter, and Vic saw O'Malley draw his pistol and take a shot at him. Vic could feel the bullet O'Malley fired just miss his head by inches. He turned and ran for cover to the bank while firing at the same time.

After O'Malley took a shot at Vic, he yelled to Mary in the kitchen to bring out some bandages as he ran behind the counter to attend to Chet. Chet had taken a bullet in his right shoulder, which had completely passed through. At least, he wouldn't have to dig the lead out. Mary came through the kitchen door with bandages and remained behind the counter in case O'Malley needed her help with Chet.

"Doc, where's the marshal? I thought he'd be in here with you and Chet," remarked Mary.

"Right behind ya, Mary," said the marshal.

"Where ya been at, Marshal?" asked Mary.

"I was at the side entrance of the café to make sure Jason didn't try to send men there. It was Doc's plan to dress like me and sit at the counter to surprise the gun hands. As you can see, it worked really well. Doc had moved Chet from the exam room to his bedroom the day he was shot, thinking they might try to kill him, so he couldn't tell us who shot him. It worked really well from the look of Vic's face. Father Luke even helped with a service for a coffin filled with rocks. Doc, are you about through treating Chet?" asked the marshal.

"I'm ready. Mary, can we move Chet upstairs in that spare room of yours? I want to get him in a bed and make him comfortable. I can't believe his stomach wound didn't open up."

"Sure, Doc, you and the marshal lift him and take him upstairs. We'll lock the door, and I'll make sure nobody goes up. I'll keep an eye out down here in case Jason sends more men over. The key's in the door so just lock him in and bring the key down to me," said Mary.

The marshal and O'Malley lifted Chet and carried him upstairs to the spare room, putting him on the bed and covering him up. Just as they exited the room, they heard Mary call to them from the foot of the stairs.

"Marshal, Doc! I just saw three gunmen cross the street on the other side of the building. I think they might try to go around behind the café and come through the back door. You two best go out the side door before those men get here so you can go up the street and fight them on your own terms."

"Mary, we can't leave you and Chet here. That would be a death sentence for the both of you," said O'Malley.

"They're not going to kill a woman. Jason knows if they do that, they'll have this whole town down on them. The townsfolk might be afraid of Jason right now but if he kills me, every woman in town will have her husband out to avenge me. Now git going! I'll make sure Chet's safe."

"She's right! C'mon Doc, let's make tracks before those three get here." The marshal went over to the side door entrance and carefully looked out the door in both directions. It was clear, and Tom motioned to O'Malley to follow him out the door. They went down the steps quickly then turned and went up to the street. They reached the street, looked around, and saw no one in sight. "C'mon Doc, let's run for it!"

They took off running as fast as they could on the boardwalk toward O'Malley's house. As soon as they started to run, gunfire erupted from the bank across the street, and Tom and O'Malley were just able to duck behind some barrels that were on the boardwalk in front of the general store while returning fire at the bank.

Suddenly, the three gunmen Mary had seen appeared at the boardwalk by Mary's and started to fire at O'Malley and Tom. At that moment, gunfire erupted from across the street at the saddle shop. One gun hand went down from the shots, and the remaining two ducked down the alleyway out of sight.

"Thought you two could use a little help," yelled Thad from the saddle shop.

"Sure could, son! Thanks for the extra gun. There are too many to stand and fight. If you can, make your way toward O'Malley's if they get too close," the marshal yelled back.

Suddenly, the two gunmen came out from around the corner they had hidden behind when Thad had started shooting. One of the gunmen started shooting at the saddle shop and the other started shooting at O'Malley and the marshal. The first shot caught the marshal in his right calf. The second or third shot caught O'Malley—a grazing wound to his right shoulder.

O'Malley grabbed Tom by the arm, helped him up, and busted through the door of the general store, out of the line of fire. "Tom, let me take a look at your leg. Jonas, do you have any bandages you can get for me?" O'Malley asked.

Jonas, who owned the general store, was stunned to see O'Malley and the marshal come bursting through his door but recovered quickly and located what O'Malley needed.

"Doc, make it quick, we gotta git outta here as fast as we can before the rest of Jason's men rush us," said the marshal.

"You don't have to tell me, Tom. The bullet went right through and missed the bone. I'll get it wrapped up and that'll stop the bleeding. My shoulder wound is barely a scratch so I just need to stuff a bandage under my shirt."

"Okay, Doc. Let's get outta here right now."

They got up and carefully looked out around where the two gunmen had fired at them. The marshal could see Thad just inside the saddle shop door. He caught Thad's attention and held up two fingers then pointed at O'Malley and himself and then down the street to let Thad know they were going to make a break for it. He then pointed at Thad and where the gunman had been, indicating he wanted Thad to cover their run for O'Malley's house. Thad nodded his agreement while reloading his rifle.

"Tom, are you going to need some help running for the house?"

"Naw, Doc, I'm fine. I might not be able to run as fast as before, but I'll be okay." They got to the door and as soon as they saw Thad was ready, they bolted out and down the street, shooting their guns and running on the boardwalk as fast as they could. Thad was able to hold the two gunmen at bay, but the others in the bank came out and started shooting at Tom and O'Malley while throwing a couple of shots in Thad's direction.

Just before reaching the end of the block, Tom took a bullet to his left shoulder and then another to the right side of his back. O'Malley grabbed him just as he started to fall and pulled him around the corner in an alley, out of the line of fire. He sat him down against the wall of the building so he could examine him. He saw Thad start to run across the street firing his rifle as he ran.

Gus stepped out of the post office and fired one of the barrels of his shotgun at the two gunmen across the street and the other barrel straight down the street at the gunmen who had come out from the bank. The shots from Gus made all the gunmen take cover, and they stopped shooting for a couple of seconds, letting Thad join O'Malley and the marshal.

"Doc, I'll cover you while you work on the marshal. How is he?"

"You just keep us covered and let me work."

"Sure thing, Doc," Thad said as he took a couple more shots at the gunmen down the street.

"Doc, just leave me here. I can't travel. You, Thad, and Gus need to make it back to your house and finish this thing with Jason."

"Tom, I've got to stop this bleeding, or you'll be in serious shape."

"Doc, I've been around enough to know the kind of wound I got. You leave me here, and I'll cover you. I figure I got about ten more minutes before I'm done, and you know it, too."

"Doc, we got to be movin' pretty quickly. I'm not gonna be able to hold them off much longer. There are three of them coming up on Gus's side of the street, and two on our side. I don't like those odds very much, but I'll stay here as long as you want," said Thad.

The marshal pushed O'Malley away and pulled out both his Colt pistols pointing them at O'Malley and Thad. "I'm ordering you two to leave right now. But before ya go, ya need to help me stand up."

O'Malley and Thad looked at each other in surprise and then did as Tom had ordered. After they got him standing, he edged slowly over to the corner of the building grimacing in pain. He then looked at Doc and Thad. "All right, you two now git outta here, and I'll cover you."

At the same time, the marshal caught Gus's attention and motioned him to get down the street. O'Malley tried to convince the marshal one more time to let them help or carry him, but the marshal would not have any of it. With that, Doc, Thad, and Gus started running down the street toward O'Malley's house.

As soon as they took off running, the marshal stepped around the corner, holding a pistol in each hand. He used the gun in his right hand to shoot at the gunmen down the boardwalk and the gun in his left hand to shoot at the gunmen across the street. The marshal was unsteady but kept walking down the boardwalk, continuously firing his Colts.

The bullets whizzed past him as he continued his slow, painful walk toward Vic's men. As he kept walking and firing, he noticed Vic was nowhere to be seen. Then the scorching pain of a bullet hit him in his right shoulder, staggering him. Through sheer stubbornness, he managed to stay up on his feet. He willed himself not to go down and kept up his firing when a bullet struck him in his right thigh, breaking his leg and forcing him to his knees. He still kept shooting and took out one of the gunmen down the boardwalk in front of him. Then he felt a searing pain in his chest and fell face first, dying instantly from the bullet that went through his heart and exited out his back.

Sarah, Alicia, Clara, and Colin heard the gunfire coming from down the street. Alicia wanted to go out and help, but Sarah made her stay put. They then saw Gus, O'Malley, and Thad running toward the doctor's house. Sarah went to the front door and opened it, yelling to Gus they were at Clara's and were safe. Gus yelled back at them to stay put and be careful. Sarah went back in and told Alicia they would stay where they are as they could help better from Clara's house.

After the marshal was killed, Jason came out to see what happened since he had stayed safe and out of sight in the bank. Vic had gone out when the marshal was shooting down the boardwalk. Vic's boys from the bank were on the boardwalk, returning the marshal's fire and allowing Vic plenty of time to take careful aim with a rifle and make the fatal shot to the marshal's chest.

Jason quickly walked over to him. "Where do we stand, Vic? Did you get the rest of them?"

"No, Jason, the marshal was like a crazy man. He had at least two bullets in him when he came at us from around the corner of that building. I saw Doc, Gus, and that kid that won the rifle contest take off down the street toward O'Malley's house."

"Well, Vic, what are you going to do about this mess?"

"Jason, there are only three of them left, but there's seven of us, eight if you're gonna join us. If they're held up in Doc's house, it'll be real hard to get to 'em. But I got me an idea on how to get 'em out of that house. Clara Jenkins has a house right across the street from Doc's. She's a real good friend to Gus and Sarah so I'm gonna send my men up the street to keep the three of them busy while you and I go to the back of Clara's house and take her hostage. I'll then take her out on the front porch with a gun to her head. Then, you watch all of them surrender."

"I'm not going to help you with this, Vic. That's what I'm paying you for."

"No, Jason, you're mistaken. You're comin' with me and get your hands dirty. It's only a woman so if you get scared, you can always use that little pocket derringer you carry."

"All right, all right, let's get down there and get this over with."

"C'mon, Jason. We're goin' through your bank and out the back door. You wait right here while I go tell the boys to go up the street and keep those three bottled up."

Vic walked up the boardwalk to his men and motioned the lone gunman over from across the street. When he got them together, he quickly explained what he wanted them to do and sent them up the street to take their positions and fire at the house from behind cover. He then went back to Jason, and they went through the bank and headed toward Clara's house.

O'Malley, Gus, and Thad entered the doctor's house, and Gus told them what positions to take, giving them their best angle on the gunmen. Gus turned toward Thad and was about to tell him what window to take when he saw blood. "Thad, your left arm's bleeding. Did you get hit?"

"Yeah, I got hit in the arm when I crossed the street to join Doc and the marshal."

"Let me get my bag from the back room and take a look at that, Thad." O'Malley went to the back room and returned with his medical bag and some bandages. He took out a pair of scissors and was about to cut Thad's sleeve when he pulled his arm away.

"Doc, these shirts are expensive. I'll just take it off, and you can look at the hole."

"Doc, Thad, do whatever you have to but make it quick. I see Vic standing with his men by the bank. I don't think we're gonna have much time before they try to come in after us."

"I get the point, Gus. Come over here, Thad, so I can get a good look." Doc examined Thad's arm closely and then said, "I was afraid of this. The bullet is still in there. I've got to get it out. Otherwise, infection will set in."

"Well, Doc, what are you waiting for? Go ahead and start workin' on it," said Thad.

"Thad, I don't have anything to give you for the pain, and it's gonna hurt like the devil."

"Just get started and make it quick, Doc, so we can get back to Jason's men."

"Gus, you keep an eye out while I take Thad in the back room and get the bullet out."

"Sure thing, Doc. I figure you got maybe five or ten minutes before the shootin' starts," said Gus.

O'Malley took Thad to the back room, sat him in a chair, and then started to probe for the bullet. He located the slug quickly, extracted it, and bandaged Thad's wound. They were back in the front of the house within ten minutes. Thad's face had been filled with pain until O'Malley got the bullet out. As soon as he removed the slug, a look of relief came over Thad's face.

"Okay, Gus, tell us where you want us," said Thad.

Gus told them where he thought they would be able to do the most harm to Vic's men while still defending the house. He saw Jason and Vic go back into the bank while the gunmen slowly made their way toward them. It bothered Gus that Vic went back into the bank with Jason. He didn't think much of Jason, but he didn't figure Vic to be a coward.

As Vic's men moved closer, they started shooting from behind some barrels they found. They were still too far away to shoot with any accuracy, so Gus told Thad and O'Malley to wait until they got closer. Gus looked down the street in the opposite direction to make sure some of Vic's men had not gotten in position to surround them. However, he noticed a lone rider coming into town, whipping his horse at full speed. Gus recognized the rider as Moses and quickly stepped out the front door onto the porch, waving his arms and yelling at the top of his lungs for Moses to stop at O'Malley's house.

As Moses approached, he saw Gus and jerked back hard on the reins causing the horse to skid to a stop in front of O'Malley's house. He grabbed his rifle and jumped off the horse. Moses ran quickly to the house just as Vic's men opened fire. Both Moses and Gus made it back into the house without being hit by the bullets whizzing around them.

"Moses, how did you know we were in trouble?"

"Well, Gus, Stu and Whitey showed up at the ranch around ten o'clock this morning. They had holed up during the night in an old line shack until the storm passed. They then decided to ride to the ranch to warn you and Sarah what Jason Long was up to before they headed back to Texas. Their trip to the ranch was way out of their way, but they thought it was the right thing to do. So I thanked them, saddled up a horse, and beat it into town to warn you. But it looks like you are already in the thick of things. So, what's the plan and how can I help?"

Gus explained what had happened this morning, including what happened to the marshal, and brought Moses up-to-date on their plan.

"I'm sure sorry to hear about Tom, but he always did put other folks' safety before his own. I brought my rifle in so you just let me know where you want me and let's finish this once and for all."

Gus explained to Moses they had three shooters and two windows so they would rotate among themselves with the third person guarding the front door and shooting from there when the opportunity presented itself.

❁ ❁ ❁

Alicia, Sarah, and Clara wanted Colin to go downstairs, but he refused as he sensed his family might be in trouble. So they told him he could stay in the same room but needed to sit in a chair away from the windows. Colin agreed to this.

All of them could hear the shooting at O'Malley's house as Vic's men got closer. There was no window in Clara's house facing the direction of Vic's men so if Alicia and Sarah wanted to fight, they would have to show themselves by moving out onto the front porch. Sarah and Alicia stood at the window looking far down the street as they could to try and catch first sight of Vic's men. Clara took a seat next to Colin so he wouldn't get overly excited, but all their attention was focused down the street.

Meanwhile, Vic and Jason approached the back door to Clara's house and found it unlocked just like the other doors in town. No one ever locked their doors unless they were merchants. Vic slowly turned the door handle and opened the door. They walked into the kitchen and looked toward the front of the house. They could hear some muffled conversation and started to walk quietly toward the sound.

The next room was the dining room with a long table used to feed Clara's boarders at meal time. At the end of the dining room, was an open archway on the left, leading into the parlor. Straight ahead at the end of the dining room, was the front door. It was obvious the low voices were coming from off the left of the dining room.

Vic, with Jason behind him, approached what appeared to be the parlor. Vic edged close to the opening and looked around the corner, keeping his body out of sight. After a few moments, he inched back from the opening and whispered to Jason, identifying who was in the room. He drew his Colt .45, turned toward the parlor, and stepped into the room.

"Well, ain't that just cozy. All of Gus's family in one room. You ladies, get on over by Clara."

"You two cowards picking fights with women now? Or maybe that's all you can handle," retorted Alicia.

"Naw, we're huntin' your pa, Doc, and that young ranch hand who decided to join the fight. And, young lady, you're goin' to be my bait for the trap. You're gonna walk out there with my gun to your head. Either those three are gonna come outta the house or Gus is gonna have one dead daughter," replied Vic.

Sarah gasped and looked at Vic and Jason. "You'll never get away with it. Don't take my daughter. Please, take me instead. Gus will come out if he sees me with a gun to my head," begged Sarah.

"He might come out, but I know he will if he sees his child in danger."

"Don't hurt sister!" Colin said in a raised voice.

"I ain't gonna hurt her as long as she behaves herself," retorted Vic. "Now, get over here, girl, and walk toward the door," ordered Vic.

Alicia went to the door and opened it as she was ordered. Vic came up behind her and put his arm around her neck with a gun to her head. Vic called over his shoulder and told Jason to keep the others covered with his derringer.

Alicia and Vic walked out onto the porch and down the three stairs to the front of the yard where the white picket gate was.

"Gus, if you want to see your daughter live through this, you three better get out of that house and drop your guns!" yelled Vic.

"Don't come out, Pa. He's gonna kill all of us, anyway!" Alicia quickly yelled out.

"Shut up, or I'll brain you with my gun barrel," Vic warned.

Colin heard Vic yelling that he was going to hurt Alicia so he stood up from his chair and started toward the front door.

"Kid, stop, I don't want to shoot you, but you can't go out there," directed Jason.

Colin couldn't hear Jason because his mind was set on one thing and that was helping his sister. Jason pointed his derringer at him to shoot, and Sarah picked up a vase from an end table and threw it at him, hitting him in the chest and knocking him backward.

By this time, Colin was out the door and down the steps, half-running, and half-shuffling, he jumped on Vic's back.

Vic was so startled he flung Alicia to the side where she fell to the ground and struck her head on a large rock by the fence, stunning her. She watched in a daze as Vic reached behind him and grabbed Colin, throwing him like a rag doll. She rose up on her right elbow and shook her head, trying to clear the dizziness and fog from her sight. She saw Vic turn toward Colin, but she was so dizzy she couldn't stand yet.

"So, you're the big brother, huh? You just stay down there, or I'll pick up a rock and hit you on the other side of the head like I did years ago."

"You no hurt sister. You a bad man!" Colin blurted out.

"You just lay there, kid, and you won't get hurt!" yelled Vic, pointing his finger at Colin. Vic then turned and approached Alicia, leveling his gun at her.

Over at O'Malley's house, the men could see what was going on at Clara's and when Vic brought Alicia out with his gun to her head, the four of them bolted for the door but when they opened it, gunfire erupted from Vic's men, forcing them back into the house.

"We gotta do somethin' before Colin or Alicia get hurt," said Gus.

"Let's see what they want and buy some time to deal with them," said O'Malley.

"Doc, they don't want to deal. They want us all dead so they get an open hand to get my land and take over this town. Thad, you're a good shot. Get to a window. Doc, get me some white cloth. When I put the white flag out there, shoot Vic if you have a clear shot. Moses, you come with me but stay here at the front door and if you get a clear shot at Vic, take it."

Thad reloaded his Henry rifle and quickly took his position at the window. "Gus, somethin's goin' on out there. Doc, you better get that white cloth and hurry," said Thad.

Gus came over to Thad's window and saw Colin attack Vic. He watched as Vic threw Alicia to one side and Colin to the other.

They could see Vic say something to Colin and then turn toward Alicia with his gun aimed at her. He brought it up as if he was about to shoot.

Thad and Moses brought their rifles up and took aim then lowered them.

"Gus! Look!" Thad yelled.

"Don't hurt sister! Don't hurt sister!" Colin yelled as he got up with clenched fists in front of him and walked toward Vic with his crooked gait. Vic whirled around as Colin struck him with weak blows to his chest.

Alicia heard Vic say, "Well, chink, it's too bad I didn't kill you when I whacked your head with that rock years ago."

Then there was a shot. Colin grabbed Vic, slowly sliding down Vic's body with a surprised and painful grimace on his face.

All at once, it dawned on Alicia. She remembered Vic, whose looks had aged, but he was clearly the same boy who had hurt Colin many years ago when they were on their way home from school. The memory of that horrible day came crashing back to her as Colin slid the rest of the way to the ground repeating, "Don't hurt sister!" over and over until he fell to the ground unconscious, with blood covering his midsection.

By this time, Alicia's dizziness had cleared up and as Vic turned and moved toward her, she sprang up so fast Vic paused, momentarily surprised. That pause was all she needed, and she quickly did a crossing kick to Vic's gun hand with the instep of her right foot, sending the gun sailing out of his hand and landing on the other side of the fence. She ended her kick by landing the foot on the left side of her body, continuing the turn and placing a side kick with her left foot to Vic's rib cage, sending him on his back.

Jason had caught his balance after being hit by the vase and still covered Sarah and Clara with his derringer. When Sarah saw Colin shot, she started toward Jason.

"Hold it, Sarah. I don't want to shoot a woman, but I will today."

"Please, Jason. Have some mercy. My son is lying out there, shot. Please let me go help him."

"Just stay where you are, Sarah. When Vic gets done, we'll see to your son."

"Doc, Doc! He shot Colin! Colin's still moving. I gotta get out there to him," yelled Gus.

"Just a second, Gus, you're all much better shots than I am, and you can't treat his wound. You, Thad, and Moses get your rifles and go to the windows. Pin down Vic's men, and I'll go get Colin. I see that look, Gus. We don't have time. If you want Colin saved, you do what I say right now."

"Okay, Doc, just give us ten seconds to get to the windows." Gus and Moses ran into the next room where Thad was. "Okay, men, when we run out of rifle shells we will return the fire with our pistols."

"No need for that, Gus. When I heard the shooting, I grabbed an extra box of shells. I'll put it on the floor between us so we can reload quickly."

"I got a better idea, Thad. Each of us will shoot and keep those boys down and when one runs out of bullets, the next one will take a turn while that man reloads."

"Sounds good, Gus."

"Doc! Thad, Moses, and I are ready when you give us the word."

"Okay, boys. Look at Alicia! My God, she's fighting Vic by herself. Start shooting!"

Thad started shooting while Gus and Moses looked out the window just as Alicia had sent Vic flying with her turning back side kick. *That's my girl*, Gus thought to himself.

As O'Malley ran across the open street, Vic's men tried to shoot, but Thad kept them at bay with his expert marksmanship. When Thad had emptied his rifle, Gus took over. When he took aim, he saw just how good Thad was with his Henry. Two of Vic's men lay on the ground writhing in pain from Thad's inflicted gunshot wounds. He glanced out the window and saw O'Malley had made it to Colin and was kneeling over him. He fired several more shots at the men to prevent them from shooting at O'Malley.

Vic had received a hard kick to his midsection but got up quickly from the ground. O'Malley had just gotten to Colin when Vic got to his feet.

"Talk about luck. Doc, you don't have to worry about helpin' that chink. I'm gonna git rid of you right now."

"Doc, you take care of my brother, and I'll give this rotten human being what he deserves."

"That suits me just fine, Miss Chink. I'll git rid of you first, and then I'll take care of your chink brother and the doctor."

Vic put his fists up and started edging toward her. Alicia started to circle around him and when he threw a right cross, she stepped to her right. As he punched nothing but air, she landed a roundhouse kick to his left kidney area. He stumbled after the kick but kept his balance and remained on his feet. He turned and faced her with anger boiling over. When he thought he was close enough, he threw another right cross, trying to hit her in the face. She once again saw the punch coming and stepped to the right, blocking Vic's punch with her left forearm and hitting him in his solar plexus with a straight right arm punch. As Vic doubled over, she grabbed a handful of his hair with both hands and as hard as she could, pulled his head down to her right knee, which she brought up with such force it crushed Vic's nose and sent him sprawling on his back, bloody and dazed.

"How's Colin, Doc?"

"I'm taking him across the street. I've got to stop this bleeding, and I can only do it back at my office." O'Malley picked him up in his arms as a low, moaning sound came from Colin. He took off with him, running as fast as he could across the street back to his house.

"Okay, Doc's comin' back. Let's give him the cover he needs," said Gus.

They started firing their weapons, shooting enough bullets with their repeating rifles to keep Vic's men pinned down. O'Malley made it without a single shot being fired at him. As he entered the house, he shouted, "Keep those men pinned down. I think Alicia can handle Vic. I'm taking Colin to the exam room so I can work on him!"

"Doc! Is my son gonna be all right?" Gus yelled back.

"I can't tell you until I get him back there. But I'll tell you as soon as I know," Doc shouted back as he carried Colin to the exam room as fast as he could.

Vic slowly got up with a flow of blood streaming from his crushed nose. He had now lost complete control of his temper and wanted nothing but to get his hands on Alicia and break her neck. He lunged at her straight on and did it so quickly he caught her by surprise, getting his hands around her neck.

Alicia reacted without thinking by bringing both arms up as hard as she could inside Vic's arms, breaking his grip. She then came down as hard as she could with knife hand strikes to Vic's collarbones hearing and feeling both bones break. She wasn't done yet. She stepped back with her right leg and as hard as she could, brought her right foot up in a roundhouse kick, striking Vic to the left side of his head, breaking his jaw and crushing his left cheekbone.

Vic staggered to his right, and she brought her right foot back, bringing it forward in a side kick to Vic's left rib cage and breaking three ribs. He amazingly managed to stay on his feet although he stumbled and staggered like someone who had been drinking all night in a saloon.

Jason couldn't believe his eyes. That petite girl couldn't weigh more than a hundred pounds but was giving Vic the beating of his life. Jason knew he had to do something drastic if they were going to win this fight. He was covering Clara and Sarah with his derringer but knew he'd have to shoot Alicia if they were going to finish this thing.

He looked at Sarah, who was watching the fight outside while keeping an eye on Jason. When Alicia kicked Vic to the ribs, he saw he had a clear shot at her so he moved his derringer from the direction of the parlor and took aim at her out the open front door. Sarah saw his movement out of the corner of her eye. The parlor fireplace was just to her left, and she glanced over and saw a poker leaning against the hearth. She slowly edged by the poker, picked it up, and threw it at Jason to stop him from shooting Alicia. The poker hit him on his left side, jarring him just as he had pulled the derringer trigger.

Vic was still standing and had recovered slightly. He was going to try one more time for Alicia. She resumed her fighting stance. Her right leg was back, and she had her hands raised with clenched fists, standing sideways toward him. As she braced for another attack, she knew exactly what to do.

Vic lunged, and she took a hop back. With her open right hand, she struck Vic just under his bloody nose, shattering the rest of his injured nose and driving his head backward.

Almost immediately, she heard a soft pop coming from the direction of the house. Vic's head jerked violently to his right and blood spurted out of the left side of his head as he collapsed in front of her like a rag doll. When she looked at the house, she could see Jason, who seemed off balance as if he had stumbled or been hit with something. Whatever happened, she was sure he had meant to shoot her.

After Jason shot his derringer, Sarah looked out the window and saw Vic taking the bullet to the head and slumping in a heap at Alicia's feet. Sarah looked at Jason, who was regaining his balance and lifting his two-shot derringer up to try for Alicia again. She screamed, "Jason" and started to move toward him to prevent his shooting her daughter.

Alicia took a small knife from her right cowboy boot, which she had gotten from the box she had left in Mary's spare room. The knife was made with a three-inch blade sharpened on both sides with an ivory handle also three inches in length. She removed it quickly and, with the same motion, threw it underhanded, hitting Jason squarely in the throat.

His eyes bulged out with a look of terror and surprise, and he grasped his throat as blood erupted from the fatal wound. He dropped his derringer and fell to his knees, trying to talk but only emitting a gurgling sound as he fell dead face forward driving the knife the rest of the way into his throat and out the back.

Alicia ran into the house and seeing Jason lying lifeless on the floor, ran to her mother and hugged her. She turned to Clara asking if she was all right.

"I'm fine, Alicia, but they're still shooting out there."

"You're absolutely right, Clara. Mom, let's get the guns and help our men finish this thing."

"I agree. I'm tired of being pushed around. How should we go about this?" asked Sarah.

Alicia quickly explained what she thought they should do, and Clara agreed to join them.

As Gus, Moses, and Thad continued to keep Vic's men pinned down, they saw Vic collapsing and Alicia running into Clara's house after throwing what appeared to be a knife.

"Can you two keep them busy for a minute so I can look out the front door into Clara's house?"

"Sure thing, boss, I just got another one," said Moses as Gus went into the hallway and looked across the street into Clara's open front door. He saw Jason lying lifeless on the floor and then saw the three women appear in the hallway, carrying guns and walking toward the back of the house. He took a step forward, and three bullets hit the door casing within inches of his head.

"I thought you two were going to keep these boys pinned down." There was no answer. "Thad, Moses, are you okay?" Gus asked as he walked back into the room he had left them in.

When he entered the room, he saw Moses bending over Thad, who was lying on the floor with blood streaming out of his left shoulder.

"Doc, Doc! I need you in here!" shouted Gus as he picked up the rifle he had left leaning against the wall.

"Gus, I can't leave Colin right now. What's the problem?"

"Thad's took a bullet to his shoulder, and it's bleedin' pretty bad."

"Gus, come back here and get some bandages. You'll have to put pressure on his wound to stop the bleeding."

Thad came to and looked at Gus and Moses. "I'm okay, boys, just lean me up against the window, and I can still shoot."

More bullets hit the house with some coming through the window. Gus and Moses returned the fire, and Vic's men ducked back behind their cover. They bent over Thad and did as he asked, propping him against the wall by the window he was shooting from when he got hit.

"Thad, I'm gonna get some bandages for your shoulder. Moses, you throw a couple shots to keep those boys down if you can."

Moses nodded, and Gus ran to the back room where he saw O'Malley working intently on Colin. "How's he doin', Doc?"

"All I can say is he's alive. I just found the bullet and am going to remove it. After that, I'll sew him up, and we will just have to wait. The bandages for Thad are on the third shelf in that glass cabinet."

Gus turned to the cabinet and took out more than enough bandages. "Doc, you call me if you need anything for Colin."

"Gus, all I need you to do is go back in there, bandage Thad up, and keep those men at bay."

"You got my word on it, Doc." He hurried back to Thad and pulled him back from the window where he had been firing, leaning him back against the wall. He quickly put a bandage on his shoulder and pressed hard as O'Malley had told him to do. He then took cloth strips to tie it off. "Thad, you rest easy for a bit, and we'll keep those boys real busy."

"I can still shoot, boss. I'll be fine."

"I know, son, and I'll let you know if we need your gun. You've done enough for now. You just rest easy for a while." He went back to the window and resumed firing until he ran out of bullets. As he reloaded, Moses took over.

Alicia, Sarah, and Clara made their way out the back door and walked down about a hundred yards toward the sound of gunfire. There was a ten-foot-wide passageway between the buildings leading to the street where they could see Vic's men crouching behind some barrels and crates and firing at O'Malley's house.

"Mom, you and Clara stay on this side. I'll go on the other side and when I give the word, we'll start shooting at them. That way, we can get them in a crossfire between us and Doc's house."

"Alicia, I see what you're doing. It's safer on this side because if those men shoot back, they have a direct line to the spot you picked for yourself. I already have had one child shot today and, for all I know, maybe dead. I'm your ma, and you're gonna stay on this side with Clara."

"But Ma!"

"No buts, young lady." Before Alicia could protest further, Sarah crossed over to the other side and took up her position. The three women readied themselves and as Alicia raised her hand and then brought it down, they started shooting.

Gus kept firing Thad's rifle until it was empty. He then crouched down and started reloading. When he reloaded the rifle, he noticed the box of shells only had three rounds left. That meant they would be down to their Colt .45s. They certainly had plenty of ammunition in their gun belts when they got to the pistols. What bothered Gus is he wasn't sure if he could hold off these men if they decided to charge at them with their pistols and rifles blazing. With Thad wounded and O'Malley tied up in the exam room, Gus was not certain how this was going to play out with only two of them left.

He lifted his rifle up to his shoulder and took aim. Just before he fired, gunshots erupted, and Gus and Moses ducked down, thinking Vic's men were on the attack. But no bullets struck the house or windows. He stood up and looked out. Vic's men were firing at something between the buildings. It dawned on him that must have been where the ladies were going when he saw them walking toward the back of Clara's house. The women were attacking the men's flanks. Gus and Moses quickly stepped out onto the front porch and took separate positions as they started firing.

Gus yelled out to the men. "Jason and Vic are dead. Do you boys want to join them?"

Gus and Moses fired some more and so did the ladies. Then Gus heard one of Vic's men yell out.

"You let us leave now, we'll not come back."

"Run for your horses now, boys, and never come back. Ladies, let this scum leave."

The women heard the verbal exchanges between the men and Gus. Talking directly to the men, Sarah said, "We won't shoot if you get your carcasses outta here right now."

The men stood up and collected their wounded. They headed down the boardwalk toward the bank. Alicia ran down the passageway to the boardwalk and looked around the corner, watching them enter the bank. She realized their horses must be at the back of the bank, and she ran back down the passageway and past her mom, saying she'd be right back.

She ran behind the buildings toward the back of the bank until she caught sight of the horses. The men came out the back, got the wounded, and mounted their horses. Then they rode out of town.

Alicia returned to Sarah and Clara, and they went down the passageway to the street while she told them Vic's men had ridden out of town. The three women then hurried to O'Malley's house where Gus, Sarah, and Alicia hugged each other on the porch.

Gus explained O'Malley was working on Colin but did not know how he was doing other than he was still alive. Just as Gus finished speaking, O'Malley walked out on the front porch. As if rehearsed, all four asked how Colin was doing in unison.

"He is doing as well as can be expected, but he's not out of the woods yet. If I had to make a guess, I'd say he will make a full recovery.

I also took a look at Thad, and you two did a pretty good job patching him up. I put Colin on a cot to rest and recover. Can you help me get Thad back into the exam room? I still need to remove the bullet from his shoulder."

"With pleasure, Doc. Here, Alicia, you hold my rifle." Gus handed the rifle to her and went in followed by Sarah and Alicia, who asked if they could see Colin.

As Gus and O'Malley helped Thad to his feet, he told them to go on back and sit with Colin.

The rest of the day was spent at O'Malley's house. While he patched up Thad, they remained to see if Colin would regain consciousness. By dinnertime, Colin had come to and said hello to his family before he dozed off to sleep.

"Folks, he's a tough kid, and I think he will pull through. I'll keep him here for a few days and then he should be fit to travel."

They thanked O'Malley and told him they'd stay in town at the hotel to be near Colin. Memories came back to both Gus and Sarah of the time Colin had sustained his head injury when he was a young kid.

Alicia told everyone Vic had admitted to being the person who had originally hurt Colin and went on to say Vic would never hurt another person again. Then, she spoke up with another idea that had just occurred to her. "There's no need for all of us to stay in town. Pa, you, Ma, and Moses can go back to the ranch, and I'll stay in Mary's spare room. That way, you three can make sure the ranch is okay, and I'll rent a buckboard to bring Colin back."

"I think your ma and I would want to be here for Colin."

"Gus, Colin's going to need rest, and it's probably better for all of you to go back to the ranch. Alicia and I will bring him back when I think he's well enough to travel. You really can't do anything more for him."

Gus and Sarah looked at each other and knew what the answer was. "My children are the most important thing in my life. Doc, if you say Colin's better off without us being a nuisance then so be it.

We will head back to the ranch after we have dinner at Mary's. Can you join us, Doc?"

"Thanks, Sarah, but I'm going to stay here with Colin. I have some food I can fix for dinner, and you're welcome to eat with me."

"Doc, we will accept your invite if you let Alicia and myself fix dinner for you. Gus, you might want to go into town and get the undertaker out to Clara's as she's going to need help over there. Gus can also check what happened to the marshal and how Chet is doing."

"Sarah, I hate to tell you, but Tom Jackson sacrificed his life so the three of us could get to my house," said O'Malley.

Sarah looked shocked and sad at the same time. Tears welled up in her eyes, but she did not cry. "Tom was a brave man. He was always fair and upheld the law. He will be sorely missed," said Sarah.

"I will accept your offer to cook dinner tonight. I'm going into town to check on Chet and make sure he is all right."

Doc, Gus, and Moses went into town to notify the undertaker he was needed at Clara's and found out he had already picked up the marshal's body. O'Malley then went to Mary's Café and found Chet resting comfortably and in good spirits. He was doing so well he asked to be moved back to the jail so he could sleep in his own cot.

Mary volunteered to make the arrangements after she made O'Malley fill her in on everything. She told O'Malley that Alicia was welcome to stay in the spare room after they got Chet moved back to the jail.

That evening after dinner, Gus, Sarah, and Moses returned to the ranch, and Alicia went to Mary's to stay for the next few days. Gus, Sarah, and Moses came to town two days later for Marshal Jackson's funeral, which was attended by an overflowing crowd paying their respects to a marshal who was well liked for his honesty, integrity, fair play, and disregard for his own wellbeing when protecting the citizens of Cheyenne.

Vic and Jason were buried unceremoniously in Boot Hill and Jason's ranch and holdings were split up into parcels and sold at an auction where some of the original owners bought them back. There were no claims on Jason's ranch as no family could be found.

With the exception of Marshal Jackson's funeral, O'Malley and Alicia spent every free moment with each other, talking about the future of the town and their own. Alicia had decided to settle in Cheyenne and not return to her teaching position back east. She informed the school of her decision and made arrangements with her landlady to ship her property out to Cheyenne.

Two days after the marshal's funeral, O'Malley and Alicia rented a buckboard from the livery and laid Colin on soft blankets in the bed part of the wagon. On the way out to the ranch, O'Malley stopped the buckboard at their favorite spot where they had so many picnics in the past. He climbed down followed by Alicia. They let Colin know they would only be a few minutes. He answered with his typical, "Okay!" and O'Malley and Alicia walked to their spot.

O'Malley looked tenderly at her and dropped to one knee. "Alicia, we have known each other for quite some time. You are sensitive, kind, and caring. You are not only physically beautiful but beautiful in every aspect of life. Also, you are dedicated to your family and those you love. I am one of those who love you with all my heart and want to spend the rest of my life with you. Would you do me the honor of being my wife?"

A smile spread over Alicia's face and tears of happiness filled her eyes. She pulled O'Malley up and said, "Yes, yes, yes! These past few months with you have been some of the best in my life."

They came together with a long embrace. They then walked back hand in hand to the buckboard to return to the ranch and tell Gus and Sarah the exciting news.

Chet and Thad made a complete recovery and as the days and weeks continued, the mayor requested Washington to appoint Chet as the new marshal. The request was approved after the facts were known and finding the town's support for Chet. When Chet received the appointment, he asked Thad to be his deputy marshal. Thad accepted the appointment, and he and Chet carried on the same tradition of fair justice that had been established by Marshal Jackson.

O'Malley and Alicia's wedding took place in late summer. Alicia turned out to be the best assistant he could ever hope for at the clinic. She also ran for mayor, and the people of Cheyenne elected her, removing the corrupt mayor who had cooperated with Jason.

With the addition of O'Malley as a son-in-law, both Gus and Sarah felt the family was unified and complete with a bright future ahead. However, a certain politician had some other ideas about Cheyenne and its surrounding territory.

www.ingramcontent.com/pod-product-compliance
Lightning Source LLC
Chambersburg PA
CBHW070834020826
48982CB00019B/1136/J

* 9 7 8 0 6 9 2 6 2 5 0 2 6 *